Coal Camp Days

Coal Camp Days

a boy's remembrance

RICARDO L GARCÍA

University of New Mexico Press
Albuquerque

First edition

Library of Congress Cataloging-in-Publication Data

García, Ricardo L
Coal camp days : a boy's remembrance / Ricardo L García.—1st ed.
p. cm.
Summary: In this fictionalized memoir based on the author's childhood, a six-year-old boy describes his life in a coal mining town in northern New Mexico during World War II.
ISBN 0-8263-2304-9
1. Hispanic American families—Fiction. 2. Coal mines and mining—Fiction. 3. Mining camps—Fiction. 4. New Mexico—Fiction. 5. Boys—Fiction. I. Title.
PS3607.A725 C63 2001
813'.6—dc21

2001001991

All photographs by author unless otherwise noted.

To my wife Sharon, this book is affectionately dedicated

CONTENTS

PREFACE

Most events in *Coal Camp Days* really happened in one of the mining camps located in the Colfax County coal fields of northeastern New Mexico: Blossburg, Brilliant, Dawson, Gardiner, Koehler, Swastika, Sugarite, Van Houten, Yankee. Each camp thrived and later died between 1880 and 1955. Because people literally lived in tents when some of the coal towns were first established, they were called "coal camps."

There is little written about the people who worked, played, married, raised families, or died in the coal camps. This book tells about some coal camp people. The fictitious coal camp name "Chicorico" was suggested by "chicorica," a Colfax County place name of unknown origin. Its anglicized pronunciation, *sugarite* [sugar-REET], was given to the canyon, creek, and coal camp five miles north of Raton.

Though the book is fiction, the people and their zest for life are real. I've tried to be true to the spirit of coal camp life as I remember it. The barely visible remnants of coal camp people—crumbling foundations, decaying slack piles, rusting pots and pans—hardly reveal their spirit. I hope *Coal Camp Days* rekindles memories of that ebullient spirit and joy for life.

Thanks to Todd Wildermuth and staff at the *Raton Range*, Thayla Wright and the staff at Johnson Memorial Library, David Vackar and staff at Vermejo Ranch, John Evans, Thelma Fuller, Charles García, Sarge Rivali, and Vesta Toller, and others who've generously shared their coal camp experiences with me. Thanks to Jill Root for sensitive copyediting and to the staff at UNM Press for shepherding the manuscript, and to the ghost-editor who helped immensely with my New Mexico Spanish. Special thanks to Sharon, whose meticulous editing gave spirit and soul to this book.

Ricardo L García
Lincoln, Nebraska

Invitation

Come climb these hills
with me,
where Dad dug coal
for us.
For thirty years he dug
these hills
and came home by these tracks—
we scrambled for the scraps
soggy in his lunch bucket.
Come walk these tracks
with me,
where Mom collected coal
for us—
fallen
from the train's sudden stops,
she hiding from company cops.
Come climb these hills,
Come walk these tracks . . .

1

DIOS DA, PERO NO ACARREA

Our days in the Chicorico coal mining camp were abundant with tales of brave and daring deeds. Always, the heroes of Chicorico were common, ordinary people who celebrated life, inspired by the dream of better days through hard work, sacrifice, and thrift. By good example, they encouraged us to make something of our lives to benefit our families and communities. Above all, they taught us respect.

On my sixth birthday we celebrated a victory over death. There were no cakes, candles, nor gifts, only a song and a story. At supper, Dad and Mom led us through a lively rendition of the "Happy Birthday" song. Then they took turns telling about my birth and first six months of life. Like me, my brothers and sisters—Juan, José, Angela, and Ramona—were all ears. My oldest brother, Arturo, was not present, though he had been at my birth in 1938. He had joined the navy in 1940. Now, in 1944, he was flying airplanes somewhere in the Pacific. But then, he had been a witness to the victory.

On May 25, 1938, six o'clock Wednesday evening, Mom proclaimed to Dad, "Manuel, the time's come. He's been kicking in my *panza* all day."

Dad sent Arturo to fetch the Company doctor, Dr. Monty. Arturo returned, puffing heavily. "Dr. Monty can't come! He's in Swastika! Some kid's got the whooping cough!"

Dad rushed next door to the Malcolms. "Dick! Mary! I need your help! Dr. Monty can't come to deliver Clara's baby."

"Let's go!" Mrs. Malcolm rose abruptly, dropping a sewing project into the chair. She clenched her right hand into a fist, smacking it into her left. "My turn to help!"

This was payback time for Mrs. Malcolm; Mom had helped deliver Petee, the Malcolm's youngest, the same year my brother José was born. She wrapped a shawl around her shoulders and grabbed some washcloths and towels made from Gold Medal flour sacks. She handed them to Dad, speaking to her husband at the same time.

"Dick, you stay here! I'll send Clara's children over. Put 'em to bed. It's getting late. Tomorrow, you watch José and Petee."

"But Dick has to work tomorrow," Manuel protested.

"No, I don't, Manuel. I'll switch with Onorio. Git! Don't leave Clara alone."

Dad and Mrs. Malcolm skittered out of the Malcolm house. Outside, the dry air was cool. The stars shimmered brightly. They crossed both backyards, entering our house through the kitchen.

Mrs. Malcolm issued her first orders: "You kids! Sleep at our place! Take your school clothes. After Mr. Malcolm feeds you breakfast, go to school with Freddie! José, you stay there with Mr. Malcolm. Manuel, take these towels and washcloths, stack them nearby. We'll need 'em. Heat plenty of water. find Clara's mending scissors. Sterilize them!"

Arturo, Angela, Juan, and José gathered their toothbrushes, sleeping garb, school clothing, and books; they left. Mrs. Malcolm went into the bedroom, where Mom was resting on her bed.

Before searching for Mom's scissors, Dad drained some of the hot water from the boiler pan of Mom's Majestic *fogón*, poured it into a pan, and placed it on the stove to boil. Fumbling through Mom's sewing basket, he found all kinds of needles, but no scissors. He looked where Mom was last sewing, spotted a receiving blanket on a dynamite powder box by Mom's chair. The scissors were on the box, beneath the blanket. He ran his forefinger along the blades. Sharp as razors, the scissors were German chrome-plated, made of finely tempered steel. He returned to the kitchen and put the scissors in the hot water, but it wasn't boiling. The fogón needed stoking.

Dad grabbed some small lumps of coal from the powder box next to the fogón. He wrapped the lumps into a roll using the May 24th edition of the *Raton Range*. He opened the fire door and shoved the roll into the firebox. Repeatedly he took deep breaths and blew, till the paper ignited.

Before long, the water on the fogón was boiling, and the water in the boiler pan was considerably hotter. Dad needed to moderate the temperature of the water in the boiler, or it would be too hot to use for my delivery. Because there was no running water in the house, Dad had to bring cold water from our backyard faucet pump. He grabbed a bucket, went outside, and drew water from the pump, carting the water back into the kitchen.

When done with the preparations for my birth, he walked out to the back porch where it was cool and leaned against the porch's railing. It was a quiet night in Chicorico. Light dimly beamed from a few of the neighbors' living room windows. The stars still shimmered brilliantly. Dad heard Mrs. Malcolm call from within the bedroom: "Manuel, best you get in here!"

Dad stole a momentary glimpse at the bright, beaming stars and entered the house, rapping lightly on the bedroom door. Meekly, he turned the doorknob, barely opening the door. He spied Mom lying on top of the bed dressed in a nightgown. He hesitated—flustered, embarrassed.

Mrs. Malcolm scowled, glaring toward the slightly ajar door, face flushed: "Get in here, Manuel! No time for modesty!"

Dad recoiled, pulled the door shut, stepping back. From deep within the bedroom, Mom pleaded:

"*¡Sí! Entre!*"

Dad was still reluctant. Cautiously . . . tentatively . . . he opened the door again.

Mrs. Malcolm detected his shyness. "Don't worry, Manuel. You're no different than Dr. Monty. He's a man, too. He can't be here. You're needed."

Hesitantly, Dad entered the room, gazing directly at Mrs. Malcolm, avoiding eye contact with Mom, meekly asking, "How can I help?"

"Clara's 'bout ready to birth! But the bed's too soft. She's not laying flat. We need to lay her flat!" The bed mattress was old, its cotton stuffing matted and broken down. The extra weight of carrying me caused Mom to slump into the mattress, an awkward position for birthing.

"We can lay her on the floor," Dad recommended.

"No! Too dirty! Heaven knows what's been on the floor."

"But Clara washes the floor once a week!"

"Manuel, the floor won't work!"

"Only other place I can think of," Dad suggested, "is the kitchen table."

"The kitchen table?" Mrs. Malcolm did a double-take. "The kitchen table . . ." She turned pensive, ruminating.

"Wipe it off! Put a blanket on it! I'll help Clara to her feet."

Dad dashed into the kitchen and wiped off the table. He shoved the chairs against the kitchen wall and stacked the folded towels and washcloths on the nearest chair. He threw a blanket over the table, brushing its wrinkles out.

"This'll be perfect!" Mrs. Malcolm declared, assisting Mom into the kitchen. "We're near the water and towels."

Mom didn't speak at first. She shuffled haltingly, holding her bulging stomach with both arms as Mrs. Malcolm and Dad guided her toward the table. Something about having a child on the kitchen table struck Mom's funny bone. She jested, "The boys aren't here to set the table!"

"Yeah! Sure!" Mrs. Malcolm chortled. "A lotta good they'd be!"

"Ha-ha—uh! Ha-ha—uh!" Mom struggled to laugh, but stopped abruptly, halting her steps and tightly grasping her stomach.

"Clara! Best you don't laugh." Mrs. Malcolm frowned, tenderly advising Mom, "Let's get you on the table 'fore you drop the baby."

Mrs. Malcolm eased Mom backwards onto the left side of the table.

As Mom slid onto the table, Mrs. Malcolm reached down and lifted Mom's legs up on it. Mom lay down and wiggled to the center of the table. The contractions came quicker and stronger.

"Mary—he's coming!" Mom excitedly announced.

"Push him out, Clara!" Mrs. Malcolm coached Mom. "Keep a-pushing! I see his head! Keep pushing! I got his head!"

Mrs. Malcolm gently grasped the back of my head with her right hand. She raised her left hand toward Dad. "Manuel, be ready to hand me a warm washcloth."

Dad poured cold water into the pan of boiling water and then drained some of the tepid water into the wash basin. He soaked a washcloth, wringing it, grabbed some towels, and returned to Mom's side by the table.

"Wow! He's a big one!" Mrs. Malcolm exclaimed, taking me in both hands and raising me high enough for Mom to see. Mrs. Malcolm took the wet washcloth, daubing at my nose, eyes, mouth, and ears.

While Mrs. Malcolm cleared the mucous from my face, Dad shook his head in surprise, "He's a real roly-poly!"

Mrs. Malcolm focused on the job at hand. "Okay, Manuel, I've got an itty-bitty job for you. I'm going to hold the boy by the legs. You give his bottom a quick slap."

"No!" Dad shook his head emphatically. "I'm too strong!"

"Hurry up! Can't wait forever!"

Dad wavered.

WAP! Mrs. Malcolm slapped me squarely on the bottom, forcing air into my lungs. I yelped.

Mrs. Malcolm stayed cool as a cucumber, still in command. "I've got one more itty-bitty job for you, Manuel." She paused before completing her instructions. "This time, you've got to do it. I can't hold the boy and cut his cord at the same time!"

"You want *me* to cut his cord?"

"Now, Manuel! Clara and I need your help!"

"*Manuel . . .* " Mom pleaded with her eyes.

Dad sputtered as he darted to the silverware drawer, found a clean fork, and rushed to the stove, mumbling loud enough for Mrs. Malcolm to hear, "This is no small job you're asking me to do!" Dad lowered the fork into the boiling water and lifted the scissors away from the pan to cool them down. He darted back. Mrs. Malcolm held me with one hand under my neck, the other under my rump.

Mrs. Malcolm cautioned Dad, "Leave lots of slack, at least six or seven inches, so's when the cord's cut, there'll be plenty left to tie a strong knot."

Dad raised the scissors to the cord, pinched the cord about seven inches from my stomach, and snipped.

"You done?"

"Yep."

Mrs. Malcolm laid me down and tied a knot in the cord, trimming the excess.

"Get his clothes and the receiving blanket Clara laid out, Manuel. Put them on the cabinet, next to the wash basin. I'll wash the boy."

While Mrs. Malcolm was bathing me, Dad assisted Mom. She was hurting. The table was hardly a place to stay after birthing a child. Dad helped Mom down from the table and supported her as she shuffled to the bedroom. Mom crawled beneath the blankets. Dad stayed, holding her hand.

After washing me, Mrs. Malcolm daubed me dry, pinning a two-inch-wide cotton belly-band around my stomach. Next she pinned on a diaper, tied on an undershirt, and slipped a flannel gown over my head. She wrapped me snuggly in the receiving blanket, handing me to Mom.

"A, mi hito, qué ojos lindos—claros y morenos."

Mesmerized, Mrs. Malcolm and Dad gazed at us as Mom lightly brushed her hand across my face and hair. Then Mrs. Malcolm broke the spell, cleaning her hands with a towel. "Manuel, take the boy. I'll help Clara here."

Dad took me into the living room, holding me close to his chest. He lulled me to sleep, singing "When It's Springtime in the Rockies." When I awoke, it was three o'clock in the morning. Dad was still holding me. By then, Mrs. Malcolm had bathed Mom, returned her to bed, and cleared the kitchen, putting the dirty washcloths and towels into the bushel basket. Already she had gathered the dirty clothes from our powder-box hamper to wash at her house. Now, at 3 A.M., she slept on the couch. Dad returned me to Mom. He sat at the kitchen table for a while, slumping on his forehead and arms, sleeping.

I slept my first morning in Chicorico. About 5 A.M., Dad awoke from his slumber at the kitchen table. His arms tingled, the circulation cut off by the weight of his head. He moved to the living room floor, using the cushion from his easy chair as a pillow. Mrs. Malcolm slept soundly on the sofa. About 8 A.M., Dad awoke again, brewed some coffee, and sat in the shade of the front porch steps. Mrs. Malcolm still slept.

Around noon of my first day, Mrs. Malcolm prepared lunch for Mom and Dad and joined them to eat. Then she left to go home. Later that afternoon, as Dad washed the dishes, Angela came home from school. She had stopped at the Malcolms to pick up José.

"Where's Juan?" Dad asked.

"Playing. He stayed to play with Freddie and Petee."

My brother Arturo was still on the bus. He attended St. Patrick's Academy, a Catholic high school in Raton.

I let out a cry from the crib.

"Daddy, what's that squealing in your bedroom?"

"A little *cabrito.*"

"Oooo," she cooed, wrinkling her nose. "A cabrito, Daddy?" Angela realized I was a boy.

Four-year-old José stopped galloping his toy horse—the one *Abuelo* Ribera had carved for him—across the edge of the kitchen table. His eyes got as big as *platos.* He didn't connect Dad's reference to a cabrito with the new baby. "A cabrito? Re-e-e-ally? Can I play with him? I wanna play with him."

Angela and Dad started laughing. Poor little José couldn't understand. He looked hurt.

"Ah-h-h! José, we're not laughing at you. Your mama hasn't named your new brother yet. You'll have to wait a while to play with him."

Later in the week, Dr. Matthew Montgomery came to the house to check on Mom and me. People affectionately called him "Dr. Monty," a name he also preferred. He lived in a regular Company house, using the front room and a bedroom for an office. His wife, Etta, helped as a nurse. They had no children. Dr. Monty served all the Company camps: Chicorico, Brilliant, Dawson, Gardiner, Koehler, Sugarite, Swastika, Van Houten, and Yankee.

All was well with Mom. As he examined me, he made small talk with Mom:

"Say, who helped you with the boy?"

"*La vecina*, Mary."

"Hmm. Good job, even the cord's tied well."

"Oh! *También*, Manuel."

"Manuel! He helped?"

"*O, sí.* I asked him to help."

"Why, I never—"

Dr. Monty started to comment on Dad's unconventional behavior, but he caught himself, shifting to praise. "Why . . . like I was sayin' . . . Mary and Manuel did a good job. I'd better watch out! They'll have my job!"

"Oh, no! You're very good."

"Why, thank you, Clara. Say—" Dr. Monty reached into his black bag, pulled out a birth certificate and a pen. "On the matter of a name for the boy?"

He started writing the details of my birth. He was so engrossed in filling out the certificate that he hadn't noticed Mom's mood shift, her eyes cast down in a blank stare. Only moments ago, she was radiant, animated with talk of her newborn son.

When Dr. Monty noticed Mom's silence, he politely nudged her out of the daze by asking again, "Clara? . . . The boy? . . . What's his name?"

Embarrassed, Mom turned toward Dr. Monty: "*No sé.* I . . . Manuel and I . . . we can't think of a name—a Christian name."

"Ho!" Dr. Monty laughed wholeheartedly, exclaiming "A Christian name! Why, I like my name—'Matthew'!" Dr. Monty waxed on, "It's from the Bible."

"*¡A, qué lindo—tu nombre!* I like it! Write it down right away! *Espérate. . . . En español se dice—Matías. Escríbale—en español.*"

"Well? Okay, then! 'Matías' it is! If you say so, Clara." Dr. Monty was taken aback, a little embarrassed, but pleased. In a flash Mom had decided to name me after a doctor whose name was from the New Testament.

Dr. Monty paused. He'd never had a namesake. He carefully wrote down "Matías Montaño." "Check it for spelling, Clara."

Mom examined the certificate, nodding yes.

Dr. Monty continued with the certificate. "I estimate he weighs about eight pounds. What do you think, Clara?"

"He *is* big."

"Yes, he is at that!" Dr. Monty finished the birth certificate, explaining, "In a few months, you'll get an official copy of the certificate from the State office. Keep it in a safe place." Dr. Monty's work complete, he tucked the certificate into his bag and prepared to leave, warning Mom, "Be sure to baptize him as soon as possible."

That afternoon when Dad came home from the mine, Mom told of Dr. Monty's visit. "All's well with me—*y con* Matías!"

"Eh?"

"Manuel, I chose to use Dr. Monty's Christian name, 'Matías.'"

"*A, qué bueno!*"

"*Y, también,*" Mom excitedly continued, "Dr. Monty said we should baptize Matías as soon as possible."

"*Válgame Dios!* He doesn't have to tell us! Soon, we'll take Matías down-home to Ribera. Baltazar and Feliz will be his *padrinos.*"

I remember very little about the first six months of life. Mom said that, when hungry, I wailed wildly and kicked my feet a lot. The only thing I remember about my baptism was the calming presence of Abuelo Ribera, who spoke to me in Spanish as he held me. In November of that year, an arctic norther blasted through Chicorico Canyon, blowing snow with a 40-below-zero wind chill. Our coal camp house was drafty and cold. I picked up a bad case of influenza, a deadly killer of coal camp children and adults.

Dad called on Dr. Monty for treatment. When my two sisters and brother died—Esmelita, Carmelita, and Abrán—Dr. Monty had been just a young, greenhorn doctor. Yet Mom and Dad didn't blame him for the deaths of their babies; even a veteran doctor could not have saved them.

Dr. Monty came to the house as soon as he could. He found me in Mom and Dad's bedroom. They stood by the crib, watching as Dr. Monty examined me. I was listless, burning with fever. In those days, influenza symptoms were treated with rest in bed, allowing the body's immune system to fight. Often, infants and the elderly died before their immune systems could combat the disease.

Dr. Monty walked out of the bedroom into the kitchen. Dad followed, leaving Mom with me in the bedroom.

"Matías is in the hands of God," Dr. Monty sighed wearily. "I can't do anything for him, Manuel." Dr. Monty gazed at the kitchen floor, overcome by futility. He put the stethoscope in his crumpled, black leather bag, removed his glasses, rubbed his furrowed brow, and wiped the tears from his deep blue eyes. He blustered softly:

"If I was any kind of man, I'd dry my tears and cure Matías. I can't! . . . Looka' here, in my bag. It has mosta' my tools. Etta gave it to me when we moved to Chicorico so's I could visit homes and care for families."

Dr. Monty opened the bag, "Looka' here—a fancy stethoscope with a pearl cover on it, a blood pressure gauge, and cystoscope—all these fancy doodads in my bag—for what?"

Dad looked on, frustrated, gazing at the instruments. His own tools were self-defining: a pick, a shovel.

Dr. Monty belittled the medicines in his bag: "An' looka' here, at these glass vials, full of pills an' powders. They're supposed to cure everything from asthma to weariness. Shoot! They're worthless for helpin' Matías!" Dr. Monty closed the bag in disgust. "I just can't get used to it. There are so many camps, so many families needing a doctor. Right now, in some other home, a baby is whooping! Or burning with a blasted fever, like Matías!"

"Here, rest a bit, sit down." Dad offered a chair to Dr. Monty.

"Aww, Manuel, it's late. You and Clara must be tired. You have to work tomorrow."

"I won't work. Dick Malcolm will tell the Super. Would you like some coffee?"

"Sure, just a bit! Put a shot of whiskey in it to calm my nerves."

"I have no whiskey."

"How about some of Onorio's wine, then?"

"Are you sure?"

Dr. Monty rubbed his trim, tiny moustache. "Yes," he nodded absent-mindedly, "I'm sure. . . . Manuel, I, too, get sick." Dr. Monty shook his head, despairing as he slumped into a chair, arms leaning on the kitchen table. "Sickness of the heart. . . . I've seen too many babies die. I became a doctor to make folks well, not to let them die! To make matters worse, I couldn't help Clara with her first two girls, or the boy, Abrán—"

"Abrán died of a spider bite, Dr. Monty. We found the spider in his baptismal gown. He cried at the *bautismo*. Many babies cry when they feel the water on their heads. *Pero*, Abrán was not crying from the water. It was the spider bite."

"Well, yes. But the girls?" Dr. Monty appeared haggard and tired. He folded his glasses into a case, putting them in the black bag. He wiped his eyes, clouded with tears.

Dad feigned placidity, but he was anxious. "We can't lose faith. The girls were baptized. They're with the Lord."

"It just makes me sick . . . just sick . . . to think Esmelita and Carmelita aren't with us now."

"Clara was the same way. Every Sunday she would go to the cemetery, to visit the dead children. In the summers, she would take fresh flowers from the yard. She would stay there all day, crying. When she came home, she would go to bed. I ordered her to stay home from the cemetery. She spent too much time with the dead. We must care for those we have now."

"This is so doggone sad, an' . . ." Dr. Monty was caught in the clutch of a deep depression, entangled by melancholy bred by the high infant mortality rates in the coal camps.

Dad was disheartened. Dr. Monty's despondency was common among Company doctors. In the past, other Company doctors left the camps as soon as they were able, going to cities and towns where there was higher hope for the survival of infants. Dad liked Dr. Monty and wanted to keep him in the coal camps. He offered Dr. Monty solace, the best he knew how.

"¡A, qué mal! ¡Su tristeza es del corazón y alma! 'This is bad! Your sickness is of the heart and soul.' You must not let it dampen your spirit." Dad poured the wine into a shot glass and then into a coffee cup. He did the same for himself, taking the coffee pot from the stove and pouring coffee.

"Manuel, how do you fight this sickness?"

"I'm not an educated doctor, *pero los viejos del país* say sickness of the heart is despair in the soul. They say we must never lose faith."

"How do you keep faith? I've told you, once again, I can't help you with one of your children. Three gone, and I haven't done you a darn bit of good. With Matías? I'm certain he'll die."

"Dios da, pero no acarrea: 'God provides, but he does not carry anyone,'" Dad recited a down-home *dicho.* He stood and walked to the icebox, took out a fresh cucumber, and cut it into thick slices. He placed them in a bowl, pouring vinegar over them. "Dr. Monty, come with me to the crib. Bring your bag with the bandages."

Dad and Dr. Monty entered the bedroom, Dad carrying the bowl with the vinegar and sliced cucumbers. Mom was sitting on the bed, holding my limp, frail body wrapped loosely in a blanket. Dad's tone of voice was confident, feigning assurance:

"Clara, Dr. Monty and I have been talkin'. We're going to use a *remedio, como los viejos en el país.*"

Mom was not fooled. The down-home remedy was a last resort—a grasp at faith. She laid me in the crib and went to the dresser, where the statues of the Sacred Heart of Jesus and the *Virgen de Guadalupe* stood, searching the top drawer for her rosary. Kneeling before the statues, she lisped,

"Dios te salve, María, Madre de Dios, el Señor es contigo. . . ."

Dad laid two vinegar-saturated cucumber slices on my forehead, turning to Dr. Monty. "Give me a bandage, to use as a bandana."

Keenly watching, Dr. Monty reached in his medicine bag and took out the scissors and a roll of gauze, cutting off a piece and handing it to Dad. Dad soaked the bandage in the vinegar, wringing out the excess. He wrapped the bandage around my forehead, gently lifting my feverish head to wrap the gauze around the back. I lay limp, hardly moving except when Dad lifted me to remove my diapers. Now I was naked, except for the cucumber headband. Dad fanned me with the blanket, hanging it at the foot of the crib.

"Now, Dr. Monty, we must leave Clara with her prayers."

Dad and Dr. Monty briskly left the bedroom. In the kitchen, Dr. Monty rubbed his chin, shaking his head.

"Never saw the likes of it, Manuel." Dr. Monty was skeptical, doubting the viability of home remedies.

"*¿Sabes qué?* En el país, los viejos have many remedies."

As Dr. Monty opened the door to leave, he bowed his head and cupped his mouth with his hand, whispering woefully to Dad, "I'll come around tomorrow morning with a death certificate."

Dad sighed, "Yes . . . come. . . . Leave the bandage?"

Dr. Monty handed Dad the roll of gauze, quietly closing the kitchen door. In the bedroom Mom's lisps could be heard, praying to the Virgin, ". . . *ruega por nosotros*. . . ."

Dad sat in the kitchen, thumbing through his *Biblia* far past midnight. Every two hours, he replaced the bandana and cucumber slices with fresh ones, hoping they would leech out the fever. Mom kept vigil, kneeling beside the bed, praying the rosary repeatedly, while I lay feverish and limp.

Mom and Dad sensed *La Muerte* in our house. The Angel of Death had come three other times in *la carreta de los muertos*, shooting with her bow and arrow, hauling away the souls of Abrán, Esmelita, and Carmelita. Down-home *cuentos* say that when it's your time to die La Muerte comes with an arrow in her bow, shoots, pierces your heart, and hauls your soul to Judgment in her death-cart. The righteous respect her, calling her *Comadre Sebastiana*. She is fair, taking the souls of the rich and the poor without favorites.

This time when she arrived, she dismounted from the carreta, laid down her bow and arrow, and slipped through the bedroom wall. (I was enthralled by this part of the story. I pictured La Muerte fading through the wall, the house chilling.) La Muerte inspected the entire household.

Down-home cuentos say that when it's your time to die, La Muerte comes for you with an arrow in her bow. Photograph copyright L. A. Richardson, courtesy of Taos Historic Museums.

Faith pervaded, now that Dr. Monty was gone. Dr. Monty doubted the power of faith. Mom and Dad invoked its energy, appealing to the Lord's better side. La Muerte observed. Dad had applied the cucumber headband, como los viejos. After reviewing the words of God in the Biblia, he slept at the table, forehead and arms resting on the open book.

La Muerte listened to Mom, who knelt at her bed most of the night, rosary in hand, whispering her prayers fervently: "Dios te salve Maria," pleading to the Virgin Mary to intercede "*llena eres de gracia*," the Virgin Mother had a son, "*el Señor es contigo*," who was almost killed right after birth, "*bendita tú eres entre todas las mujeres*," so Joseph, the Virgin Mother, and the Baby Jesus fled to Egypt, "*y bendito es el fruto en tu vientre, Jesus.*" Now Mom prayed for her son's life.

La Muerte remembered. She had taken three of Mom's children already. The Lord could wait for the fourth. Her work done, she floated through the wall, placed the arrow in her quiver, mounted the carreta, and whisked away. . . .

At dawn, the sun rose from behind Hennigan's Peak, casting a warm glow over the prairies east of Chicorico Canyon. I burst out in a strong, strapping cry:

"*WAAAAAAAA!*"

Mom was startled out of her sleepy stupor. She had slumped into a sitting position next to the bed, head pressed against the chenille bedspread.

"Manuel! Manuel! Matías *vive! Ven acá!*"

Dad jerked out of his slumber, bolting into the bedroom. Mom took the blanket off the crib, wrapped it around me, unbuttoned her blouse, and lifted me to her breast. Dad delicately peeled away the cucumber bandana, daubing my forehead dry. He returned to the kitchen, throwing away the vinegary bandage and cucumbers. They were overjoyed. I was alive and well!

While Mom cuddled me, Dad prepared her favorite breakfast, *huevos rancheros con jamón*, warm tortillas, and coffee. Dad took a slab of bacon from the icebox and cut eight very thin strips of bacon, placing them in a deep, black frying pan. Mom liked her bacon very crisp, with most of the fat fried out. Dad watched as the strips crackled and sizzled, no longer spattering hot grease. He walked out to the henhouse and brought back six freshly laid eggs.

After lifting the sizzling bacon onto a plate, Dad broke open the eggs by jamming each against the pan's rim, dropping the egg whites and yellow yolks into the frying pan. The bacon grease spattered again. Dad leaned back, shielding his eyes with the spatula. After the spattering stopped, Dad sprinkled some of Mom's Chimayó chili powder over the yokes. As the bacon and eggs simmered, Dad laid three cold tortillas on the fogón, flipping them over several times. After the last flip, he glazed a thin layer of chokecherry jelly over the tortillas and poured a cup of coffee.

Using a cutting board for a tray, Dad placed three of the eggs on a plate along with four bacon strips. He set the tortillas, coffee cup, saucer, and a fork on the board. He stepped cautiously, carrying the food to Mom, who was sitting on the edge of the bed holding me. Mom had smelled the bacon and eggs frying, the strong coffee brewing. She smiled, eyes gleaming with sheer joy. Dad placed the cutting board tray on the dresser. She handed me to Dad and sidled a chair up to the dresser.

As Mom ate breakfast at the dresser, Dad sat on the bed, rocking me in his arms, serenading:

"When it's springtime in the Rockies, I'll be coming home to you. . . ."

Mom finished eating; she took the empty dish and cup to the kitchen. Returning, she listened as Dad continued his serenade, still rocking me in his arms, singing the Rocky Mountain Springtime song. Mom couldn't wait any longer. She wanted to embrace her *niño*. Eagerly, she extended her arms. Reluctantly, Dad relinquished me back to her, leaving both of us in the bedroom.

Dad ate his breakfast and washed the dishes. He felt like a king. All was well in the realm. He relaxed in the living room, lighting a pipe, perusing back copies of the *Raton Range*. In each, he read headlines about Nazi terrorism against Jews in Europe. In the November 15, 1938 edition, a photograph of a starving Jewish mother and daughter caught his eye. They lived in a tarp tent beside a road, evicted from their home. Already, stories of Jewish dislocation were percolating out of Europe. Hungry, despondent Jewish people were being evicted from their homeland.

Dad placed the newspaper down. He had no idea Germany, Italy, and Japan would soon be at war with the rest of the world—that so many Jews would be persecuted. In November 1938, folks in Chicorico were crawling out of the Great Depression. Conditions seemed a little better than before. Numb from the Depression, they didn't feel the winds of war.

As Dad pondered the terrible stories, he heard Dr. Monty's light rap at the front door. Dad opened the door; the sun was about half way in the sky.

"Entre, *por favor.*"

"Manuel, how's Clara?"

"Sleeping. She prayed all night."

"She okay?"

"*Cansada, no más.*"

"I'm sorry to hear that." Dr. Monty fumbled through his black bag, groping for a death certificate. "I know it's here, someplace."

"You need no death certificate."

"Wha—?"

"Matías lives!"

Dr. Monty dropped his bag and hurried to the bedroom. Mom was sprawled out, sleeping diagonally on the bed. I was resting on my back, wide awake and stark naked, fingering my toes. Dr. Monty touched my forehead, joyously exclaiming, "Why he's cool as a cucumber!"

"Yes. He has no fever."

"Thanks be to God!" Dr. Monty sighed, "and to the remedio He taught you!"

Dr. Monty examined me, feeling under my armpits and touching my stomach as Dad looked on, beaming from ear to ear.

"Never saw the likes of it! Matías has no fever. His temperature's normal. He's supple and nimble, just as he should be." Dr. Monty sighed heavily, bursting out:

"By goll! Matías looks wonderful!" Dr. Monty clasped both of Dad's hands, vigorously shaking them. "By goll! You did it, Manuel! You did it! You did it!"

Dr. Monty repeatedly pumped Dad's hands, shaking them up and down with both of his hands. "Manuel, you were right to say we should never give up! We must care for the living." Dr. Monty pulled Dad into the kitchen, sitting at the table, still clasping Dad's hands.

"Tell me about the remedies you learned, er . . . down-home."

For the remainder of the morning, Dr. Monty sat in the kitchen taking notes, listening as Dad explained the remedios he learned en el país, down-home in San Miguel del Vado. Before long, Dr. Monty's scant knowledge of college Spanish started to show: "Manuel, what I need is a good dictionary. Some of these herbs—I'm not sure what they are."

"Haah!" Dad laughed, ironically. He went into the front room, searching the bookshelf we called our library. "Here it is!" Dad came back into the kitchen, holding his 1903 *Appleton's New Spanish-English Dictionary*, the successor to *Velázquez's Abridged Dictionary*.

"It's well-worn, Manuel."

Dad proudly thumped the dictionary's leather-bound cover. "Got it in 1917. Taught myself English with it."

"I'll be."

"Where were we? A, sí—*cilantro.*" Dad looked up the word, with Dr. Monty watching: "Here it is, 'coriander'?"

"Oh, sure, 'coriander'!"

"Cilantro prepared as a tea," Dad explained, "is good to relax, especially for nervous children, and when you're worried and can't sleep. Or, when you eat too much."

"It's a sedative of sorts."

"Another good tea is made from mesquite."

"You mean those mangy mesquite bushes?"

"Oh, yes! Tea made from the seeds, or bark, of mesquite is good for the runs."

"Diarrhea?"

"Y, tambíen después de mal panza—to settle your *tripas.*"

Dr. Monty paged through the dictionary till he found the word "tripas."

"Oh, yeah, sure—'intestines.' I should've known."

"Cilantro y mesquite, they taste good, and they won't make you sick."

"No side effects?"

"Nada."

All of us children loved the cucumber story. I was bothered to know La Muerte had been in our house for the fourth time. I wondered how José felt about her presence, but I didn't ask.

2

RESPETO DE LOS DERECHOS DE TUS VECINOS ES LA SALVACIÓN DE TODOS

Memorial Day was special in Chicorico. The mine was closed, school was out for the year, and Dad always planted a garden in our backyard. For me, Memorial Day, Tuesday, May 30, 1944, was extra special because Dad and Mr. Heard were taking me fishing. Having Dad home during the week was unusual. That morning he rose early, waxed his 1941 Chevrolet Special Deluxe, picked some lilacs from the bushes out front, and drove Mom, Ramona, and me to the Mount Calvary Cemetery in Raton to decorate the graves of our *Angelitos de Dios*—Abrán and two sisters, Esmelita and Carmelita, who died in infancy.

As we drove out of Chicorico, the sudden, solitary trill of a meadowlark reverberated over the coal camp's quiet hush. Memorial Day was special to everyone. Chicorico folks were proud of their direct involvement in the war effort. Almost all the families had men or women in the armed services somewhere in Europe or the Pacific. Two Chicorico families had lost their sons in the infamous Bataan Death March.

Chicorico's presence in World War II was indicated by armed service flags hanging in the windows of most homes, the number of stars on each flag representing the number of armed service personnel in the family. The coal of Chicorico was shipped to the Colorado Fuel and Iron Works (CF&I) in Pueblo, and to the Kaiser Steel Corporation in Fontana, California, where iron was smelted into steel for the war effort.

We arrived at the Mount Calvary Cemetery, located on the prairie slope at the southwestern edge of Raton. The Memorial Day ceremony was just about to begin. A lot of people congregated around the grotto in the center of the cemetery where a veterans memorial was erected. Chairs were provided for the veterans and other participants in the parade through downtown Raton that was now just ending at the cemetery. They were all seated, waiting for the ceremony to begin. The rest of us stood in a circle around the perimeter of the chairs, facing a podium and a microphone. Mom and Dad lifted Ramona and me in their arms, raising us high enough to see over the crowd.

The Raton High School band started the ceremony by playing "The Star Spangled Banner." Everyone rose. The men who wore hats held them over their hearts. Mom took Ramona's right hand and placed it over her heart, signaling me to do the same. Dad couldn't hold his hat and me! He flicked his head sideways several times for me to take his hat. I grabbed it, careful not to crease the brim.

A lot of the people sang along with the band; Dad and Mom mouthed the words, barely audible:

"O-oh, say can you see,
By the dawn's early light . . ."

Goose bumps . . . shivers . . . more goose bumps erupted across my arms, spreading over the rest of me.

"What so proud–ly we hailed
At the twilight's last gleaming . . ."

I shuddered and twisted my shoulders to chase the shivers away. Those words, that song, felt good, but they gave me goose bumps, the shivers. I tried to join in the singing:

"Whose bright stripes and bright stars . . ."

Too hard, those words. Too high, those notes. I faltered, mouthing the words, like Mom and Dad. Others painstakingly warbled on, voices straining. Some voices cracked, wavering for the higher notes.

Right after the band completed the anthem, it struck up another patriotic tune. Folks cheered up, buoyantly singing:

"My country 'tis of thee,
Sweet land of liberty,
Of thee I sing! . . ."

Sing! Sing! Sing! Mom and Dad sang their hearts out. I joined them. I could actually sing this song! The words were easy to say, the notes easy to reach! I warbled the words loud and clear! What fun! The goose bumps and shivers vanished. I felt warm all over.

When the band completed "America," Probate Judge Fred Voorhiis asked everyone to sit. Dad and Mom lowered Ramona and me to the ground. We remained standing, as there were no chairs for us. I handed Dad's hat back to him. Mr. Voorhiis introduced the main speaker:

"It's my pleasure to give you one of our own—a veteran wounded by a Japanese bomb while he manned his gun on a ship in Pearl Harbor. He lost his left arm and was honorably discharged. Now he works in the Brilliant mine—Nash Trujillo!"

Shouting, thundering applause erupted! Those sitting stood up, turning to the standing crowd, vigorously clapping. Mr. Nash Trujillo looked very young in his sailor suit, the left sleeve pinned to its shoulder. He cleared his throat and people sat again.

"Howdy, folks! Er, I ain't too good at speaking. Our boys are really fighting hard in Europe and the Pacific. Two Colfax County boys are in the Italian invasion—Frank Bartholomew and Joe Sluga. Frank's from Koehler and Joe was from Sugarite, before it closed down. There's a whole slew of guys fightin' in the Pacific. I'm glad to be back home. I was scared all the time the Japs were bombing us. Making war is no ball game. Boys die . . . get burned . . . or blown to bits. No, I ain't sorry I enlisted and did combat against the Japs. A lot of the boys on that ship were killed. I was lucky. But I'm no hero. Or a public speaker, you can tell!" Thundering applause mixed with laughter!

"Hey, I'm not important. I'm lucky to be alive, doing my part working the Brilliant mine. I can't kick. And, we're gonna win this war!"

Thundering applause again! Everyone sitting stood up, joining the vigorous clapping. Mr. Trujillo was our hero. He wasn't ashamed to admit he was afraid for his life. Embarrassed by the long, loud outburst of applause, he gawked and awkwardly curtsied, waving with his one good arm. The applause intensified, muffling his expressions of gratitude: "God bless you! God bless America!"

After Mr. Trujillo sat down and the applause subsided, the American Legion, the Disabled Veterans, and the Veterans of Foreign Wars demonstrated the changing-of-the-guard ritual. The men were dressed in full uniform from World War I or II, including their guns. After the ritual, twenty-one men prepared for a gun salute. Judging by their uniforms, the men represented the army, navy, and marines, except for Mr. Alva Stockton, who wore the blue Civil War uniform of the North.

Mr. Stockton had served as a Union soldier for the Colorado Volunteers under Major John M. Chivington in 1862. Mr. Stockton volunteered to join them. The Colorado Volunteers repulsed the only Confederate threat to New Mexico in Glorieta Canyon east of Santa Fe. Mr. Stockton was one of the soldiers lining up for the twenty-one-gun salute. His ninety-eight years showed; he doddered, watching every step.

Mr. Voorhiis called the men into formation, asking everyone in the audience to stand. Ramona and I squirmed to see. Dad and Mom noticed and lifted us again. Mr. Voorhiis ordered, "FIRE!" The soldiers shot their rifles successively into the clear, blue sky—a salute for the fallen dead.

The air was filled with smoke and smelled of burnt gunpowder. A few babies cried. Mr. Voorhiis dismissed the men. They marched back to the chairs, but stayed standing. Mr. Voorhiis turned his eyes upward to the flag, placing his American Legion hat over his heart. Everyone followed suit. Mom lifted Ramona's and my hands to our hearts, pointing to the flag. Dad handed me his hat again. Everyone stood silently, some with heads bowed. A lone trumpeter played taps lowly. . . .

From Dad's arms, I could see quite a bit. Mount Calvary Cemetery sat on a high incline just east of another coal camp, Brilliant, which nestled in the foothills of the Sangre de Cristo mountains, just like Chicorico. To the

Erosion took its toll, although the Norman Cross was still apparent on the hand-carved tombstone.

east, the prairies undulated for miles to Johnson Mesa, Hennigan's Peak, and the Chico mountains, all formed by volcanic action centuries ago.

Veterans' graves were decorated with small American flags. The cemetery was strewn with flowers. People used the day to decorate their family graves with lilacs, plum and cherry blossoms, and other handpicked flowers from their yards. Headstones reflected the multiethnic complexion of the coal camps, with names and memorial phrases inscribed in English, German, Greek, Hebrew, Italian, Spanish, and several different Slavic languages.

We found the graves of Abrán, Esmelita, and Carmelita. Dad had carved a headstone for each of the children. For each grave, he had found a pink sandstone rock about the size of a gallon bucket. With a large nail, he carved a Norman Cross into each rock, and then etched the names of Abrán, Esmelita, and Carmelita with dates of birth and death. Erosion was taking its toll, obscuring the names and dates on the sandstones, although the Norman Crosses were still very apparent.

"*¡Ándale!* We have to plant the garden before Mr. Heard comes over."

Dad and I pulled the dried weeds that had grown around the headstones. Dad's rush to clear the graves was a ruse. Usually, he insisted on thoroughness. He rushed us to prevent Mom from lingering at the graves of her dead children. It had taken many years to break her depression so that she no longer spent every Sunday visiting the graves. Just as I pulled the last of the weeds from around the headstones, Dad led a prayer for our passed-on sisters and brother. He picked up Ramona, and Mom took my hand. Being careful not to step on any graves, we walked back to the car and left the cemetery. Other people were still milling around, lingering at gravesides, remembering the living and the dead.

Now home, Dad immediately started to plant a garden in our backyard. Chicorico patriotism was apparent in most backyards. People took to heart the government's promotion of Victory Gardens. Canning and preserving occurred all summer as vegetables ripened. Our backyard was like most others—a rectangular lot with a coal shed, an outhouse, a water pump, and a chicken coop with a henhouse. Earlier, when Dad and Mom first moved to Chicorico, they had planted cosmos and wild mountain flowers around

Each coal camp house had a view of the canyon's walls and the hills for a backyard.

our house. In the front yard, they had planted lilac bushes and a cottonwood tree. These were now mature.

Chicorico houses were situated in rectangular lots running up and down the canyon, facing the railroad tracks and main road. Chicorico Creek meandered down the canyon, snaking under the tracks and the main road as it wound its way to the Canadian River. Each coal camp house faced north or south, had a view of a canyon wall, and had the hills for a backyard. On a ridge high up in the hills to the south, a deep reservoir had been dug. Fed by a natural spring, the reservoir provided pure mountain spring water for all the homes and Company buildings.

The Company's production manager—we called him the "Super"—and the Company doctor were provided houses with hot and cold running water, full baths, a flushing toilet, tub, and sinks. The rest of us took water from a pump located in our backyards. We toted water to drink, bathe, cook, clean, and irrigate the garden. We also heated water when needed. Mom's fogón had a small boiling pan attached to its left side, which kept a few gallons of water warm so long as the fogón was stoked up.

After removing the rocks, most families grew vegetable gardens in the rich, fallow soil of their hillside homes. Dad cultivated a small eight-by-four-foot patch each year, recycling the vegetable plants into mulch. Our yard was especially rocky. Over the years, our rock pile grew higher. In the winter, the rocks grew, it seemed. The cold days must have percolated them to the surface.

"When it's spring time in the Rockies . . . ," Dad hummed as he spaded the soil, believing that humming was good for clearing his catarrh. Much of the backyard was a haven for field mice and bullsnakes. The prairie grasses grew wild. Only the eight-by-four patch Dad cultivated appeared tame, subdued by years of plowing and harrowing to raise vegetables. We rarely saw bullsnakes, but they kept the mice population down. When we saw one, we weren't allowed to kill it. We were to chase it away. The same applied to rattlesnakes, but we were never tested. We never saw rattlesnakes in the yard. José said rattlesnakes avoided bullsnakes, and the bullsnakes claimed the yard as their territory.

Dad leveled the surface of the soil, which was soft and crumbly. Surprisingly, it was not too sandy or grainy. Instead, it was dark and crumpled easily, saturated with compost Dad had decomposed for many years. There were always small stones in it. While spading, Dad broke down the big clods and dug up the stones that had grown since the last spring. I pitched the new stones onto the rock pile in the corner of the yard.

The newly upturned clods writhed with wiggling worms. The clods looked alive, they had so many worms in them! Dad's composting over the years paid off in better soil for gardening and worms for fishing. I grabbed the worms and put them in a coffee can. Mixing in compost, Dad raked the garden surface smooth and flat. He sent me into the house for the seed onion, and cucumber, zucchini, and garden lettuce seed packets. When I returned, Dad already had plowed furrows and was ready to plant.

"By early July, the onions and lettuce will be ready."

Using his pocketknife, Dad cut slits in each seed package as he dropped seeds along the furrows. He folded soil into the furrows, lightly tamping over the seeds.

"Your mother will make us a salad *muy sabroso.* She'll slice the young onions and mix them with the lettuce, throwing in *quelites* she'll pick from the *llano.* For dressing, she'll mix olive oil and vinegar."

Dad planted the cucumber and zucchini seeds in mounds two feet apart. "They won't be ready till the end of August."

As he finished planting the seeds, he stabbed the packets, making a sign for the head of each furrow showing where the lettuce, the cucumber, and the zucchini seeds were planted. Dad stood up, arms akimbo, proudly surveying the straight rows of newly planted lettuce, cucumbers, zucchini, and onions. He put a hand on my shoulder.

"Make sure the plants have plenty of water. And pull the weeds before they choke the plants. Now! Let's find some more worms."

Dad spaded clods of dirt and grass in different parts of the backyard. I broke down the clods, searching for worms. Dirt seeped under my fingernails and my palms collected a thin sheen of dust.

When Dad thought we'd collected enough worms, we stopped to clean ourselves. We slapped the dirt and dust out of our pant legs, kicked our shoes against the pump stand to shake loose any clinging mud, and ran water from the pump over our hands. Dad shook his hands, casting water in every direction. He went into the house to dry his hands and prepare for our fishing trip.

Rubbing my hands under the gushing water, I picked the dirt from beneath my fingernails. I daubed my forehead with some water, twisted my mouth under the faucet, and let the water gush into my mouth, swallowing in huge gulps. I rubbed my face on my shirt sleeve and dried my hands on the pant legs of my bib overalls. I joined Dad in the house.

Ooga! Ooga! Mr. Heard honked the horn of his blue 1928 Ford Model A pickup. Mr. Julian Heard was the father of the only African American family remaining in Chicorico. His father came to Chicorico to work in the coke ovens in 1910, bringing the family from West Virginia.

I rumbled out the door with the fishing poles. Dad walked, carrying a tackle box and can of worms.

"Put your tackle in the back, Manuel. I've got plenty of grubs if'n you don't."

"¡Ándale, *pues!* Matías and I found plenty of worms."

Mr. Heard opened the door from the inside. I crawled in. Dad followed, closing the door.

"But will the bullheads take to 'em?"

"Sí. *¿Cómo no?*"

There was plenty of room in the cab for the three of us. The Model A was the first pickup produced by Ford, designed for utility, with a sparse interior design, mostly a small oval instrument panel in the center of the dashboard decked with a tiny speedometer and gauges. Mr. Heard saw my legs dangling over the middle of the seat. He gently moved them to the right of the gearshift to make room to shift. He dropped the pickup into gear and drove out of the canyon, heading for Highway 85 and Stubblefield Lake. The lake was one of six built in the late twenties to irrigate the farms between Maxwell and Springer.

"Mr. Heard, what's a bullhead?"

"A bullhead? Well, it's another name for a catfish."

"Are they like trout?"

"Matías, you ask too many questions!" Dad was embarrassed by my verbosity.

"That's okay, Manuel. Round these parts, kids only know about trout."

"Mr. Malcolm says trout are the best."

"Hito, Mr. Malcolm likes trout; Mr. Heard likes catfish." Dad pressed his lips, showing his irritation.

"Well, Manuel, trout are the best fighters. They're harder to catch," Mr. Heard rejoined. "When a bull hits, he just gloms on—hook, line, and bait. Trout nibble around a lot. You have to know how to set the hook, when they're nibbling. When they bite, they fight like heck! They're nimble critters."

"Mr. Malcolm says he'd never go cat fishing, he—"

"Sometimes Mr. Malcolm gets carried away with fishing stories!" Dad nudged me in the leg with his knee, glaring at me. That was his way of telling me to be quiet.

The conversation turned to family. Mr. Heard told about Eddie, his oldest son, who was in the Army somewhere in Europe. He didn't know where.

"I sure fret about that boy. He's the only son I've got. Sure miss him." Mr. Heard's daughter, Marian, was my age.

"I know. Our boy Arturo's in the navy. He flies a bomber. We can't worry, just pray for our boys."

When we reached Stubblefield Lake, Mr. Heard drove across the dam to its eastern side, near a water diversion canal. The canal served as a spillway when the dam was full. He parked close to the bank where the dam and the canal intersected. We were on a high spot and could see across the lake. On the other side of the lake, two antelope grazed with a herd of cattle. On the western horizon, the snowcapped Sangre de Cristo mountains silhouetted the sky. At the base of the Sangre de Cristos was the front range, the foothills where most of the coal camps nestled. Between the foothills and the lake, the prairies undulated in rolling dips and swells. Something frightened the antelope. They sprinted, disappearing into the rolling prairie.

"Hito, when we get down from the truck, there'll be no talking. I'll show you how to fish. Watch and learn."

As soon as the engine died, Mr. Heard and Dad scurried from the pickup, inspected the bank, located fishing spots, unloaded the tackle and poles, tied leaders and sinkers to their lines. Dad rigged up a pole for me. Mr. Heard motioned to Dad to use the grubs for bait. Dad impaled a grub on his hook and one on mine. He motioned me to watch him cast his line into the water. I watched. Dad cast the line like a graceful baseball pitcher following through a smooth, even pitch. He laid the pole down, securing it with rocks.

Dad held my pole, swung it over his right shoulder, and whipped it forward. The sinker, hook, and line careened into an arch, flying high over the water—plunk! The sinker sank, pulling the hook and line with it. Dad handed me the pole. I was fishing!

I sat down to wait and discovered that fishing was a waiting game. You bait your hook, throw your line in the water, and wait. With a little bit of luck, a fish will swim along, bump into your bait, and glom onto it. With a lot of luck, a fish in a school of fish will swim along, bump into your bait, and glom onto it! Then you pull it in, tether it on a stringer, bait your hook, and cast your line again, quickly and accurately, to approximately the spot it was before, hoping all along the school of fish is still hanging around, waiting for your next cast!

The best part of the waiting game was the silence and tranquility of lake, land, and life surrounding them. As I waited, a colony of gulls scavenged along the shore, ancient holdovers from centuries ago when the area was covered by a large ocean. When the ocean receded, leaving behind lakes with fish and plants, the gulls remained. We sat in silence for a long time.

Glomp! Mr. Heard's line bounced, rippling the surface of the water. He reeled slowly, lifting the bullhead out of the water and over the shore. It looked easy. The bullhead hardly moved.

Glomp! My line bounced! I started to reel fast. The pole bent into a bow. Heavy! Dad came by my side, breaking the silence, directing me in soft tones, "Slow, reel slow. Don't jerk the line; it'll break. Take your time. Bulls don't fight, just like Mr. Heard said."

What a thrill! I wanted to reel fast, to jerk that bull in right away! But Mr. Heard knew best. He'd already caught one. I kept reeling, slowly pulling the bull closer. Dad looked on, concentrating on the end of my line. Now I could see the fish's face above the water, staring at me with his mouth open. He'd swallowed the hook and its face looked like the face of Winston Churchill's bulldog I once saw in the *Raton Range.*

Dad reached in the water and pulled the bullhead out. It just hung there, hardly moving. Dad broke silence again:

"To remove the hook, put your fingers over the gills, then squeeze the head. His mouth will open. This one swallowed the hook. Have to cut the line. Use my knife. It's in my pocket."

I reached in Dad's pocket, got the knife, opened it, and reached over to the bull's mouth.

"*Con cuidado.* See these whiskers? They're horns." Dad pointed to the bullhead's tentacles on its head. "They'll pick you. You might drop the bull."

Before I cut the line, Dad ran the stringer through the bull's gill. Dad motioned for me to cut the line. He threw the stringer into the water and tied it to a stick. He showed me how to tie a new leader and hook on my line. I hurriedly grabbed a plump, squirmy grub and stuck it on the hook. Dad lifted the pole over his right shoulder and whipped it forward, watching the sinker and hook arching over the water. Plunk! The sinker plopped into the water and sank. Dad handed the pole to me. I was fishing again!

Dad and Mr. Heard never spoke. They sat quietly all afternoon, waiting for the bullheads to glom onto our lines. I soon enjoyed the silent ritual. When a catfish seized onto one of our hooks, we'd reel it in slowly, remove the hook, place it on the stringer, re-bait, cast, sit down, and wait.

As I waited for a bite, I gazed across the placid surface of the lake. A few puffy clouds reflected in the turquoise blue water. The air smelled like fish. Patches of sky were momentarily darkened by hordes of geese winging their way north in V-formations. Contented and happy, my mind drifted. I loved the fishing ritual. It was a lot like mass. You had to be quiet in mass, and after watching the adults, you could tell what you had to do. And, no talking!

Fishing was better than mass. In mass, you had to be quiet and listen to the priest. The room was always too hot, winter or summer. One time last summer, at mass in Saint Joseph's in Raton, a little girl fainted. The church was very hot and crowded. We were packed into the pews. A lot of people were standing in the back of the church and along the sides. Nobody noticed the girl faint, until her parents stood to go to Holy Communion. Then she fell into the aisle! She was squeezed into the pew so tightly, she couldn't fall over when she fainted till her parents got up.

Out here was better than mass, under the sky with the cows and the antelope, watching the different birds, waiting for a bite. If you were quiet, you'd see a water strider skittering across the surface of the lake, or a mud hen showing her babies how to dunk for minnows.

I glanced at Dad and Mr. Heard. Both had their eyes on their lines, fully engrossed in fishing. About four o'clock, Mr. Heard stood up and went behind the pickup. He unloaded some sticks and paper, lit a small campfire. He placed a charred coffeepot over the fire. At home, Mr. Heard had filled the pot with water and coffee, cowboy style, in which the coffee is boiled in the water. After a while, he brought two cups of coffee, offering one to Dad.

"Sorry, no milk, Matías."

"That's okay," Dad injected before I could respond, "he can sip my coffee if he wants."

"Here, wait!" Mr. Heard abruptly stood up and went back to the pickup. "I've got another cup for Matías."

He brought back a cup of coffee and handed it to me. I looked over to Dad for approval. Dad winked, nodding yes. Normally, Mom and Dad wouldn't let us drink coffee, except when Mom made oatmeal cookies. We were permitted to dunk them in coffee. These gentlemen were nice to me. I felt like a prince in the presence of two kings.

I sipped the hot coffee. Secretly, I didn't like the thick, syrupy, acrid taste of the strong cowboy coffee, but I didn't say anything. Real men just swallow without wincing. After all, I was being allowed to drink the divine elixir of adults. I continued sipping cautiously. We sat quietly. Finally, Mr. Heard broke the silence:

"How many you catch, Manuel?"

"I have four. The boy has two."

"Pretty good. I got five. Think we fished out this spot?"

"For today, *yo creo.* Ready to call it a day?"

"In a while. If'n you don't mind, I'd like to set a spell longer." Mr. Heard sat between Dad and me. "When I'm out here in the wide open spaces, I could cry for joy! I feel so good. You always hear that cowboys hanker to sleep on the prairie. Bet it's beautiful with all them stars!"

Dad didn't respond. After a while, he murmured wistfully, "My brother, Jesús, he's a *vaquero.* I gave him my piece of the ranch and came to Chicorico to work in the mine."

"Manuel, I grew up being a miner. Been mining since I was thirteen. That's all I ever knew. And I don't like it, being underground and all."

"All these years you been mining, and you don't like it? Why—"

"That's all I know," Mr. Heard interrupted Dad. "And it's good money for a colored man."

"¿Como?"

"Manuel, before the union, colored men didn't get paid near what other men were paid. You know that."

"Sorry, Julian. Been a while we've had to think about that, hasn't it?"

"You bet!" Mr. Heard perked up. "Ever since 1937 when we organized. Union's been the best part of mining, far's I'm concerned. . . . But let's cut the politics, getting too serious. I'd ruther been workin' on a ranch."

"*A*, Julian, ranching's hard work."

"At least it's outside, where you can see the sun, hills, the critters roamin' around. Do you ever miss the ranch?"

"Sometimes, like now. But there's no money in the ranch. It will only support one family. There's no doctors or schools, either. For a family man, Chicorico's better."

"I know what you mean," Mr. Heard was in agreement. He raised his hand up to Dad's shoulder, "If'n I was alone, I'd be a cowboy and . . . "

As Mr. Heard was telling Dad why he would like to be a cowboy, I noticed that Mr. Heard's palms were almost white! The rest of him was black. I first noticed when Mr. Heard was shifting gears in the truck. Now, when he laid his hand on Dad's shoulder, I noticed again. His palms were almost white. The rest of his skin was pretty dark. Without knowing why, I blurted out:

"Mr. Heard, why are you so black?"

"*¡Cállate la boca*, Matías! Do not ask such questions!" Dad scolded, vexed and utterly embarrassed. As for me, I was surprised at Dad's stern, curt scolding. He was a soft-spoken man who rarely raised his voice in anger. And Mr. Heard didn't seem at all bothered by my question.

"Shoot, Manuel, I am black, mostly," Mr. Heard laughed, "except maybe the palms of my hands and the bottoms of my feet." Mr. Heard held up his palm, showing it to Dad.

Dad glanced at his light-skinned palm, chafing from embarrassment. He couldn't laugh along with Mr. Heard. Instead, he apologized for my faux pas.

"Please pardon my boy, Julian. He's just a boy."

"Bright boy, I'd say! He's right observant!" Mr. Heard tried to relax Dad. His voice sparkled, and with a gleam in his eyes, he turned to me, "Why do you ask about my color?"

"I don't know. Just asking." I shrugged, glancing at Dad. Simultaneously, his face oozed with pain and embarrassment. Yet Mr. Heard remained calm, almost amused.

"Matías, you asked a fair question. I'll give you a fair answer." Mr. Heard gathered his thoughts for a moment, "Now—what's a bullhead?"

"A catfish."

"Well, yeah! A bullhead is a catfish, and a catfish is a—?"

"A fish."

"That's right! Now, what's a rainbow trout?"

"Well . . . it's a fish, too!"

"Good boy! Now—bulls and rainbows are fish. They're pretty much the same, as fish. Wouldn't you agree?"

"I . . . I . . . guess so."

"No guessing to it! Bulls and rainbows—they both need to eat to live; they both need water to swim; neither can live outside water."

"Yes! Yes! This is true!" Dad sensed where Mr. Heard was taking me with the parable.

"The only thing different about bulls and rainbows is on the outside—the color of their skins! Bulls are sort of bronze and yellow. Rainbows are speckled with the colors of the rainbow."

"What does all this have to do with you being dark?"

"Por Dios, Matías! *Con respeto.*" Dad cautioned me to ask questions respectfully.

Without flinching, Mr. Heard continued the logic of his parable:

"You know, Matías, folks are pretty much like fish. Folks have different colored skins. Inside, we're still folks, just like bulls and rainbows are just fish. That's all they are—fish. God makes us all with different colored skins is all."

"And we're all made by the same God!" Dad chimed in, now less tense. "In the eyes of God, we're all in His family. We are His children."

"A-men," Mr. Heard uttered softly.

Dad gazed at Mr. Heard, placing his hand on Mr. Heard's shoulder: *"Un hombre muy bueno."*

After finishing coffee, we reeled in our lines, removed the leaders, hooks, sinkers, and loaded up the pickup. Mr. Heard put the fish in a bucket of water. I don't remember much about the return trip home. I must have dozed a little—except Mr. Heard described a recipe for frying the fish.

"When you're frying the bulls, sprinkle a little bit of chili powder on them. When they're turning crispy, sprinkle a little bit every time you turn 'em over. Add a little bit of salt and pepper too. Say, how many did you catch?"

"Between me and the boy, six."

"That's hardly enough for that big family of yours! Take mine!"

"Oh, no Julian. You gave us grubs, and the ride to the lake."

"Oh, go on now! You'd do the same. Besides, my missus don't like bulls. Says they're too fishy-tasting, like mud suckers. She likes rainbows."

"You tell Dahlia she doesn't know what she's missing."

"Won't do no good. No matter how you fix bulls, they're still suckers to her."

When we got home, Dad showed me how to gut the fish. Beside a tree stump in our backyard, Dad demonstrated how to cut the fish open—a messy, smelly job. Some of the bullheads were still alive. They watched as he gutted them. When Dad drove his knife into their bottoms and sliced open their breasts, they wiggled momentarily before they died with their eyes open.

Dad took each fish after it was gutted and whacked off its head with a sharp hatchet—the very hatchet used to de-head chickens. After deheading the fish, he asked me to bury their entrails and heads in the garden. They made good fertilizer. He busied himself washing the fish underneath the pump's faucet. When finished, he took the fish in the house while I buried the heads and entrails. I ran some water from the pump to clean my hands. I swirled water in the fishing bucket, tossing the dirty water in the garden.

When I returned to the kitchen, Angela, Juan, and José were setting the table. Mom watched, giving them directions. Dad was frying the fish, religiously following Mr. Heard's directions and using Mom's chili powder. Mom was particular about her chili. She only bought the best powder made from chili peppers grown in Chimayó. It was pure chili powder without pepper or any other seasoning. She also used Tío Baltazar's chili when he gave it to her.

As we sat for supper, we bowed our heads and closed our eyes, giving thanks. Dad led the blessing in Spanish:

"*Bendito sea Dios, bendito sea Jesucristo, bendito sea la nombre de María, Virgen y Madre, bendito sea sus Angeles y sus Santos.*"

Dad shifted to English. "Thanks be to God for giving us this day to plant our garden. Thanks be to Mr. Heard for giving us his catch. We pray for Arturo who's in the war, y tambíen, Edward Heard." Dad finished the blessing by leading us through an Our Father and a Hail Mary for Arturo and Eddie.

As we ate, Dad repeated Mr. Heard's parable about bullheads and rainbows, how their skin colors were different, but they were still fish. They were more alike than different—just like people. No matter what our color, we were all equal children of God.

"*Respeto de los derechos de tu vecinos es la salvación de todos*—'respect for the rights of your neighbors is the salvation of everyone,'" Dad quoted Benito Juárez, the first President of Mexico, ending the parable.

3

SHOOTING WITHOUT RESPECT FOR LIFE

The next day, I sauntered to the Company store to pick up the mail. The store's front doors were gigantic, with windows running almost the full length of the doors. Inside, display counters were filled with an array of garden and home utensils, and clothing. The Company store also sold food, including produce, meat, and dairy products requiring refrigeration.

Angela was busy doing inventory in the back. I went to the post office in the northeast corner of the store. Mrs. Chicarelli was the postmistress. Her son Geno was my best friend. I think she got the job as postmistress because she could read Italian, Spanish, and English. She waved, pointing:

"Come to the side door." She was a nice lady, always smiling, and her eyes danced when she spoke. She wore her hair in a bun.

I opened the side door and was charmed by a chaotic concerto of chicks, chirping their hearts out!

"Your dad's chicks're here."

There must have been twenty crates of chicks in the back of the post office. Each crate contained ten chicks. They were chirping up a storm, in chaotic synchrony in their cardboard shipping crates. They had been shipped from Garden City, Kansas, on the Santa Fe Railroad and probably hadn't eaten during that time. They sounded starved. I peeked into one of the crate holes. The chicks were yellow fuzz balls, with cute, beady eyes and beaks sharp enough to break a window.

"Sure you can hold it level?" Mrs. Chicarelli handed me one of the crates, peering at me. "If you tip the box, they'll all fall to the side. You might break a leg."

"Don't worry, Mrs. Chicarelli. I do big jobs at home too."

"Ho-o-o," she chuckled, "You're just a whipper-snapper."

"I know." Acting like a whipper-snapper was some kind of hero, I grabbed the crate. She held the door open, then scurried ahead to hold the front door.

"Hey, little brother! I'm glad you're taking the chicks." Angela spied me as I was leaving. "Tell Mom I'll bring the mail after work."

At home, I took the chicks to the back porch. "Mom! Come see the chicks!"

She came out to the porch.

"*¡A, qué lindas!* You better feed them right away. Give them water, too, but don't put them in the coop with the others. During the day, leave them to wander in the yard. They won't go far. At night, put the crate in the coop for them."

I took the chicks to the chicken coop and opened the gate. The rooster tried to run out. With my foot, I shoved him back into the coop, still balancing the crate. He squawked, running to a corner and puffing up as if to fight. I ignored him, closed the gate behind me, and put down the crate. I went into the henhouse. Most of the hens were setting, watching with mild curiosity as I searched for the chicken feed.

I found the chicken feed in a Purina Chow gunnysack of mashed and mixed seeds. I tucked some in my pockets, returned to the crated chicks, and fed them through the holes in the crate. They gobbled every last chicken feed seed. I poured water in one of the Mason jars Mom used for canning chokecherry jelly, pouring the water into the lid and placing it on the ground. I took the chicks out of the crate. They mobbed the lid, crowding out each other as they struggled to drink.

While the chicks drank, I went into the henhouse and fed the hens. I left to fetch water from the pump for their trough. While I was fetching water, the hens spotted the chicks' water. Stampeding the Mason jar lid, they crowded out the chicks, drinking their water. Then the hens turned on the chicks, pecking at them! I chased the hens away, put the chicks back into the crate, and placed it outside the coop. I filled the hens' water trough. They mobbed it, and I rushed out of the chicken coop! Now I understood why Mom cautioned me about segregating the chicks.

I just needed to tend to the garden before I was a free man. The garden needed a little watering. We didn't have a hose to irrigate the garden. Instead, I had to run water into a bucket and carry the water to the garden. Dad had rigged up a sprinkler—a half-gallon Rex lard tin can with a small wire handle. With hammer and nail, Dad had punched a whole lot of tiny holes in the can's bottom.

I dipped the can in the bucket, then carried it up and down the garden rows, sprinkling over the furrows. The water in the can trickled out of the makeshift sprinkler onto the garden. When the can emptied, I repeated the procedure.

As I carried the last bucket of water to the garden, I heard birds chirping on the other side of the llano. I paused to watch the birds. It was springtime in the hills. The birds had returned from their winter's roost, looking for a place to build nests to lay their eggs. They did this every spring.

"Shoo! Go away!"

I had spotted a bullsnake in the garden—a long fellow. I grabbed a stick and chased him away. He slithered into the llano's tall grass. I returned to sprinkling, but was rudely interrupted, a loud ruckus coming from a rotting ponderosa tree trunk! I ran across the llano and found the bullsnake crawling up the tree trunk. He was after the fledglings in their nest.

"Shoo! Go away!"

I poked the snake with a stick. He slithered through the grass and disappeared under some rocks. I went back to the tree trunk covered with ivy and moss. Mushrooms were growing on the moss. I carefully tilted the mushrooms. Within the recesses of the rotting tree trunk, there were two flicker fledglings, chirping away, waiting for their mother to feed them. They had just been born. They were sitting in their eggshells, wrinkled and gawky, but they sure could stretch their throats and chirp. They were famished, like the chicks in the post office. Beside the two fledglings lay two unhatched eggs, flecked and speckled in pink and blue. Carefully I withdrew my hands, the mushrooms springing back in place.

I finished watering the garden and scrutinized it for weeds. It was too soon to have any weeds, but I wanted to do a good job for Dad. Again I heard a ruckus coming from the flicker's nest. I ran across the llano. Closer, I didn't hear the fledglings anymore. When I arrived, the bullsnake was in the nest, looking fat and satisfied. The fledglings were gone. He had eaten them. Adding insult to injury, he had broken open the unhatched eggs and curled up to rest in the nest—with egg on his face.

I ran back to the yard to get some pebbles out of the rock pile. Stuffing pebbles into the front, back, and bib pockets of my overalls, I dashed back to the nest, bombarding the tree trunk with the pebbles. Some of the pebbles hit the bullsnake, bouncing off to the side. He started to crawl out of the tree trunk. I picked up my stick and poked the snake in the belly. He wound his long, sinewy body around the stick, scaring me! I dropped the stick. The snake unwound itself and crawled away. I looked around for some more pebbles.

By now, José had spotted me throwing the pebbles. He dashed over to help. Fully armed with pebbles, he handed me some. *Ping! Ping!* No use. We kept missing.

"It's hard to hit a moving target," José observed.

I described what had happened, showing José the now empty nest where once a family of flickers lived.

José hunched his shoulders, nonchalantly explaining, "That's Mother Nature for you. One animal eats another, and then another eats that one. Everything's tied together, like a long chain."

"A-a-a-ck! Who'd eat a snake?"

"Lots of birds, mostly hawks and eagles. Say, want to come with me?"

"Where?"

"To the coke ovens. We'll kill some rattlesnakes."

"Rattlers? Heck, no!"

"Ah, don't be a big baby," José scoffed.

I was really afraid of rattlesnakes, but my big brother José was asking me to play with him—better yet to share an adventure with him. What I didn't know was that in the past week, Juan, Freddie, and Petee had turned down his offer to hunt rattlesnakes. They thought he was crazy to want to fool around with rattlers.

"What'll you shoot them with—pebbles?"

"S-u-u-n! My arrows have real Indian arrowheads. I'll shoot 'em with my bow and arrow. Wait here. I'll get 'em."

José had a strong bow he'd found in somebody's trash. It was worn down pretty smooth, but still had a strong, willowy spring to it. I always wished I had found it; I could have been the greatest Indian of all times, although José thought he was. Angela brought him some cotton string from the store. It was stout, just like the tightly woven string used by surveyors and carpenters to plumb straight lines.

While José went for his bow and arrows, I filled my pockets with stones from the rock pile—the biggest, roughest stones that would fit in my pockets. I couldn't be totally defenseless, although I was pretty well weighed down with the stones.

José showed me his four arrows. They were good looking, straight as can be. He made his own arrows. Dad brought him some dowel rods from the carpenter's shop at the mine. José had searched for arrowheads out on the prairies east of Chicorico. He found an abandoned hunting camp with plenty of arrowheads. Most were flint; some were obsidian.

Using Dad's pocketknife, he cut a slit at the top of the dowel and slipped an arrowhead into it. Using white cotton thread dipped in piñón pitch, he tied the arrowhead securely to the dowel. At the other end, he cut a bowstring groove for shooting.

For feathers, he hunted the hills for crow and turkey feathers. When he didn't find enough feathers, he went into the chicken coop and plucked feathers from two of the chickens. They weren't very cooperative. By hook, crook, or pluck, he found his feathers and glued them with pitch onto the end—just like the Indians using pitch from the bark of piñón trees.

"Why do you need me?"

"It's more fun when I have help. When a snake runs under a rock, you go behind the rocks and lift it up."

"You're crazy!"

"You don't pick up the rock, just tip it back. The rattler can't bite through the rock. Heck, you're safer than I am. I'm in front of the rock. Come on."

I really was afraid of rattlesnakes. Yet, my desire to be brave like José, and the flattering thought he chose me to share an adventure, spurred me on. Ever since Dad told us our great-grandfather might have been *genízaro*—Mexican Indians brought to New Mexico as servants for the Spanish colonists—José pretended to be an Indian. I liked the idea too.

We walked east from Chicorico in the direction of the coke ovens. The buffalo once ranged far and wide over these prairies. The Comanches stalked them as the buffalo drank from Chicorico Creek. The buffalo and the Comanches were long gone by the time of Chicorico Coal Camp. All that remained were the deserted hunting camps, discarded arrowheads, and broken pottery.

East of the coke ovens and the Colored People's Cemetery antelope and coyotes used to range freely on the prairie. Now it was a rarity to see or hear them. But sometimes, in the spring right about dusk, we might hear the coyotes raising a howl. Their yelps were the shrill, high-pitched barks of frisky young puppies yelping in sharp, short staccato barks: "*Yip! Yip! Yip!*"

José and I were like a hunting party. We had to bring back food to feed our families back at the camp. We were sent because we were the best and the bravest. Stealthily, we crept up to the abandoned coke ovens. I fingered the rocks in my pockets. They were a comfort. A while ago, I was getting tired of carrying the weight and was tempted to throw them away. Now I was glad to have them. José and I were destined to be heroes. Everyone in the camp would sing of our adventure, dancing to our victory.

Now at the coke ovens, José prodded with a stick around the ovens' foundations. The beehive ovens were in different conditions of disrepair. Over the years, people in Chicorico had carried away many of the ovens' bricks for landscaping their yards with pathways or small walls for their flower gardens. We saw little field mice nesting in the foundation cracks.

José whispered enthusiastically, "Where there's mice, there's snakes. Rattlers are attracted to the mice. Snakes like to eat 'em. . . . We just have to poke around."

"How will you know if it's a rattler?"

"You'll know."

"But how?"

"Rattlers don't like people. They avoid us. But if you get too close, they rattle."

José continued poking his stick.

"How will I know it's the rattle of a rattler?"

"Son of a gun, *chili con pan!*" José exclaimed in Spanish rime. "Don't you know nothin'? When you hear a rattler, you'll know it. There's nothin' that sounds like one."

With a stick, he started poking under rocks and cracks in the oven foundation, earnestly searching for rattlers. I started searching, but I took a more lackadaisical approach. I held back, using only my eyes to search.

"José! Over there!" I pointed to a boulder on a small ledge. "I think I saw something crawl under the rock."

"Are you sure?"

"It moved fast." A rush of blood. My toes tingled. I was snared by the excitement of the chase.

"*Shh*—let's look-see."

José put his stick down quietly. He stuck his arrows in the ground in front of him. He put one of the arrows in his bow and started to pull back on the string of the bow, whispering:

"Go behind the rock. When I shake my head, pull the rock back, re-a-l slo-o-w. The rattler will be cornered under the rock. I'll shoot him."

I skirted a wide circle, tiptoeing gingerly as I veered around to the back of the rock. When someone walks near them, snakes can feel the vibrations of a person's feet. I stood in back of the rock, leaning to tilt it back. The rock was pocked with holes, making it easy to grip with my fingertips. I gripped the rock and tipped it slowly . . . warily, tipping high enough for José to shoot under it where the snake was hiding.

I looked toward José to see if he was ready to shoot. He was standing close by, both feet firmly planted on the ground in the classic archer's pose, except the bow was almost touching the ground. It was taller than José. Holding the bow in his left hand, he pulled the arrow all the way back, the limber bow arching. He was ready to shoot, his right fingertips holding the arrow and bowstring at his right eye.

The rattler must have seen José. It crawled out from under the rock, away from José, directly toward me. Its forked tongue darted in and out of its mouth as it stealthily crawled away from José, unaware it was slithering toward my toes. I panicked, dropped the rock, and turned to run up the ledge.

Wang! José shot the arrow at the slithering rattler. The arrow missed the snake, glanced off the rock, bounced, and slammed into my lower back—*puum!* It penetrated my bib overalls and shirt just above my right hip. Pain! Sharp . . . cold . . . prickly pain!

"O-o-o-o-o-o-o-o-o-o-o-o! You shot me! You shot me!" I screamed, dancing wildly about.

As I danced, José repeatedly exclaimed, with a look of utter disbelief and despair, "I *shot* you! I sh-ot y-o-u! I–I-I shot you!"

Still running wildly about, I continued to scream, "It hurts! It hurts! You shot me! O-O-O-O-O-O-O-O-O!" The pain was tingling and throbbing at the same time. Gone was the adrenaline rush of only a few moments ago, when the blood rushed to my head and my toes tingled. Now, I imagined hearing the *glug-glug* of blood cascading out of my back. Utter panic overcame me; I yelled frantically:

"I'm gonna die! I'm gonna die! It hurts!" I started to run toward Dr. Monty's house, which was nearby on the east end of Chicorico.

"Don't run! You'll make it worse!" José was chasing after me, trying to catch me. He finally caught my arm, the arrow dangling from my back.

"Stop it! Don't you know? Running makes it worse. When the Indians shoot a buffalo, it doesn't die right away. Instead, the buffalo runs and runs until he bleeds to death."

I slumped to my knees, still screeching, "I'm gonna die, José. You can have my marbles. Tell Ramona she can have the dog." The "dog" was a black, chubby stuffed toy, about twelve or fourteen inches tall. When I was about a year or so old, he first showed up, especially in baby photographs, always in some strange place as though he had just wandered in. My brothers and Angela would tease me, saying he was some stray who had just shown up and taken a liking to me. I was obligated to take care of him. I was passing the responsibility of the dog onto Ramona.

José gripped my arm tighter. "You're *not* going to die!"

By now, the pain was radiating over my entire back. It felt like when I was three years old and accidentally sat on an anthill. I hadn't noticed the ants crawling all over my body. They got under my shirt and crawled all over my back, biting it. When my back started to hurt—sharp, piercing sensations—I ran to my mother. She removed my shirt and discovered the ants. She brushed them away. I was all better. Mothers have a way of fixing their little boys. I wished she were here right now, but I didn't dare tell José. I had to be like Prince Valiant, the gallant hero. No Mama's boy stuff.

José calmed me down a little, observing, "You're barely bleeding."

The arrow was dangling in my back. It had pierced my overalls and shirt before entering the skin. "It hurts, José! Please pull it out!" The arrow hung loosely and blood appeared on my shirt where the arrow had pierced. "Pull it out!"

"Pull it out? S-u-u-u-n! Haven't you seen the movies? That will make it worse. It'll rip your skin. I have to push it through you."

"N-o-o-o! Take your hands off me!" Terrified, I struggled to pull free of José, especially when he said,

"I ain't gonna break the arrow while it's in you. That's the other way it's done."

José had second thoughts. "I guess you're right. We got to stop the bleeding. And get you to Dr. Monty." Awkwardly, he tried to stand me on my feet, afraid he might cause further damage with the arrow.

"You're gonna have to stand up and walk. Here, I'll hold my hand around your wound to stop the bleeding."

"Is my blood gushing out?" I moaned one step at a time.

"Aw, quit your moanin' and groanin.' S-u-u-u-n! It's hardly coming out."

We started walking. My pockets bulged with pebbles.

"Stop." José noticed the pebbles. "Shoot. We'll never get there—empty them."

"No!"

"Yes!"

"Make me!"

"Naw. Meet you at Dr. Monty's." He dashed away, putting distance between us.

"Wait! Don't leave me here alone!" I emptied my pockets, one pebble at a time, reluctantly surrendering my weapons of last resort.

José returned, grinning, "Let's go."

That was the longest one-half mile I had ever walked. With my brother holding his palm up against my back, we looked goofy. I was stumbling over tufts of grass, and José was struggling to keep his hand cupped around the wound in my back. I staggered along, sniffling and whimpering occasional sobs, making them sound like groans. The ground was practically flat, but I felt like I was climbing the highest peaks in the Sangre de Cristo mountains.

José didn't talk on the way to Dr. Monty's. He concentrated on keeping his hands in place without stumbling, sunk in the doldrums of fear and regret.

When we arrived at Dr. Monty's, he was busy with someone else. Mrs. Monty took one look and ushered us into the other room. She laid me on a table on my stomach. José didn't want to let go of me, but he did reluctantly. The arrow stood straight up. With scissors, Mrs. Monty cut through the bloody overalls and shirt, cutting a large circle of cloth from around the arrow.

"Matías, I'm going to pour some alcohol where the arrow pricked your skin. This will hurt at first, but it will clean the wound." She poured and daubed around the arrow's shaft. I closed my eyes, cringing with pain as she poured.

I could hear José quietly sobbing. José had been very brave and grown-up from the time he shot me until now. Having turned his responsibility over to an adult, he was free to express his fear. Anxiety and guilt trickled out of him in stifled sobs:

"I'm so sorry. I didn't mean to shoot my little brother. . . . Is he okay? . . . Will he be crippled? We were just hunting for rattlesnakes. . . . I didn't mean to shoot him."

"What gives here?" Dr. Monty barged into the room, his voice strong, calm, and confident.

"Matthew," Mrs. Monty explained, "somehow, José shot this arrow into Matt's back."

José was still sobbing softly, "I'm sorry. I didn't mean to shoot my little brother."

"Never mind. Run! Get your mother!"

As José left the room, Dr. Monty held my shoulder lightly. "Now, you have to be a big man, Matías." Dr. Monty lowered his voice, inspiring confidence in me. He was very calm under pressure. "Remember—you and I have the same names, because we're tough. We're not gonna let a little old arrow scare us. What do you say?"

"Don't tell Dad, okay?"

"Huh! Whatta you talking about?"

"If Dad finds out José shot me, José will be in big trouble."

"Why, Matías. Here you are, shot in the back. And you're worried about your brother!" Dr. Monty was incredulous. "Listen, I'm going to poke around a little bit where the arrow goes in your back. You can cry if it hurts. You tell me, okay?"

"Okay," I sputtered, still feigning bravery.

Dr. Monty took a knife from the chrome steam case. The case blew very hot steam and water over the knife blade, sterilizing it. I could barely feel the slice of the sharp blade as Dr. Monty cut slits at the shaft of the arrow. He gripped the arrow's shaft between his fingers near the arrowhead's front end and slowly pulled it out, pressing heavy gauze over the hole. He applied pressure over the hole, stopping the bleeding. He tossed the bloody gauze while Mrs. Monty poured iodine over the wound. She wiped the excess iodine, then laid gauze over the hole, pressing down on the wound. The gauze turned red from the iodine.

Dr. Monty held the arrow in front of me, scrutinizing it from arrowhead to feathers, running his eyes back and forth, meticulously examining every section of the arrow. He touched the tip.

"That's some arrowhead—obsidian . . . really sharp." The arrowhead was well-shaped obsidian—naturally formed glass—with a sharp point and sharp edges, but it was small. "Must've been traded from Indians in the north," Dr. Monty ruminated. "There's no obsidian in these hills." Dr. Monty gazed at the arrowhead for a moment longer, then turned to the work at hand.

"Good thing it wasn't a direct hit," Dr. Monty continued, "because it would've penetrated deeply—it's so small and sharp."

"José wasn't shooting at me. He was shooting at a rattler. The arrow glanced off a rock and hit me."

"Hope both of you learned a lesson. Leave the rattlers alone and don't shoot at anything unless you intend to kill it." Dr. Monty threaded a needle as he spoke. "Now, I'm gonna sew you up. Shouldn't hurt much. Just need three stitches."

"Wow! A three-stitch wound!"

"Don't be bragging about your wound. I've seen much worse. Yours is only a scratch. I'll numb it up first."

He rubbed a numbing liquid on my back. Aaaah! The pain subsided for an instant, then WOW–OW!—the Novocain injection seemed to go through my back into my stomach. But as quickly as the needle stung, the pain vanished. Dr. Monty started to sew, but I couldn't feel a thing.

"Another lesson to learn: keep away from a weapon's line of fire."

"But it was only a bow and arrow!"

"No *buts* about it! Don't you know why Comanches used arrows? To kill buffalo. And buffalo are ten times bigger than you!"

"Oh."

"Qué pasó con mi hito?" Apprehensively Mom entered the room.

"Oh, Mrs. Montaño, Matías is a tough pistol. He'll be okay."

"But what's the matter?" Mom wasn't easily placated. José stood silently by Mom's side.

"Didn't José tell you? Here, look at the wound."

"No! He said you called for me."

"Well, Matías, you tell your mother."

I glanced at José. His eyes avoided mine. I looked at Mom. She was anxiously reading my face, searching for an answer. I started to explain. "José didn't mean nothing by it, and—"

José abruptly blocked me from speaking while blurting out a confession, "I accidentally shot Matías with one of my arrows. It was an accident. Matías ran back, just as the arrow glanced from the rock."

Mom glowered at José. If looks could kill! Mom turned to me. Her furious scowl turned to a concerned frown. "Is he telling the truth?"

"Yes! Yes! Cross my heart and hope to die!"

"Matías, don't make jokes. This is serious business." Again Mom read my face, peering into my eyes to discern any nuances. "You're not just saying that, are you?"

For a split second, I thought of making up an elaborate joke about how we were playing cowboys and Indians, and how José made me be the cowboy so he could shoot at me. Then I would say I was joking and everyone would laugh. But Mom had just cautioned me about joking. I glanced at Dr. Monty for advice. He, too, was waiting for my answer.

"Matías, tell your mother the truth," Dr. Monty advised. "Let the blame fall where it belongs."

A lump came to my throat. I swallowed. How could I tell the whole truth? I panicked and ran, and that's when the arrow hit me in the back. I was running away, like a coward. Hesitantly, I reported the truth, hoping more notice would be placed on the accidental shooting and less would be placed on my cowardly act.

"José tells the truth. He was shooting at the rattler. I turned and ran. The arrow hit the rock and bounced, just as I turned to run."

"So-o. It was an accident."

"Yes," I curtly responded, not wanting to get José in big trouble. José looked pleased. He owed me big time.

"Mrs. Montaño, both José and Matías told me the same thing. I don't think they made it up."

Mom sat down, mollified, relieved to know José hadn't shot me on purpose.

"But you shouldn't play with sharp arrows and rattlesnakes."

Dr. Monty assured Mom: "It sounds worse than it was, just a slight prick in the skin. Good thing it wasn't a direct hit, or it might've punctured his kidney—that's trouble."

"Will you come to check on Matías?"

"No need to. He can run and play. He'll be okay. Just keep the stitches clean. Clean the wound with warm water, once a day. Here's some gauze and tape. Change it daily. Let the wound heal. Here are two pills for pain. They have a little bit of codeine in them. Give him one at bedtime if he's in great pain, and another six hours later . . . only if he wakes up and needs it. More'n likely, the stitches will itch more'n hurt. Don't let him scratch them. No matter how much they itch. Next week, sometime," Dr. Monty turned to me, "come over. I'll remove the stitches. Might be a small scar where I stitched. And no scratching!"

With that advice, Dr. Monty helped me to my feet. I felt a bit shaky when all the blood rushed from my head to my feet. I stood, wobbling, getting my balance. José grabbed my hand. I jerked it away, refusing his help. When we left Dr. Monty's house, the sun was still blazing at full bloom, although suppertime was approaching. We followed the tracks home. I felt no pain; the spring in my gait returned. I felt so good, I skipped from tie to tie on the tracks while Mom escorted José home. I heard José complaining to Mom:

"Ow! You're hurting my ear!"

Then Mom switched to the other ear, dragging José by the ears as we made our way home along the tracks. José blurted out another confession, whining loud enough for me to hear:

"I'm sorry! I didn't mean to shoot Matías. I hate my bow and arrow!

I'll throw them away. I'll break them into a million, zillion pieces. They'll never be used again. I promise! I promise!"

I was in my glory, a hero coming home from battle with my patched-up wound—a three-stitch wound would leave a scar, a permanent red badge of courage. I felt cocky, having the tear in my shirt with blood smears on my pants pockets. I felt great! The only kid in Chicorico to be shot by a real Indian arrowhead who lived to tell it. And the enemy was defeated. He promised to lay down his arms and destroy them. Not only was I brave, but I got the enemy to disarm. Ah, peace on earth.

Of course, that evening at supper, Dad had to hear of the misadventure. He scowled, but seeing the misery in José's face, decided José had been punished enough, especially when José remorsefully mumbled:

"Dad, I'm so sorry. Matías, I'm so sorry. Mom, I'm so sorry we scared you so much. And . . . and, I got rid of my bow and arrows! Destroyed! They'll never be used again!"

"Sí, Manuel," Mom turned to Dad. "José promised to break the arrows and throw them away."

"Well, what's done is done," Dad sermonized, "but you shouldn't have been hunting rattlers. They're living creatures. You must respect them. You were acting just like the Japs and Germans, shooting without respect for life." Dad eased up. "Oh, well, you've broken the arrows. You've disarmed. Good. If only the Germans and Japanese would put down their weapons. There would peace on earth. And Arturo and Eddie Heard would be home with us having supper."

Here we were eating supper when the topic of the war raised its ugly head. We fell silent, a depressing reality. Everything reminded us about the war, from coal production to the draft. We dreaded seeing two Red Cross workers delivering a telegram from the president of the United States to someone's house in Chicorico, opening with a formal note of condolence that was always the same: "*We regret to inform you. . . .*" Without reading that telegram, we knew it told of someone's death, or that he was missing in action, giving little hope he'd ever be found to bring home to be buried.

Supper ended in a somber mood. "*Vamos rezar a Dios y la Virgen*

María," Dad decreed as he led us through the Lord's Prayer and a Hail Mary in Spanish. When done, we crossed ourselves and left the table. Promptly Juan and José started clearing the table, to wash and dry the dishes. I started helping, but Mom interrupted me:

"Matías, tonight, you don't have to help your brothers. But, do me a favor?"

"Sure, Mom." The magnanimous hero couldn't refuse his mother.

"Take some toilet paper to the outhouse." Mom handed me two rolls of paper, which Angela must've brought home from the store. Everything in Chicorico was rationed, including toilet paper.

I took the rolls from Mom and walked outside to the outhouse. Sure enough, the old toilet paper roll was almost empty. I placed the rolls on the potty bench and walked over to the garden. I was surprised—that bullsnake again! This time I grabbed Dad's hoe. I wasn't going to kill him, but thought to give him a good scare.

Hoe handle in hand, I hacked the hoe into the ground, slamming it down close to the bullsnake, hacking in a circle around the snake, careful not to hit him. I meant to terrorize him, to frighten him so badly he wouldn't come around anymore. The bullsnake stopped in his tread, lying absolutely still without moving a single muscle. He blended well with the grasses and could barely be seen.

I changed my tactic. Gently, I nudged the end of the hoe on his tail. The bullsnake crawled away, slithering toward the coal shed. I chased him, prodding his tail with the hoe just to keep him crawling. He slithered through a crack in the coal shed's board wall. I lifted the shed's loading lid and peered inside. I couldn't see anything but the coal, gleaming in large chunks. The snake was somewhere beneath the coal.

I started to close the lid; something caught my eye on a small rafter inside the shed, between the wall and ceiling: an old shirt stuffed into the ledge. I stretched to reach the shirt. With the tip of my fingers, I felt something in the shirt. The rafter was much wider than it first appeared. Something was wrapped in the shirt.

I'd forgotten about the bullsnake. He was history. The shirt intrigued me, hidden away as it was. I carefully pulled the shirt out from under the rafter. This was one of José's old hand-me-downs that had seen better days, with holes in the elbows and buttons missing, ready for Mom's rag box. Yet it was carefully rolled. I laid it on the ground behind the shed and unrolled it. Inside the shirt were José's arrows. The arrowheads and feathers were lovingly wrapped with toilet paper for extra protection from the rain and snow.

Wow! José lied. He didn't destroy the arrows. He pretended to be sorry. Yet he didn't throw the arrows away. But, he really WAS sorry. But, he loved his arrows. I glanced around. No one was in sight. I knelt on the ground by the arrows to take a closer look. The faded, plaid cotton shirt provided a rustic background, making the arrows look ancient. They looked quite authentic with real arrowheads chipped from flint or obsidian, and on the other end, the variously colored feathers from wild turkeys, crows, and chickens. The arrowheads and feathers were glued onto the shaft with piñón pitch. The shafts had been lovingly sanded as smooth as satin.

I sat down by the arrows, studying them for a long time. They were skillfully constructed, crafted by a caring hand. "These are too beautiful," I thought, "to be destroyed." After a while, I realized someone might come out to find me, and the arrows would be discovered. I rolled the arrows back into the shirt, returning them to the coal shed's ledge. Placing the shirt and arrows exactly in the spot where I'd found them, I noticed José's bow was stuffed deeper into the ledge. I carefully put the fondly bundled arrows back in place, concealing the bow entirely.

4

SIGN AT THE MINE: "NO WOMEN OR BEARS ALLOWED"

My claim to fame was toppled by a real hero known for brave and daring deeds. Our trout fishing expert and neighbor, Mr. Dick Malcolm, was the first coal miner to serve as fire boss in the Chicorico mine. He cast the die for being a good fire boss. A fire boss was highly respected by the miners. His job was to inspect the mine before each shift to make sure the mine was safe to work. In the Chicorico mine, the fire boss had to be especially careful about damp-gas and faults in the mine's bedrock ceiling.

Damp-gas was the methane released when coal was dug or blasted, and carried in the dust that settled on the mine's floor and walls. When it accumulated, explosions were possible. Damp-gas was easily stifled by simply sprinkling water on the dusty walls. Faults in the bedrock and coal seam were harder to detect. The fire boss would tap the ceiling's roof with the end of a pick handle, listening for hollow spots indicating a break or fault. Faults were buttressed by using log props to support the ceiling.

The miners selected a conscientious veteran who knew the craft of mining and could detect unsafe working conditions. The stories about Mr. Malcolm were legion. After the union was organized, he was the first fire boss to be appointed by the miners. No hazard got past him, be it poor wiring, weakened cross-ties, a possible faulty bedrock, or gassy conditions. He was tough on hazards.

During supper one Saturday, Juan anxiously awaited to tell about one of Mr. Malcolm's latest feats. To Juan, it was bigger than life and took more than a grain of salt to digest. Dad made Juan wait a bit before telling the tale. For Dad and Mom, supper was a crucial gathering of the family where serious concerns were discussed, with no petty bickering allowed. All topics were allowed. Important issues or family matters received the greatest attention. Yet suppertime talk was always convivial—the time and place each day we could be heard by the whole family.

Just before supper, Dad would ask us to sit with him in the living room to listen to Gabriel Heater, a radio news commentator. We concentrated on what the news commentator reported because Dad would test us as we ate. At supper after the blessing, the news was discussed. Most of the news was about the European and Pacific war efforts. We learned about geography, different peoples, and cultures. We also learned much when the commentator talked about the war's economic and financial underpinnings, especially about war bonds and other emergency means for funding the war.

"José, these are bad times in Europe. Tell us about it." Dad led the discussion.

"We're on the beach in France. The biggest invasion of the war."

"How do you know?"

"Gabriel Heater said that! From the Armed Forces Radio News."

"We're having it the worst," Juan chimed in, "at Omaha and Utah Beach."

"The English had an easier time at those other beaches," José injected.

"Gold, Juno, and Sword," Angela recalled the names of the other beaches. "Their invasion was much easier. They're calling the invasion 'D-Day.' It's a tremendous attack—the largest ever. Soldiers from

England, Canada, Australia, America. Our soldiers have run into fierce resistance by the Germans."

"And what about the paratroopers?" Dad checked our memory.

"Oh! They went over first." Angela had a sharp memory for details. "Dad, is it true, that Arturo flew the paratroopers for D-Day?"

"*¿Quién sabe?*" Dad sighed. "We don't know where he is."

"That's why we think he's there," Mom sounded worried. "Y, tambíen Edward Heard. He wrote his mother. Mrs. Heard could barely read the letter. There were many holes in it, where words were cut out."

"How come?"

"Because we're at war with Germany and Japan," Dad quickly answered. "Spies might get the letter and find out about our troops."

"Arturo's service flag finally came. I'll hang it after supper." Mom held up the four-by-six-inch service flag, with a blue border, a red inside border, a blue background, and a white star. The single star signified we were a one-star family with one person in the armed services. A gold star signified the person had died. For some reason, we had just received the flag although Arturo had been in the navy for a long time.

"Where will you hang it?"

"In the living room window."

"Good." Dad stroked the flag fondly, rubbing his fingertips across the weave of the star. "Now we can show all who pass by the house, we have a son in the war."

Juan was more interested in the here and now. He could hardly wait for the serious discussion to end. Whenever he was nervous or impatient, he would tap rhythm with his left foot under his chair. I sat next to him and could feel the vibrations. He was aching to tell about Mr. Malcolm.

"I hope everyone's done?" Juan pretended to be calm. He didn't want to upset Mom or Dad by appearing impatient. Then he'd never tell his story.

"What's the rush, Juan?" Angela quizzed, "I have new duties at the store. I now work at the cash register as well as assist Mr. Ruker, the manager."

"Clara?" Dad glanced at Mom, wondering who would help Mom in the house. This was the first he had heard that Angela worked in the Company store.

"O, sí, Manuel. I told Angela to find work. She doesn't like working in the house. Anyway, I have the boys to help."

"And Ramona?" I chirped. Ramona hooked her little finger in the side of her mouth, smiling.

Mom jumped to Ramona's defense: "O, no! She's too little."

Mom's comment about Ramona made me grin, causing me to speak without thinking, "Ramona has no chores."

Mom immediately read my thoughts; she knew I was jealous of Ramona. "Don't worry, her time will come." Ramona kept smiling; I'm not sure she understood my jealous motives, but she knew we were talking about her.

Dad ignored me, turning to Angela. "And, what do you do at the store?"

"Many things—help with shelving, help with inventory. I'm a cashier as well."

"So you handle people's money?" Dad frowned.

"Yes. And their scrip . . . when they use it."

"Do you keep some of the money for yourself?" I insinuated, meaning to joke.

"Certainly not! How dare you say that!" Angela snapped defiantly, glaring at me. Integrity was no joking matter for Angela.

"Honey," Mom interrupted, "don't be too harsh on Matías."

"Well, I'm honest. I would never shortchange a customer—not on purpose. Mr. Ruker trusts me so much, he may have me keep the books."

"That's good," Mom softly commented. "Mr. Ruker wouldn't say that if he didn't trust you."

"My word is my bond, Mother. I pride myself. I can be trusted to handle money."

"Yes! Yes!" Mom was a calming influence, "I'm proud of you. If you need help, your father keeps the books for the union. He can show you."

"That's okay!" Angela cheered up. "I've been watching Dad, and the

Sisters at St. Patrick's are teaching a class in bookkeeping." Angela was a good student. The nuns liked her a lot.

"I'm sorry—just joking." That's all I could say. I felt badly, but I meant no harm. I really liked Angela. She was nice to me. I was the first child Mom had asked Angela to help with. She'd even changed my diapers. And, when Ramona was born, Angela assisted Mom by serving as my full-time nanny. As Mom grew stronger, and no longer had to stay in bed after Ramona's birth, Angela still helped with my care and really made me feel special.

"Try not to joke so much, Matías," Angela reminded. "Sometimes jokes hurt people."

Juan poked me in the ribs. By now, his left foot was really tapping! He was anxious to tell his story. By horsing around, I was taking precious time from Juan.

"Did you hear about Mr. Malcolm?" Juan butted in. "He shook hands with a bear!"

"N-a-a-ah! Huh?" José and I exclaimed in disbelief.

"Yes! Yes! This morning, he finally did it." Juan's face was beaming with a smile from ear to ear. He really wanted to spin his tale, but he had to wait for an okay from Dad.

"Did what?" Dad gave Juan the opening he needed. Now he could tell his tale.

"Yesterday this bear was looking for chokecherries in the bushes. That's what Mr. Malcolm told me. He spotted it when he went to work early; he was fire boss for the day shift. He said the sow was alone without any cubs. Anyway, she found some chokecherry bushes by the mine entry. He never paid her no mind; he went into the mine and inspected it. When he gave the okay, the men came in the mine to work. He noticed the bear was up the slope above the mine entry, eating some chokecherries. He went back into the mine to start working.

"Mr. Malcolm figured after she ate all the chokecherries off those bushes, she smelled more chokecherries right inside the mine. She followed her nose. Bears can smell pretty good. They have good noses. Her nose took her right up to the mine entry. The shaft was posted:

NO WOMEN
OR
BEARS ALLOWED!!!

"The miners say women and bears bring bad luck in the mine. Women bring the worst luck. But bears are plenty bad too. Anyway, she couldn't read the sign. So she did as she pleased . . . went right into the mine. Inside, she found some of the miners' lunch buckets. They all smelled yummy. She liked the lunches that had chokecherry jelly sandwiches in them. With both paws, she tore into the lunch buckets. They didn't stand a chance. She ripped them open and ate everything down to the last crumb, 'specially the chokecherry jelly sandwiches, that's what Mr. Malcolm said. . . ."

Juan paused for dramatic effect, waiting for our thoughts to catch up to his story. He paused long enough for the tension to mount before continuing. "She was still hungry. So she walks into the mine where some of the miners were working. *¡Hijo mano!* Man alive! Did they get scared!

"'Oh, brother!' one miner said. 'A bear in the mine is bad luck. A woman in the mine is worse luck. But a woman bear in the mine? Double-bad luck!'

"The miners were so scared they wouldn't do any work. The bear might eat one of them. Or, two of them!"

Another pause by Juan . . . "But, Mr. Malcolm wasn't scared. No sir-e-e-e!" Juan shook his head and beat his chest, pretending to be Mr. Malcolm. "Mr. Malcolm told the miners:

"'Now, boys, in all my years as fire boss, there's nothing I can't handle. Just leave her to me.'

"Whew! The miners were glad that Mr. Malcolm was with them. He went on talking:

"'This here sow's no different than any other woman. I noticed if you're good to yer woman, she'll be good to you. This sow can't be that much different.'

"So Mr. Malcolm went right up to the bear and gave her a hug. . . ." Juan paused again, only this time he was grinning from ear to ear.

José and I exclaimed in disbelief:

"S-u-u-n!"

"No, sir! N-a-a-h!"

Dad held back a laugh, grinning instead. Ramona was animated. Mom and Angela weren't interested, but they were polite and didn't say anything.

"Not only that," Juan continued, "he told the bear:

"'You're sure pretty. You have a pretty nose. And you have such shiny, curvy claws. And you have such a soft, brown coat.'

"Right away, the sow seemed to like Mr. Malcolm because he said so many pretty things to her. He could tell she wasn't a mean bear. She was just hungry. So Mr. Malcolm sez:

"'Tell ya' what? Let's make a deal. Every day we'll leave you some food—outside—for you to eat. Only promise—don't come in the mine anymore. What say? Deal? Shake on it?' Mr. Malcolm reached his hand out. . . . The sow grabbed his hand. They shook on it. Right away, after they shook hands, the sow turned around and walked out of the mine. The next morning she came by. Mr. Malcolm had all kinds of food waiting for her. She ate it and went away."

"Na-a-a-w!" José doubted Juan's veracity. "That's a whopper if I ever heard one."

Juan stuck to his guns, pretending to be telling the truth and nothing but the truth. He didn't stammer nor let his voice quiver when he defended the story. He capped the story by quoting Mr. Malcolm:

"'A nod and a handshake,' Mr. Malcolm said, 'is all a man needs in Chicorico.'"

"What a classy story!" I really liked Juan's story. "Someday, I'm going to be a miner. Maybe I can be a fire boss and have adventures like Mr. Malcolm."

"Hito, Mr. Malcolm told Juan a *chiste*," Dad explained. "Sometimes, Mr. Malcolm likes to joke. He's good at pulling your leg. But, he's a very good fire boss, believe me. He's respected by the men."

Juan got defensive. He thought Dad accused him of lying. "But Dad, you're a fire boss too. Things like that *can* happen?"

"Oh, yes! He might've seen a bear. When he was fire bossing, he might've spotted a bear sniffing around the entry. When the bear didn't smell much—maybe some gas—she probably went along, away from the mine, searching for chokecherries, or berries she could eat."

"Aw, heck, Dad." Juan got recklessly brazen, "That's a boring story!"

Silence . . . stone-cold silence . . . a shock wave of silent tension rippled across the kitchen table. Juan's curt, brazen comment shocked us all. He actually insulted Dad. But we relaxed, realizing the insult had rolled right off Dad, like water rolling off a duck—lucky for Juan. Dad was more concerned about our romantic illusions of coal mining. He admonished us:

"You boys don't know what you're talking about. You think mining's glamorous!"

"But, Dad," I whined, "I want to be a miner like you. You have a swell job."

"¡A, mi hitos!" Mom surprised us. She was dismayed and just as opposed to mining as Dad. "You boys are too smart to be miners. We want you to get a good education, make something of yourselves."

"But Dad's smart," Juan defended Dad. "And he's a miner." He knew he had insulted Dad. Now, he was trying to vindicate himself by twisting Mom's words around.

Juan might be sly, but Dad was much smarter and wasn't easily fooled by him:

"Your mother's not saying I'm not smart. It's just you get old, your body wears out. It's better to work with your head. When I was probate judge, I made more money in two days than I did in a week in the mine. And I didn't work as hard. Here, let me show you my record." Dad turned to Angela, "Bring my book for 1940. It's on the first shelf of the library."

Dad was in politics for a while. The miners elected him to the state legislature for a two-year term, 1936–1938. Then he was elected probate judge for Colfax County for a two-year term. Angela brought the diary to Dad.

"*Mira, aquí,*" Dad pointed at a column of figures. "For the month of May 1940:

Made money in the mine $42.71
Made money in court 71.78
Marriages & Notary Public 23.80

"Now, look here, at July and August, the same thing. I worked harder in the mine and made less money. Money won't buy you happiness, but why kill yourself in the mine when you can have a better job with an education?"

The figures didn't lie. They jumped off the page, showing a real disparity. Working with your mind paid almost twice as much as working with your back. And you could work longer with your mind. Although working indoors all day didn't sound like much fun, either. Yet we pondered the figures as Dad read them aloud. When he reached the last column, Dad surprised us again. He actually married people.

"I didn't know you married people, Dad. You're not a priest." José studied the figures, especially the ones showing that Dad had performed marriages.

As a probate judge, Dad was authorized to probate wills, notarize papers, and conduct marriages. He translated the marriage ceremony into Spanish. He had Mrs. Chicarelli translate the ceremony into Italian, and she taught him how to read it aloud. For Slavic or Greek, he used English, although the Greeks often brought their own priest from Walsenburg to marry them. Most couples came from nearby Colorado or Texas. Both states required a blood test that took three days to process. New Mexico did not require the test. Instead of waiting three days to get married, couples from southern Colorado and west Texas came to Raton, where Dad married them. Nestled in the foothills of the Rocky Mountains, Raton also made an ideal honeymoon site.

"But? Only priests marry people." José was still confused about the difference between civil and religious marriages.

"I told everyone I married to go to the priest or a minister. I could only marry people under the law. I told them they weren't married in the eyes of God."

"*No importa,*" Mom injected. "What's important is you kids need a good education to get somewhere—to make something of yourself.

Already, Angela is talking of college to be a teacher. That's why we buy books for you to read. Have you read the new book? It came in the mail last week." Dad and Mom took every opportunity to buy books for us. Some were discarded from the Raton Public Library. Most were ordered from publishers who advertised in the union magazine, the *United Mine Workers of America Journal.*

Before we could answer Mom's question, Dad announced, "Tomorrow, Clara, after mass, I'll take the boys to the mine when no one's working."

"No! Manuelo! The mine's dangerous."

"The boys need to see the mine; mining's no work for a man. They'll see it's not so glamorous. . . . I'll take my fire boss lamp."

Mom wasn't placated. Yet our romantic illusions about coal mining worried her, although she didn't have anything against hard work. Mom didn't want us to grow up to be coal miners. She was too familiar with men whose bodies were wracked by the pain of arthritis and black lung disease from working too long in the cold, wet, and gassy coal mine. She was also too familiar with widowed mothers and children who had to fend for themselves, their husbands and fathers killed in the mine. Mom relented:

"Well, okay. I don't like it, Manuelo. Maybe it's best the boys see for themselves. Promise to be careful."

"I'll be careful," Dad promised as he lovingly gazed toward Mom.

Before Mom could change her mind, we all rose from the table, gave her a hug, and hopped to our after-supper chores straight away. Juan took warm water out of the boiler tank of the Majestic fogón. He washed and José dried the dishes. To replace the water they were using, I went to the pump outside and brought in two full buckets. I stood on a powder box and poured them into the boiler tank. We'd use it tomorrow. When done, I went into the living room.

Mom and Dad were sitting on the couch, listening to "The Jack Benny Show" on the radio. Mom had already hung the one-star flag in the window. She crocheted doilies as she sat listening. They were very intricate and would have to be starched and ironed when she finished them. Dad smoked his pipe. The smoke emitted a sweet smell, like cherry blossoms in spring. Dad purchased the sweet-smelling tobacco after Mom complained of the rank odor of the Prince Albert tobacco.

I liked to browse through the books in our library—a large pine six-by-six-foot bookshelf Arturo had made in manual training. It had six shelves and covered part of the wall. Above the shelf were three pictures: one of Pope Pius XII given to Mom at mass, and one of John L. Lewis, president of the United Mine Workers of America. The third was a group portrait of the Chicorico miners standing eight rows deep in front of the Chicorico mine entry. Miners sat in the front row. Right in the center was the Super, Mr. William "Bill" Pratt, the only man not wearing miner's gear. He wore a wide-brim hat, shoved back on his head. He held a sign:

Chicorico Miners & Superintendent
Chicorico Coal Company
Nov. 4, 1925

The photograph was taken just before the men entered the mine. Dad stood in the fourth row, fifth man from the right, with a broad grin on his face. Mr. Chicarelli, Mr. Malcolm, and Mr. Heard posed formally as though standing at attention for an important event. Most of the min-

Most of the miners were relaxed, ready to enter the mine.

ers were relaxed, their caps and lights rigged, ready to enter the mine. They looked exuberant, their eyes and smiles filled with the hopes and promises of a good day.

The living room was Mom and Dad's family showcase. The books, the furniture, and the photographs told something about the family's history. I sat in a brown, soft stuffed chair. The cushion was broken down. Yet it wrapped around my legs and back, engulfing me. On the wall above was a wedding portrait of Mom and Dad. Their portrait was made from two separate family snapshots taken before Mom and Dad knew each other. When they married in 1920, they couldn't afford to pay a photographer to take their picture. In 1925, a traveling photographer came to Chicorico, Mr. Louis R. Dold. He was famous for photographs of the striking miners' tent colony before and after the April 20, 1914, Ludlow Massacre.

Mr. Dold was making the rounds of the coal camps with a camera, tripod, and plates. After photographing the group portrait for the Chicorico Coal Company, he offered his services to the miners. Dad invited him to the house. Dad wanted to have a wedding portrait made by combining two photographs. Mr. Dold was sure he could meld the two photographs into a wedding portrait.

When the portrait was completed, Dad looked very handsome. He was wearing a dark suit, a shirt with a turned-up collar, and a bow tie. His hair was neatly parted on the side. Mom looked resplendent and beautiful. She had a radiant smile. Her eyes glowed, exuding sweetness. She was wearing a delicate, white lace blouse with fancy hand embroidery. Around her neck, she wore a locket. Her hair was not parted and fell to the nape of her neck. The photographer was very skillful; it was a lovely wedding portrait. He mounted it in an oval, dark mahogany frame with concave glass. All for the cost of two dollars.

I spent the evening looking through the new book, *The Book of Adventure*. It was one of a series of nine books called the *Young Folks' Library* that Mom ordered through the *United Mine Workers of America Journal*. One came every other month. They were hardbound with tan and black gilded covers and a few well-placed pictures. They were not watered-down children's books; they contained condensed versions of classic sagas, written in the prose style of the original stories. The pictures at the front of the book were in color. In the text, they were in black and white. I couldn't read the words, but I liked reading the pictures and imagining what the story was about.

Juan liked the books equally well. He sat with me after he'd finished with the dishes. Both of us fit in the chair, though it was a bit crowded. He had read all of the books in our library. He explained the latest story he'd read:

"There's another story in the new book, it's confusing. It's about a silly knight who attacks windmills, Don Quixote de la Mancha. He has a partner, Sancho Panza, who's more reasonable. They're both from Spain—where our people came from."

"Why did he attack windmills?"

"I don't know."

"Was he crazy?"

"I guess."

5

MINING'S NOT THE MOVIES

Sunday after mass Dad took us to the mine. We invited Freddie, Petee, and Geno. On the way to the mine, we walked two abreast along the tracks, stepping from tie to tie. At times, one of the guys would break his stride and jump onto one of the rails, trying to balance as he walked on the slippery, narrow rail.

Geno started showing off. He was my age, but much taller and very sure-footed. He hopped on a rail and started walking precariously with stiff knees, doddering like Charlie Chaplin: "Hey—guys. Looka me go!"

We stopped to watch. He spread his arms to each side for balance, stepping slowly and deliberately like walking a tightrope, wobbling as he placed each foot down carefully before lifting the other. The rail's surface was smooth and slippery, but once he got his balance, he skittered nimbly up the track without slipping until he turned around to see if we were still watching, foot slipping off the rail.

"Ow-eee!" he squealed, sitting down on the track and grabbing his ankle.

We scurried forward. Dad knelt on one knee, "Hurt yourself?"

"Aw, heck no!" Geno recoiled. "Just my ankle—scraped it on the rail."

"Wanna go home?"

"Go home? N-a-aw," Geno sputtered. "It's just a little scratch—really." Now he was protesting, not wanting Dad to take him home. He wanted to go to the mine. Besides, he didn't want anyone to think he was a sissy. He would have to carry his pain quietly or miss the chance to go into the mine.

I helped Geno to his feet. He limped a little when he first started to walk, but soon forgot about the scrape and fell into a bouncy gait with the rest of us as we continued our trek up the tracks with Dad.

The tracks were our *Camino Real.* We walked everywhere on them: to the coke ovens, school, baseball field, Company store, clubhouse, mine. The tracks, built to a high standard of precision, ran straight through Chicorico Canyon from the east to the west. The two rails were kept at the same elevation so the train wouldn't tip off. The rail bed was made of stone ballast, and the ties were laid on the bed ten and three-fourths inches apart. Steel spikes clamped the ties snug against the rails, using four spikes per tie, fifty-seven kegs of spikes per mile. The ties were saturated with creosote that bubbled from the heat of the sun, emitting a tarry odor. We rarely paid attention to the tracks' symmetry; we just walked on them.

Today, we were absorbed in our adventure, going into the mine. Juan re-told Mr. Malcolm's bear story. When the guys heard the tale, they pummeled Dad:

"Maybe we'll see a bear?"

"Maybe we should've brought food?"

"Maybe she'll bring her cubs?"

"Maybe, just maybe," Dad chuckled.

At the machine shop, Dad rigged us up with hard leather miner caps and battery-powered lamps that hooked to them. The caps were too big for us, but they sat back on our foreheads and didn't obstruct our view. Dad helped Geno and me hook the battery case to the hammer-loop on the right side of our overalls. The guys took turns helping each other.

Just before we entered the mine, Dad glanced to the sky. We looked, too. There wasn't much there in the vast, turquoise sky, empty except for a few puffy clouds scattered on both horizons. The sun was there though we couldn't look at it. At the mine's entry, Dad motioned us onto a motorcar, an electrically powered Jeffrey Trolley Motor. Like a trolley car, the motorcar ran on rails.

We sat on the top casing; it was shaped like a big Milky Way candy bar with three headlights, a wide, rectangular iron frame enclosed in a steel casing with a niche for a driver and two other men. Other riders sat where the guys were sitting now—on top of the metal casing in back of the front end. Dad, Geno, and I were in the front end. Dad was the driver; we'd be the first in the mine.

Dad lit his fire boss lamp, handing it to me: "You and Geno, watch the flame. If it flickers a lot, tell me right away."

With great pride, I set the lamp between Geno and me. We were proud to be given such a job. Even to be temporary assistant-to-the-fireboss was a big honor.

Ernnn! Ernnn! Dad turned the ignition. *Spu-too! Spu-too!*

The electrical engine sputtered and coughed, like someone trying to wake up after a long sleep. Dad stopped twisting the ignition key.

"Sunday—day of rest," Dad jested, "even for the motorcar." We chuckled, anxiously waiting for the motorcar to wake up. Again he twisted the ignition:

E-R-R-N-n-n-n-n-n-n-n-n-n-n-n-n-n-n-n! The engine roared, fading to a low hum, ready to go. Dad shifted into forward gear. The car followed the tracks into the mine.

The sunlight from the entry faded. The walls engulfed us, swallowing us with only the light of our lamps and the motorcar. The lights on our caps allowed us to see only where we looked. Everyplace else was dark. The tunnel lights were shut off. The motorcar's lights lit the rails in front of us. Deeper and deeper we drove, plunging into darkness, surrounded by rocks, coal, and dirt . . . damp . . . dank . . . dark. Our headlamps followed the jerk of our heads, capturing glimpses of the manmade cavern.

Water pools formed where underground springs dripped. As we

The sunlight from the entry faded and the dark engulfed us as we entered the mine. Courtesy of the Raton Museum.

passed from section to section, the dark rushed in behind us, engulfing us. Geno and I watched the lamp's flame. It didn't flicker, but felt good in the mine's smothering darkness. I could hear myself breathe, and when I spoke, my voice was stifled in the dark, swallowed by the pitch-black air, like hollering into a canyon and hearing no echo.

La Muerte was here—in the shadows, in the chinks of the rock walls . . . silent . . . grave, curious about our presence. I shuddered as she and the carreta swept into my mind. I thought about the blue turquoise sky outside the mine, and the scattered puffy clouds. Thoughts of La Muerte faded.

Dad stopped the motorcar next to the room where he had been working on Saturday. The room was once a solid seam of coal. Miners had dug out and hauled away the coal, creating the room. About twenty feet square, the walls and roof were made of the very coal being mined. The miners already had rigged up lights for the room. Dad switched them on. Suddenly light flowed throughout the room. We were standing in the midst of an ancient coal seam.

Under the bright lights, Dad showed us the Joy loader, a small tractor-like vehicle for loading the coal blasted from the room's walls. The miners called it the "joe-loader." From its rubber belt, coal was conveyed out of the room to cars hooked to the motor car, which pulled out the loaded cars.

Dad found his pick, grasped it like a conductor's baton, and started a lecture:

"We do drift mining here at Chicorico. We bore into the drift of the coal seam," he pointed, "digging a tunnel into the side of the mountain, following the coal seam. Think of the mountain as a double-layer cake with chocolate icing in the middle. The bottom layer is covered with chocolate icing. The top layer is resting on the icing. You are the coal miner, a teeny-tiny *hormiga,* smaller than a termite, digging out the chocolate icing. As you dig and carry the icing, the top layer might fall down on you—*Squerch!* No more you!

"So, you have to work slow but sure. You must prop up the ceiling as you go along. One hormiga can't do the whole job. You work with others, as a team. Each must work with all his muscles, doing his job right. He must be careful, do a good job so others won't be hurt in accidents by his carelessness. Now that you are digging in the icing—the coal—the rest of the crew follows. Behind the coal diggers—the men who pick and blast out the coal—timber-men saw logs into cross-bars and props, notching the logs to fit them together to hold up the roof." Dad was making sweeping gestures with his pick.

"Track-layers put down rails in new areas and take them from over-mined areas. Joe-loaders fill up the waiting coal cars, and a motorman hauls away newly dug coal. Outside, tipple-men sort and clean the coal. Stones, dirt, and shale are thrown away, making big slack piles. The tipple-men separate the coal by size, bigger chunks for use in the steel mills, smaller ones for everyday use. Nowadays, more and more men work on the outside.

"All the time, it seems, there are new machines, in and out of the mine. We use electricity a lot, too. These make the work easier, but there's danger with these new machines. Some are very heavy, causing great vibrations; they loosen the rock ceiling. Others make a tremendous noise, making it hard to tap the ceiling with a pick to hear hollow spots, danger areas. Someday there will be no need for men like me. A continuous miner machine will do everything—undercutting, boring, and loading coal. Company dynamite specialists will do the blasting."

"Will you get laid off?" Juan was agitated by the thought of Dad's possible obsolescence.

"Lot of men will. Me? Maybe."

"No '*maybes*,' Dad!"

"Juan, *no le vale la pena*. Mining's hard, dangerous work. I'll be forced to do something better, outside. Let me tell you, we're still like the old-timers, but they didn't have a union crew. Every man was an independent miner with three jobs: undercutting, boring, and blasting after excavating the dirt and rocks and propping up the ceiling. Come, here. Close to the wall, where I'm undercutting." We moved by the wall of coal, sitting on the cold, damp floor. Dad continued his lecture:

"Down here at the bottom of the wall, I'm undercutting. You see the deep wedge?" Dad pointed to a long, deep wedge running horizontally along the coal seam. "I'm cutting into the coal. This is done by lying down on your side—like this."

Dad lay on his side and chiseled into the wedge he'd started yesterday. In the days before sump pumps, miners often lay in water as they etched out the wedge.

"Once you etch a deep wedge in the coal—oh, two or three feet deep—you stop. You measure up the wall about six feet and bore some holes, usually two or three. See this auger?" Dad handed Juan the auger.

"It's heavy!"

"It's a five-foot-long drill made of steel," Dad explained.

"Give it to me. Hey, it's really heavy!" Freddie exclaimed. José and Petee took hold of it, agreeing.

Dad took the auger back, stuck it on the wall, and commenced to drill, leaning on the auger handle with all his weight.

"Just like drilling wood; coal's soft, easy to drill. Coal used to be wood, you know."

"Yeah!" Juan chirped. "Long time ago, this used to be a big swamp. Right where we're standing."

"How long ago?"

"I dunno. But there were dinosaurs then."

"Lot of fossils, too. We're standing in a very old swamp," Dad chuckled.

It was hard to imagine we were standing in a swamp, except for the room's damp, dank feeling.

"Why are you drilling the coal?" José was more interested in mining than dead wood.

"To blast the coal into chunks. The deeper the hole, the bigger the blast."

"How?"

"With dynamite."

"Wow!"

"Once you have your holes deep enough, you load dynamite powder into them. We store the powder in wooden boxes in the machine shop."

"Oh, yeah." Geno recognized the purpose for the wooden boxes his dad brought home. Like Dad and many of the other miners, Mr. Chicarelli brought home the empty powder boxes. They were handy as furniture of all sorts.

Dad continued his lecture:

"You can't let the powder get wet. It won't explode. When we're ready to make a shot, we take the powder out of the box and stuff it down the holes. With a steel rod, like this one," Dad picked up an iron rod, "you pack the powder into the holes, good and tight. Then, you stick a fuse into the dynamite. You yell *'FIRE IN THE HOLE!'* The men take cover away from the wall, except you. You light the fuse by putting your lamp's hot glass to the fuse. You take cover—*wumpff!*"

"N-a-ah!"

"What 'ja expect?"

"A big KA-BOOOM!"

"Like bombs in the war movies."

"Mining's not the movies. The sound is muffled by the coal. After the blast, chunks of broken coal fall to the floor, kinda like a shattered clay jug. The chunks are ready to load."

The guys fidgeted, roaming around the room for a few minutes. Geno and I sat still on the damp, cold floor, bewildered and disappointed, our curiosity blunted. I looked out of the room, down the dark tunnel we'd come through. I saw her again: La Muerte flitted into the shadows as I turned my head.

"Boys, it's not pretty in here after a blast. The blast throws coal dust into the air. That's why we wear goggles."

Noticing Geno's and my dejection, Dad decided it was time to go. He put down his pick and got back onto the motorcar:

"Time to go." We followed. Dad dropped the car into reverse.

On the ride out, Dad continued his lecture:

"Mining has two main hazards, cave-ins and dust. Miners tunnel into seams of coal under millions of tons of rocks and dirt. Any faults in the coal, or the rocks, could cause the roof to shift and fall. Everything, anybody, can be instantly crushed, like a tiny hormiga. And, like I said, when you're blasting, the shots throw coal dust into the air. It's very explosive. Any little spark can make it explode. We call it 'damp gas.' That's where the fire boss has to do his job. As he's inspecting, if there's too much gas in an area, he makes an outside man wet down the dusty walls to keep the dust down."

Dad treated the whole mine as his lecture hall, but his office was a dark, bleak room hewed from coal. Within that gnawed-out room, he spent each day undercutting the coal seam, boring dynamite powder holes into it, blasting and loading coal without seeing the natural light of day or night. When he could, he'd take a break, sit with his lunch bucket to eat, and then return to his diggings until his shift rotated.

I had imagined an army of men working in common cause, conducting a crusade to produce coal to support the war effort. Yet Dad described his work as a solitary pursuit to earn money to put food on our table. Every day he lay on his side to undercut the bottom of the coal seam with his pick. Then, he set to work drilling holes for the round of charges. With the auger, twelve turns to the inch, he drilled a six-foot hole for each charge, repeating the same procedure devoid of romance. Four holes along the roof, two on each side, and four holes on the bottom.

Missing were the men toiling collectively at their noble tasks, greeting each other in strapping camaraderie, toiling to make a better world. Where did they gather to spin their yarns of deeds great and small? Of winning union battles and chasing bears from the mine? The ambience of a collective, convivial spirit, working in common cause, could not be felt within the silent, stone shuck of the coal seam.

As we emerged from the mine, the sun showered us with warm light, flowing over our heads and cascading over our bodies. We perked up, dazzled by the brightness.

"Men weren't meant to be miners. If God wanted it so, he would've built a pick in our hands instead of brains in our heads."

Nervously, we laughed at Dad's observation of the Divine Plan.

As we put away our caps and lanterns, Geno noticed a hand-car sitting under the tipple. "Mr. Montaño, what's that?"

"That? A hand-car. The section gang uses it to move about on the job." A section gang is a repair crew that maintains railroad beds and tracks. They were working at the other end of the canyon, past the school. Chicorico Creek had washed out a bank near a little railroad bridge. With more rainfall, the bridge could collapse.

"Can we ride it?"

"Please, Mr. Montaño? Can we?"

"Can we? Plea-ea-ea-ssse?" Petee and Freddie chirped, like a chorus of hungry baby robins begging for worms.

"I don't know." Dad looked at the rest of us. Our eyes were aglow. Dad appeared ambivalent, but he had a playful glint in his eyes. There was a little boy in Dad—a fun-loving man. I sat on the hand-car, pretending to rest. Dad took the hint.

"All right. The train's not running. It can't hurt. I always wanted to ride one, anyway."

We piled on. The hand-car was operated manually. Muscle power made it go. Two persons stand face-to-face, holding its I-shaped lever. In teeter-totter motion, one person pushes down on the lever while the other pulls up; as they establish a push-and-pull rhythm, the lever causes the wheels to turn, moving the hand-car on the tracks.

"Freddie and José, you get on one side. Petee and Juan, you the other. Now, Freddie and José, push down on the lever, real hard. Petee and Juan, pull up. Back and forth, up and down—and we'll go."

"U-h-h-h-h!" The guys grunted, pushing, pulling mightily. We barely moved.

"Too many men here. You boys aren't strong enough to make it go. Matías! Geno! We'll walk to the house. You boys should be able to pull your own weight. Take the car, con cuidado, down to the store, where the road crosses over by our house."

"Aw heck, Dad," I begged.

"I wanna ride too." Geno begged also.

"Okay. I'll take you cabritos for a ride. You bigger boys take the car to the railroad crossing by the store. Wait for us there! When we get there, I'll take over. I'll take the cabritos on a ride to the section gang, where the car belongs."

As the boys pulled away, Juan yelled. "How fast can we go?"

"Haah!" Dad shouted. "As fast as you can make it!"

"Mr. Montaño!" Geno was concerned. "That's too fast!"

"No te penes, Geno. The boys aren't that strong. Yo, boys! Be sure to stop by the house! I'll take the car to the section gang. . . . Matías y Geno, come, walk these tracks with me."

Dad walked the tracks every workday to the mine and back. The grade of the rail bed from the mine to the store hardly dropped; the grade dropped more rapidly from the store to the bridge where the section gang was working.

We walked home on the tracks, the same way we came to the mine. Most of the time, we walked on the ties. There was a road along the tracks. Yet it was easier stepping tie-to-tie, especially when it rained or snowed and the dirt road got muddy and slippery. We could barely see the guys; they got smaller and smaller as they pumped their way slowly down Chicorico Canyon. Walking hands in pockets, Geno and I didn't have much to say. The trip into the mountain scared the mine out of us.

"I can tell you boys are down. The mine made you blue, eh? You don't have to be miners—if you get a good education. We work hard in the dark and wet ground. For what? To put food on the table. Sure, I get good pay, but my job can be taken from me. When the Company wants, it can kick me out of the mine. Or, close the mine. When you have an education, you are equal to any man. That can't be taken from you."

When we arrived at the railroad crossing where the store was located, the guys were waiting for us. Little did Dad know they had hatched a plot to get another ride on the hand-car.

"How goes the ride?"

They warbled:

"Snazzy!"

"Swell!"

"Classy!"

"Is it true," José asked, "that Tío Baltazar is in the section gang?" Uncle Baltazar Ribera was my mother's brother.

"You know that already, José. Pero, why do you ask?"

"No reason. Give him an *abrazo* for me, bueno!" José did have a reason to ask. Tío Baltazar's whereabouts were crucial to the plan for another ride.

"*¿Cómo no?*" Dad took over the car. Geno and I got on.

"I'll push and pull it. You boys sit down. Hold onto the side. Enjoy the ride." At first, the wheels turned slowly and the car barely moved. It was easy for Geno and me to count ties. As the grade dropped, Dad pushed down harder. We moved faster; the ties passed more quickly under the car. Before long, the ties moved under us too fast to count! Besides, we couldn't count past ten. We waved at Louie Leal and Marian. They were playing at Louie's. They jumped away from their play, running toward the tracks, watching as we rolled by.

Now we were gliding by the school houses. Mrs. Hilliard was sitting on the front porch of her house with Miss Blackerby. We waved. Miss

Blackerby would be our teacher this year, when Geno and I started first grade.

"Hang on, boys!" the principal, Mrs. Hilliard, yelled. "Expect to see you in school come September!"

Geno and I waved at Mrs. Hilliard and Miss Blackerby. I felt ten feet tall. What fun to ride the tracks on a Sunday afternoon—to see our friends and our teachers. We were like heroes in a parade. We crossed the bridge where the section gang was repairing the fallen banks of Chicorico Creek. None was at work. Like the miners, they didn't work on Sundays.

A little further down the tracks, the section gang camped on a railroad siding. They had a mobile camp, a small train of three very old Pullman cars painted silver. One car held tools. The men slept in another, and the third car was used for eating and relaxing during off-hours. When they completed repairs, a steam engine would pull the three-car camp to the next job.

Dad pumped the hand-car onto the siding. Tío Baltazar came out to greet us. He invited us into the Pullman diner where the men ate. It was clean and tidy, with the musty smell of men who sweat a lot. The diner was practically empty, except for three men playing cards with the cook. Tío Baltazar explained that most of the men were out and around, searching for arrowheads. Tío had a pretty good collection himself. However, he no longer sought them. They were everywhere, wherever the Apaches or Comanches had once made camp. Now he liked searching for pottery shards around more permanent settlements. They were more difficult to find.

"The news is not good from home, Manuel." Tío Baltazar lowered his voice.

"*Qué lástima,*" Dad sighed, drawing his breath.

Tío Baltazar continued, but he was difficult to hear. He was so soft-spoken, like Mom. "Tell Clara, our father is not well. *Tiene una toz muy mala.*"

"*Ojalá*, that he will be better?"

"He's an old man, ninety-eight years. Clara better go see him." Tío Baltazar rested his arms on the little table, revealing the crucifix tattooed on his left arm. The two men gazed at each other with an unspoken understanding about Abuelo Ribera's serious condition. I was too young to share their feelings.

"O, sí. I'll tell Clara," Dad acknowledged Tío's implied message. Then, he turned to us as though nothing were wrong: "Let's go, boys. Give Tío Baltazar un abrazo."

Geno and I took turns hugging Tío Baltazar, who escorted us out of the diner. He walked with us on the tracks for a short while, then returned toward the diner, wishing God be with us, adiós.

That Monday after Dad and Mr. Malcolm went to work, José, Juan, Freddie, and Petee met in the llano behind our house. They finalized their plan to get another ride on the hand-car. Juan was the leader, but he shouldn't get all the blame for the Big Lie they were about to perpetrate. They were all *mentirosos*—liars when it suited them.

They walked down the tracks to where the section gang was repairing the embankment by the bridge and approached my Tío Baltazar. The guys agreed: Juan would do the talking. He was good with words and could be very persuasive.

"*Hola, Tío. ¿Cómo le va?*"

"*Aquí, no más, trabajando.*" Tío Baltazar put down his shovel and took off his hat, wiping the sweat from his forehead.

"I am sorry to hear about Abuelo Ribera." Juan expressed concern for our Grandfather Ribera.

"I have to get to work boys. Can't talk now. Thanks for coming down." Tío Baltazar glanced at the foreman.

"Dad sent us for the hand-car. He needs it at the mine."

"*¡Qué va!* Why would he send boys to do a man's job?"

"Yesterday he showed us how to run the car. Last night, he told us to bring the hand-car back—that he needed it at the mine."

"But he didn't tell me when he was here yesterday with your brother and Eugene."

"Dad said he forgot. After he came home, he remembered he would need it."

"I don't know. I'll check with the foreman."

Tío Baltazar approached the foreman. Considering Juan's request, both swung their arms in short jerks and shuffled their feet on the rocky soil. These men couldn't imagine why the guys wanted the hand-car. For Tío and the foreman, it wasn't a toy. The guys knew that Tío and the foreman were trusting men, like Dad and most other working men of their generation. The Ten Commandments were laws to live by.

"Okay," the foreman nodded as Tío Baltazar turned to return to the guys.

"Take the car to the mine, right now." Tío Baltazar gave instructions. "Don't go near the tipple. Tell the man at the tipple to put it where Manuel wants it. Now go. Before the train comes for coal."

The scheme worked like a charm. The guys got on the car and slowly pumped it away, heading up the tracks toward the mine. The first part of the trip was slow going. The grade rose gradually. To lighten the load, they threw everything off the hand-car, including a pick, shovel, crow bar, and a long, thick stick—the handle of the hand-car's brake. To stop, the long stick is placed in a ring next to the right back wheel. When the stick is pulled back, the brake rubs against the wheel, slowing down the hand-car.

Once reaching the store, the grade leveled off, and they could go a little faster. When they got close to the tipple, Freddie observed:

"Here we been working like dogs. For what? We didn't go fast."

"It's all uphill," José commented, "all hard work."

"S-u-u-n! It's downhill going the other way." Petee realized.

"We told Tío Baltazar," Juan injected, "that we would leave the car here."

"Well, we will," José implied. "He'll never know we took another ride."

"How do you know your tío won't see us?" Freddie asked.

"We'll stop before we get to the bridge. Then bring it back."

"Let's go!" José gave the marching orders.

There they stood, stooped over the hand-car's handle, face to face, their skinny elbows jutting out of their bib overalls. They were immersed, intent on flight—to glide, to slide, to roll down the tracks—

Pu-u-sh-pull—Pu-u-sh-pull—the hand-car crawled.

They pushed and pulled harder. The car moved slightly faster.

Push-pull! Push-pull!

They gained speed, chanting in unison:

"Push-pull! Make the car go!

Push-pull! Make the car go!"

Faster! Faster! the hand-car sped!

"Push-pull! Make the car go!

Push-pull! Make the car go!"

Fully engrossed, they hardly noticed the midpoint, the crossing by the store.

"Faster!" Juan screeched.

"Yeah! Faster!" Freddie yapped.

"Give it gas!" Petee yelped.

"¡*Dale* gas!" José howled.

They chanted in unison:

"Push-pull! ¡Dale gas!

Push-pull! ¡Dale gas!"

Their prime purpose: to rush and roll rapidly. They rushed past the store. The incline dropped; down they went, iron wheels turning, proud guys huffing and grunting, yearning for more speed. Faster! Faster! The hand-car sped! Now they bobbed up and down, up and down, in syncopated rhythm. The harder they bobbed, pushing and pulling, the faster the car moved, sliding, gliding down the tracks.

Geno and I spotted the guys as they careened past our house. We blitzed toward the tracks.

"Give us a ride?"

"Wait for us!"

Poof! They were gone, like a sand devil dancing down a dirt road, disappearing in its own dust. They couldn't give us a ride, even if they wanted to! They couldn't stop! Earlier they had thrown the brake handle away along with some picks and shovels. This was part of the grand scheme the guys hadn't considered—how to stop the fast-moving car without brakes.

The guys sped by the schoolhouses, knowing they'd soon get caught red-handed. They hurled toward the bridge where the section gang, including Tío Baltazar, was working. The guys panicked.

"Where's the brakes?"

"Holy Toledo!"

"Every man for himself!"

"Bail out!"

The hand-car was still moving at a breakneck speed. They leaped to both sides of the track and tumbled head over heels across the ballast and rolled down the slope of the bar ditch into the mud puddles of stagnant water at the ditch's bottom. The car coasted over the bridge and slowed to a stop near the men hard at work. Tío Baltazar and the foreman mounted the car and moved it onto the siding. When the foreman and Tío Baltazar looked around to help the guys, they were gone. Wasting no time recovering from the jump, they scampered up the tracks putting distance between themselves and the section gang. They hurried by Geno and me, shouting with clenched fists:

"Don't tell nobody!"

"Talk and you're dead!"

"Eat my knuckles!" Juan threatened, shaking his fist.

They disappeared into the piñón and juniper covered hills, their knees and elbows bruised, their clothing muddied from rolling into the bar ditch. Geno and I yelled, teasing them as they fled:

"Liar, liar,
Pants on fire!"

That ditty's lyrics were fighting words, unless, of course, the facts supported the charge. Geno and I decided to keep our mouths shut anyway. The thought of eating a fist-sandwich didn't have much appeal to us.

That evening after supper, the guys organized a game of hide-and-seek in the llano behind our house. The whole gang was there: the Malcolm brothers, Marian, Geno, Louie, Dennis and Donald Giocomo, Frank, Clarence, and Mary Francis Rivali. A tree on the side of the llano was the "IT" post.

The first round of hide-and-seek went smoothly for me. I found a downed tree overgrown by scrub oaks. I crawled beneath the scrub oak's foliage, a perfect hiding place.

"All the oxen-come-in-free!" Juan shouted, after finding Petee and tagging him IT. I popped up from beneath the branches; not thinking, I yelled:

"Ya–hoooo!"

Everybody heard me, including Petee. He put his hands over his eyes, leaned his face against the IT tree, and began counting, "1–2–3–4. . . ." When he got to twenty, he shouted, "Ready or not! Here I come!"

Petee uncovered his eyes, poking around, dilly-dallying as though he didn't know where I was hiding. I could tell by the way he kept glancing through the side of his eyes that it was all show. He was coming after me. He drifted toward my hideout.

Meantime, Marian, Geno, and Louie all ran in free. I panicked and jumped from my hideout, pushing the willowy scrub oak branches aside. *WAP!* A branch swung back, slapping me on the cheek, stinging like a bee bite. I hesitated, then ran as fast as I could, trying to beat Petee to the IT tree. Petee outran me.

"You're IT!" Petee triumphantly yelled as he tagged the tree, shouting to everyone, "all-a oxens come in free!"

"Shucks." Petee caught me. I was IT! I waited for everyone to come in, noticing no one was dumb enough to yell "yahoo," giving up their hiding place. Being IT was going to be hard, especially since the older kids could outrun me. When everyone was in, I imitated Petee, covering my eyes with my hands and leaning against the tree, counting aloud:

"1–2–3–4–5–6–7–8–9–10—" I raised my head. "Hey? What comes after ten?" I saw everyone trying to hide. They returned to the IT tree.

"No fair!" Freddie whined, "You peeked."

"Well, what else could I do?"

"Cool it!" Juan yelled, "Matías can barely count to ten."

"Yeah! I was peeking, fair-and-square!"

"Peeking fair-and-square! Baloney! If you can't count to twenty, you can't play." Freddie was piqued.

"Don't make a Supreme Court case out of it!" Juan realized tempers were hot. "There's gotta be a way we can all play together."

"Well, I don't wanna be the bad guy, but we won't have time to hide if the little kids can't count to twenty."

"Goll-llee! I wanna play!" Geno wanted to be in on the action.

"Me, too!" Marian chimed. "I can't count to twenty!" The other little kids were quiet. I knew they couldn't count to twenty, but were afraid to speak up.

"Well, count to ten—twice!" Petee suggested. "It takes just as long to count to ten twice!"

"I knew we'd find a way to play without fighting. How 'bout it, Matías?" Juan was pleased.

"Okay."

"Hey! Good idea!" Juan cheered up. He was worried we wouldn't get to play.

"I don't care," Freddie agreed, "just so it's not me."

I resumed by counting to ten, twice, without speeding up my counting pace—or peeking to see where everyone was hiding. Honesty is the best policy, especially if you want the other kids to let you play. I don't mind saying the honesty policy makes hide-and-seek a tough game when you're six years old. I was IT for a very long time. Whenever I found one of the bigger guys, he could outrun me to the IT tree. And the kids my age were very good at hiding.

After a while, José became bored with the monotony of the game. It wasn't much fun for him. There was no thrill because I was lousy as IT.

"Hey, Matías?" José asked, "Mind if I take over?"

"Wh-a-at?" Juan dubiously questioned.

"S-u-u-n," José pretended to complain, "I never get to be IT."

"Matías has to catch somebody before he can stop being IT." Juan was holding me to the rules.

"Well, I wanna be IT. It's boring this way. Matías never catches nobody."

"For crying in a washtub! Nobody wants to be IT!" Juan was astonished at José's request to be IT. The fun of hide-and-seek was tricking the hunter. Yet José was bored with the fact I was not very good at being IT. I wasn't too excited about my record-breaking term as Chicorico's longest-standing IT. This was not my idea of setting a record.

Juan relented: "Well, I don't care. You'll have to catch a coyote like me before I'm IT. Start counting, José!"

Yip! Yip! Yip! Yip! Everyone yelped like coyotes at Juan. José covered his eyes counting, 1–2–3–4. . . .

As I was hiding behind our outhouse, I spied Tío Baltazar walking up the tracks toward our house. "Oh, oh!" I thought. "He's come to tell Dad! The guys are in deep trouble!" I gave up my hiding spot, running to greet him:

"Tío Baltazar!"

"Hola. *¿Qué tál?*"

"Aquí, no más jugando."

"¿Y, sus hermanos?"

Gulp! He knew about the guys! I feigned nonchalance:

"Okay, I guess."

As I took him into the house, he winked, reciting a down-home dicho: *"Vale más poco y bien ganado, que mucho y enzoquetado,"* 'It's better to get a little and stay clean than to get a lot and get muddy.' That down-home saying made sense. The guys should've been satisfied with the hand-car ride they got on Sunday.

"¡Entre! ¡Entre!"

Mom and Dad rose to greet Tío Baltazar. They were pleasantly surprised and delighted to see him. Ramona ran right up to Tío. He lifted and hugged her, setting her down.

"You should come for dinner," Dad encouraged Tío Baltazar. "Don't be such a stranger. You're *familia.*"

Tío Baltazar furrowed his brow; a grim pallor swept over his face. *"Hermana mía, mira la telegrama."* Tío Baltazar handed Mom a neatly folded telegram.

Mom unfolded the telegram to read:

June 22, 1944–Ribera Station–Baltazar Ribera at Raton section gang–*Baltazar, Padre Pablo está muy enfermo. Venga a la casa adelante. Feliz*

"¡Por Dios!" Mom exclaimed, wrinkling her brow. She explained to me: "Your abuelo is very sick." She handed the telegram to Tío Baltazar.

Tío Baltazar turned to Dad. "I'm leaving on the Super Chief, tomorrow from Raton. Give me a ride tonight? To the station."

"¿Cómo no? Where will you stay in Raton?"

While Dad prepared to leave, Tío Baltazar explained he'd sleep in a section gang car in Raton. His crew was split up. Most of the section gang was in Raton, working on a bigger job. As they left the house, Mom hugged Tío Baltazar. "Tell Papá, I'll come as soon as I can."

Tío Baltazar didn't say a thing about the guys and how they lied about delivering the hand-car. He had graver matters on his mind than the guys' reckless pranks. At least he didn't say anything in front of Mom. . . .

When Dad returned from Raton late that night, all of us were in bed. I heard Dad speaking to Mom, surprised to hear Mom raise her voice.

"Manuelo! Why didn't you tell me!" Mom harangued Dad, chewing him out.

"The boys might've been hurt in the car." Mom rarely raised her voice against Dad, but nothing got between her and the safety of her children.

"Pues, they didn't get hurt." Dad tried to vindicate himself.

Mom ordered Dad, "Tomorrow, you must talk with them. They lied to Baltazar. He trusted them!"

"Honey, boys will be boys—"

"Our boys don't lie! Tomorrow! Manuelo, promise!"

"Bueno, *mañana.*"

I don't know what Dad told Juan and José. I do know the Malcolm brothers and my brothers had to stay in the house for a week helping their mothers, a punishment far worse than a spanking.

6

IF ANY SHOULD NOT WORK, NEITHER SHOULD HE EAT

Three days after the trip to the mine, Mom enrolled me in school. Proudly, Mom showed Mrs. Hilliard my birth certificate, verifying my age. Mrs. Hilliard took the certificate, commenting, "Lord, six years have passed since you had Matt. Hmm—that first year was a struggle, as I recall."

"Yes," Mom nodded, "but he's strong now. Just needs to be more careful."

"Ho! Don't I know." Mrs. Hilliard glanced at me. "What you doin' hunting rattlesnakes?" I didn't get a chance to answer. Before I could brag about my brave and daring deed, Mrs. Hilliard returned the certificate to Mom, addressing her as though I weren't there.

"He'll be getting his shots in October. Unless he's had 'em?"

"No," Mom nodded.

"Well, I can finish the rest of the paperwork in a bit. Miss Blackerby will be Matt's teacher."

With that, Mrs. Hilliard and Mom turned to telling about family.

"What do you hear from Arturo?" Mrs. Hilliard inquired.

"Only good news. He's back in flight school, learning to fly big bombers, so he's still not in the war zone. And your sons?"

"Good to hear about Arturo. My boys don't write much. They're all in the army, but they're not with the same outfit. I raised them to be pretty independent. I'm not surprised when they forget to write their mother."

"It was hard, *¿Qué no?* Raising four boys alone?" Mom knew about raising boys. She had four.

"Oh, it wasn't so hard, but lonely without Marvin." Mrs. Hilliard sighed; taking a deep breath, she turned pensive. "I remember the day I lost him . . . like it was yesterday—been more'n ten years ago. It was an ordinary day, in early February. It was my first year as principal. I was trying hard to do a good job. My teachers and I were making grand plans to celebrate the birthdays of George Washington and Abraham Lincoln. We thought it important that the children know about American heroes.

"The day was going smoothly. I remember the children—Miss McBride's first graders—were being called in from recess. She was ringing the bell. Like always, some of the boys were straggling behind. Miss McBride really rang that bell, so hard I thought it would surely break!

"As the laggards were coming toward the schoolhouse, I heard a rumble, like a thunderstorm moving into the canyon. But it was early February. There were no thunderclouds in the sky. I looked at the clock, 10:15—a thunderous, rumbling, shaking of the earth! I thought it might be an earthquake. The floor shook, practically knocking me down, china rattling on the cupboard. I prayed as I caught my balance:

'Oh, Heavens, an accident at the mine. Lord, make it not so.'

"I rushed to the mine. Flames were belching out the entry! It was so hot! The rescue squad, wearing gas masks, was standing back more than a hundred feet. The steel gate used to block the entry was melted from the fire's intense heat. The air was filled with the stinky, rank smell of burnt grease, pitch, and—worst of all—human flesh. Bodies of men were sprawled at the front entry where the explosion had thrown them. They must've been going into the mine when it exploded. The living were writhing, wiggling, squirming. Others lay still. They were dead.

"The squad wrapped the injured men in blankets and dragged them away from the front entry. Grabbing a jar of water, I ran to the injured men and raised one miner's head. His hair was seared, face scorched. He stared at me without speaking. I gave him a drink. I moved down the row. The burns seemed to get worse with each man. I had to retreat, get away from those men. The smell of their burnt flesh was repugnant. It made me sick to the stomach. I was ashamed, but the smell was terrible."

Mrs. Hilliard paused, tears welling in her eyes.

"Maybe, you shouldn't speak *de este tiempo, terrible,*" Mom suggested, consoling Mrs. Hilliard.

"Thank you, Clara. But I want Matt to hear this. So he'll know about coal mining." She continued: "Dr. Monty was there, frantically trying to relieve the pain of the miners. Most miners were in shock, a blessing for them. After my stomach settled, I just watched the squad evacuate the dead miners from the entry. This was dangerous. The squad could get burnt. The roaring fire could kill them. They didn't dare wait for the fire to die down; the coal within fed the fire! The bodies would be charred beyond recognition. The men in the rescue squad were brave, compelled to save the bodies from cremation even though they couldn't save the lives.

"The rescue squad worked tirelessly. One man ran too close to the flames, grabbed a dead miner, and started dragging him away. The dead man's clothing was covered with smoldering dirt and splintered boards. The rescuer stooped to remove the smoldering debris, but he was too close to the raging flame. He fainted, falling beside the dead miner.

"Two other rescuers saw what happened. They darted to the fainted man. One rescuer pulled the fainted man away while the other dragged the dead man—without removing the smoldering dirt and splintered boards. I ran to the fainted man and wiped his face with a wet rag to revive him. That's when I realized. Mr. Hilliard was not among the living—or the dead—outside the mine. That meant he was in the mine with no hope! The putrid smell of burnt flesh made my stomach sick again."

Mrs. Hilliard suddenly sobbed. She had painted a vivid image . . . running miners . . . burning clothing. I remembered our trip to the mine and envisioned La Muerte, a black specter fading in and out of the flames.

It was horrible! Uncomfortably, I shifted from one foot to the other. Watching a grownup woman cry, I wanted to cry, too.

"Oh, Clara, you were so lucky! Your man was sick in bed." Tears welled into her eyes. Mom tried to console Mrs. Hilliard, but she interrupted, "N-o-o, that's all right, Clara. . . . I'll be all right." She slipped a handkerchief from the desk drawer and blew her nose.

"Would you have another?" Mom asked, groping through her purse, tears in her eyes.

Mrs. Hilliard handed Mom a spare handkerchief. "Let's have a good old-fashioned cry!" Mrs. Hilliard laughed, blowing her nose again.

Good-naturedly, Mom giggled, blowing her nose. Both mothers wiped their eyes.

"Well, back to work." Mrs. Hilliard composed herself, shuffling papers at her desk. She escorted us to the door. "Did Manuel plant his garden yet?"

"Yes," Mom nodded as I chirped, "I helped him." I was glad to be leaving. Enough talk about mine explosions.

As we walked along the tracks returning home, Mom filled in other details of the Chicorico mining accident. The death toll of 95 would make the 1933 Chicorico explosion the nation's worst mine disaster since 1928, when 135 were killed at Mather, Pennsylvania. In 1923, 122 men were entombed in the Number One mine in Dawson, a Phelps Dodge coal camp south of Chicorico. A blast that killed 361 miners at Monongah, West Virginia, in 1907 held the all-time record as of June 19, 1944. Lucky for us, Dad was sick in bed that sad day in February when Mrs. Hilliard lost her husband. She raised her four boys alone. Each joined the army upon high school graduation, never returning to Chicorico. She was a four-star mother, and prominently displayed her service flag in the living room window.

At home, Mom had me change into play clothes—bib overalls, old shoes, and faded shirt. My education as the son of a coal miner continued:

Freddie offered to trade his nickel for my dime.

"Wanna trade? My big, fat nickel for your little, skinny dime?"

"Which is more?"

"Well, which is bigger?" He handed me his fat nickel.

"Hmm." I studied the dime and nickel, noticing the nickel was bigger. "Well, the nickel's bigger."

"Well, then, how 'bout it?"

"Well, okay."

We exchanged coins, and he bolted away, repeatedly taunting:

"Want a nickel?
Suck a pickle!"

"Hey! You cheated me!"

"Sish!" he yelled back, running to the Company store to spend his ill-gained dime, "I cheated you fair and square!"

"Cheated fair and square!" I indignantly shouted, remembering I had used similar words to justify peeking when I was IT playing hide-and-seek. Yet I managed to get along with the guys once I figured out they never lied; they just bent the truth a lot, and I had to be cautious. That same day, Juan and José formed a cartel with Freddie and Petee to work together to share in the profits. Grudgingly, they allowed Geno and me to join. Juan cooked up the idea of making fake coins.

"Let's go behind the clubhouse." Juan led the charge. "There's lots of bottle caps in the trash."

We scurried behind the clubhouse to the trash barrel. There were a lot of bottles and cans in the trash barrel. At the bottom, we found a bunch of Coors and Coca Cola bottle caps. I liked the Coors caps with their picture of Golden Mesa in greenish bronze tones. We found a few Grapette, Delaware Punch, and Orange Crush caps.

We stuffed as many caps as would fit in our pockets and carried them to the track crossing by the store. Our timing was good. The train would soon be passing by to the mine. We placed the caps about two inches apart on both tracks. We weren't allowed to stand next to the tracks when the train passed, so we went to our front porch to wait for the train.

The Santa Fe Railroad track bisected Chicorico, running east to west through the canyon to the mine, running from Raton to Chicorico and back. Through a system of track switching and sidings, one engine managed to pull empty coal cars from Raton and to return with loaded coal cars. After the miners hauled the coal out of the mine, it was dropped in the tipple's chutes for cleaning, culling, and loading into the train cars. The main mine shaft still penetrated the side of the hill at the west end of the canyon, following the coal seam deep into the canyon's wall where a geologist and pioneer miners had first made camp with their families to mine these hills.

The tipple, a tall wooden scaffolding located at the mine entry, was raised over the tracks to clean, cull, and load coal onto the trains. At peak production when the miners worked three shifts around the clock, the tipple operators loaded a train of twenty coal cars per day. Beside the tipple was a stone barn once used for stabling mules and donkeys in the days when the animals were used to haul coal. Now it served as a machine shed, a carpenter shop, and a lamp house where mining gear was stored.

Every working day, a train of empty coal cars crept up the tracks. Reaching the mine, the engine pulled the empty cars into a siding and uncoupled. Then it went to the tipple, where it coupled with the coal cars from the day before. Slowly the engine pulled each car beneath the tipple. Newly dug and washed coal gushed down the tipple's chutes into each empty coal car. Each was filled slightly above the brim.

At this point, the engine switched, pulled the filled coal cars down the tracks, and temporarily parked them beside the empty coal cars. The engine uncoupled from the filled cars and coupled again to the end of the empty coal cars. It pushed them onto the main track and beneath the tipple where they waited, ready to be loaded with coal for the next day's haul. The engine backed down the tracks, re-coupled with the loaded coal cars, and pulled them to Raton. The train repeated this cycle every working day.

Chug!–Chug!–Chug!–Chug!–Chug!–Chug!–Chug!

Before long we heard the chugging, whizzing, and popping of the train's mighty engine—a two-million-pound, black, iron and steel steam engine fueled by coal that heated the steam to drive the pistons to turn the huge iron wheels to pull the coal cars. Every time the train passed our house, I was filled with awe and fascination: tangles of steel, pipes, pistons, valves, gears, and wheels . . . winding gradually up and down the

The tipple was raised over the tracks to cull and clean the coal to load into the trains. Courtesy of Raton Museum.

tracks. It dragged its long, serpentine tail behind: a gargantuan dragon hissing vapors of steam, tossing bits of cinder, and bellowing clouds of smoke. Its shiny steel wheels rolled taller than most of us; its tangle of cylinders, pipes, and tubes throbbed, pulsating like the protruding, straining muscles of Joe Louis . . . strong, mighty, grand.

Chug! Chug! The engine, causing the ground to shake, slowly puffed its way up the tracks. The *tat-a-tat-tat* rattling of the windowpane announced its approach.

Crunch! The bottle caps were smashed into smithereens, pulverized into fragile, thin, tin leafs of filigree. As soon as the rest of the train passed, we darted to the tracks to find our fake money. We gathered most of the caps. Some were so pulverized they fell apart when we picked them up. We took the ones that held together to the store where Angela was tending the cash register.

"Hey, Sis! I figure these are worth quite a bit? Let's see—" Juan brazenly began.

"What in Heavens are those?" Angela cut him off, smirking.

"Bottle caps. We made them into coins."

"Why, they're worthless!" Angela laughed aloud, "They're nothing but flimsy pieces of tin! They're as worthless as a Christmas tree on the Fourth of July—that's how worthless they are." She came down hard on Juan and the rest of us, squelching our delusions of making money.

"But?"

"But, nothing!" Mr. Ruker injected. "Sorry boys—that's not money."

"Scrip's not real money, either," Juan lamely argued.

We groped, standing around hands in pockets, despondently gazing toward the floor.

Mr. Ruker looked sympathetic.

"By gall! Whyn't I think of this before?" His eyes brightened as he grabbed a leaflet from a spindle. "CF&I in Pueblo put out a call for scrap iron at two cents a pound!"

"There you are," Angela injected, "collect scrap iron and make real money."

"I'll give you full value—two cents a pound."

"Great!" Juan was pleased. "Here, let's shake." Juan extended his hand, shaking Mr. Ruker's.

"Be careful," Angela cautioned. "Don't cut yourself on the rusty metal—blood poisoning. Here, take these gloves." Angela handed us some brown, cotton jersey gloves—her seal of approval of our mission.

"Let's go, guys," Juan commanded. "We got work to do."

We needed a wagon to haul our tonnage. We nailed a piece of rope to each of two powder boxes. Following the guys, Geno and I each dragged a box. We split up into two crews, walking on both sides of the tracks, searching down the tracks away from the Company store. We scrutinized every inch of the tracks. Slim pickings: old spikes, rusty nails, one spike plate.

"We'll never make any money this way, by the time we split it up." José was dejected.

"Yeah," Freddie agreed. "Not worth a hill of beans."

"Beans would be worth more!" Petee scoffed.

"And more gas!" We had a good laugh with Juan's joke about the gassy beans.

"Let's go down by the coke ovens," José suggested.

"I don't know," Petee was doubtful. "Didn't you see a rattler there?"

"Yeah!" I blurted, "José shot me with a real Indian arrowhead!" No one was overly impressed by my claim to fame. First Mrs. Hilliard, now the guys, discounted my brave and daring deeds. I was no hero to them.

"Well, that's different. Matías and I went looking for the rattler." José held onto his idea of searching the coke ovens. "We found the rattler; he didn't find us."

"I don't care!" Petee exclaimed. "Don't get me wrong. I'm not saying I'm scared of rattlers."

"Huh? You're pretty dumb, if you're *not* scared of rattlers," Juan noted. "But, if we're gonna make money, we gotta take risks."

"All this talk ain't worth a hill of beans," José impatiently remarked. "It won't get us any junk. I say let's go to the coke ovens!"

"Okay, lead the way," Petee cautiously agreed.

Juan, José, and Freddie took the lead, trekking toward the coke ovens. Leery of rattlesnakes, Geno and I followed the guys' exact footsteps. For scrap iron, the coke ovens weren't much better. When they were abandoned, most of the iron rod-work was removed. Petee found a very long poker, Freddie a ventilation lattice.

"Eureka!" José yelled from the drainage ditch behind the coke ovens. "Come here, there's gold down here!"

We bolted to where José was standing. There right in front of him, embedded in the bank, was an old car rusting away. Someone must have shoved it over the bank and left it to rust. Over the years, people had pilfered it for spare parts. The engine, coils, springs, axles, and wheels were gone. The chassis, fenders, and other tin parts were rusting beyond worth, but the frame was still intact.

"Wow!" Juan exclaimed. "A bonanza! But we're not rich yet. We have to haul the frame to Mr. Ruker."

"Say," Freddie asked, "doesn't your dad have a hacksaw?"

"Hey, ya!" José jumped in, "and plenty of blades!"

"Okay, José and Petee, go get the *serruche* and blades." Juan took over.

José and Petee left for the saw and blades. By the time they returned, Juan and Freddie had pretty well figured out the best way to saw the frame into pieces.

"Okay, everybody, put on your gloves." Again Juan took charge, describing the work detail:

"Freddie and I will take turns sawing the frame. Petee and José will load the boxes and pull them to the store. Matías and Geno can help them."

We watched as Juan and Freddie took turns sawing the frame.

"Be careful," Juan cautioned Freddie. "Saw without twisting the blade. It'll break."

I enjoyed watching the guys working, but my mind wandered as I gazed at the coke oven ruins. All that remained were the oven's foundations, overgrown by weeds and grass. A few beehives—the kilns where the coke was baked—were still standing. It was hard to imagine this decaying place of tumbling brick kilns as a busy workplace, bustling with men and mules burning, loading, and hauling the coke to the tracks where it was loaded into coal cars to be hauled to the steel mills in Pueblo.

"Ready to haul the scrap!" Juan hollered, ordering us to load it up.

The steel pieces were cut short and small. Geno and I loaded them into the powder boxes, distributing the weight evenly so neither box would be too heavy. We pushed the boxes while José and Petee pulled. Pushing and pulling the boxes around rocks, tufts, and yucca plants was all hard work. At the tracks, we lifted the boxes on the rails. The boxes glided like a sleigh across the snow with José and Petee each pulling a box and Geno and I pushing from behind.

When we got to the store, Mr. Ruker was surprised. "Boy, howdy! Where'd you find all that junk?"

"There's plenty more where that came from!" I bragged.

Angela was beaming with pride. "Atta boy." She ruffled my hair.

"Put your junk on the scale. Angela, weigh it. I'll give the boys two cents a pound."

"Wow!" Geno exclaimed, "how many pounds with this load?"

"Twenty. I'll keep a running tab." Angela was all business. She took a pencil from behind her ear and wrote the amount on a paper pad.

"We'll be back," José called as we left.

When we got back to our metal mine, Juan and Freddie had sawed off more pieces of the frame. We loaded the pieces into the boxes. Back and forth we hauled, five times. Each time we hauled about twenty pounds. Each box held about ten pounds, which would have been easy to push, except that Geno and I did most of the work. The guys barely pulled the boxes, causing us to strain.

"Rank has its privileges," José commented when I complained.

On the last trip, Juan and Freddie came with us. They were vibrant, skipping lickety-split, waving arms in high hopes, rhapsodizing about how they were going to spend the real money . . . visions of candy bars and ice cream cones every day for the rest of the summer.

"I got a blister," Freddie complained. "Gloves weren't much good."

"Me, too, on my hand. We shoulda been careful." Juan spit on his blister, licking it with a coating of saliva.

"Yuk!" Freddie was disgusted.

"Try it," José advised. "Dogs lick their wounds, and they get better."

"Sish! Maybe so—for a dog."

"Well it works," Juan said. "My blister feels better already. Try it."

Freddie was skeptical, but the blister stung.

"I'm no dog, but I'm not proud. If it works, it can't hurt nothin.'" Freddie spit on his blister and licked it. "Hey, it does feel better!" He slobbered all over the blister.

"Whoa!" Juan yelped, "Don't drown it!"

At the store, Angela weighed the last haul.

"Twenty pounds again. That makes one hundred pounds, all-told."

"One hundred pounds—I never figured you boys to work so hard. How much do I owe these hard-working boys, Angela?"

Angela poked the pencil in her hair and showed Mr. Ruker the figures on the pad, "At two cents a pound, times one hundred pounds, comes to $2.00."

Mr. Ruker was so pleased he quoted from the Bible:

"If any should not work, neither should he eat."

"Huh?" Juan was stumped. He didn't understand the relevance of Mr. Ruker's quotation. Neither did the rest of us.

"You'll understand when you're older. Boy, howdy, two dollars is a lot of money. But a deal's a deal."

Mr. Ruker went over to the cash register, turning the crank. "Here's thirty-three cents each. Extra two pennies are toward the gloves Angela gave you."

The success of our cartel led to its demise. The guys thought they could make more by working as individuals. They broke up the cartel. After that, each went his own way taking odd jobs, just like the old days of mining when men individually contracted to mine. I liked the idea of people working together in common cause, sharing the wealth, even if it wasn't much. I was delighted when Juan approached me to work with him.

"Want a job? We'll split even-steven."

"What's the job?"

"Mr. Malcolm's chickens got out of the coop. He wants us to round them up and return them."

"How much does it pay?"

"A dime. You'll get a nickel."

"Wow!"

A nickel bought a lot. At two-for-a-penny, you could get ten candies for a nickel.

"Mr. Malcolm has twelve chickens and one rooster. You stay away from the rooster. I'll look for him. You look for the hens."

"Okay," I thought. "This won't be so hard." Mr. Malcolm's chicken coop bordered the llano just like ours. Sure enough, the chickens had strayed into the foothills and were easy to catch. I stalked each stray—sneaking behind, grabbing her legs, and carrying her to the coop. She'd flutter her wings and squawk a lot. Before long, I had all twelve chickens back in Mr. Malcolm's coop.

"Juan!"

"Over here! In the Malcolm's outhouse."

I walked over to the Malcolm's outhouse. It sat over a pit in the ground and was supported by a wooden two-by-four foundation. Several years ago, Mr. Malcolm moved his outhouse to a new pit, a very deep pit. He didn't want to move it again. It was a hard, all-day job requiring help from Dad, my brothers, and the Malcolm boys.

Juan poked his head out the outhouse's doorway. "The rooster's in here—in the potty part!"

"Oh."

The rooster was down the pit standing on human waste.

"He's down there? *There?*"

"Yes! Down there—*there!* Now! How we gonna get him out?"

"I dunno. Anyway, I found all the chickens, in the hills behind the llano."

"Well, good. Now all we need to do is get this rooster out. Let's put our heads together and think. Maybe something will come up."

We could hear the rooster fretting inside, strutting back and forth across the pit's floor. "*Puc-k! Puc-k!*"

"I got it!" Juan's eyes flashed like exploding light bulbs. He clenched his fists, flexed his biceps, suggesting: "Well, why don't I lower you down. You pull him out. I'd go down, bu-u-ut, my shoulders are too wide, and you're not strong enough to hold me. I can hold you. Unless you're afraid."

I was afraid, but I couldn't let him know. And I wanted that nickel. "Okay! Don't drop me!"

"Drop you! Holy smokes, I'm strong as a buffalo."

I wiggled through the hole. Juan held my left arm with both of his hands, leaving my right arm free to grab the rooster. As soon as the rooster saw me lowering into the hole, he backed into a corner and strutted to another.

"I can't reach him; keeps running from me! And my arm's hurting."

"Here, I'll swing you around. He'll be confused and stay still." Juan was correct. The minute I started swinging around, the rooster stood still.

"Stop swinging me," I screamed. "It hurts. Quit!"

Juan let go of my arm. I dropped down *KERPLOP!!*

I landed on my feet. *Ph-e-e-e-e-e-e-ew!* Reeking, rotting, putrefying human waste. I was ankle deep in a stinky pit. I stopped sinking. The bottom was surprisingly solid as I sloshed around ankle deep.

Slosh-thunk! Slosh-thunk! With each step, I had to tug carefully. The gooey bottom was very sticky. I had to curl my toes, then lift my foot and shoe together, or the shoe would stick in the gooey waste and my foot would slip out. Stepping cautiously, I'd forgotten about the odor, but it was still there. I yelled:

"Get me out of here!"

"I have to get a rope. Be back in a second." Juan disappeared in search of a rope.

"Don't leave me here!" I screamed. "Don't you dare!"

But he was gone, probably for all of two minutes. It felt like twenty-four hours. Juan re-appeared, poking his face down the hole.

"Here, take the rope. I'll pull you up."

"But what about the rooster?"

"Holy smokes, I forgot about him!"

"Well, I can't! He's flapping around down here making a mess! Make a lasso and throw it down."

"There you are stuck in the hole, and you're playing cowboys!"

"Just do it!"

"Okay, okay, hold your horses!" Juan threw the lasso, but kept the other end of the rope. It had a lot of slack. I grabbed it and tried tossing the loop over the rooster's head. He ducked to one side.

"Try to snare him," Juan advised. "Put the lasso on the ground. Shoo the rooster on it, then pull."

I laid the lasso on the waste and cautiously approached the rooster from the opposite side. He backed away, stepping in the lasso's noose. I yanked, knocking him down. I grabbed him by the legs, his wings flapping, splashing waste every which way. A few drops hit my lips. I wiped them on my shirtsleeve. I checked the noose. It was tight around the rooster's legs.

"Bravo!" Juan yelled as he pulled up the rooster. He grabbed the rooster and ran to the Malcolm's coop.

José stuck his head down into the hole. He'd come from the house when he heard the commotion.

"We got the rooster out!"

"Yeah, what're you doin' in there?"

"José, why would the rooster jump down the toilet hole?"

"Huh? He wouldn't go by himself!" José scratched his head. "And, how'd you get down there?"

"Juan put me down."

"Figures," José mumbled. "Rooster probably got down the same way."

Juan came back puffing. "It's a done deal. Rooster's in the coop."

"I want more out of this job." I surprised myself, asserting my independence when I was the one in the pit.

"We split even-steven. We agreed."

"I got all the chickens. You didn't get even one. Then I came down here to get the rooster too."

"Well, you were the best man for the job."

"Not only the best," I retorted. "I was the only one that worked. Besides, I'll tell Dad—"

"Tell him what?"

"How'd the rooster get in the hole?"

"You want a nickel? Go suck a pickle! How do I know?"

"You know, 'cuz you put him here!"

"Go fly a kite! I'm no dodo! I wouldn't drop him in the hole."

José smirked quizzically at Juan, asking suspiciously, "Would-d-d-dn't yo-u-u?"

Juan paused, gawked into the pit, his eyes glassing over. "Okay! I'll give you the dime when I get it from Mr. Malcolm."

"Okay, let's pull him out."

They dropped the looped end of the rope.

"Put the loop under your armpits."

I did as directed. José and Juan grunted, contorting their faces, tongues hanging to the sides of their mouths. The rope tightened, lifting me, slowly, haltingly, *spl-l-unk!* My shoes broke free of the gooey waste. I curled my toes to hold onto my shoes. Juan and José continued to lift, grabbing my wrists, waist, hoisting me through the hole. Right away, Juan walked me to the pump.

"Sit down here!" Juan ordered. "Don't move. I'll be back."

José sat with me. "You sure stink."

In a few seconds, Juan returned. "Take those dirty things off," he ordered again. After I took off my shoes, socks, pants, and shirt, he had me rinse my feet under the faucet and helped me put on some dry clothing, draping the wet socks, shoes, and pants on the clothesline.

Juan filled a bucket with some soap and water. One at a time, he removed the shoes, pants, and socks from the line, dunked each into the bucket, rubbing them clean on Mom's washboard, rinsing each article under the gushing water of the pump. He wrung the water out of each, hanging them on the line. He rinsed my shoes the same way, holding them under the gushing faucet. I didn't have any others, except my dress shoes, which I wasn't supposed to wear to play.

"José, help me. I didn't bring Matías's dress shoes. We'll have to carry him into the house, or his socks'll get dirty."

"Here," José suggested, "put your arm around our shoulders. Then, pick up your feet. We'll carry you to the porch. Then you can walk in the house."

I put my arms around their shoulders and raised my feet. José and Juan slowly toted while I held onto their shoulders, suspending my legs slightly above the ground. I enjoyed being toted by my brothers, like a wounded hero in combat. As they set me down on the porch step, José quizzed Juan, arms akimbo:

"Say, Juan, what gives?"

"*¡No mí agüite, quelite!*" 'Don't bug me, pigweed!' Juan insulted José.

The insult didn't bother José. "We-e-ll, what gives?"

"*¡Nada!* Be quiet," Juan scurried us into the bedroom. "Promise you won't tell."

"Tell what?"

"Promise first."

We promised.

"I let the chickens out of Mr. Malcolm's coop. And I hid the rooster in the toilet. Didn't think he'd fall in the hole."

"Son of a gun, *chili con pan!* That takes the cake!"

"Haven't you heard of make-work?"

"What's that?"

"I created a job; I *made* work."

"Holy smokes, that's cheating!"

"It's only partly cheating. Once I made the work, someone had to do it. That was honest work."

"I'll say!" I defended my actions. "I didn't know Juan cheated. And I worked hard for the dime."

"Yeah," José quipped sarcastically, "you guys cheated fair and square."

Angela announced at supper that evening:

"There's going to be a meteorite shower tonight."

"*¿Qué es eso?*" Mom quizzed.

"Like falling stars, I think," Angela surmised. "I've never seen one. May we stay up to see the shower?"

"When will it be?"

"Not sure, maybe midnight."

"That's pretty late. I have to work tomorrow."

"Dad," Angela offered, "you and Mom can go to bed regular time. I'll watch the kids."

"We-l-l-l? Okay. But be real quiet."

We were delighted to stay up late on a summer evening. Outside, the crickets were twittering a symphony. The air was cool and dry, with only a few pesky insects to bother us. Around 10 P.M., Mom and Dad went to bed. We went out on the porch. Juan and José got involved in astronomical observations.

"The sky's so clear," José observed, "you can almost touch the stars."

"With a sky-hook," Juan stated matter-of-factly, "you can touch the stars."

"Naw! There's no such thing."

"Uh-huh, a 'sky-hook' looks like a meat hook—one of those used to hang the cow's carcass in a meat locker."

"Jimen-ee-whizz!" José retorted indignantly. "What do you take me for? I'm no dodo. I know what a meat hook is."

"Well, look. A sky-hook is much bigger. You tie a rope to it and throw it in the sky."

Juan stood up, pretending to twirl the rope and sky-hook around his head before tossing it into the sky. "When it hits a star, give the rope a quick jerk, and—" Abruptly, he stopped and shouted:

"Look-it! Look-it!"

We glanced skyward. It was raining fire in the sky! The gleaming meteorites were blazing fireballs—spinning and streaking, crisscrossing each other, swirling in silvery trails of star dust, fizzling into the ebony, star-spangled sky. . . .

The shower ended. I was transfixed, gazing . . . waiting . . . wishing for another shower to spout. For all the sudden blaze and fury, the starry skies from rim to rim of the canyon hills remained within the cloudy Milky Way, just as spangled as ever. Overhead there were no charred remains, no falling ashes, only the infinitely deep, dark spaces among the sparkling stars.

The shower over, we reluctantly filed into the house, quietly undressing and crawling into bed. Falling asleep was difficult—too much excitement that day: enrolling in school, Mrs. Hilliard's explanation of Mr. Hilliard's death . . . the burnt miners . . . the sickening smell of burnt flesh . . . the miners' faces burnt to the bone . . . then, playing too hard, getting cheated out of my dime, crushing bottle caps on the tracks, collecting scrap iron, falling into the outhouse pit, viewing the meteorite shower—the sky ablaze.

Huh! The entire sky was ablaze again! I jumped out of bed. José and Juan were already at the window, awestruck. Outside, the sky was burning yellow and red. It wasn't the sky! It was the Chicorico mine. Flames belching from the entry. Dad running out of the mine. His overalls burning! Flames trailing behind him, his skin burning—La Muerte chasing Dad! The faster he runs, the faster he burns. La Muerte loads her bow with a long arrow to shoot Dad. He explodes into a huge fireball! N-o-o-o-o-o-o-o-o—

My right leg twitched, jerking me out of the nightmare. Sitting up in bed, I looked around. No fire in the sky—Angela, Juan, José asleep. Got up. Sneaked to Mom and Dad's bedroom. They were sleeping. Went out to the porch. Crickets were chirping . . . stars were beaming. Goose bumps prickled my arms. I felt angry. I wished I was little again—then I didn't know about La Muerte.

7

BIEN O MAL, TODO ACABA

Tuesday, July Fourth, Dad and Mom surprised us.

"I get a one-week paid vacation. The union negotiated with the Company."

"And, we're going down-home," Mom excitedly added.

We loved to visit down-home at Mom's homestead near Ribera. It gave us a chance to be real cowboys, riding horses and buckboards while helping our cousins with chores. Tío Baltazar, Mom's brother, and Tía Feliz were my godparents. They baptized me at the San Miguel del Vado Church, the same church where Mom and Dad were baptized and married. All of us kids were baptized in the San Miguel church.

While Mom and Dad prepared for the trip to Ribera, I hunted down Geno, asking him to do my chores.

"I'm pretty busy, Matías," Geno hedged. "Won't have time."

"Aw, com'on," I begged. "The garden and the chickens might die."

"That's a lot of work," Geno complained, counting on his fingers, "I mean! One, taking care of the chickens; two, watering the garden; and three, weeding to boot! That's a lot of work."

"Well, yeah. But I'd do the same for you."

"Not really! We don't have no garden to weed or water. Just chickens."

"What about Twal?" She was Geno's German shepherd.

"Oh, ya, her."

"She's just as much trouble."

"Okay! But I ain't weeding no garden."

"It's a deal! Let's shake on it." All that was needed was a nod and a handshake in Chicorico. Geno drove a hard bargain; I wasn't surprised he refused to weed the garden. I hated weeding! He wanted me to wait for his dad so we could light his firecrackers, but I had to hurry home.

The road to Ribera followed the Santa Fe Trail most of the way. At high rises on the prairies, we could see the trail's ruts—furrows etched by the freighter wagons of traders as they had traveled round trip from Independence, Missouri, to Santa Fe, 1821–1880. From Chicorico the route ran to U.S. Highway 85, south on 85 passing Hoxie Corner, Maxwell, Springer, Wagon Mound, Las Vegas, and Sunshine gas station. There we took County Road 3 leading to Ribera.

As a village, Ribera sprang up when the railroad came through in the 1880s. There wasn't much left of it—a dilapidating blacksmith's shed, a few old homes, a post office, a small grocery store, and the Santa Fe Railroad station.

Mom's family homestead sat about two miles east of the Ribera railroad station. Her home was on a small ridge overlooking the Pecos River. The house was built in 1805 in the fashion of a Spanish hacienda, incorporating Pueblo Indian architecture—a flat roof, *vigas*, and adobes. The house was shaped like the letter *L*, with a flagstone wall enclosing both ends of the house, creating a courtyard complete with trees, an adobe *horno* for baking, and an open portal, which led into both sides of the house.

Dad drove into the courtyard. Our cousins Trinni and Willie greeted us. They were the same ages as Juan and José. Tío Baltazar was down in the fields, irrigating. He farmed the bottomland abutting the Pecos River

Mom's house down-home incorporated Pueblo Indian architecture—a flat roof, vigas, and adobes.

directly east of the house. This summer he was raising tomatoes for the market and chili for the family. Tía Feliz came to the portal with her daughters Josie and Clarita, Mom's namesake.

"*¿Como está abuelo Ribera?*" Dad asked politely.

"*Es muy enfermo.* Entre, entre."

"Come, go with us!" Trinni suggested to the guys. He and Willie were hitching up the buckboard.

"Where you going?" José asked.

"*Allá,*" Willie pursed his lips, cocking his head. "To chop some *leña.*" He pointed with his lips toward Bernal Mesa, where firewood was plentiful.

Dad nodded okay. Mom, Angela, Ramona, and Dad went into the house to see Abuelo Ribera.

Juan and José clambered onto the buckboard. José reached down for me. I put my foot on the front wheel spokes, grabbed José's hand, and pulled myself onto the front seat.

"Get in back," Juan ordered. "Hold onto the seat when the ride gets rough."

"Hey!"

"Hay's for horses!" Juan was firm. "You'll get to ride up here when we bring back the wood."

"I get to ride shotgun sometime!" José demanded.

"Okay! On the way back."

"No brakes?" José noticed, remembering the roller coaster ride through Chicorico on the hand-car.

"*¡Breques! ¿Pues, por qué?*" Trinni smirked. "These old nags? They can barely walk!" I felt sorry for Thunder and Lightning—two very old beer-bellied swaybacks whose days of raising a storm had long passed.

"*KIX! KIX!*" Trinni clicked his tongue, shaking the reins. Thunder and Lightning lurched slowly, pulling the buckboard toward Bernal Mesa. We rode through the village of San Miguel del Vado, the original village for the 300,000-acre San Miguel del Vado Spanish land grant given to fifty-one families from Santa Fe in 1803. Mom's family was among the original homesteaders; Dad's family already lived in the area. In its heyday, it sported the San Miguel County Courthouse, a large Catholic church, a bilingual Catholic school, a Wells Fargo stagecoach station, grocery and mercantile stores, a host of blacksmith sheds, and the Santa Fe Trail trading post.

After the Santa Fe Railroad bypassed San Miguel and the county seat was transferred to Las Vegas, the village dwindled, shops closed, and most people moved away. Only *La Iglesia de San Miguel* remained, the first building constructed in 1803. The church faced the original Santa Fe Trail, which crossed the Pecos River one hundred yards due east. As Santa Fe traders approached San Miguel from the east, they could see the church's steeples and front doors. Traders steered their wagons directly toward the church, fording the river over basalt bedrock.

We forded the river. The buckboard pitched, rocking the buckboard side to side. A half-inch beneath the buckboard's floorboards, the reddish brown current rushed past. I tucked my fingers between the floorboard's planks, feeling the cool, rushing water. As the horses emerged on the other side of the bank, they snorted, vigorously shaking themselves. They liked the cool water and would've dallied if Trinni had allowed.

"*Kix! Kix!*" Trinni shook the reins, motioning the horses to move along a little faster. They broke into a gait temporarily and then slowed down to a snail's pace. We continued east on a logger's trail once used by Hispanos to cut and transport logs from the mesa. When the Santa Fe Railroad was building through these parts in the early 1880s, logs from the mesa were used for bridges, trestles, and ties for the rail bed. Years ago, Abuelo Ribera used this very trail and buckboard to haul logs for the railroad. Now the trail was used to run sheep back and forth to the top of the mesa.

"Whoa! Whoa!"

A herd of sheep plodded toward us, trailing a cloud of dust that rose and then settled on the grass as the congested sheep butted each other,

As Santa Fe trail traders approached, they could see the steeples and front doors of La Iglesia de San Miguel.

bleating, struggling to keep their heads above the congestion, hooves pattering on the powdery path. Behind the sheep a *borreguero*, with gnats circling his face and diving at the sweat of his brow, rode a strawberry roan. It was Dad's brother, Tío Jesus!

"Tí-o-o!"

We yelled, the strawberry roan reared on his hind legs. Waving his hat, Tío Jesus leaned back in his saddle. He was thin, wiry, dark as molasses with jet-black hair to match. Like José, he had a long, sharp nose; his cheeks were high on his face, and his brown eyes flashed intently. He wore a cowboy hat banded with a rattlesnake skin, holding a turkey feather. He dismounted; his spurs jingled as he swaggered through the sheep toward the buckboard.

"¿Cómo le va?" he greeted us, taking off his gloves and tucking them in his belt.

"*¿Cuantas borregas, tienes?*" Trinni led the conversation.

"¿Aquí?" Tío Jesus reflected on the question, answering deliberately, "*Nomas treinta.*"

"No más treinta. ¿Por qué?"

Again Tío Jesus considered the question carefully, deliberately:

"Pues, *aquí el coyoté es muy mal.*"

"Lots of coyotes here, huh?"

"Aye, Matías! With you here, it's one more coyote!"

We laughed! Tío Jesus was a kidder!

"Bueno, got to go. Tell Manuel to come down by the *ranchito*, tomorrow. I need his help to repair the sheep shed!"

He mounted, tipped his hat, clicked his tongue at the roan, and rode on his way with the sheep, the dust trailing after them.

We continued up the logging trail till we found a patch of trees recently burned by a lightning fire. Such fires usually scorch the treetops, leaving dead-standing trunks. The guys busied themselves trimming branches, splitting and then chopping the trunks into smaller logs.

There wasn't much for me to do. I walked further up the trail. At first, I could hear the guys chopping and loading the logs onto the buckboard. Further up the trail, their voices faded. Pollen dust, blowing from the upper branches of the piñóns, crept into my nostrils. High from the side of the mesa, the wind swept across the trees. I sat on a boulder, listening to the murmur of the sweeping wind.

Ba-a-a-a-a!

Barely audible—the bleak bleat of a sheep.

Ba-a-a-a-a-a!

Louder now, the bleat came from a meadow surrounded by bushes. I jumped from the boulder, weaving through the bushes in the direction of the bleat. A lamb! Probably from Tío Jesus's herd. A coyote paced around her. The frightened lamb, frozen with fear, couldn't retreat nor run. I broke through the bushes, grabbing a branch of a *lemíta* bush.

Wang! The branch didn't break. Supple and strong, it jerked my arm. I yanked at it, trying to break it off. It snapped; the coyote glanced at me and jumped into the bushes.

"*Whew!*" I thought. "*He's gone.*" I crossed the meadow toward the lamb. Before I was even a third of the way, the coyote popped out of the bushes again and faced down the lamb. A smaller coyote darted behind the lamb, nipping her thigh. The lamb turned toward the small coyote. She was surrounded! Both coyotes were oblivious to me.

The big coyote paced, facing the lamb, concentrating on the kill . . . mouth pulled back into a sneer, sharp pointed teeth protruding; the hair on his back bristled. I threw my stick at him; it fell short. Snarling, the coyote jumped for the lamb's throat! Knocking her to the ground, he clamped his teeth on her throat; she screeched as the coyote's sharp teeth ripped her throat. The small coyote bit her on the backside, struggling to pull her into the bushes. The big coyote, still clenching her throat, yanked her in the opposite direction.

They were in a tug-of-war as I stood helplessly by, flustered. My eyes stung from salty sweat. I was afraid, and my sweat showed it! The big coyote yanked at her throat, jerking his head back and forth. Suddenly, he let go, snarling and springing at the small coyote's throat! The small coyote yelped and dashed into the bushes. The big coyote dragged the dead lamb beside a rotting tree trunk. While the victorious coyote chewed, lapping the blood flowing from the lamb's throat, the small coyote timidly joined the feast, nibbling at her thigh.

I ran back to the guys and told them what happened. Willie and Trinni grabbed their axes. I led the way to the killing-meadow. The coyotes were gone, without leaving much behind. Small tufts of lamb's fleece clung on bushes where the coyotes had dragged her away. José tried to follow the coyotes' trail, but soon the ground turned rocky. The coyotes' footprints disappeared where the coyotes had carried the carcass across a sandstone shelf. The varmints had made a clean getaway.

Disappointed, we walked back to the buckboard. The guys were pumping me with questions, hardly giving me a chance to answer:

"Were both coyotes males?"

"Was the smaller one a pup?"

"How come you didn't holler?"

"Weren't you scared?"

"I don't know!" I was irritated they would question my courage. "And NO! I wasn't scared!"

"A-í-í-í-í!" José shrieked, winking at me.

I thought, "I wasn't scared, but I was afraid. That's why the coyotes ignored me. They sensed I feared them." José, like the coyotes, sensed I was afraid, but he didn't push it.

The return ride back was easier for Thunder and Lightning. The trail sloped all the way to the river, which we crossed. Trinni stopped the buckboard and invited us to swim. Willie unhitched the horses, who went right into the water. The guys took off their clothing and jumped in. I was game and started to undress till I saw a ball of water snakes swarming in the water by the shore. I put my clothes back on.

"Come in!" José yelled, "those snakes aren't poisonous!"

"No-o-o, *gracias*. I'll stay on the buckboard." I wasn't keen on snakes.

The guys laughed boisterously, frolicking in the cool water of the Pecos, diving to the shallow bottom and buoyantly bobbing to the surface, shaking the water from their hair and eyes. . . . They finally tired, came onto shore, and lay in the grass. Shortly, they dried and dressed. Trinni whistled.

Nada.

Thunder and Lightning ignored the whistle. He whistled again!

Nada.

Willie undressed and waded into the river after the horses. He slapped Thunder and Lightning in the rumps! They lurched, acting surprised, and begrudgingly plodded out of the river while blowing water from their nostrils. Trinni and Juan hitched them up while Willie dressed. We hopped on the buckboard—José insisted on riding shotgun—rode past San Miguel del Vado and returned to Tío Baltazar's.

"¡Ándale, hitos!" Mom hurried us as we unloaded the logs. "Supper's almost ready."

All the kids got to eat on the portal. The adults ate in the kitchen, except Abuelo Ribera, who ate in bed. His bedroom was next to the kitchen so he could hear the adults as they spoke. On the portal, Angela was in charge of the kids so there was no horsing around while we ate. We couldn't talk with food in our mouths; we had to eat with one hand on our laps, except when we were cutting meat. Angela made us use our right hand, except Ramona, who was left-handed. And she wanted us to talk about current events, which none of us knew because we hadn't listened to the radio. I re-told the story of the lamb and the coyote. José listened intently. I think he was a little jealous.

After supper, the guys went out to bed down Thunder, Lightning, the hogs, and cows. Angela and Josie washed and dried the dishes. Ramona and Clarita played with some dolls. Tío Baltazar and Dad sat in the living room smoking pipes. Tía Feliz and Mom joined them.

Tía Feliz reached into her blouse between her bosoms, pulled out a bag of Bull Durham tobacco, rolled a cigarette, and lit it. She offered the cigarette to Mom; Mom declined. Instead, Mom reached into her purse for a pack of Lucky Strikes. Tía Feliz offered her the lighted cigarette. Mom took Tía's cigarette, raised it to her own, touched its tip, and puffed, inhaling rapidly. After returning Tía's cigarette, Mom leaned back in the chair and blew smoke toward the ceiling, relaxing.

Tío turned up the volume on the radio. President Franklin D. Roosevelt was presenting a fireside chat on the eve of the country's birthday. As always, the president was optimistic but honest. He spoke of eventual victory in Europe. He said that the Normandy invasion was advancing, but the German soldiers were seasoned, well-trained fighters. They were putting up stiff resistance. Fighting was tough, and deadly. But, as our troops liberated each French village or town from the grip of the Germans, men, women, children came out in droves, hugging our soldiers, waving our flag, singing our praises.

The fireside chat was exhilarating, sparking a lively conversation. Some of the boys from the nearby villages of Villanueva and Anton Chico were in the Normandy invasion. They survived D-Day.

The cigarette and pipe smoke got too thick for me. I excused myself, walking back to the vacated kitchen.

"¿Maa-tí-as?" I barely heard Abuelo's feeble voice calling from his adjoining bedroom.

"Sí, Abuelo, it's me."

"*Aprovecharse.*"

Abuelo was in bed, and I could barely see his face. The coal oil lamp had a short wick and cast very little light. I drew nearer; he looked frail. He raised his gnarled, knobby hand, waving me to come near. I took his hand. With great effort, he pulled me near him next to the bed. His voice shook, quivering, as he lisped in Spanish.

"*Una día, se va a ser un hombre. Y luego es su tiempo pa' ayudar a mi Clarita. ¿Ella trata a usted muy bien, que no?*"

"¡A sí! *¡Mamá me trata muy bien!*"

"Ay, que bueno. *Respeto pa' sus parientes es muy importante. Ayudar a ellos en los años ancianos—como su Tío Baltazar me ayuda ahora.*"

Pablo Antonio Ribera was ninety-eight years old, born in 1846 in this house. He grew up during the American takeover of his homeland here in Ribera. He helped the Yankees fight the Confederates in 1862 at Glorieta Canyon, just ten miles from here, where he met Alva Stockton—Colfax County's only other living Civil War veteran in New Mexico.

When the Santa Fe Railroad came through, he negotiated to have the station named "Ribera." He got a decent price on the land the Santa Fe Railroad bought from him. The railroad cut right through his ranch. He was guaranteed compensation for any livestock injured by the train as well as compensation for any other damage.

He hauled logs to make ties for the railroad in the same buckboard we used to get firewood. Gradually, Tío Baltazar took over the ranch and leased the grazing land to Tío Jesus. Tío Baltazar raised crops for the market and the family. He also kept a few pigs and cows for milk and meat.

I had never heard Abuelo Ribera speak so much. By nature, he was a reserved man.

"Time for bed, Matías!" Mom came in as Abuelo was still telling about the ranch.

"*Buenas noches*, Abuelo." I started to leave.

Abuelo shook his head. Something was wrong. He didn't want me to leave. He wouldn't release my hand. Instead, he covered it with both of his, grasping feebly. He wanted to tell me something. He tugged my hand, barely moving his lips. I leaned close, barely feeling his breath:

"*Bien o mal, todo acaba*"—'Good or bad, all things pass'—Abuelo lisped the down-home dicho.

Finally, Mom lightly grasped his wrists, gently tugging,

"¡Tut-tut, Papá! Matías needs his rest."

Reluctantly, Abuelo Ribera released my hand, laid his head back on the pillow, and closed his eyes.

Mom escorted me into my cousins' bedroom with a dimly lit oil lamp. I could hear more than see the guys. They were sound asleep, crowded together in bed. They were breathing deeply, sleeping hard. Tía Feliz had laid a blanket and a pillow in the corner of the room. I undressed and lay on the blanket. Mom covered me with another blanket.

"Say your prayers, niño cariño."

Mom brushed a kiss across my cheek and left the room. My cousins' bedroom was cool but pleasant. The pitch-dark room was much like my Chicorico bedroom where light streaks through the window only when there's a full moon. Somehow, the bedroom's darkness was not suffocating like the darkness of the mine. Outside, an occasional bell clanked as sleeping cows lulled. Far off, an owl hooted. I drifted into slumber toward Bernal Mesa where we gathered wood . . . the smell of piñón pollen . . . the soothing murmur of the wind. I lurched! All of a sudden, the wind gusted viciously, blasting and jerking the piñóns, swaying their crowns! I sat up. The guys were asleep. *That sudden rush of wind. Must be another nightmare coming on.* I lay down. The icy room soon returned to its pleasant coolness. The sheer curtains flapped at the open window.

Cock-a-doodle-do-o-o-o. . . . The distant crow of a rooster trickled into my restless dreams, gently erasing them. I awoke, stood up, and peeped out the open window, after pulling the sheer curtains aside. I watched the wispy pink sky fade with the sun as it rose above the rim of the piñón-covered mesa. The sunlight flowed over me into the room. I closed the curtains. Again, the insistent rooster crowed, but the guys remained sleeping, sprawled on their beds and twisted in their blankets. They were honestly tired from their hard work the day before. Getting wood had flat tired them out.

I dressed and went into the kitchen. Tío Baltazar, Tía Feliz, and Mom were sitting at the table. Dad had risen early and gone already to Tío Jesus's place to help repair the sheep shed. Mom and Tío Baltazar were softly crying.

Tía Feliz noticed me at the doorway. She held a finger to her puckered lips:

"Shh, come here." She took me into Abuelo's bedroom.

He lay in bed, eyes closed. I nudged his cold hand, lightly:

"Abuelo?"

Nada.

"Abuelo?"

Nada. . . . Tía Feliz, tears trickling slowly down her cheeks: "*Pobrecito*, su abuelo, last night he left to Heaven."

Abuelo . . . dead . . . no! Last night, he talked of his life! Todo acaba—all things pass. He wanted me to stay! Todo acaba . . . late, last night . . . gust of cold, violent wind! No dream! La Muerte—in the cold wind, not the raging fire of the mine—took Abuelo.

"Bu-ut? Bu-ut, only last night?"

"Yes, he spoke with you for a long time. You must tell us all that he told you. You were the last to speak with him."

"He talked about a lot of things."

"Ah, sí, su abuelo liked to talk with you and spoke of you often. He said that the Ribera blood in you was strong. Now, say a prayer for your abuelo," she spoke in hushed tones. "Then, go tell your father and your Tío Jesus. We'll need their help."

I crossed myself, muttering a Hail Mary for Abuelo, feeling a great loss. I hesitated, not wanting to leave his side.

Tía Feliz noticed, taking my hand, "Come. Have some breakfast before you go."

After breakfast, I scurried to Tío Jesus's place, only about a half mile down the road. He lived alone in the house where Dad and he were reared. I found them working on top of the sheep shed. It was in bad shape.

"Dad, Tío, I have bad news."

"Trinni told me about the lamb."

Tío Jesus thought *that* was the bad news.

"No! No! Abuelo died last night!"

They crossed themselves, bowing their heads, then crawled down from the roof. Tío Jesus spoke in his deliberate, direct manner:

"This was expected! *'De la muerte y de la suerte no hay quien se escape.'*" Tío quoted a down-home dicho: "No one escapes death or their fate." "Don't take me wrong, Matías. I'm saddened by the news. But your abuelo was a lucky man."

"Lucky to die?"

"Lucky to live so long and well." Tío Jesus continued, "He was born in the same house he died in, ninety-eight years later."

"Ah, sí, Jesus! Pablo had a good life. *Vamanos*, let's go see how we can help."

They put their tools in the shed and locked the corral gate. Tío went into the house to get his hat. I really admired the way Tío was a dashing, swarthy vaquero. But I really didn't like what he had said.

"Dad, how come Tío's so blunt?"

"Ha! Ha! Look who's talking! You're a lot like him."

"Huh?"

"Jesus is a straight-shooter. Always speaks his mind. Sometimes, you're that way. Remember how you asked Mr. Heard blunt questions—about being black? But don't worry, when people know you, they'll know you're a straight-shooter."

The dashing vaquero emerged from the house with a long bullsnake curled around his arm. He leaned over, shaking his arm. The bullsnake uncurled and wiggled away.

"Tío! The bullsnake?"

"Haah! He's a fat, lazy one!" Tío pointed to the bullsnake as it ambled under the porch.

"Did he crawl into your house?"

"I keep him there. He eats *ratoncitos!*"

"Como el jardín," Dad explained. "To keep the mice away."

"Haah!" Tío jested. "He keeps your mother away, too!"

"Verdad," Dad chuckled.

Tío Jesus kept the bullsnake in his house to keep mice out. Years later, I found out Mom wouldn't step into his house until he removed the bullsnake. As we walked to Tío Baltazar's, I took Tío's hand. He grabbed me by the armpits and hoisted me on his shoulders:

"Ride 'em, cowboy."

The view from Tío Jesus's shoulders was awesome. Ahead, I could see Tío Baltazar's home. Behind it, the hill sloped gently and the road wove by it to the Ribera-Montaño cemetery, ending where the graves began. To the west, swelling buttes jutted abruptly. The piñón-topped buttes were rimmed by sandstone outcroppings. To the east, neatly lined furrows of recently planted tomato and chili plants ran to the *Acequia Madre*—the Mother Ditch—that irrigated water from the Pecos River into the furrows.

Tío Jesus lowered me as we entered Tío Baltazar's house. Tío and Dad comfortingly hugged Tío Baltazar and Tía Feliz. Then, Dad embraced Mom, holding her for a while without saying anything. . . . Dad asked what he could do to help. Tío Baltazar asked Tío Jesus and Dad to dig a grave and build a pine box vault for Abuelo's coffin.

Tío Baltazar borrowed Dad's car to drive to Las Vegas to make arrangements with Salazar's Mortuary. Mom and Tía Feliz would accompany him to the mortuary to arrange for someone to pick up the body, embalm it, and return it home for the burial. This would take two days. Abuelo would be buried three days after his death, the custom downhome. They would select a coffin and measure it so Dad and Tío Jesus could build a big enough vault.

"Matías, we're going to the *camposanto.* Bring us some water, soon." When Dad found Tío Baltazar's pick and shovel, he left for the cemetery. Tío Jesus went to his place to get his pick and shovel to help.

After they left, I took two empty gallon jugs from Tía's pantry. I selected these two because they had rings on their necks, making them easy to carry. I went to the well. Tío's pump was black, shaped like a sea horse. I pulled on the long handle, pumping until the warm water drained from the pipes. I filled the jugs with cool water and headed to the camposanto. When I arrived, Tío Jesus and Dad had already marked off the area to dig beside Abuela Ribera's grave. I didn't know her, or either of Dad's parents. They died during the influenza epidemic of 1918.

"Here's the water!"

"Gracias, Matías!" Tío Jesus replied. "Put it by some tall grass, to keep it cool."

The camposanto was almost at the top of a bluff. I wandered to the high point of the bluff where I could see most of the valley, including the spreads of Tío Baltazar and Tío Jesus. Bernal Mesa bordered the valley to the east, and Rowe Mesa was to the north. The Pecos River ran diagonally through the valley, a perfect spot to homestead.

Originally, Indians lived in this valley, which was situated south of where the Pecos Pueblo Indians lived for at least five hundred years. Sometime in the late 1700s, Mexican Indians from Santa Fe were allowed to settle this valley. Earlier, the genízaros had been brought from Mexico to Santa Fe as servants. When the Catholic Church prohibited slavery in the Spanish colonies, the Indians were freed and sent to the valley. In 1803, when Mom's family settled in the valley along with fifty-one other families, most of the genízaros had left. Those genízaros who remained in the valley intermarried with the Spanish settlers. Dad's family was not among the Spanish settlers of the San Miguel del Vado Land Grant. Dad surmised his family may have been genízaros, already living in the valley when the Spanish settlers arrived.

I meandered back to where Tío Jesus and Dad were digging. They dug methodically. Digging was slow, hard work. Both were sweating profusely. The sun was at full blaze with no breeze to cool the hot air. They took turns with a pick and a spade. Dad would pick for a while, Tío Jesus would shovel, and vice versa. Then they'd rest, drinking water. They sent me back several times for more water. Each time I returned, the hole was even deeper. To finish the deeply dug grave, Dad and Tío took turns dropping into the hole to dig or shovel. When finished, they rested flat on their backs on the mound of dirt that rose beside the hole, watching the hawks and ravens circling overhead.

Supper that evening was somber. Josie and Angela had prepared and served it. The adults were quiet. After supper, Juan and José washed and dried the dishes while Trinni and Willie took care of the animals. Tía Feliz supervised Josie and Angela in the preparation of food for the next evening's *velorio.* Tío Jesus excused himself and went home. Tío Baltazar, Mom, and Dad sat in the living room. This evening, they didn't smoke or talk very much. Mostly, they sat in the living room with their somber faces turned toward the floor. Clarita and Ramona played quietly without disturbing the adults. I sat with Mom and Dad for a very long time. Finally, Dad excused himself to go to bed.

"In the morning, Baltazar, give me the dimensions of the casket, bueno?"

Tío Baltazar nodded his head and stood up to go to bed. Everyone followed.

The next morning, Tío Baltazar gave Dad the casket's dimensions. Dad walked to Tío Jesus's, who was already selecting boards to build the box. They carried the boards and nails to the grave and measured the hole. It was both wide and long enough to hold the vault for the casket. They built it there at the grave site. Making sure the lid would fit the box, they laid the lid on the dirt pile and then gently wedged the pine vault into the grave. They left a hammer and some nails with the lid for use after the formal interment. Jabbing the shovels into the dirt pile, they took their picks and went home.

On the way back to Tío Baltazar's, I asked:

"How come you don't pay the funeral man to dig the grave? Or make the box?"

"If you want the job done right, do it yourself!" Tío Jesus boasted.

"Besides," Dad offered, "it costs a lot of money to bury a man."

"You'll have to pay for me," Tío quipped.

"Pay! What for? We'll tie you to the saddle of your roan and slap him a good one! He'll take you on a long ride, till the coyotes find you!"

"A-yí-yí-yí-yí!" Tío trilled in falsetto. "Pero—use my Mexican saddle, bueno?"

Both laughed. I didn't.

Abuelo's velorio lasted late into the evening. His casket was placed in the living room, and chairs were arranged around the casket so his family could sit with him for the last time: Baltazar, Luz, Beatrice, Agripeña, Clara. Abuelo was dressed in a black suit, white shirt, and black tie, his black leather vest buttoned. His thin, gold rimmed glasses rested on his nose. Early in the evening the adobe room was cool, but as *compadres*, cousins, and grandchildren—*todo la familia*—congregated, the room turned hot, stuffy from candles whose burning wax and wicks stifled the coolness of the room.

As people came into the living room, they paid their respects to Abuelo and then sat down, waiting for prayers to begin. Most of the men and women sniffled intermittently. Tears welled up in Mom's eyes. She struggled to keep her composure and strained to hold back tears. They slowly trickled from her eyes. She daubed the tears away with the corner of a handkerchief, only to daub again. Dad shed no tears, although he kept clearing his nostrils with his handkerchief. His neatly starched and folded handkerchief was soon damp and crumpled, bulging in his back pocket.

Tío Baltazar knelt on the floor. Everyone followed. He recited a *verso* invoking the intercession of the Virgin Mary. The adults knew the verso and recited with him:

Madre mía de los Dolores
Tú has de ser intercesora
pa Pablo Ribera.
En la hora de la muerte
Tú sí defiendas, Señora.

Then Tío Baltazar led everyone through the rosary. With each decade, he recited the same *ofrecimiento:*

Los Ángeles en el cielo
Alaban con alegría
Y los hombres en la tierra
Responden:—¡Ave María!

After the rosary, Tío Baltazar invited the men into the kitchen. Tía Feliz invited the women to the portal. Everyone tarried in the living room, hesitant to leave Abuelo alone. Eventually, the men did drift into the kitchen to talk over coffee or whiskey. They sat quietly, each lost in private contemplation, hardly speaking except to mutter something complimentary about Abuelo. The women sat on the portal, recalling how well Abuelo Ribera had provided for his family, certain that Abuelo had died in the grace of God. Josie and Angela moved quietly between the two groups, politely serving the food they'd prepared.

Now was my chance to visit Abuelo. I found him alone, just as I had two nights before when he called me to his bedside. He had told me so much just two evenings ago. And now, he would not speak. I slipped into the room. We were alone and together in the same room, just like two nights ago. The coffin was on a table, too tall for me to see Abuelo. Candles flickered and cast thick, bouncing shadows across the floor and on the ceiling. I felt proud to be alone with Abuelo. He had trusted me to care for Mom and Dad when they were old. He had passed the responsibility to me.

I pulled a chair close to the casket and stood on it, reaching into the casket and touching Abuelo's hands. They were neatly folded over the lapels of his dark suit; a leather-bound Bible nested in his hands. He had been a quiet, calm man, and in the coffin he looked relaxed, almost normal except his eyelids were shut.

"Bien o mal, todo acaba." Good or bad, all things pass . . . Abuelo's last words. The down-home dicho eased my mind.

Early in the morning, the pallbearers placed the casket on Tío Baltazar's buckboard. After brushing their mangy coats, Trinni hitched up Thunder and Lightning. They looked pretty slick, those two old stallions who'd rather swim than haul logs! They sensed the solemnity of the moment, hauling their master for the last time. Trinni drove the buckboard. The pallbearers, Dad, Tío Jesus, and four other family friends—Gaspar Leyba, José Sena, Max Urioste, Juan Mascareñas—walked beside the buckboard.

Abuelo was carried on the buckboard from his home to the church for the final blessing. A Mexican priest, Father Nava, led the Ribera family in a slow procession to the church with many of the other villagers following. Father Nava led us through the rosary:

"Dios te salve, María, Madre de Dios, llena eres de gracia; el Señor es contigo; bendita tú eres todas las mujeres, y bendito es el fruto en tu vientre, Jesus."

Mom was holding her rosary. I recited along with her as she and most of the procession responded:

"Santa María, Madre de Dios, ruega por nosotros pecadores, ahora y en la hora de nuestra muerte, Amén."

Our voices cascaded down the road from Ribera to San Miguel del Vado as we responded ten times for each decade to Father Nava's invocation of the Virgin Mary.

Directly behind Father Nava, Willie pulled a carreta with a handcarved sculpture of La Muerte. This wooden sculpture, usually stored in the church, was a *santero's* rendition of the same angel who had visited our home four times, and only two nights ago had come for Abuelo's soul.

Her skeleton frame, too well sculptured for me, sat on the carreta. Tufts of stringy gray hair from victims long deceased hung limply from her grinning, tilted head. Even though her eyes and nose were empty sockets—dark hollows of nothing—she appeared to be aiming the cocked bow and arrow she held in her bony hands. I deliberately tried not to look at her, but she seemed determined that I would.

The procession approached La Iglesia de San Miguel. The church was built in 1803 as a sanctuary and fortress against Indians, who actually lived in peace with the genízaros. A thick adobe wall surrounded the churchyard, which was filled with graves of the original settlers.

Abuelo's casket was carried through the large church doors, down the aisle to the altar, and then opened. I always liked this church whose ceiling was logged with pine vigas. Along the walls were *retablos* of San Miguel, the patron saint, and a *santo* of San Miguel stood in a niche on the wall. Votive candles at his feet illuminated his long, wiry body.

The church was cool. Father started mass with an incense burner hooked to a chain. He swung the burner over the casket while reciting the Biblical reminder "of dust we come and to dust we return."

"*Polvo y polvo,*" he repeated four times as he swung the burner in the four directions of the map. The smell of incense floated throughout the church and smelled like the Holy Palms Mom burnt in our fogón. Abuelo Ribera's last words resonated in my mind: *todo acaba . . . todo acaba.*

Father chanted parts of the mass; others, he lisped in Latin. Concluding the mass, he stepped down from the altar to the main floor, standing beside Abuelo's open casket. He called Abuelo's children—Tío Baltazar, Tías Luz, Beatrice, Agripeña, and Mom—to stand with him beside the open casket, reciting the final absolution and sprinkling Holy Water:

"*Dale, Señor, el descanso eterno y la luz perpetua.*"

Tío Baltazar rested his hand on Abuelo's. Mom stepped forward, bent over the casket, and kissed Abuelo's forehead; the other tías followed. Father Nava fastened the casket shut and sprinkled it with Holy Water. He stepped in front of the casket, motioning the pallbearers to carry it out of the church. Father Nava followed, leading everyone out. Juan rang the Angelus bell slowly . . . softly.

The pallbearers placed the casket on the buckboard. The procession resumed:

"Kix! Kix!"

Trinni clicked his tongue. Thunder and Lightning lugged the buckboard, proudly holding their heads high, leading the cortège.

At the graveside, everyone huddled near the freshly dug hole. Father Nava presided at the west end of the grave. With both arms, he lifted a large, black crucifix to the sky, facing east. As he raised the crucifix, Abuelo was lowered cautiously, the ropes bracing the casket squeaking, bearing Abuelo into the earth. The squeaking stopped. The casket rested in the pine box. Tío Baltazar dropped some piñón needles onto the casket. Father lowered the crucifix, stepping back.

Tío Jesus dropped the lid into the hole, then jumped down onto the lid, clutching the hammer and nails. He knelt on the lid, nailing it shut. Dad reached down and pulled him from the hole. They grabbed a shovel and promptly started shoving dirt back into the grave. The first few clods of soil sounded like the muffled roll of drums, pounding erratically on the pine box. Mom sifted a handful of soil into the grave. . . .

8

NO HAY MAL PAN CON BIEN HAMBRE

Mom and Tía Feliz baked ten loaves of bread in the horno the morning of our departure. They got up before the chickens, washed out a small *cajete*—about half the size of our galvanized tin bathing cajete—mixed flour, water, yeast, shortening, sugar, and a little salt. They took turns stirring the dough in the cajete with a large, long wooden spoon, kneading and punching the dough, squeezing it with their fingers, and rolling it into a ball.

They covered the cajete with a flour sack. Together, they heaved the cajete on top of the fogón's warm uppermost shelf. Tía brewed some coffee while Mom served some *bizcochitos.* They sat on the portal, visiting about family and friends while munching on the cookies and sipping coffee. It was 6:00 A.M.

At about 7 A.M., Tía punched down the raised bread dough; Mom punched it into ten dollops of dough. They kneaded each dollop into loaves and put one loaf into each of ten pans. When done, they placed the pans back on top of the fogón's top shelf, placing a flour sack over the pans. They warmed up some more coffee and relaxed in the portal, waiting for us to rise before making breakfast.

Before breakfast, Tía Feliz ordered Trinni and Willie to prepare the horno for baking the bread. Juan, José, and I were curious about stoking up the horno, since we'd never seen it done. The horno, a dome-shaped adobe oven, sat in the courtyard and looked like a miniature version of a coke oven kiln. The dome's top had a small hole in it for ventilation and a larger hole serving as a front door. Trinni and Willie searched the woodpile till they found some small, dry logs that still had pitch in them. The newly cut logs were too green for burning.

Using a hatchet, they hacked off small chips of bark from the logs, leaving the core of the log scarred but intact. They spread the chips onto the horno's floor, placing the logs on top of the chips. Willie struck a match to the pitch of the chips. Gradually, they ignited. Trinni jammed four adobe bricks into the horno's front door so the chamber oven would warm. The cracks between the adobes allowed just enough air into the horno for adequate ventilation. We went in for breakfast.

Every forty-five minutes, Trinni and Willie would place more chips and logs in the horno. They were burning the logs down to very hot embers. About 10 A.M., Tía came out to the horno, asking Willie to remove the adobes from the front door. She floated her hand over the oozing warmth of the embers.

"Horno's ready," she concluded, rubbing her hands.

We went back to the kitchen. It took us several trips to carry the raised loaves to the horno. After Mom had handed us all the raised loaves, she came with us to the horno. Willie opened the oven door. With a spade, he leveled the embers, tamping them down lightly to create a smooth surface. Tía had a *pala de horno*, a very large wooden paddle that served as a spatula to place and remove the bread pans in the horno. Its handle was round and looked much like a shovel handle. The spatula end was broad, about eight inches wide and twelve inches long. Tío Baltazar made this special tool for Tía as a wedding gift.

We handed the pans to Mom one at a time. She positioned the tin pan on the spatula. Tía carefully shoved the spatula into the horno, cautiously sliding the tin pan off the spatula onto the embers. When all ten pans were in position, Willie blocked the front door with the adobe bricks. We went back into the house.

In about an hour, we checked the loaves. Willie removed the adobe bricks from the horno's door and stepped back quickly; the hot air surged out the door, almost searing Willie. Tía waited briefly for the first rush of hot air to dissipate before shoving the spatula into the horno; she shimmied a bread pan onto the spatula, pulling it out of the horno. Mom lightly tapped the loaf's crust, smelling it. Then Mom held the spatula's handle while Tía tapped the loaf's crust, smelling it. Mom put the loaf back into the horno and removed another, repeating the ritual with the second loaf, each mother tapping and smelling the loaf.

"*Unos cuantos minutos.*"

"*Un algo más.*" Tía nodded yes, agreeing with Mom.

About a half-hour later, Mom and Tía removed the bread pans from the horno. This time when Willie removed the adobe bricks from the door, the wonderful odor of baking bread rolled out of the horno. The bread crusts were slightly browned; my mouth watered to see and smell the bread loaves in their pans. Using the huge spatula, Tía carried two loaves at a time into the kitchen and placed them on top of a cutting board. Mom rolled the pans over and tapped their bottoms; the loaves fell top down onto the cutting board. Tía and Mom waited until they cooled to wrap them in some of Tía's clean towels made from cotton Gold Medal flour bags.

We helped Dad load the car while Mom was waiting for the bread to cool. Then Tía gave Mom five loaves. Before long, Dad was in the driver's seat, and we were ready to go.

"Manuel, tell the *hefe* I'm staying here until after the harvest. Then I'll come back to work."

"Bueno, it's just as well you stay here to take care of family matters, también." Dad gave Tío Baltazar an abrazo and turned to Tía Feliz. She gave Dad an abrazo, kissing his cheek.

"*Dios tí bendigo, hermano cariño.*" Mom embraced Tío Baltazar firmly, prolonging the hug. Then she hugged Tía Feliz as Tío Baltazar opened the car door for Mom.

As we pulled out of Tío's courtyard, Dad jested playfully:

"*¿O-yeh?* Baltazar, bring us some chili when you return!"

"¡Como no, Manuel!" Tío Baltazar chuckled, rapping Dad on the shoulder.

As we drove up the incline away from Tío Baltazar's, I gazed out the window toward the camposanto at Abuelo's grave, now a huge mound of dirt over his tomb. Mom saw me looking and glanced herself. Tears leaked from her watery eyes.

Leaving Mom's homestead was solemn. She was in a melancholy mood, realizing Ribera was no longer home now that her father had passed away. For years, she had referred to Ribera as "down-home." Though her home was in Chicorico with Dad and us, she could no longer return to the homestead and be with either of her parents. Sadly, she could not count on her house in Chicorico to be home. It belonged to the Company. Yet Mom made sure it was our home in spirit and deed.

Dad tried to kid around to distract us, irritating Mom. Then he tried his time-honored trick of inventing tall tales with a twist:

"Remember the time I spotted a railroad train roaring down the highway, smoke bellowing from its stacks, and headed right for us?" . . . So, we churned out stories on the road returning to Chicorico. Dad baited us with one of his old tall tales, and my brothers tried to one-up each other with a better twist to the plot. Dad told a chiste about a rodeo cowboy named Punk Cheeney who got in an argument with a Latin teacher over the pronunciation of the word *rodeo.* Even Angela got involved in the storytelling fest. Mom quietly listened. Time passed quickly. In Wagon Mound, we stopped for gas and were treated to soda pops. By 6:00 P.M. we were back in Chicorico.

I ran to the backyard, noticed the chickens had been fed and were in the coop for the evening. The garden needed weeding, but it had been watered and was looking good, the sprinkling can neatly in place. Geno had lived up to his bargain. Now I would have to return the favor when his dad took the family on vacation. We helped Dad and Mom unload the car, except for Juan. He was in the kitchen, stoking a fire in the fogón. When we finished unloading the car, Mom called us to the kitchen.

"Vamos, tomar un snacké," Mom suggested. "Wash your hands."

We washed our hands and sat at the table. Mom unwrapped one of the freshly baked loaves and sliced it, placing the slices into the oven. The bread slices soon warmed. We took turns spreading butter and then chokecherry jelly on our slices. Angela served us some water. Mom and Dad had coffee.

After the blessing, Dad ordered:

"Tomorrow at supper we must talk about the news. Now, let's enjoy your mother's bread—baked in the horno down-home."

Ardently, we devoured the most scrumptious bread in the world. I told Mom:

"Umm-yum! You make goo—oood bread!"

"No hay mal pan con bien hambre." Mom's eyes twinkled with the down-home dicho: "There's no such thing as bad bread when you're hungry." She felt better back in her own kitchen.

I awoke the next day after Dad and Angela had gone to work. The guys were also gone, probably looking for odd jobs to make money. Mom and Ramona were in the kitchen. As I ate breakfast, Mom told me to tend the garden. Dad wanted all the weeds pulled, roots and all.

"Y tambien, pull the weeds from the bricks out front." Dad had taken bricks from the abandoned coke ovens and laid a brick path from our front gate to the steps of our front porch. Each summer, weeds grew between the cracks.

"That's hard work, Mom."

"Sí, pero remember? Anything worth doing is hard."

"That's what Dad said."

"I know, honey. He told me to tell you. When you're done, we'll pick the onions and lettuce. Then we'll gather some quélites."

The garden was cluttered with weeds, choking the lettuce. The only way to pull weeds by the roots is to get on your hands and knees, grab the stem at the ground, and pull! If you grab a bunch of weeds by their tassels and pull, you'll leave most of the roots in the ground. They'll return to haunt you as hardier, tougher chokers of the vegetables! I resigned myself to go slow but sure. It was hand-to-weed combat. One weed at a time! I pulled and tossed each weed into a pile to carry away when done. As I pulled, I thought, "What the heck's a weed? They're sure tough buggers! Why not eat the weeds? Anyway, horses and cows eat weeds all the time!" By now my knees really ached. The little rocks and hard dirt pressed through my pants, pricking my knees. I decided to take a break from the stoop labor to ask Mom about weeds.

"Some weeds can make you crazy," she explained. "Others are poisonous. Some will choke your plants. *Pero, ¿se come quélites? ¿Y tambien la té de yerba buena del llano?*" Mom gazed out the window toward the llano, reflecting on the paradox of the weed, thinking aloud many of the same thoughts I had:

"Some can make people crazy. Others are good to drink as tea. Hmmm."

"Gee, Mom. My thoughts, too!"

Should've kept my mouth shut. The spell over Mom broke; she sensed I was stalling. Her pensive mood flashed to the task on hand:

"Don't eat the weeds! Pull them out! Out front, tambien!" Mom stood up, abruptly ending the seminar on the paradox of the weed, playfully scolding:

"¡Andale! Andale!"

She scolded playfully, but she meant business. I returned to the weedy garden, thinking that farming was hard. Not as hard as coal mining, and not as heroic either. When I finished pulling the garden weeds, I went out front and pulled the weeds from between the cracks of the bricks. This was not as difficult; the roots of the weeds hadn't grown as deeply as had the garden weeds.

I finished weeding the front path, telling Mom. She inspected my work carefully, complimenting:

"Good job, hito. Come, let's pick quélites."

She brought a bucket and knife from the house, handing me the bucket. Ramona tagged along; Mom didn't want to leave her in the house alone. We searched the llano behind the house, looking for quélites. Mom carefully inspected each quélite to make sure none was spoiled by bugs or animals. She picked the good ones, putting them in the bucket.

When the bucket was practically full, we returned to the pump to cleanse the quélites with fresh, cold water.

"Mom, are quélites weeds?"

"Weeds! *¡Qué va!* I would never feed you weeds. Quélites are spinach."

"Oh."

"Como los dandelions. Down-home they're eaten like lettuce. In Raton, people pick the dandelions from their lawn and throw them away like weeds. What a waste!"

"Gosh."

Mom was smart. She knew a lot about food and how to prepare it.

"Before supper, I'll show you how to pick lettuce and onions from the garden. For now, you better go in the house. Take Ramona. A storm's coming."

I took Ramona's hand, walking into the house. Inside, I scanned the southwestern sky. A gathering of clouds darkened the horizon, slowly rolling over the tops of the hills, descending down into Chicorico Canyon. Hurriedly Mom finished washing the quélites and came into the house. A distant rumble . . . the roll of thunder, like a giant bowling ball bouncing across the hills, reverberating and echoing between the canyon walls. Flurries of lightning flashed where the clouds gathered. The sky darkened. I was frightened.

Mom sent me into her bedroom to get the Holy Palms, given to us on Palm Sunday at mass. These palms were blessed by Father Stanley to burn in emergencies such as storms. Mom had placed them in a vase on the dresser, next to our small statue of the Sacred Heart of Jesus. I clutched a handful of palms. Mom threw them in the fogón. They burned instantly, emitting the fragrant odor of incense.

Mom crossed herself, sitting at the table:

"En el nombre del Padre, del Hijo, y del Espiritu Santo." She recited the Lord's Prayer in Spanish.

As we prayed, I peered out the window. The wind had picked up. The sky was much darker. I noticed the chicks weren't in the henhouse. They were cloistered together, almost smothering one another, in one corner of the chicken coop. The hens and rooster had retreated into the henhouse, but the chicks didn't know enough to get out of the storm. Or they were afraid to go into the henhouse. They couldn't jump into their crate, once inside.

"Mom! The chicks! They're in the rain!"

Promptly Mom peered through the window.

"Come, hito! Let's put them in! Ramona, you stay here! Watch from the window."

Mom dashed outside. I followed. The wind had picked up. Squalls swept down the side of the hills, over the llano and into our yard. Mom unlatched the chicken coop gate and beckoned me to enter quickly. Inside the coop she dashed over to the chicks, grabbed one in each hand, and carried them to the henhouse.

"Open the door, hito. Hold it open."

She gently dropped each chick through the door, scurried back to retrieve two more chicks, and toted them to the henhouse. Holding the door open was difficult: the wind and rain swirled furiously, pelting gales of rain against it. We were drenched. Mom's hair and dress were sopping wet, but she continued the daring rescue. Just as she placed the last two chicks inside the hen house, *Ker-pop!*

Lightning smacked a nearby large piñón, splitting the tree to smithereens! Its sap, rising to the bark, exploded, hurling strips of glowing crimson bark in all directions. The embers whirled high into the sky . . . falling, wiggling to the ground. Wisps of burning wood and exploding sap permeated the gusts of rain, drifting to the chicken coop; the rain still pelted furiously.

"Get in the shed!" Mom urged, tailing behind me, closing the door.

"Pray with me, hito!"

The rain and wind shook the henhouse. The wooden planks creaked, allowing rain to seep onto the trembling walls. Mom sat on the ground and hugged me tightly, pressing me against her blouse. She was confident, her heartbeat slow and steady. The chicks huddled on the hem of her dress. The hens sat calmly, placated by our presence, although the rooster was skittish, crouching in the corner. Mom's close embrace mollified me, her strength comforting. I was secure and warm in her arms, although we were drenched.

We recited the Lord's Prayer three or four times, huddled in the henhouse, the chicks cuddled on the hem of Mom's dress:

"Padre nuestro, que estás en los cielos; santificado sea el tu nombre. . . ."

After awhile, the rain simmered into pitter-patter rhythms, falling much more gently.

"Escucha!"

Mom whispered, relaxing her hug, pointing to the ceiling. The wind had died down; now the rain fell in a slow, steady rhythm. To the northwest, we could hear the faint roll of thunder. The storm had passed through and was on its way to the next canyon. Mom released me, gently tugging her dress from the chicks. They hopped away from the dress, chirping as they skittered. Mom cupped her hand and scooped up one of them, running her index finger over the chick's head.

"Que suave al tacto—como lana." Mom extended her hand toward me to pet the chick.

Worried I would cause harm, I touched her head gently. She chirped! I jerked my hand away.

"*¡No tenes miedo!*" Mom assured me. "She's a baby. She's talking to you."

I touched the chick again, and she chirped. This time her chirp didn't startle me. She wasn't afraid of me. I was her caretaker and provider. She was small, cute, and fragile, soft to the touch: "Gee, Mom. She *is* soft!"

"Yes," Mom replied. "Her soft feathers will soon grow much larger."

Mom set the chick down and stood to leave the henhouse. The rooster still appeared skittish, still cowering in the corner, and seemed to be glad we were leaving. The hens were in their nests and didn't seem overly concerned about our presence or our leaving.

Finally, the rain stopped, and the sun beamed brightly through the few remaining clouds. Fast-passing summer storms—"gully washers," Dr. Monty called them—were common in Chicorico. One would rush through, hurling rain and flashing lightning, although a lightning strike was unusual. The clouds would continue on their way and the sun would return. The ground and grass would be damp for a while. Most of the rain would run off rapidly to Chicorico Creek, which surged with water, cresting for a short time before receding back to its usual trickle.

We inspected the shattered tree. The tree was split in two, charred where the lighting had made its direct hit. The lightning had shattered its crown, but the trunk was intact, although there wasn't much left of it standing.

"Make good firewood," Mom observed, "when it dries. Come, Ramona's worried about us. See her at the window."

Ramona came running out on the porch. She had watched much of the doings from the kitchen window, as Mom had told her to do. The lighting strike scared the wits out of her. From the kitchen window, she couldn't see we were safe and sound in the henhouse. Tears streaming, she was choking on her sobs.

"Don't cry, honey. We're okay."

"Yeah! Ramona! We had a big adventure!" I chirped, trying to appease her.

She ran down the steps and hugged Mom around the legs, but recoiled when she felt Mom's wet dress. Mom took her hand; Ramona wiped her eyes with her fists. We returned to the house, where Mom helped me dry off with a towel. She put out dry clothing for me and went into her bedroom to dry and change. "You can go play now," Mom shouted through the closed door.

I wandered across the llano into the hills, checking for animal tracks. At first, I didn't find any. They had been washed away by the rain. I groused around the edge of the hills. It was a perfect time to be in the hills. The sun was hot and unforgiving, but a cool breeze occasionally whiffed through the trees, cooling the air. I had never been to the reservoir by myself. I decided to hike to it, without asking permission to go there alone. Mom wouldn't have permitted it.

At the reservoir, I found some fresh deer tracks. After the rainfall, the deer must have wandered near the edge of the reservoir and left their tracks in the muddy ground at the edge of the rocky bench. One deer broke away from the others. I followed his trail for a long time as it wound higher into the hills. In the summer, the deer tended to go higher up the hills. They came down in the winter to feed where less snow covered everything.

I continued following the deer's trail. This was new terrain, much higher than I had ever been before, about 7,500 feet above sea level. The ponderosas were big at the trunk and majestic, dominating the hillside. Tall, stately trees with huge crowns and red-brown bark, they were scattered among marshy meadows where the snow accumulated in the winter. I didn't see any signs of the guys playing here. The canyon floor and the hills below, with their dense underbrush, piñóns, junipers, cottonwoods, and scrub oaks, made a much better place to play war games.

Here in the high country, I saw signs of wild animals, especially droppings. Some were deer droppings. Others, I didn't recognize. They weren't cow droppings because ranchers did not run cattle on Company land. Probably what I saw were elk droppings, but I imagined they were bear droppings and started to make a lot of noise to let the bear know I was in the area. The trick with a bear is not to surprise it. A bear will not attack a man unless it is surprised or feels threatened. This rule doesn't apply to grizzly bears. The worst place in the world to find yourself is between a sow and her cub—brown, black, white, or grizzly.

With all the noise I was making, I ruined any chances to see any kind of game, even turkeys or deer. The second they heard my voice, they would be gone in a flash. I continued following the deer trail until I came to a large outcropping of boulders, a natural dike—a vertical sheet of rocks formed by cooling lava many centuries ago. Instead of reclining horizontally, the rocks stood vertically, forming a wall. This part of the dike was exposed, forming into a peak.

I crawled up the dike to its peak, looked to the west and saw the Sangre de Cristo mountains, still slightly frosted with snow, shimmering in the afternoon sun. The mountains rose abruptly, looming over the front range of the hills where I was standing. Glimmering in the summer sun, the mountains appeared to be very close, although they were hundreds of miles away. Wow! I had an eagle's view of Chicorico Canyon.

I heard a hum coming from the Chicorico mine tipple down on the bottom of the canyon floor. Because I was high above the mine entry, I could see the entire operation outside the mine. At the mine's entry, men and machines scurried, dumping, culling, cleaning, and loading coal into empty coal cars.

I clambered down the dike and found a big stick to use as a sword. I climbed back. Standing tall on the dike's peak, I tapped it with the stick, knighting the dike:

"I dub you 'Eagle Nest,' my secret hiding place. We shall tell no one, not even Juan and José." I flung the stick and listened to it crash into the bushes below.

Every day, after I had done my chores, I would sneak off to Eagle Nest to watch the culling and washing of the coal in preparation for shipping. The rough coal was hauled over the tipple and dropped onto a conveyor belt where tipple workers sorted it, dropping the various sizes into different chutes. The coal hauled out of the mine was all sizes and shapes and full of impurities, mostly dirt, rocks, and shale. The big chunks were used in smelters; the medium-size chunks were used for stoking railroad trains and very large furnaces; the smallest chunks—some even the size of gravel pebbles—were sold to people for use in their houses. The coal was run through a washer where it was cleaned. As the coal left the washer, it glittered as it was dumped into the coal cars.

I spent many, many hours at Eagle Nest with the Sangre de Cristos in clear view most of the time. No matter how many times I sat and watched, I never tired of the jingle-jangle din of the coal processing operation—from rough, crude lumps to glittering chunks of coal bound for smelters and furnaces. The coal was high in "BTUs," or British Thermal Units, a unit used to measure heat energy. Chicorico coal, low in sulfur, burned hot for a very long time and was excellent for smelting metals and economical for heating.

The powdery residue of slack tailings were hauled in little gondola cars to the far north side of the canyon and dumped into huge piles. Trails of smoke seeped from hot holes in the tall, cone-shaped, growing slack piles. The slack piles were a continual fascination. They grew by slow degrees into large, black mounds of coal dust, shale, and rocks, trailing smoke into the sky as they smoldered. The gondola car carried their loads to the top of the pile, dumped them, and returned to the tipple for more slack to repeat the cycle.

I went home straightaway after discovering Eagle Nest. I didn't want to raise any suspicions about where I'd been. Mom had already picked the lettuce and onions and prepared a salad for supper. The salad was made from the freshly picked quélites, onions, and lettuce with a dressing of olive oil and vinegar. Dad sprinkled black pepper over his own salad, passing the shaker around the table. I was game and sprinkled a lot of pepper on mine. I don't remember what we had for a main course, but I could've eaten the salad alone. For dessert, we had some of Mom's freshly baked bread with the last of our chokecherry jelly. At supper, Dad announced:

"Next Sunday, we must pick some chokecherries; they're ready." Dad had inspected the bushes on Chicorico Creek where we went every year to pick them.

The next Sunday afternoon, Dad took Juan, José, and me with him to pick chokecherries. We loaded two cajetes in the trunk of the car. We planned to fill one cajete to take home to Mom to make chokecherry jelly. The other tub was reserved for Mr. Onorio Chicarelli to make chokecherry wine. As we picked the chokecherries, a bird swooped down over the bushes and slammed smack-dab into the windshield of Dad's car. It fell to the ground, fluttered for a moment, and then flew away.

"See what happens when you eat too many ripe chokecherries!" Dad warned us, "You get drunk—like that bird!" Actually, Dad knew that the bird wasn't drunk. If the chokecherries were *that* ripe, they wouldn't be good for picking. Dad just didn't want us to eat too many chokecherries so there would be plenty for making jelly and wine.

"Naw!" José didn't believe him. "That bird just didn't see where it was going!"

"José!" Dad acted playfully surprised. "You know birds have very good eyes?"

"Well, yes, but—"

"But, nothing! That bird was drunk!"

"How come we don't get drunk, when we eat chokecherry jelly?"

"Because when your Mother cooks the chokecherries to make jelly, they can't ferment."

"Oh." José scratched his head. I thought Dad was joking, but like José, I didn't know the meaning of the word "ferment" either.

"When you're done helping your Mother with chokecherries, come over to Mr. Chicarelli's. To make some chokecherry wine." The Chicarellis lived two doors west of our house, next door to the Malcolms.

Mom and Angela were ready to make the jelly when we returned home. We picked the chokecherries off the stems, culling out the bugs, twigs, and leaves. After we washed them, Mom cooked them in a large pan. When they were sufficiently cooked, Mom poured them in a cone-shaped ricer, the one she used sometimes to mash potatoes. Juan handled the pestle, pulverizing the chokecherries and dripping the juices through the perforated ricer into a large pan.

After Juan pressed a batch of chokecherries, I scraped the pits and skins from the ricer, throwing them into a bucket. The waste was gooey and sticky, emitting a tart aroma, causing me to lick my fingers. My red fingers tasted good at first, until the juices flowed down my throat. I gagged, grabbing my exceedingly dry throat, and darted to the washstand! I scooped up some water from the drinking bucket, gulping it down!

"Haah!" Juan jested. "The cherries choked you!"

I had just discovered the acrid aftertaste of chokecherries that gave them their name! Chokecherry juice, in its natural state, is very dry. Yet, once boiled with sugar and pectin, poured into a Mason jar, and sealed with paraffin wax, chokecherry juices jell smooth and tangy. Spread over freshly baked bread or freshly made tortillas, chokecherry jelly is *muy sabroso*.

Mom and Angela took over the operation to finish making the jelly. When we'd pressed all of the chokecherries and thrown away the pulverized pits and skins in the garden, we went over to Mr. Chicarelli's wine cellar. Sometime ago, Dad had helped Mr. Chicarelli dig a wine cellar under his house. All the Chicorico houses sat on a raised foundation with a crawl space underneath. Some people used the space for storage; others, like Mr. Chicarelli, dug a basement. Mr. Chicarelli used the basement for making and storing wine.

During Prohibition, people in Chicorico kept Mr. Chicarelli's wine cellar a secret so the revenuers wouldn't smash his wine barrels. Several businessmen made offers to buy his wine to sell at speakeasies in Raton. He could have made a big profit by selling wine, but he knew it was unlawful to make and sell alcohol. He never sold his wine, but he was generous to a fault, giving it to any adults who asked. Mr. Chicarelli grew up in Sicily, and as a young man, immigrated to Chicorico to work in the mine.

Geno greeted us when we arrived at the basement, warning, "Shh. No talking while Dad's workin.' He don't like it!"

Mr. Chicarelli was showing Dad what needed to be done.

"Manuel, we can get three, maybe four squeezes out of these chokecherries. The first squeeze is the best."

Dad poured some of the chokecherries into a press.

"Now, watch, Manuel. With grapes you don't add yeast or sugar at first. Grapes have their own yeast and sugars. Not so with chokecherries." Mr. Chicarelli added lots of sugar, and a little bit of yeast, turning the press's handle and squeezing the chokecherries. The press made a grinding, crunching sound as the juice dripped down into a wooden vat, a wine barrel cut in half.

Mr. Chicarelli took the pulverized chokecherries out of the press and put them into a bucket, sprinkling more sugar and yeast onto them. He added some fresh chokecherries to the pulverized cherries and handed the bucket to Dad, who poured it all into the press. Again Mr. Chicarelli turned the press's handle, squeezing the juice into a vat, placing the pulverized cherries into a bucket, adding fresh chokecherries and crumbling additional yeast and sugar into the bucket. When done squeezing all the chokecherries, Mr. Chicarelli transferred the juices into a wooden wine barrel that had a spigot on one end.

"Now, Manuel, we squeeze again one more time. We add a lot of sugar to bring out the juices in the squeezed chokecherries. Makes the last squeeze very sweet, too sweet for me."

"Me, too," Dad agreed.

After the third squeeze, Mr. Chicarelli decided to stop. The chokecherries were decimated shucks of skin and pits.

"They're no good! Too dry! Now, we just leave the juice in the barrels. In a year, they're ready to drink." Mr. Chicarelli turned to José and Juan:

"You boys want a drink?"

Surprised but thrilled, Juan and José turned to Dad. Dad winked, nodding yes, warning:

"*¡Un poco, no más!* None for Matías or Geno."

Their chests swelled, their heads puffed up even bigger! They were big men now, some kind of heroes. Geno and I were put in our place—too little to drink wine.

Mr. Chicarelli poured some of the first-squeeze wine into two small glasses and gave it to the guys. They tipped their glasses and took a big swallow, gulping down the entire jigger, exclaiming:

"Ugh-h-h!"

"E-ho! It's sour!"

"Ha! Ha!" Both fathers chuckled, then Mr. Chicarelli offered, "Here, try this!"

Mr. Chicarelli poured from the third-squeeze barrel. This time José and Juan lifted the glasses warily to their lips, sipping slowly. As soon as the sweet, syrupy chokecherry juices touched their lips and tongues, they took giant swallows! This time they really liked the taste.

"Euum! Yum! That's good."

"Tastes just like cherry soda! Give us another?"

"Enough, boys. The sweet one will ruin your liver—too much sugar."

Both chuckled. Dad nodded in agreement with Mr. Chicarelli, who turned to Geno and me:

"You're too young to try the wine. When you're older, you can have some. Take my word, there are times when a little bit is okay. But too much is bad!"

Dad and Mr. Chicarelli both knew the guys weren't drinking wine.

It was really chokecherry juice. Yet they wanted to teach us respect for alcohol. As we got older, neither ever forbade us from drinking wine. Instead, they reminded us to be cautious about what we ate and drank—the kind of caution that taught us moderation.

As we were walking home along the tracks that evening, Juan and José started horsing around, acting like winos, hiccupping and stumbling along the tracks, slurring their words as they sang the marine corps song:

"From-uh du halls of-of Mon-n-n-tezuma-h to da c-shores of Tripoli. . . ."

Dad laughed, turning to me: "The chokecherry juice was too fresh to ferment. They're drunk with the thoughts of drinking chokecherry wine, but they're not drunk with wine!"

Now I knew what "ferment" meant!

9

TWO WRONGS DON'T MAKE A RIGHT

Summer was in full bloom. Each day started cool and early, languishing late into evening. For the last two weeks of July, we had sunlight till 9:45 P.M., giving us plenty of time to play and work the livelong day. When we weren't doing chores and odd jobs, we played with the same total absorption we devoted to chores.

One afternoon, Marian and I had just finished an oatmeal cookie at her house and had come to ask Mom if I could go to the store with her and Mrs. Heard. Marian had a nickel tied in the corner of her handkerchief, where all little girls carried their money. Mom insisted on tying my pennies in the corner of a handkerchief too. Sometimes she'd pin the handkerchief to my shirt. She feared I'd lose the pennies, especially when I put them in my pockets, already jammed with nails, snails, and other treasures. Mom winked:

"Little boys have to be careful, with cheaters like Freddie." Mom was right; it was good protection from the Chicorico swindlers.

Marian was going to share her purchase with me. Angela had leaked the rumor the store had a shipment of Hersheys, but just one box of twenty-four. We were anxious to get there before they ran out. Mrs. Heard was going to take us. She needed some flour, anyway. To do her part for the Hershey bar, Mom gave Marian some sugar ration stamps. We had plenty of sugar ration stamps, with seven of us at home. The Heards had only three people at home; they got fewer stamps.

As we left the house, we saw José sitting on our steps, looking lost.

"Hey, José! Marian's got a nickel."

She shook her handkerchief. José didn't even look interested.

"We're goin' to the store with Mrs. Heard."

"To buy a Hershey," Marian chimed in.

"That's nice," he sighed nonchalantly. "I'm waiting for Petee. We're supposed to play cowboys."

I didn't think too much about José's response, although it was strange for him to mope around waiting for anybody to play anything. A couple of days later when Mom shooed Geno and me out of the house, there was José again, sitting on the steps.

"Mom said we had to play outside. We're gonna build a race course for our hoops. Wanna help us?"

"Naw! Petee and I got plans."

Geno and I grabbed our hoops and ran off to the llano.

I didn't think about José any more that day, but he sure was acting strange the next day. First of all, he got up early—really early; I think he and Dad were the only persons up. I didn't know this until the smell of freshly brewed coffee woke me, and I noticed José wasn't in bed. Afraid that I was missing something, I tumbled out of bed and staggered into the kitchen.

"What's going on?" I asked.

Mom and Angela were at the table with Dad. Mom was fixing Dad's breakfast and Angela was eating some Wheaties before she left for work. José came into the kitchen from outside, bringing in the water for the kitchen and the stove. And the coal bin was full already. This was strange.

"What'cha doin', José? Is something wrong?"

"Aw, I just couldn't sleep. So I thought I'd get my chores done early, so's I can play all day."

Dad and Angela left for work. José went out to water the chickens. Ramona was up by now, and Mom fixed breakfast for the two of us, scrambled eggs—my favorite. While Mom was washing breakfast dishes, I went outside to do my chores. Getting them done early and having the whole day to play sounded like a pretty good idea. Mom and Ramona came out of the house and were on their way to Mrs. Malcolm's while I was feeding the chickens. Then I noticed something strange.

José was crouched down behind a clump of wildflowers up on the hill. He appeared to be spying on the Malcolms. I remembered him brooding on the steps the last few days. Now, he was crouched behind some wildflowers spying on the Malcolms' house. He certainly was doing strange things lately. "Oh, well," I thought, "better just worry about myself."

Before I could finish feeding the chickens, the Malcolms' back door opened. Petee came out. He looked around to make sure no one was watching. He didn't detect José, crouched even lower behind the clump of wild flowers. When it appeared the coast was clear, Petee took off for the hills, with José sneaking behind him.

Another two days passed, and José was again awake and finished with his chores early. This time he stayed in the house until Mom and Ramona left for Mrs. Malcolm's for coffee. Not having any girls of her own, Mrs. Malcolm really enjoyed Ramona. Sometimes when Mom and Ramona came home from their morning coffee visits, Ramona's head was crowned by her hair woven into a coronet of French braids. That was how Mrs. Malcolm put a tiara on the little princess' head! I admit! I was a little bit jealous of Ramona. She was pretty cute. As soon as they left for next door, José ran into our bedroom.

"What ya doin' in here?" I heard Juan asking.

"Nothin'," José replied. Then he came out carrying his belt, which he only wore with dress pants. Other times, we wore overalls and didn't need belts. Next, he was digging around in Mom's kitchen shelves until he found an empty Rex lard can, one with a wire handle. Out the front door he went; clearly, he didn't want Mom or me to see him.

Petee met him in front of the house. Petee had one of Mrs. Malcolm's kerchiefs tied around his waist with an empty lard can hanging from it. He was holding a second can in his hand. José put on his belt and hooked his can onto it. Something was going on! Looking around to make sure no one was watching, they took off into the hills.

I couldn't stand it; I had to know what was going on. I decided to sneak along behind them. This was fun. *Ta-dum!* I pretended to be "Ike MacArthur," U.S. superspy on a secret mission—my mission to discover the Nazis' plot. I jumped from clump of grass to rock, ducking behind bushes, dodging Hitler's top generals. This was FUN! José and Petee had no idea I was spying on them. They wouldn't have liked the idea they were the Nazis.

There they were ahead of me, finally stopping in a grove of wild plum trees.

"Su-u-u-n-n-n-n!" I heard José groaning as he tugged at his can so hard he pulled out the handle, tumbling off his belt. He threw the can on the ground in disgust:

"I told ya! I told ya! We shoulda picked those plums the other day, when I followed you up here."

"But they weren't ripe!" Petee whined. "I wanted them to be perfect; there were so many of them to surprise Ma an' Dad an' Freddie. There were so many. I never should have let you come with me." The disappointment in Petee's voice was almost a sob.

"Oh, for cryin' in a washtub! I didn't make this mess."

"Don't you suppose I know *that!*"

"It was a bear—a really big bear. Look! You can see all the plum seeds in his scat."

"Scat? That looks like *poop* to me!"

"It is poop, dodo! But we Indians don't use such bad words."

"Well, I ain't no Indian!" Petee sarcastically replied. "Call it what you want—it's still poop!"

Both guys were very disappointed; they'd come prepared to pick lots of plums. That's why they'd tied the cans to their waists to leave both hands free for mass picking.

"Our pledge didn't do much good," José lamented, "but it still goes for next summer. Only next time, we'll beat the bears to 'em." Petee and José had pledged themselves to secrecy and now decided they needed to renew the vow. On their sacred honor, they would tell no one else about their discovery of paradise—the Chicorico version of the Garden of Eden.

To seal the covenant, they made a blood-pledge. I watched as José found a cactus plant and removed a picker from it. He pricked a very small hole in his index finger and handed the picker to Petee. Petee did the same. They squeezed their index fingers with their thumbs, forcing a tiny drop of blood to secrete; they touched fingers, meshing their tiny drops of blood together. They were now bound by a blood-pledge, showing how much they prized the plump, wild plums of paradise.

Chicorico's long daylight hours were perfect for after-supper softball games. Most of the guys congregated at the baseball field, and before long a game was on! The baseball diamond being too big, the guys rigged up a smaller diamond. They used the regular home plate, but used pieces of wood for the other bases, shortening the distances between plates. We little kids would tag along. We'd watch the game or bring our hoops or find some other means of entertaining ourselves. Some girls would come, too. Of course, they weren't allowed to play, but they could watch and cheer for their favorites.

I'll always remember one particular Wednesday evening in August. Juan and José had finished dishes in record time and rushed off to the baseball field. Having nothing better to do, Geno, Marian, Louie, and I followed them.

The team captains had already been chosen when we arrived. Juan was usually one of the captains. The other, Wayne Starkovitch, was always a captain; he claimed that right because he was the oldest. Juan and Wayne were busy choosing their teams. Most of the players were about Juan's age, some a little older, and some a little younger. José and Petee, even though they were younger than most of the players, almost always were chosen to play because they were so good. Juan had both of them and Freddie on his team. Both teams selected, the captains were about to toss the bat to see which team would be up first.

"We wanna play." I was proud of my spunk, speaking up for us little kids.

"What!" exclaimed Bob, the pitcher on Wayne's team. "You can't even throw the ball five feet."

"Can so!"

"Yeah! We wanna play," chimed in my friends.

We all crowded around home plate.

Wayne's little brother, who was going into second grade when school started, joined us. "I'll tell Ma."

Wayne was supposed to be watching him.

"Yeah! Yeah! Yeah!" All of us little kids chanted.

Wayne and the other guys didn't want to get in trouble. They formed a quick huddle, mumbling among themselves. Juan announced as the huddle broke:

"You guys can be backups for the outfielders. We'll each take three of you."

"But, here's the rules," added Wayne. "You only shag balls the outfielders miss, and you don't get to bat."

"Okay," we all readily agreed. After all, there were all kinds of six and seven year olds who were never allowed to play, even when the teams didn't have nine players.

Juan chose Geno, Louie and me. Wayne's little brother and two of his friends were chosen for the other team's backups. Marian wasn't even considered, even though she could throw faster and farther than any of us. That just wasn't fair, but I wasn't going to complain. The guys might change their minds.

"You can be my backup, Matías."

José was the right fielder, so I got to be in no man's land way behind him. Geno was the center field backup for Freddie, and Louie was the backup for the left fielder, Clarence Rivali.

Juan tossed the bat. Wayne caught it. Then Juan placed his hand above Wayne's. They continued, alternating hands, progressing up the bat until there was no more bat handle left. Our team was up first.

Freddie struck out. Another guy hit a pop fly to the second baseman.

Juan was up; he hit a single down the third base line. The next batter hit a line drive to center. Juan took off, touched second, and slid into third. The batter was on first. Two men on; José was up to bat. First pitch was a ball; José swung at the next pitch and missed. He swung at the third pitch—

POW! A line drive to the shortstop, Wayne. He grabbed the ball and easily tossed it to the first baseman. José was out. Wayne's team came in to home; we took our places on the diamond, the field, and no man's land.

The guys were all pretty good; we little kids didn't get to do very much. We shagged a few hits. They were always home runs—otherwise the outfielders would've caught them. It was the bottom of the third. I noticed Marian wasn't sitting with the girls; she was behind home plate. I felt bad for her; we should've insisted she be a backup too. There were two outs, a runner on second, and the count was one and two.

POP! HIGH FOUL BALL. Marian was there. She caught it! And with a pleased look on her face, she forcefully flung it to Juan, our pitcher. I always admired the way Marian could throw a ball—not like most girls. She had a strong overhand throw.

"Yow-ee, kid!" our catcher yelled, "I could'da caught it!"

"Leave her alone!" the batter yelled. "She just kept you from havin' to chase it!"

"Okie-dokie!" Our catcher grimaced, yelling at the batter, "but you're out!" The catcher wanted to count Marian's catch as his.

"Heck no! Dead ball!"

By now the batter and the catcher were nose to nose. Our team was running in from the field, and Wayne's team was gathering around the batter and catcher. It looked like a sure enough fight brewing.

"Forget it!" Juan yelled. "Let's play ball." Juan was more interested in playing ball than losing precious time fighting; besides, our team was leading five to three.

"We'll cancel that last fly ball!"

"Okay! Juan's right," Wayne shouted to his team. "Let's play ball!"

Relieved the fight was curtailed, all the guys returned to their positions and began their baseball chatter:

"Play ball!"

"See ya in St. Louiee!"

"Batter up!"

Our team started back to their positions. Wayne's team moved back to the sidelines, and the batter took his stance next to the plate.

Zoooooom! Juan really hurled that ball over the home plate. The batter took a feeble swing at it. Strike! He was out. Our team was up again.

One . . . two . . . three. We were out and back in the field for the bottom of the fourth. It was getting pretty boring for us backups. I looked over at Geno; he was kicking at some dirt clumps and tracing patterns with his foot. He noticed I was looking at him. We feebly waved at each other. I looked over to Louie and noticed he was gone. I looked back toward home plate and saw he was there with Marian. This was a long inning—lots of balls, foul balls, and a few hits, but no scores.

Wayne's backups didn't even bother to take the field for the fifth inning. Geno came out to no man's land with me at the bottom of the fifth; but before the first two hitters were on base, he was back by the diamond, playing with the other little kids. It looked like they were playing shadow tag, and they seemed to be having a lot of fun. I truly wanted to join them, but I'd been the one who asked to play. Juan, Wayne, and José had to do a lot of fast talking to get the other guys to agree to let us play, even if it was only backup.

Blapp! Finally, a hit in my direction, arching high overhead. The ball whizzed past José, and it was still coming . . . coming . . . just above my head and right through my hands, bouncing outside the field and rolling into the ditch. I ran after it. Where'd it go? . . . Ah! There it was, in the ditch, lodged in an old bag of rags someone had thrown there.

Not wanting to stick my hand in the bag, I kicked at it. The bag fell open; the ball tumbled out, but so did an odd assortment of tattered woman's clothing: a pair of white, high-heeled shoes, a stretched-out girdle, and an old hat. The hat must have been an elegant Easter bonnet at one time, lots of flowers and net. Stuck in the straw crown was a beautiful pin—silver, three inches long, and with the biggest pearl I'd ever seen. The pearl glistened in the rays of fading August sun. I'd never seen such a resplendent pin. Mom could never afford such a luxury. I'd take it to her. I grabbed the pin, stuck it in my shirt, and scampered out of the ditch with the ball.

"About time, kid!"

"Yeah! Where ya been, anyway?"

"Lay off!" Juan yelled. "No one could'da done it no quicker!"

I could count on my big brothers to look out for me. I might have tarried a bit too long when I found that pin, but it was a swell pin. I was definitely going to give it to Mom.

I wound up and threw the ball to José. It went pretty far but dropped about twelve feet in front of José. I wished I could throw like Marian! Both José and I ran to the ball. We got to it at the same time. I picked up the ball and handed it to José.

"Look at this classy pin! It's a real pearl."

"Let's see." José keenly examined the pin. "Naw! It ain't a real pearl!"

"Well, it sure looks real! It's real silver, too!"

"Hey, José," one agitated player yelled, "let's get this game on the road! Throw the ball, for gosh sakes!"

All the guys were anxious to continue the game. Wayne's team was leading, six to five. I started running back to my position; José stuck the pin hurriedly in his overall's strap and hurled the ball to Juan.

The rest of the game went quickly. I stuck it out in no man's land. No more runs were scored. I couldn't get that pin out of my mind. What if there was a whole treasure trove of stuff? What if there were some diamonds there, or even a gold ring? I might get rich. I just had to get back into that ditch to check.

I decided to take a last look at the castaways. I ran over to the ditch, pilfering through the heap of worn women's clothing. Didn't find anything interesting. Heading back to home plate, I spotted my brothers, Freddie and Petee, and a few other guys way off, crouching in a circle.

"Hey, kid? Come here!" They called a little kid over to them.

All the little kids, including my friends, were as curious as can be. They all started to run over to where the guys were crouched in a circle. Freddie and some other big guys lined them up, away from the circle. They wouldn't let them go into the circle until they escorted them to it, one at a time. This was sure strange. Shortly after the kids were escorted into the circle, they would break out of it and run towards their houses. Knowing I was missing out on something, I started to run toward the circle.

"O-o-o-ow!" I heard Louie cry as he broke out of the circle and ran home.

I saw Marian, Geno, and a few other kids already running to their houses. Something was wrong. I started to run faster!

"Watch out! Here comes Matías!"

The circle broke up. The big guys ran every which way. A red-faced José came from the circle and handed me my pin.

"Here's your pin. Go home. I'll join you later."

"Hey, it's bent! What's going on?"

"You can straighten it! I'll see you later." And he ran off with the other guys.

I took the pin, straightened it out as much as I could, and slid it through the strap on my bib overalls.

It was a cool evening. Chicorico's elevation, 6,666 feet above sea level, made for hot days and cool evenings. The crickets were just starting to chirp. Fireflies whirled in random spirals, fading as quickly as they appeared. The air smelled crisp and clean. Far off, I could hear the excited bark of Geno's dog, Twal, greeting him as he approached his house. Stars slowly made their appearance, glowing as the sunlight faded.

I felt so good. This had been a perfect day. I had spied on Petee and José's failed mission. Geno and I had played all afternoon in the llano; after supper I had played ball with the big guys. I had the classiest pin in the whole world to give to Mom—just the way an August evening should be, absolutely, totally wonderful.

I must have loitered too long on the way home. It was darker than when I usually came home after evening play. All the lights were on at our house. Usually, some were turned off to save electricity. Closer, I heard men talking in our living room. The front and back door were both wide open, cooling off the house for sleeping. I went through the back door so I wouldn't bother the men who were visiting Dad. I was positive

Ramona was with them, using her charms, smiling and looking pretty—easy for her to do. The men were probably giving her pennies and nickels. She always had that effect on Dad's friends. I envied her; I'd like to get a nickel on my looks, just once.

Actually, the men weren't paying Dad a social visit. Nor were they admiring Ramona. They were angry. I couldn't hear their words, but in retrospect, it was easy to infer this conversation:

"Manuel, one of your boys stuck Geno with a pin!"

"Yes, Manuel, my Marian, too!"

"And my Dennis and Donald."

"And my boy Stan said it was a bi-ig pin."

"My Mary Frances, too."

"They made the kids sit on it."

"I'll get to the bottom of this!" Dad tried to defend his sons. "But, I don't believe my boys would do such a thing!"

"My boy got stuck, too," Mr. Leal protested. "By one of the Malcolm boys!"

"I'll have a talk with the boys!"

"Well, Manuel," Mr. Malcolm pitched in, "best we talk to my boys, too."

"Yes, your boys, too!" one of the fathers added.

Dad and Mr. Malcolm were stumped. They couldn't imagine their boys picking on little kids.

Mom was standing in the door between the kitchen and living room. She couldn't believe her ears. Those poor little kids. All that hurt! All that crying!

In the meantime, I walked into the kitchen with no idea of what was going on. Mom looked sad; I would cheer her up with my pin. I held it out to her. She glowered at me! I smiled lamely, hoping she'd get over my tardiness. She motioned for me to come to her. She grabbed the pin from my hand.

"¡Por Dios!" She exclaimed, "It's bent!"

Dad was startled and jerked up from his chair. "Matías, how could you!"

How could I what? I didn't understand. Something wasn't right. I panicked and bolted for the kitchen door, trying to hide behind it. I heard the fathers trying to pacify Dad:

"Go easy on him, Manuel."

"Yes, he's just a little boy!"

Wham! Mom slammed Ramona's little brown play broom on my head. It barely touched; my baseball cap protected my head. *Wham!* The broom slammed on my head again. There was nothing playful about Ramona's play broom—it hurt! I wailed:

"WA-A-A-A-H!"

The men were still trying to pacify Dad.

"Manuel? Maybe my boys put him up to it!" Mr. Malcolm sputtered, worried that Dad would lose his temper.

"I'll get to the bottom of this!"

"Better cool off, Manuel." Mr. Heard tried to calm Dad, "Take a breather, 'fore you hurt the boy!"

Needless to say, I was scared. I was no hero, thinking Dad—a mighty powerful miner—would swat my backside with his leather miner's belt. Mom was doing a pretty good job of proving the point, using Ramona's play broom. Heroes don't crouch behind kitchen doors wailing.

"WA-A-A-A-H-H-H!"

Wham! Again, the broom. Mom missed! Now she was trying to prod me from behind the door by sticking the broom handle under it.

"Maybe you'll think twice before sticking pins in kids!" That didn't work. She poked—*womp! womp!*—poking the broom at me instead of whacking with it.

"Come out of there!"

Mom and Dad thought I was the pin-sticker! I sputtered, slipping from behind the door:

"N-o-o-o-o! Mo-o-o-m!"

Wham! Ramona's broom struck my bottom.

"Ouch!"

Wham! Again the broom hit me in the *como se llama* where God designed bad little boys to be hit!

"Owoooo!" Again I squealed, running out the back door.

"You come back!" Mom yelled.

I ran behind the outhouse. I waited for a while. Mom didn't come after me. The men were filing out of the house, sounding placated. They were talking and laughing with each other as they bid Mom and Dad goodnight.

Dad and Mom blamed me—betrayed . . . dishonored. Having done no wrong, I was stinging, but not from the broom. The sting ran to my very bones. I brought Mom a present, and she thought I brought her my weapon. The guys double-crossed me. . . . I'm no pin-sticker. Evil beat Good, unlike the comic books. . . . I needed to clear myself with Mom and Dad. Timidly, I went back into the house. They were sitting in the living room, Mom reading the *Raton Range*, Dad the *United Mine Workers of America Journal*. I went to Dad:

"I didn't stick nobody with a pin! I found the pin, and showed it to José; he—" I stopped, not doing well. Dad's scowl turned more fearsome with every word.

Dad was silent for a long while, fidgeting with the *Journal*'s pages. He crimped a page's corner, putting the *Journal* in his lap.

"I don't know who stuck who, Matías. God knows the truth." He paused, deliberating. "If you did it, don't let it happen again."

Dad resumed reading the *Journal*. Mom pretended to be absorbed in the *Range*, although she nervously fidgeted, crossing and uncrossing her leg, while I was speaking to Dad. I went to our bedroom, throwing myself down on the bed, my mind racing, re-enacting the evening. Getting on the team, shagging balls . . . finding the pin . . . showing it to José . . . pilfering the trash again . . . seeing the guys crouched in the circle on the field . . . walking home so peaceful . . . hearing the men talking in the living room . . . offering Mom the pin. . . . What a mess, worse than two trains crashing head-on.

I was crushed. Mom and Dad believed I was the varmint. For a long time, my mind spun like tires spinning in the mud, getting nowhere fast. I'd never get any sleep if I kept turning the evening over in my mind. I better try to sleep. Before undressing, I went into the kitchen and poured some warm water from the fogón's boiling pan into our white, tin wash basin. I had a bad case of accumulative dirt. You can't shag balls and poke around other people's trash without accumulating dirt.

I washed my face and hands, went outside, throwing the dirty water in the garden. It was cool; the crickets chirped briskly. The stars beamed brightly. I felt better. Because I'd used the last of the warm water, I had to refill the fogón's pan. First I pumped water into the wash basin to rinse it. Then I filled it again and took it inside to pour the water into the fogón's pan.

Returning to the bedroom, I undressed, turned off the lights, and kneeled beside the bed. I prayed ten Hail Marys in Spanish. By concentrating on getting the words correct in Spanish, I cleared out some of the mean-spirited thoughts running through my head. After finishing, I glanced at the window. The stars spangled the canyon sky from rim to rim. The crickets chirped in complete, rhythmic symphony. Far away, I heard the winsome bark of a dog.

I decided to think about good things—Eagle Nest. A misty vision of a baby eagle, nesting down for the night. Its father and mother were guarding as it fell asleep. I continued the vision as I crawled in bed, pulling the sheet over me. The adult eagles nestled into the nest, snuggling down. . . .

Thunk! An arm dropped onto my chest. Not really awake, I wiggled out from under it and turned on my side. Juan turned on his side. We were nose to nose. Ugh! His breath stunk. Restlessly, I turned. Now I was facing José. Juan doubled up, moving closer. The mattress formed a pit next to him, tipping me half on my back, half on my side, and ever so slowly sucking me into it. I squirmed, climbed higher on the pillow, and conked out again.

I woke . . . hot . . . suffocating. Juan was next to me on his back, snoring. José had his arm flung over me, holding me down. I was thoroughly twisted in the sheet. "Hey! This isn't my week to sleep in the middle!" I guessed they'd sneaked in after I was asleep. I twisted, turned, and jimmied around, trying to release myself from my mummy shroud and to disturb them in their sleep! When I was free, I tugged the sheet over Juan; I sat up and crawled to the foot of the bed, groping for the blanket I had pushed back when I'd gone to bed. I grabbed it with both hands, pulled it up, and wrapped it around José. I wanted both of them to be miserable.

Both continued to sleep, but I'd made them restless; both turned and struck out for the cooler edges of the bed. Anyway, now I had some breathing space, but there was no peace. Here I was right in the middle of two supertraitors. I tossed and turned for what seemed like hours . . . and eventually dozed off again.

I awoke—late morning! The sun beamed through the east window, flowing over the bed. I'd slept hard and deep. I hadn't noticed when Juan and José arose. I heard Mom working in the kitchen, with Ramona firing questions:

"Mama? How come you spanked Matías?"

"Oh, honey, don't worry about it!"

"Did he do something bad?"

"Yes. Maybe not."

"Why'd you spank him, then?"

"Maybe Matías stuck other children with a pin."

"O-o-o-o! That's not nice!"

"Honey, don't worry about it. Maybe he didn't do it."

"Well, how come you spanked him?"

"Sometimes parents do things that seem right, but maybe they're wrong. Oh, honey, let's forget about it."

I popped into the kitchen.

"*¡Buenos días, perezoso!*" Mom greeted me pleasantly. "Take some cornflakes, sleepy-head?" Mom poured some cornflakes into a bowl, taking the milk out of the refrigerator. Usually I served myself.

"I have to see Mrs. Malcolm. Would you watch Ramona?"

I nodded yes.

"Ramona, stay with Matías. The boys are outside in the llano." Mom turned to me. "Here are some warm tortillas, hito." She reached into the silverware drawer. "Use this knife to put butter on 'em."

"Thank you, Mom. I'll watch Ramona. Don't worry."

Sometimes, Mom would visit over coffee with Mrs. Malcolm after we'd all had breakfast. She left for next door. I noticed Freddie and Petee were playing marbles with Juan and José by the llano. Before sitting down, I took the butter from the refrigerator. With the butter knife in hand, I tried to saw the hard slab back and forth, barely etching a line on it. The butter was hard as a rock. I set down the knife.

"Grrrrrrr!"

"What's wrong?"

"Oh! The butter's too hard." I grabbed the butter, rubbing it back and forth across the tortilla, making sure gobs of butter melted onto the warm tortilla. I took out another tortilla and repeated the procedure. I noticed Ramona holding the butter knife.

"Watch out!"

"Wh-a-a-t?" Ramona was rubbing the knife's blade with her fingers.

"Oh, forget it. That knife won't even cut butter. Just don't touch a real knife on the blade."

"I know that! I'm no dodo."

"I know—just worried. I told Mom I'd watch you."

Ramona giggled, running her fingers across the knife's dull blade. . . . *Zing* went the string of my sanity as a wild idea impelled me to blurt:

"Ramona, take the knife to the guys! Tell 'em to hold it by the handle! Then, you take it by the blade!"

"What for?"

"Guys think you're just a *polla.* This'll show how brave you are."

"Okay!"

Ramona grabbed the knife, put on her little mouse-head slippers, and walked out toward the guys. The second she stepped out the back door, I dashed out the front door, sprinting to Mrs. Malcolm's. I burst into the kitchen, hollering:

"Mom, come quick! The guys are stabbing Ramona with a knife!"

"¡Por Dios!" Mom jumped out of her chair, almost dropping her coffee cup. Mrs. Malcolm pushed her chair back, knocking it down. They lunged past me, darting to the backyard. Ramona was standing by the guys. Petee was holding the knife by the handle, pointing it toward Ramona.

"Pete! Put that knife down!" Mrs. Malcolm screamed.

"No-o-o-o-o!" Mom screeched.

"W-a-a-a-a-a-h!" Ramona wailed, provoking both mothers. Mrs. Malcolm grabbed Petee and Freddie by the collars, swiftly kicking their bottoms. Mom grabbed José and Juan the same way, swiftly kicking their bottoms.

I laughed! The guys were getting a swift kick in the pants! Revenge was sweet! Mom glared at me, Ramona still crying. I put my arm around her, feigning comfort:

"There, there, Ramona."

"I didn't do nothing bad! W-a-a-ah!" Ramona took my hand.

"Mom's not mad at you. She's mad at the guys."

Ramona's cries softened; she rubbed her eyes, listening as Mrs. Malcolm gave the guys the third-degree:

"Which of you is the craziest! Sticking pins in the young'uns! And now this?"

"But, we weren't sticking Ramona with the knife. She—"

"Well!" Mrs. Malcolm cut Petee off. "'Fess up! Whose idea was it? About the pin sticking?"

The guys guiltily waited for somebody to speak up.

Juan offered an explanation: "Last night, when Matías showed the pin to us, and then we were playing ball, everything went 'ka-whoey!'"

"We went along with one of the other ballplayers. He thought it would be funny." Petee shifted the blame. "He told us to stick the kids."

"Humph! Where's your common sense? Pete, what'll happen if you jump in the lake?"

"Why, I'd 'swallow a snake and come out with a belly ache!'"

"Hogwash! T'wouldn't happen! You'd drown! You can't swim!"

"Mother! I wouldn't even jump in the lake!"

"Of course, you wouldn't! You got a mind of your own! Why didn't you use it?"

No answer.

"Well?"

Mom scowled at the guys. They stared at the ground. Both mothers grabbed their sons and marched them into the house, where they stayed for the whole day. Ramona followed Mom into the house. Vengeance was mine! Reveling in the guys' misery, I picked up the knife and went back into the house. The cornflakes were soggy and the milk warm, just the way I liked them.

After breakfast, I took off to Eagle Nest. Once there, I basked in the reverie of revenge as I watched the tipple culling, cleaning, and loading coal, and counted the gondolas dumping their loads of slack on the smoldering pile. After a while, I began to feel blue, euphoria gone. The glory, the sweet taste of revenge, had turned sour, a bitter taste in my mouth.

There was no solace at Eagle Nest. I had double-crossed my brothers, using my little sister. My mind whirled—two wrongs don't make a right. I left Eagle Nest reluctantly, trying to get my conscience off my back, realizing I'd have to live with these awful feelings. I couldn't change what I had done.

Walking home, my guilty conscience obscured the beauty of the late summer afternoon. The sun was making ready to fall into evening, casting long shadows. As I neared the llano, I spotted Dad walking down the tracks from the mine, lunch pail swinging on his arm. I ran out to greet him.

"How's my cabrito?"

Usually we competed to get Dad's lunch pail when he first came home. We would scramble up the tracks to greet him, begging for the food scraps soggy in his lunch bucket. Today, I was the only one on the tracks to greet Dad. I took his hand; we walked down the tracks and into the house.

"Manuel," Mom greeted Dad, "glad you're home. Mrs. Malcolm and I found out who the pin stickers were."

I felt like a rat. I put Dad's lunch pail on the table and opened it. Dad had hardly touched the potato chips. I munched on the soggy potato chips as Mom and Dad talked.

"It was Juan, José! And the Malcolm boys! Some bad eggs put 'em up to it."

"Did you talk to the boys?" Dad was busy hanging up his miner's hat and his wide leather belt. In their bedroom, Mom had already filled the cajete for Dad's bath.

"O, sí. We punished the boys."

"Bueno!" He turned to me. "Matías, last night I told you 'only God knows the truth.' Today He revealed the truth. Hope you feel better."

"Uh-huh." I muttered assent, but I didn't feel better, nor worse than the night before. I was just as miserable.

Dad lay on the bedroom floor.

"Dad?" To allay my misery, I urgently wanted to confess.

"Yes, hito?" Dad was relaxing, flat on his back. He spent most of the day crouched in cramped quarters; it felt good to lie on his back, his muscles stretching.

I couldn't bring myself to confess. Dad didn't need my burden. He enjoyed his bath too much. I'd learned the hard way—two wrongs don't make a right. Instead of confessing, I offered:

"Here, Dad, I'll untie your boots."

"Say! You can have the goodies in my lunch bucket all the time!"

I untied the laces of his steel-toed boots. My fingers instantly turned black from the thick coal dust on the boots' strings and tongues. I peeled the white cotton socks off his feet.

"Bueno, out you go so I can take my bath!"

I retreated to the living room and sat on the library reading chair. Dad enjoyed his bath, cramped as he was in the cajete, scrubbing himself with a bar of Ivory soap, singing his favorite song, yodel and all:

"When it's springtime in the Rockies . . ."

10

WE ARE OUR BROTHER'S KEEPER

The last weekend of summer—Labor Day—promised to be full. I helped Dad pick the last of the onions and cucumbers. We uprooted the remaining garden weeds, tossing them in the garbage barrel. Dad spaded the soil and hacked the remaining plants into mulch. I burned the dry summer weeds in the barrel. The drier weeds popped and crackled. When the fire subsided, Dad spilled the ashes onto the garden patch, raking and harrowing them into the soil. He handed me the spade and pointed to the rake. I put them away and returned to the patch. Dad was inspecting our work.

"Bien o mal, todo acaba." Dad recited Abuelo Ribera's down-home dicho. "The garden served us well. Now it must rest." We tarried over the fallow garden, and then went into the house and washed.

"Want to go to the clubhouse?" Dad dried his hands. "I need to get a haircut."

"Yes!" I emphatically answered, quickly drying my hands.

We walked out of the house, up the tracks, over a bridge, and through a grove of spruce trees surrounding the clubhouse. We entered through a heavy, dark oak door. Directly inside was the barbershop, with a candy-striped red and white pole hanging at the entrance. The radio was broadcasting a baseball game.

"*¡Olá*, Manuel!" The barber, Chuey Torrez, greeted Dad.

"Olá, Chuey. *¿Como estás?*" Dad sat in the barber chair. Sitting down, I picked up a *Life* magazine, reading the pictures, listening to Dad and Mr. Torrez, the baseball game broadcasting in the background.

"What'll it be today?" Mr. Torrez wrapped a huge cape around Dad's neck.

"Pues, like always. A close shave and a trim."

Mr. Torrez pumped the chair's lever, lowering Dad into a reclining position. He wrapped a damp, hot towel around Dad's face to soften his beard.

"Who's playing?" Dad sounded like he had the towel in his mouth.

"The Yankees, who else?" While Mr. Torrez waited for the hot towel to soften Dad's whiskers, he fidgeted with his combs and clippers, neatly arranged on a white marble counter.

"What about the Browns?"

"Haah! They dropped out of first place. They won't last." Mr. Torrez returned to Dad's side.

"The season's not over—"

"Hold it, Manuel. We'll argue some more after the shave. No talking. You're moving your head too much." He squeezed a palm full of lather, daubing it on Dad's face. "I'm gonna try some new shaving lather, 'William's Shaving Cream.' Movie actors like Raymond Massey swear by it. Lem'me know what you think."

"Ugh! Can't you use the real McCoy? What's wrong with plain soap and water?"

"Bueno!" Mr. Torrez wiped off the William's Shaving lather. He dropped a soap bar into his lather mug, added hot water, and used a brush to agitate it into lather. He smeared the lather on Dad's face.

"Ah, better already! Don't care for store-bought lather."

"Let's see how it softens the bristles."

Mr. Torrez sharpened his razor, stroking it back and forth over a leather strop hooked to the barber chair. He dropped the strop; it flopped, dangling sideways. With agile, flowing strokes, Mr. Torrez adeptly shaved Dad's bristly beard, cutting straight swaths through the lather, up the neck, underneath the chin. He removed excess lather from the razor by lightly brushing the long blade across the palm of his left hand. After the neck, he shaved the right and left sides of Dad's face. Mr. Torrez laid down the razor and wrapped a warm towel around Dad's face, rubbing his face clean.

"So what'cha think?" Mr. Torrez stood back, wiping the excess lather off his hands.

"As always—perfect." Dad smiled, pleased with Mr. Torrez's light touch. "You have a surgeon's touch with that razor. But, hey, don't get a big head. Not sure about your Yankees. The Browns've been leading the league since June. They slipped out of first place only the other day."

"Yeah, the Yankees are first. They moved on top right away, playing like the Yankees, sweeping the Philadelphia Athletics 10–0, and 14–0. They even did it without DiMaggio." Mr. Torrez bragged about the Yankees while trimming Dad's hair.

"We shall see."

"I think the Yankees'll stay on top."

"You're loyal to the Yankees, Chuey! I like loyalty!" Dad paid Mr. Torrez for the haircut. "Keep the change."

"Oh, sure, I like the Yankees, but I'm loyal to you, Manuel! You're a good customer. Stay, listen to the game?"

"Well, for a little while." Dad sat next to me. Mr. Torrez sat in the barber chair.

By game's end, Mr. Torrez was less gabby. The Yankees had lost. After the game, Dad and I went home to prepare for our trip to Ludlow and the first day of school. Mom and Angela were busy washing and ironing clothing. Dad dug up a can of Shinola shoe polish. With a small patch of cotton rag, he smeared polish on one of his shoes, spit on it, and rubbed it vigorously with another cotton cloth. When he finished both shoes, he held them up for us to see:

"*¡Mida!* Spit-shine so you can see your face in 'em. Now you boys do the same."

He handed me the polish. I used my fingers to apply the polish. The wax was smooth and soft like whipped butter. I rubbed polish all over the shoes. Pressing hard with my fingertips, I smeared shoe polish into every crack, especially pressing hard over scuff marks. I set the shoes aside to wash my hands. My fingertips were as black as coal. Mom's heavy-duty lava soap couldn't even do the job. The soap was caustic, but it made my fingers and hands feel soft and smooth. Even though I rubbed so hard I almost removed my fingerprints, my Shinola black-dyed fingertips stayed black as coal.

"Haah!" Dad chuckled. "When you go to school, tell Miss Blackerby you were working in the mine. Now, get on the powder box. I'll cut your hair."

I didn't want Dad to cut my hair. Dad cut hair like he sheared sheep, rough and rowdy, using a pair of very sharp German scissors and a World War I set of hand clippers that yanked more than clipped.

"Why can't I get a haircut at the clubhouse?"

"You can—when you can pay for it with your own money."

Dad lifted me on top of a stack of two powder boxes and wrapped a Diamond M flour sack towel around my neck. With the German-made scissors, he cut the long hair first. I watched my brown locks slide on the towel, tumbling to the floor. Some hair stuck and I flicked it down to the floor.

"Quit squirming so much," Dad scolded as he trimmed along the neck, etching a high hairline around it and my ears. Last, he cut the front bangs even shorter, leaving a curly lock hanging down the middle of my forehead.

Dad filled his palms with Mom's olive oil, vigorously rubbing it into my scalp and what was left of my hair. Parting and combing the lock he'd left, he slipped a silly cap, made from one of Mom's discarded lisle cotton dress hosiery, over my head:

"Cap stays on till supper."

Dad tersely ended the haircut, removing the towel. I was free to play, but I chose to stay in the house to avoid any ribbing. I decided to finish spit-polishing my shoes. My spit-polished shoes looked great, thanks to Dad's clear directions. Juan and José, who were in similar silly caps and too embarrassed to go outdoors, were sitting on the floor reading comic books. They liked the bright shimmer of my shoes and asked me to shine theirs. I gladly consented.

At supper, Dad wanted to talk about Labor Day.

"Angela, tell the family about Labor Day."

Dad may have warned her ahead of time. She seemed prepared as she straightened herself in the chair:

"Labor Day honors America's working men and women. It's a national holiday observed on the first Monday of September. It started with the early Labor movement, when the Knights of Labor—the first labor union—had a parade in New York City. They chose the date halfway between the Fourth of July and Christmas."

"Tomorrow," Dad injected, "you'll learn about 'Louis Tikas.'"

"Who's he?"

"A union organizer at Ludlow. He tried to bring peace between the strikers and the Company; the Company shot him."

"Don't forget about Mother Jones." Mom told us about Mary Harris Jones, a tough, spunky advocate of unions. "She came to Ludlow to make peace. The Company wouldn't let her speak. They locked her in the hospital. She just wanted to speak to the striking miners, but the Company wouldn't let her."

"Why not?"

"You'll see for yourself. Tomorrow, after mass, we'll drive to Ludlow."

"Can't we come home and change?"

"No!" Dad insisted. "It's a formal occasion."

The drive to Ludlow was short but not without peril. We had to drive over Raton Pass, whose first seven miles wound up a forty-five-degree incline. The south shoulders dropped twenty feet to the Santa Fe Railroad tracks. To the north side, the hills crowded the roadside. Guard railings were few and far between. I'd never seen Angela so tense. I guess she thought we were all going to drop off the mountain. Mom, on the other hand, loved the view. Dad, who'd been a little tense too, relaxed as we descended down the Colorado side of the pass. Near Starkville, Dad pointed to a slack pile and a large corral filled with mules.

"They use mules to haul the slack."

"They're still using mules?" Juan was surprised.

"*O, sí.* They use 'em in the mine, too."

"How come?"

"*No se.* But they're the only mine that still uses mules."

We slowed down as we approached Ludlow. There were many cars parked around the Ludlow Monument fence. Their license plates were from New Mexico, Colorado, Wyoming, Utah, and Montana. These were miners and their families from the coal fields of the Rocky Mountains as far north as Decker, Montana; as far south as Madrid, New Mexico; and as far west as the Salt Lake Valley and Rock Springs, Wyoming.

On the exact location of the Ludlow massacre, the monument was built in the middle of a large grass and brush pasture. The Ludlow mine itself was located in the sandstone and piñón covered foothills west of the monument. There was no coal camp in sight. Ludlow was a ghost town. Once the mine was closed, the coal camp was dismantled and sold for scrap—lock, stock, and barrel—just like the other camps in the area.

Ludlow was once a thriving coal camp in the southern Colorado coal fields. Miners were recruited to this remote area from Greece, Italy, Mexico, and the Balkan countries, and locally from the Hispano homeland in New Mexico. Many languages were spoken and many cultures celebrated in Ludlow. On any given day, one could eat a meal with homemade bread, fine wine, delicate pastries, and hand-stuffed sausages while listening to a lively accordion tune from such disparate places as Montenegro, Greece, Italy, or Mexico.

Now the prairie had reclaimed the land where Ludlow once resided. On the hillside near the mine entry, the slack piles were overgrown with vegetation and no longer smoldered. Closer to the monument, half buried in the sandy, dry soil, an occasional rusting pot or pan might be found wedged up against a tuft of buffalo grass. Were there no monument, there would be no visible evidence of the 1901–14 Southern Colorado Coal Field Wars, which raged violently in this dry, overgrown prairie. The Ludlow coal camp had been at the center of the battlefield.

To the people who returned every Labor Day Sunday, Ludlow was a place of spiritual renewal—holy ground consecrated by the souls of the miners and their families who lived, worked, and died here. This is why we came to Ludlow every Labor Day Sunday—to be renewed by the spirit of the people who gave their lives so miners and their families could have a better life.

The people in attendance were not dejected, although the event that brought them here was solemn. Instead, they rejoiced in the annual reunion of coal miners and their families, gathering on Labor Day Sunday to link up again for the afternoon. As at the Ludlow coal camp, many languages were spoken and many cultures were represented at this communal affair. There were no strangers at Ludlow.

Everyone shared the legacy of Ludlow, dressing formally for the occasion. The women wore their best dresses. Some wore suits, the jackets bolstered with large shoulder pads. Others wore flamboyant hats and elegant pearl necklaces. All wore gloves, high-heeled shoes, and sheer full-length hose. Some wore the open-toe high-heeled shoes popular among singers and movie actresses. The women appeared to be very comfortable in their stylish dresses and suits as they chatted with their old acquaintances.

The men did not seem as comfortable in suits and white shirts. Some wore vests or ties. Others wore open collars, like Mr. Chicarelli, who wore a brown leather vest under his jacket. Mr. Malcolm wore a bright blue and red silk tie spangled with large, pink magnolia flowers. His vest was made of bright black satin. Both Mr. Chicarelli and Mr. Malcolm carried a gold watch in their vests and a gold chain hung from one vest pocket to the other.

"I got married in this tie. I'll be buried with it," Mr. Malcolm remarked, adding sheepishly, "'Course, it's the only one I got!"

Mr. Heard looked fit to kill, Dad said. Mr. Heard wore a black suit

Ludlow was a place of spiritual renewal.

and vest, and a black tie to match. He also wore a black hat. His white shirtsleeves were cuffed with gold links, which matched his gold watch and chain hanging on his vest. Dad wore a gray hat with his gray double-breasted suit—his speech-making suit, he called it. I'm glad Dad made us dress up. All the kids looked very classy, and while I wasn't prone to brag, my shoes were the best polished—a spit-shine à la Dad.

No doubt about it, this was a happy family gathering, an uplifting reunion. Folks knew each other, and those who at first appeared to be outsiders soon found they had friends or relatives in common. I remember Juan saying the Chicorico pioneers came from the coal camps in southern Colorado. He mentioned Ludlow as one of the camps. Now, the folks here all came from some other coal camp. Many were born in a coal camp, and many were related. All were neighbors at one time or another. They were asking about family members and their whereabouts, sharing good and bad news about births, marriages, and deaths.

Dad and Mom drifted to a far corner of the monument's fence with Silver Lorenzo, District 15 president of the United Mine Workers of America, and some other miners and their wives. They were talking in earnest. In 1944, there were a lot of strikes in mines throughout the United States. There was a rumor President Roosevelt might nationalize the mines and eliminate the right to strike.

Angela walked Ramona and me closer to the monument. It faced west, the direction from which the Ludlow tent colony was fired upon. The three of us looked up at its imposing pillar. The monument was made of marble, with an elegant rectangular pillar standing on a base of four blocks of ascending marble. A classical Ionic design was selected for the monument's frame. The Seal of the United Mine Workers of America was embedded in the pillar's crown. On each corner of the crown were spiral scrolls.

Beneath the pillar, on the first rectangular block, stood a sculpture of a coal miner, dressed in street clothing, his sleeves rolled up around his muscular arms. On the second block sat a sculpture of his wife, holding their child in her arms. The faces of the miner, mother, and child conveyed the dignity, honesty, and courage of ordinary coal camp people.

Holding our hands, Angela led us to the monument's south side and read aloud from its bronze plaque:

> On April 20, 1914 the state militia unleashed an unwarranted attack on striking coal miners and their families living in a tent colony at this site. Eleven children and two women suffocated in a cellar beneath a tent when flames engulfed the overhead shelter. Militia rifle and machine gun fire claimed the lives of at least five strikers, an eleven year old boy, and an 18-year old passerby.
>
> The unexpected attack was the fateful climax of miners attempting to achieve freedom from oppression at the hands of coal company officials. Miners were forced to live in company owned camps, buy from company owned stores, and educate their children in company dominated schools. Miners worked unduly long hours under hazardous conditions for meager pay.
>
> On September 23, 1913, miners struck in protest of these conditions, calling for recognition of the United Mine Workers Union. Eventually, the alleged peace keeping militia became infiltrated with company gunmen, leading to this—the Ludlow Massacre.

In language we could understand, Angela explained that the rights to form a union and bargain collectively were crucial to the Ludlow strike, which led to the Ludlow Massacre. The massacre was a tragic episode in America's struggle toward democracy in the workplace. Mom and Dad brought us to the site of the massacre because the struggle at Ludlow was central to our lives in Chicorico.

"Attention! Your attention!" Mr. Silver Lorenzo walked toward the monument, calling to begin the program. "Come up front so we can start!"

The crowd cordially gathered, still chatting and visiting. Angela escorted us to the front of the monument where Dad and Mom were standing. Juan and José followed.

Mr. Lorenzo stepped onto the monument's first block.

"Last year we had Reverend La Mont Miller, a Methodist pastor. He's with us today. This year, the Reverend Father Stanley will lead the invocation." Mr. Lorenzo dropped an arm and pulled Father Stanley onto the first block. As Mr. Lorenzo stepped aside, Father Stanley, dressed in a black cassock and Roman collar, raised both arms to the blue summer sky:

"Our Father who art in Heaven, we know that those who died here . . . are with You in Heaven. Please help us . . . to have the courage to remind all of Your children—even government and business officials—that those who died here . . . were Your children, killed by the hands of their brothers. . . . No matter how much money or power we have, we are all Your children . . . and must care for each other. . . . We are our brothers' keepers. . . . Amen."

Everybody resounded "A-MEN!"

Father Stanley stepped down. Mr. Lorenzo now pulled Dad up onto the block:

"As District 15 president, I have the honor to introduce Manuel Montaño; he's an old-timer from Chicorico." Mr. Lorenzo stepped off the block.

Dad was alone before the crowd. He took a deep breath, buttoned his double-breasted suit:

"*Mi plebe*, I can add little to what Father Stanley said. So let's read together the inscription on the monument. Please join hands."

We formed a human chain. I held Ramona's hand to my left. Mr. Heard took my right hand, and so on. All the families were linked. Dad led everyone, reading in unison:

IN MEMORY OF
THE MEN, WOMEN, AND CHILDREN
WHO LOST THEIR LIVES
IN FREEDOM'S CAUSE
AT LUDLOW, COLORADO
APRIL 20, 1914

Dad paused. Everyone remained holding hands, expecting Dad to continue. He spoke from the heart:

"The people that died here . . . died for the only thing working people have—their families. They paid a high price . . . so we could have a union that's recognized by the Company.

"Now, the times are good. We're working full time producing a lot of coal for the war. Of this, we should be proud. Our work is helping win the war. But, we must be careful we don't strike for bad reasons. In other parts of America, miners are striking too much. They know coal is needed for the war. They're taking advantage of their companies. The miners are being greedy. If we aren't careful, the president will nationalize the coal mines and cancel the right to strike! After the war's over, we may never get back that right. Then where will we be?

"We'll be right back here! In Ludlow! Begging the Company to recognize our union! And the people who died here at Ludlow? They will have died for nothing. . . ."

Silencio . . . a long, awkward pause . . . everyone still standing, holding hands, absolutely silent.

Finally, Mr. Lorenzo yelled, "Good speech, Manuel! Let's give him a hand!"

Thundering applause, shouts from the convivial crowd:

"Bravo! Bravo!"

Dad sighed, his eyes watering, "*¡Mucho gracias*, plebe! I see the ladies have made some food for us! How about women and children first?"

"How about men of God?" Father Stanley harped. Everyone laughed. Of course, Father Stanley was allowed to go first, followed by Reverend Miller. All of us kids pushed to get in line behind them.

The adults didn't rush. They lingered in line—talking, laughing. Father Stanley and Dad had given the occasion a serious tone, but the speeches were over. The time to enjoy was at hand.

Mrs. Heard handed Dad a full plate. Dad joined Mom, sitting on the block where he'd just delivered his speech. Ramona and I joined them. Already we had finished eating a plate of beans and a hot dog. I lifted

Ramona to the block and crawled up. We sat quietly as Mom and Dad ate. They hardly spoke.

I grew restless so I walked to the pit where the women and children had hidden to be safe from the militia's bullets but were suffocated by a tent fire that had been ignited by the militia. I lifted the pit's rusty metal door. The pit was dug deep, seven feet at least. I went in. Sunlight beamed through the gaps in the roof's planks. In one corner, a spider straddled the walls with an intricate web. I broke off a twig from a sagebrush that had blown into the pit. Twig in hand, I stalked toward the web, intending to kill the spider. Busy mummifying a beetle it had just killed, it didn't notice me. I paused. The air . . . stale . . . dry. My skin prickled. La Muerte had been here. I dropped the twig and bolted out.

Little by little, in small numbers, family members collected themselves, loaded their cars, and left. We were one of the last families to leave. Just before leaving, Dad and Mom stood before the monument. They crossed themselves and prayed. Then Mom placed her arm through Dad's, silently walking to the car.

On the road back to Chicorico, Dad and Mom were in a talkative mood.

"I'm glad we never had problems in Chicorico," I commented, "like they did in Ludlow."

"Oh, honey!" Mom explained, "things were hard at first in Chicorico. When we came in 1920, your Tío Baltazar and Tía Feliz came with us. They lived next door. We didn't have any children. We did a lot of things together. Your Tía and I would collect coal that fell off the train. When a Company guard saw us, he would take it away. So we hid from him."

"How come the guard took the coal away?"

"Company property, he said. We would have to buy it."

"They were being greedy," Dad added. "The Company was very bad about politics. The Company men were all Republicans. If they found out you were a Democrat, they'd fire you."

"That's not fair."

"I know, honey," Mom agreed. "One time while the men were working, a Company man came campaigning to all the houses. Your father told me to agree with the Company man about politics. Anyway, the ballot is secret. He came to our house and told me to vote a straight Republican ticket. I told him I would; he went away."

"Mom, you told a lie!"

"God forgive me, hito," Mom replied contritely, "but your father would've been fired if I told the truth."

"Hito, I think God will forgive your mother."

"The Company man went to your Tía's house," Mom continued. "He told her to vote Republican. Your Tía got mad and said, "'In America, you can vote for anybody you want to!'"

"That's true, right?"

"Yes, honey. But, Chicorico was not like America in those days. That man came back with some other men and threw all of your Tía's and Tío's things out of the house. They made your Tía get out, también, and they locked the door. When your Tío came home, she was outside the house with all their things. He had been fired."

"They stayed with us that night," Dad explained. "The next day they took the train to Ribera. He was blacklisted and couldn't get a job in any of the camps. Or even with the Santa Fe section gang."

"But now he has a job with the Santa Fe," Juan said. He had been listening intently.

"A few years ago when the war started, he got a job with the section gang. They were hard up for men. So they threw the list away."

"Is it really better now, Dad?" Juan was concerned.

"Much better, because we have a union. When Roosevelt was elected president, he passed a law that put teeth into collective bargaining. So we tried to organize a union. Don MacGregor from the Industrial Workers of the World—the "Wobblies," they were called—came to see us.

"Mr. MacGregor used to be a newspaper reporter for the Denver *Express.* Before the massacre, he was in charge of collecting news at the Ludlow strike. He got mad at the militia and the goons hired by the Colorado Fuel and Iron Works; he joined the striking miners, and he got fired from his news reporting job. He survived the Ludlow Massacre and became an organizer for the Industrial Workers of the World—the IWW.

"He spoke to us about the rights of working men. If we had an IWW union, the national offices would help us overthrow the Company. He told us that by sticking together we could insist upon and get our rights. The men liked what he had to say about sticking together in a union, but they didn't like the part about overthrowing the Company."

"Why not, if they're so bad?"

"Well, he was a Communist. He was too radical. He wanted to overthrow America, to get rid of capitalism. We didn't want a revolution, just a safe job to put bread on the table. But it worked to our favor to have him speak to us. When the Super found out, he got afraid we would join the Wobblies. So he called a meeting with us to form a Company union, based on cooperation.

"We liked the idea so we elected officers. I got elected president. Everything was okay for a while. Nothing really came up. We would have meetings, but we didn't do much. Then, one day a fire started in the mine's Number Two section. Some of the Company men hadn't washed down the dusty walls like they were supposed to. Luckily, no one got hurt. Some miners complained to the Company union. So our Company union wanted to have the Company men fined, to punish them for being careless.

"The Super said he would have their wages garnished to the amount of $200.00. That was a steep fine! We were satisfied. Those men would stop to think before being careless again. A month later, on a Friday night, one of the Company men got drunk at the clubhouse and bragged he didn't pay the fine. When I heard about it, I went to the Super and demanded to see the Company books. The Super wouldn't let me see the books.

"'Take my word for it, Manuel. He was drunk, just braggin'! He didn't know what he was saying.'

"I believed the Super. One day as I passed by the Company office, the bookkeeper, Pasquale Buscarini, called me to his desk. He looked around and whispered, 'I dropped a paper. Would you pick it up?'

"I was confused. Pasquale could've picked up the paper himself. I could tell he wanted me to read it. I picked it up. The paper showed that neither of the Company men had their wages withheld. Pasquale begged me not to tell on him, or he would lose his job. He was a good man."

"Boy, oh, boy, the Super lied!"

"I called some of the Company union officers over to the house, only those who were miners. I told them what happened. They were angry. They used to believe the Super, but now they couldn't believe the Company union would protect the miners. No use to say anything to the Super. They told me to contact Silver Lorenzo, the president of District 15, in Denver."

"Honey," Mom joined us, "it was very hard for your father. He was afraid to call Silver Lorenzo on the telephone. A telephone operator might listen and tell the Company. Then he'd be out of a job."

"What'd you do?"

"We had an old Essex. It wouldn't get me to Denver. So I took the train. When I bought the ticket at the Raton depot, the ticket agent asked me:

'Going to Denver, huh? To the Lakeside Carnival?'

'What's the Lakeside Carnival.'

'A park, with a lot of rides.'

"His insinuation made me mad. How dare he! I was going to tell him I had business, but then I thought it might be better if people thought I was going for fun. So I told him I might just do that.

"When I got to Denver, I got a room at the Brown Palace Hotel—very fancy place. The next day I visited Silver Lorenzo in his office. He was a real gentleman. I asked him:

'Are you a communist?'

'Heck, no! I hate communists!'"

We all laughed.

"Silver agreed to come to Chicorico to talk with the men—if the men wanted him to come down."

"Oh, so all went well?"

"In Denver it did. When I got back, the Super called me into his office. The ticket agent must have told the Super I was going to Denver and that I really didn't know about Lakeside Carnival. Probably some-one spied on me, because the Super knew I had met with Silver Lorenzo.

He told me if I called a meeting to organize a union, he would fire me. I didn't say anything back to him. Then he said:

'I don't want any trouble. If you're going to organize a union, don't meet on Company property! That's all I have to say.'

"I told Father Stanley what happened. He told me we could meet at the St. Joseph *sala.* I called a meeting of the men interested in a real union. All the officers came, and some others. They agreed to meet with Silver Lorenzo. I wrote to him and arranged a meeting time.

"When Silver Lorenzo came, he brought an accountant and a lawyer. The accountant taught us how to keep books and manage the union office. The lawyer explained how we could bargain collectively with the Company to reach agreement on a contract. If we went with the United Mine Workers, he would personally serve the union papers on the Company, forcing them to recognize the local union."

"Say, Dad," I was curious. "What ever happened to Mr. MacGregor, that communist?"

"*¿Pues, quién sabe?* He disappeared. I never saw him again. . . . Like I was saying, the following Sunday we called another meeting at the sala to discuss the union idea with all the men. About half of the Chicorico miners came. Many were afraid to come. If word leaked that they were at such a meeting, they feared losing their jobs. Some of the men didn't like the union idea. They thought it was too radical, like the Wobblies. I told them that Silver Lorenzo hated the communists. I told the men that with the union we could negotiate for a fire boss and a weigh-master-checker, and we could bargain for wages for deadwork.

'What if the Company doesn't do anything?' one miner asked.

'Well,' Julian Heard declared, 'we'll strike!'

"Everybody turned somber, dropping their eyes to the floor. The men knew what could happen to miners who strike. They could get killed—like Ludlow. Or evicted from their homes. I worried! Maybe Mr. Heard had been too radical. Maybe he shouldn't have mentioned the strike right away. Anyway, the men talked among themselves for a while, weighing the pros and cons. I decided to keep quiet. Let them talk. They must believe in the union, or it wouldn't work. After a while, different ones said:

'I'm for it!'

'Let's try it!'

'We got nothing to lose!'

'Bueno, hey!'

"I was relieved. They wanted to try it. They elected the same officers as the Company union officers. Only we didn't have to beg the Company to negotiate!"

"Boy, you're a real hero, Dad!" Proudly I patted his shoulder.

Dad glanced at me, without commenting. He continued driving, not saying anything. Everybody was quiet. Dad was in a pensive mood. We rode in silence for a long while, passing time by watching for a *perdido*, cars with only one headlight. We also watched for deer and other animals. After a while, Dad cleared his throat, speaking softly, shaking his head side to side.

"I'm no hero. The men and women of Ludlow, they're heroes."

On Labor Day, there wasn't much for us to do. Dad decreed a day of rest for everyone, including Mom. She didn't have to cook. We could get along with self-made sandwiches and a watermelon he'd cut.

Tomorrow would be the first day of school. Because the first day of school was important, Dad had already purchased yellow Number Two lead pencils and Big Chief tablets for José and me. The tablets were red. Like the buffalo nickel, they were embossed with the head of an Indian chief, only the Big Chief wore more feathers in his bonnet.

This was to be my first year in school, and Angela's last year. She busied herself organizing clothing for school and work. Ramona, Dad, and Mom relaxed, listening to the radio in the living room. I'm not sure where José and Juan went, probably with the guys playing marbles or spinning hoops. I stayed in the living room for a while, reading the pictures in the books in our library.

"Matías, *¿qué haces?*" Dad peered over his newspaper.

"Reading the pictures in the books. To be ready for school."

"Go play, honey," Mom chuckled.

I skipped out into the hills and headed to Eagle Nest.

11

GIVE ME YOUR TIRED, YOUR POOR

Mom woke me for the first day of school. Already, Angela and Juan had caught the bus to attend St. Patrick's Academy in Raton. Mom dressed me in a plaid flannel shirt and a pair of corduroy bib overalls, and brushed the dust off my spit-shined shoes. My outfit was a bit warm, but the shirt and pants were bought especially for school. Mom insisted on fastening every button, even the collar. José and I left to school, skipping down the steps onto the brick path heading toward the tracks. I peered back. Mom and Ramona were silhouetted behind the screen door. Mom pushed the screen door open, waving goodbye.

José poked me in the ribs:

"Pay attention! This'll be the only time I bring you to school. You know the way, anyhow."

As we walked the tracks, we encountered Geno and Marian with their mothers. Suddenly José puffed up his chest, telling Mrs. Chicarelli and Mrs. Heard:

"Mom had to stay with Ramona. So I'm taking Matías to school."

"Well, how nice." Mrs. Chicarelli's eyes twinkled, dancing from side to side.

"You're a good man, José." Mrs. Heard's flattery caused José to puff his chest even larger. "Would you be so kind as to escort Marian home tonight?"

"And my Eugene?"

"Definitely! Wouldn't want her to get lost." Now, José's head was so big, it almost exploded. "I'll bring Geno home, too. And at lunch time, too."

"Thank you kindly. There'll be cookies and milk waiting for all of you after your first day in school."

A large rabbit-wire fence encircled the schoolyard. Our school was really nine different Company houses all in a row—run entirely by women. In the past, there may have been a young man or two, but not since anyone can remember. Mrs. Hilliard, the principal, lived in the first house, which also served as her office. Next to Mrs. Hilliard's home was the first grade; the eighth grade was the last house in the row; in between were the other grades.

Even the janitor was a woman, Mrs. Anna Perkovich. She raised her family of four boys and two girls alone. She had been expecting her youngest son when her husband, Mr. Judo Perkovich, was killed in a mining accident. Mrs. Hilliard offered her the janitor's job, providing a way for Mrs. Perkovich to stay in a Company house. She did her job well, cleaning the schools, stoking the stoves, and shoveling the snow in the cold winter months.

"Good luck! Do what the teacher says!" José was gone in a flash, leaving us standing in front of the first-grade house with our red Big Chief tablets and bright yellow Number Two pencils.

"Ah, come on!" Marian charged up the steps.

Geno and I followed slowly through the front door. Instantly, I was overwhelmed by the newly varnished floors and desks and the resplendent colors of the flags hanging on the wall behind Miss Vesta Blackerby's desk. I'd never seen the yellow New Mexico flag, embossed with a red Zia Indian sun. The American flag was simply beautiful. The red, white, and blue of the stars and stripes dazzled me. . . . Goose bumps prickled on my arms, just like Memorial Day when we sang the national anthem. Hanging on the walls were portraits of George Washington, Abraham Lincoln, and the Statue of Liberty.

Marian was speaking to Miss Blackerby. Marian turned, waving us forward. We reluctantly approached Miss Blackerby. She stood up:

"My! My! You boys sure look dapper!"

I was lovestruck! She was striking, standing erect and tall with milky white skin and turquoise blue eyes, her wavy red hair draped down onto her shoulders. Her hands were delicate and fine-boned, with long, narrow fingernails painted red. She wore high-heeled shoes and nylon hose, the kind with seams in the back. She walked around the desk and placed her hand on Geno's head:

"What may we call you, young man?"

"Geno. Geno Chicarelli." Geno—not as impressed—answered right away.

"Oh, you're Italian? Mrs. Chicarelli's your mother?"

"Yes, ma'am."

She turned to me, her hand still on Geno's head. She gently lifted her hand, reaching to pat my head. I swerved, ducking.

"Oops! Don't be afraid, young man."

"I'm not afraid." I really felt dumb for ducking.

"And what may we call you?"

"Matías Montaño."

"You're Mexican?"

"No, ma'am! I'm American."

"Mrs. Montano's your mother." She mispronounced our family name.

"Yes, ma'am. And my brother's in the navy. He's a chief petty officer." I really wanted to impress this lovely lady.

"How nice." She addressed both of us:

"Sit where you'd like. If you talk too much, I'll make you sit by me."

I thought that might be nice and then grinned, embarrassed. Geno and I spotted two desks by the south window. Perfect! The desks were made of maple and held up by a black cast-iron frame. Their legs were firmly bolted to two boards that connected the desks to form rows. The seats were on hinges and could be raised and lowered. Sitting at my desk, I marveled at the top's smooth surface, newly sanded and varnished just like the glowing oak floor. Even the pencil groove was smooth. I remember Mom telling Mrs. Malcolm how Mrs. Perkovich spent most of her summer spiffing up the floors and desks for this first day of school.

On the upper right hand corner of my desk, someone had etched the word "KILROY." I ran my fingers across the etched word, feeling only the smooth, velvety grain of the varnished maple. The thickly veneered word was etched beside the inkwell, a small round hole seemingly without a purpose. I nudged Geno, pointing to the inkwell. Geno ran his fingers around the inkwell's lip on his desk and looked at me with a blank stare, shrugging. He didn't know either. "Ventilation," I thought, "like Tía Feliz's horno, for the open metal storage drawer below."

Miss Blackerby announced:

"When I call your name, please raise your right hand. I'm making up a seating chart. So, where you're seated right now will be your seat all year—unless you talk too much. Then, I'll make you sit by me. Try not to scratch your desktop. Mrs. Perkovich spent a lot of time sanding and varnishing the desktops so that you'd have a smooth surface to write on."

She sat at her desk with an empty seating chart and the official class roster, calling names. By the time she was through, many of our first names had been changed to American names. Juan Armijo became "Johnny"; Maria Duran became "Mary"; Marco Antonucci became "Mark"; Consuella Pappas became "Connie." Geno became "Eugene." For the most part, the other kids accepted their new names. I was none too happy with the name "Matthew," even though that was Dr. Monty's first name.

"Miss Blackerby, 'Matthew' isn't my name!"

"We must all learn to raise our hands," Miss Blackerby explained, "when we want to speak."

I raised my hand.

"I like 'Matt' much better, myself!" Miss Blackerby snapped. Her curt reply startled me.

I cooled down, but I still had my say:

"No! I like my name . . . *M-a-t-í-a-s.*" I spelled it clearly. Some kids giggled. Geno frowned, whispering:

"Shut up! You'll get in trouble."

"Now, Matt," Miss Blackerby emphatically slapped her thigh, "we all need an American name." She paused to get her breath, "Matt is a perfectly good American name."

I clammed up—respecting Miss Blackerby's wishes, though I disagreed about my name. She addressed the whole class:

"Boys and girls, America is a big melting pot. Foreigners come from all over the world. When they come to our country, they must take on American ways and American names. And they all learn to speak English. So I want all of you to try to speak English. You may want to speak in your mother tongue—Italian, Slav, Mexican, Greek—but you mustn't. You'll never learn to speak English if you always talk in another language. So be good little boys and girls—try to speak English and use your American names."

I seemed to be the only one making a fuss about the name. Dad and Juan had warned me; they also told me to respect the teacher. Questions quickly flashed through my mind: aren't we all foreigners, except the Indians? Wouldn't we have to take names like Juan read to me—Pocahontas, Geronimo? Confused, I realized I couldn't learn everything on the first day. Besides, Juan said he still didn't understand, and he was in the ninth grade. I decided to grin and bear the name "Matt."

Miss Blackerby continued explaining:

"Now that we've finished taking attendance, we'll start the day by singing two songs. Follow me. The words'll come easy. Everyone stand up good and straight, face the flags. Sing along as I sing 'America.'" She turned toward the flags, placing her right hand over her heart, singing: "My country 'tis of thee, sweet land of liberty. . . ."

We started faintly, not sure of the words, or melody. When we got to "Land where my father died," we got into the spirit, warbling loudly, trailing slightly behind Miss Blackerby. By the time we finished, I was thinking about the song from Memorial Day at Mount Calvary Cemetery in Raton. My mind wandered to that cool spring morning—the smell of freshly cut flowers, everyone singing together. . . .

"Very good, boys and girls!"

Her praise made me feel better about being an American. "Now let's sing the New Mexico song." She started: "O fair New Mexico, I love, I love you so . . ."

She stopped, recognizing we couldn't get into the swing of the song. Most of us had sung "America" at Memorial Day ceremonies, and with the war it was on the radio all of the time. But we had never heard or sung the New Mexico song.

"That's okay, boys and girls, we'll have a lot of time to learn the song. Take your seats."

We obeyed, sitting down.

"Do any of you know any songs you'd like to sing?"

Everyone got quiet. Most of us were pretty shy. Then Marian volunteered:

"I know one."

"Please stand at your seat and sing."

Marian stood up, placed her hands to her side, and cleared her throat. I was amazed to hear what came out of her mouth, an old cowboy song:

"Oh, give me a home
Where the buffalo roam. . . ."

We clapped vigorously when she was done.

"Thank you, Marian. That's a beautiful cowboy song. Where'd you learn it?"

"My daddy sings it all the time. He wished he was a cowboy."

"Boys and girls, 'Home on the Range' is President Roosevelt's favorite song. Well, anybody else with a song?"

Nobody else volunteered to sing. We sat at attention, ready and eager to learn. Class started in earnest. Miss Blackerby explained the alphabet. She had a row of letters on large cards hooked to the chalkboard.

Pronouncing each letter, she asked us to repeat the sound in unison. After we drilled the alphabet several times, she asked:

"Who would like to try the ABCs?"

Wang! Wang! A whole bunch of hands sprang up, including Marian's and mine, waving to Miss Blackerby, eagerly chiming: "I know! I know!"

"Marian, you try."

"Ohhhhhhh!" everyone exclaimed as Marian stood. We wanted to be called.

"A, B, C, D . . . Z."

Marian correctly recited the alphabet. She sat down. Others were called upon. Miss Blackerby didn't see my hand and didn't call on me. After calling about half the kids, she announced:

"Boys and girls, let's take a fifteen-minute recess. After recess, I'll call on the rest of you. So be thinking about the alphabet. I'll teach you a song with the alphabet. Now you can go out and play. Stay in back of our schoolhouse. I'll watch you. When it's time to come in, I'll ring this bell." She lifted a brass-plated hand bell with a black wooden handle.

"One aisle at a time! I want you to line up at the door. Then we'll march outside."

As we were leaving the room, I tucked my Big Chief tablet and yellow Number Two pencil inside my desk drawer. We lined up, and she led the march outside. We stood around for a few minutes, trying to figure out what to do. Geno came to me, tapped my shoulder.

"You're—IT!" I tried to catch him. He dashed away. Marian joined us. Before long, the playground was filled with kids playing games. It felt great to be running around, like on the llano. For fifteen very short minutes, we were free to play.

Ding! Ding! Miss Blackerby rang the hand bell, calling us to line up at the front door.

While waiting in line for a few stragglers, I asked:

"Would you like to hear a song now?"

"Certainly, Matt."

I stood as straight as Marian, holding my hands to my side, and sang a popular song played on the jukebox at the Sweet Shop:

"Give me five minutes more . . .
Give me five minutes more
Of your charms—"

"Oh, Matt, that's so cute." She blushed.

"Pleea-zzze?" Geno begged. "Can we have five minutes more of recess?"

Everybody laughed! Miss Blackerby giggled, motioning us to follow her into the room. I liked Miss Blackerby. She meant business, but she had a sense of humor.

As promised, Miss Blackerby called on the rest of us to recite the alphabet. Most of us couldn't recite the entire alphabet. Miss Blackerby led the entire class through the alphabet again. She pointed at each letter, which was printed on a separate card and tacked to the bulletin board running across the top of the chalkboard. She pronounced each letter clearly and then asked us to pronounce it. We spent the rest of the morning taking turns reciting the alphabet. The few kids who knew the entire alphabet by heart, such as Marian and Becky Ruker, coached small groups of us until we could recite it too.

After all the small-group practice, Miss Blackerby called us back together as a group to teach the "Alphabet Song."

"It's a catchy tune, sung all over America!" Miss Blackerby prepared us to sing. "As I sing, I'll point up, or down, for you to raise or lower your voices, or just hold it steady, like this: A–B c–d E–F–G . . ."

Wow! What a song! We really liked it. Miss Blackerby repeated it. We instantaneously sang along with her! The drilling we did in our small groups paid off. Wasn't long, we were all singing our hearts out, proud to be singing the entire alphabet.

Miss Blackerby sent us home for lunch. José came by and walked with Marian, Geno, and me. We told José about the "Alphabet Song." Of course, he knew it! Breaking out in a strong, spirited voice, he led us through the song as we marched home; arms-over-shoulders, we marched on the tracks yelping our newly learned song—"ABCD . . ."

At home, Mom served lunch for José, Ramona, and me on our front porch. The porch was shaded and cool. It was pleasant sitting on the front porch of our house eating lunch with my family, although we didn't have much to say. A train passed in front of the house. The engine was a real smoker, bellowing cindery, sooty smoke from its belly, a 1928 2–10–4 type used for heavy-duty freight. It crept by the house. The engineer waved. I gazed at the train, counting the number of coal cars up to ten, again and again. I thought of how I could be watching that train edge up to the tipple if I were at Eagle Nest.

When we returned to school for the afternoon, Miss Blackerby handed out reading books.

"These are your books for the year," she explained. "Don't write in them. Later in the year, you may take them home. For now, we'll keep them in our desks."

The engine was a real smoker, bellowing cindery, sooty smoke.
Courtesy of the Raton Museum.

She moved her chair to the front of her desk, opened her book, and instructed:

"I know most of you can't read right now. Try to follow along silently, watching the words as I read them. Also, look at the pictures—see?"

She raised the book, pointing to the first page, showing a little boy, a girl, and a small dog. We opened our books to that page. She read aloud:

"See Dick. See Dick run." She held the book high, pointing to the boy pictured running. She turned the page.

"See Jane. See Jane run." Again she raised the book up high, pointing to Jane pictured running. She turned the page.

"See Spot. See Spot run."

She continued with the story.

By two o'clock, I was restless. Sitting at a desk and listening to Miss Blackerby wasn't the same as sitting on the shore of Stubblefield Lake waiting for a catfish to bite, nor was it the same as sitting at Eagle Nest watching the processing and loading of coal into the coal cars. As dismissal time neared, Miss Blackerby had us put our books in our desks. I reached for my Big Chief tablet. It was gone! So was my yellow Number Two pencil! I raised my hand.

"Yes, Matt?"

"Miss Blackerby, I can't find my Big Chief tablet. Or my yellow Number Two pencil."

"Hmm. I'm sure they don't have feet. They can't walk away. Did you look carefully in your desk?" She walked next to my desk and stooped to look into the drawer.

"It's not here! Look for yourself!"

"Oh, goodness! Are you sure you brought it?" She brushed her hand in the drawer, feeling for the tablet and pencil. She found none.

"Oh, yes. Mom gave it to me. She told me to put it in my desk, which I did."

"Did you have your name on it?"

"No."

"Did you mark it somehow, showing it's yours?"

"No."

I looked around. Lots of kids had the same Big Chief tablets and yellow Number Two pencils on their desks. My heart sank into my stomach. Someone had stolen my tablet and pencil. Confused and hurt, I was lost for words.

"You probably left it at home." Miss Blackerby discounted the theft, returning to her desk.

"Line up at the door, boys and girls. Walk out slowly. Don't run down the steps."

Before I recovered from the shock, I found myself in a daze outside the schoolhouse. José greeted me:

"How'd it go, little brother?" José was waiting with Geno and Marian.

"Okay—I guess."

"Hey! Cheer up! School's out! Let's go." José took Marian's hand. Geno and I followed behind. When I got home, I ran into the house, changed clothing, and dashed back outside before Mom could catch me. I didn't want to tell her about the theft. I was ashamed. I moped around the back porch and dawdled aimlessly in the llano. I was tempted to run to Eagle Nest, but time didn't permit. Dad would soon be home for supper.

At suppertime, Mom asked us about school.

"It's going to be my best year!" Angela was effervescent. "I was appointed to be the editor of our yearbook, *The Quill.*"

"¡A, qué bueno!" Mom was pleased.

"I get to write the poem for it, too!"

"This is good," Dad added, "for when you become a teacher."

"Yes," Angela bubbled. "And, I'll save the money I make on Saturdays to go to college."

"I know you will," Mom was clearly pleased. "¿Juan, y tu? *¿Como se fue?*"

"Pretty good. The nuns are good teachers. I'll learn a lot."

"Hey, I brought Matías, Geno, and Marian home—all by myself!" José had to get in a word edgewise.

"Good, good, José." Mom brushed off José, looking at me, smiling, hoping to hear good news:

"Y Matías?"

"I liked it."

"Hey, I heard somebody stole your tablet." José didn't like the brushoff so he rubbed it in. "And your new pencil!"

"Shut up!" I mustered, trying to kick his shins.

"Matías!" Dad scowled. "Watch your language. Show respect."

"I'm sorry, Dad." I tried to act contrite, but I was rankled. "Someone did steal my tablet and pencil."

"Did you tell Miss Blackerby?" Mom inquired. "Sometimes children complain, but they don't stand up for themselves."

"Yes, she didn't do nothing!"

"She didn't do anything," Angela corrected my grammar.

"Yes! She didn't do anything."

"Pues, what could she do? I should've put your name on the tablet."

"Why would someone steal them?"

"Because people are envious."

"Even kids?" I asked naively.

"Especially children! They learn from their parents," Dad explained sympathetically. "We'll get you another and put your name on it. *No tí penas.*"

Still rankled and confused, I wanted to flee into the hills to Eagle Nest.

"Let's finish supper and rest," Dad suggested. "Tomorrow, we have work to do."

"All except Ramona." I was envious. "She doesn't have to go to school."

School settled into a routine of singing, listening, printing, reciting, and recessing. I liked recess the best. We started each day singing "America" and "O, Fair New Mexico" When Miss Blackerby asked volunteers to sing, no one volunteered—other than Marian; she sang "Home on the Range" each time. Eventually, Miss Blackerby changed the routine, asking for Show or Tell stories from home. We really liked this new morning routine. When Geno told about how his Dad made chokecherry wine, some of the boys started acting goofy, hiccupping and pretending to be drunk. Miss Blackerby gave us a stern lecture:

"Imbibing isn't funny. It's not good to drink and get drunk. You boys should never make jokes about it!"

When I told how José shot me in the back with an arrow that had a real Indian arrowhead, the guys wanted to see my scar. They didn't believe the story. For an instant I was a hero again. But Miss Blackerby didn't let me show my scar. Instead, she ordered us to tell true stories only.

"I'll believe Matt," she said, "or any of you, unless your story proves to be untrue." Miss Blackerby paused; a perplexed aura engulfed her face. "What I don't understand is why would anybody go hunting rattlesnakes? That's inviting trouble, seems to me." She furrowed her brow, perplexed about the excitement stirred over my rattlesnake-hunting episode.

"Seems to me, you're courtin' trouble hunting rattlesnakes. It doesn't make good, common sense."

Miss Blackerby surprised us with a really good story about when she first taught in a one-room country school:

"When I first started teaching near Branson, Colorado, I lived in a rickety wooden shack, out in the middle of the prairie. Every day when I got up, I kindled the fire in the stove and crawled back into my cot, waiting for the stove to warm up the shack. When the shack warmed up, I'd get up and dress. Then, I'd draw water from the well and heat it on the stove to wash and fix breakfast.

"Sometimes, I'd spy a rattlesnake curled up around the base of the stove, especially on cold winter mornings. I'd use a hot poker to shoo it out! I'd stand pretty far back, putting an arm's length—and then some—between the poker and the snake!"

Miss Blackerby grabbed the poker from the room's pot-bellied fogón, extending her arm, reaching toward the fogón, pretending a snake slept at its base. Some of us in the back stood up at our desks to see where she was poking.

"Real slow-like, I'd shove the poker toward the snake. It would feel the hot poker coming toward it and slither away, lickety-split! It'd slither through the cracks in the rickety wood floor. The next evening, when the ground outside got cold, and my wood stove was burning nice and cozy, it might slither right back up while I was sleeping. Next mornin,' I'd shoo it out again!"

Spellbound, at the edge of our desks, we waited, anticipating. . . .

"That wasn't so bad. The rattler wasn't going to harm me. He just wanted to keep warm. But outside, it was bad! Really bad! I had to walk two miles to school every day on a dusty path. The path had a lot of rattlesnakes. Half the time, I couldn't see them, they blended with the ground so well. But at nighttime, when there were school functions, I'd have to walk that path when it was pitch dark. There were no electric lamps along the path to light the way, and I didn't have a flashlight. The father of one of the children gave me a small Derringer pistol. It held only three bullets, but it would do the job of killing a rattlesnake. With every step, I courted danger. I might step on a rattlesnake. I walked slow-like, watching my every step. If I happened to step on a rattler, then I'd have to shoot it before it bit me. Needless to say, I've always been leery of rattlesnakes."

"Miss Blackerby," I was dumbstruck, popping up my hand. On cold winter mornings, I used to stand behind the fogón to dress. Imagine stepping on a rattler barefooted!

"Yes, Matt?" Miss Blackerby blinked her eyes. I'd lurched her from a trance. She set down the poker.

"Did you ever get bit by a rattler?"

"Heavens, no! Thank the Lord!"

I was relieved. So were the other kids. For such a good looking and intelligent woman, Miss Blackerby proved to be pretty brave. From that day on, I respected her. After her story, she called for more stories. Yep, more snake stories! But I held back the story about Tío Jesus' pet bullsnake that he kept in the house. Miss Blackerby might think I made it up.

Learning to read was a marvelous journey down a mysterious trail. Each of us had to unravel the mystery and find our own way down the trail. For me, every word was a riddle asking to be solved. *What did it mean?* The word was right there in clear view, its meaning locked in the letters waiting for me to unravel. I quickly learned that together the letters meant something or pointed to something, like the scratchy footprints of birds in snow.

Miss Blackerby used a "see and say" method for teaching vocabulary and spelling. One at a time, she held up cards with a large word printed on them. She'd flash the card, saying the word, asking us to say it.

"Dick."

"Dick!" We'd respond in unison.

"Jane."

"Jane!"

"See."

"See!"

After flashing about ten words, she'd point to sentences on the chalkboard containing the words we had learned to recognize. She'd recite each sentence aloud, pointing to each word as she read. She'd have us repeat the sentence in unison. To check on us, she'd call on us individually to read the sentence. She explained how we should attack a sentence:

"Try to sound out each word in chunks. If you aren't sure, back up and try the word again. Skip the word if it's too hard. Go on to the next word till you finish the sentence."

At first, we stumbled over the trail of words, tripping over short sentences, but we persevered, hobbling down the bumpy trail. Wasn't long and we were reading the sentences vigorously, with confidence and self-assurance. It was fun to read. In a few weeks, she had us reading aloud from our *Dick and Jane* books. Now that I could read the words of the *Dick and Jane* story, I liked it much better.

Arithmetic was like reading, but the numbers were not as mysterious as words. We learned the quantities of the numbers much the same way we learned to read words, by recognizing and memorizing what quantities the figures represented. The numbers were very exact. Words were not and could have more than one meaning. For coal miners, numbers were much better. In the days miners were paid by the tons of coal they dug, numbers were very important. Either a ton of coal was dug or it was not.

The weigh master would weigh each car of coal. A miner had to watch the weigh master carefully to make sure he put down the correct numbers of pounds. At the end of the day, the numbers would show how much coal a miner had dug that day. Dad kept a journal showing how much coal he'd dug each day to predict how much cash he would get on payday. He also kept an accurate account of the amount of scrip we'd used.

Many miners didn't pay attention and before long they owed their souls to the Company store. With the union, a miner's pay was converted to hourly wages. Even though shifts were set at exact times, Dad kept an accurate account of the time he'd worked each day.

"Numbers don't lie," Mom and Dad would both say, "but liars do!" That wasn't a down-home dicho, but it told the truth.

In the first *Dick and Jane* book, we learned that Dick and Jane had fun watching Spot run and play with a ball. Sometimes, Father played with them, showing them how to fly a kite. In the second book, we read how Dick and Jane's family had a newcomer, a sister called Sally. She was about three years old with blond hair and blue eyes. She was cute and reminded me of Ramona, although Ramona had black hair and eyes. Being kind of curious, I raised my hand and asked Miss Blackerby:

"Miss Blackerby, where did Sally come from?"

"Matt, I like the way you raise your hand before speaking out. You're learning to do the right thing." She evaded my question.

"Thank you, Miss Blackerby, but where did Sally come from?"

Everyone got still. Miss Blackerby pursed her lips, bewildered by the question.

"I'm afraid I don't understand your question?"

"You know, in the first *Dick and Jane* book, there were only Father, Mother, and Dick and Jane?

"There was Puff the kitten, too," Marian smugly injected. Marian was just like Angela—full of details!

"And Spot too!" Becky chimed in. She was good at details too.

"This is all correct."

Miss Blackerby still didn't get the drift of my question.

"Well, in the first book," I continued, "and in the second book, Mother wasn't big in the family way, like when my Mom had Ramona."

A bizarre hush swept the room! No one coughed or sneezed or raised their hand. A fly buzzing in the next schoolhouse could've been heard. I sensed a frantic panic beneath Miss Blackerby's calm demeanor, much like the way Dad acted when I asked Mr. Heard why he was so black. The other kids sat absolutely motionless, except Geno, who whispered:

"Holy smokes. Now you're in big trouble—up the creek without a paddle, you dodo!"

Big trouble? I just wanted to know how Sally came to join the family. Down-home it was common for people to adopt and raise children of their relatives as their own.

"Oh, Matt," Miss Blackerby blushed, turning deeper red as she spoke, sputtering, "you should ask your parents such questions."

"Okay, ma'am. Maybe they can figure it out."

Everyone seemed relieved, even Miss Blackerby.

I waited till after supper that evening to ask Mom and Dad. I was confident they would know the answer. After supper, I asked Mom and Dad to sit with me in the living room. I showed them the two reading books. I read the first one to them, emphasizing the different words. They really were impressed.

"¡A, qué niño!" Mom was very pleased I could read all the words.

"But, see here, in the second book, Dick and Jane have a sister, Sally."

Mom and Dad looked over the second book.

"Yes!" Mom added, "I see the family has three children."

"Father must have a pretty good job," Dad added. "He wears a suit all the time, even when he plays with the children." Very few men in Chicorico ever wore suits to work and play.

"Mother wears very nice dresses, and an apron, too!" Mom was enjoying the books.

"But, where did Sally come from?"

Mom and Dad were puzzled. They skimmed through the first book, looking at the pictures. They skimmed the second book, still bewildered about the introduction of a third child.

"¿Quien sabe?" Mom continued, *"posible, era una hija adoptiva?"*

"Yes, maybe she was adopted. Or, perhaps much time has passed between the first book and the second? Hmm?" Dad hunched his shoulder, implying he didn't know the answer either.

Dad and Mom again skimmed the books.

"If much time has passed, no one seems to be older," Mom conjectured. "Why do you ask, Matías?" She turned to me.

"Because when I asked Miss Blackerby, she told me to ask you."

AH-HA! Suddenly a hundred light bulbs flashed over Mom's and Dad's faces! They giggled, placing the book down. Neither said anything. Guess the answer wasn't important. . . .

On a Friday in late September, Miss Blackerby took us to Brilliant to see the large Statue of Liberty in the school's foyer. Since many parents were first-generation immigrants, Miss Blackerby thought we'd enjoy seeing a replica of the statue. Brilliant was another Chicorico coal company camp, once called "Swastika." In the early 1900s, the Company chose the name Swastika Coal and Coke Company, after the Indian swastika meaning "good quality." Turned out, ancient peoples of Africa, America, Asia, and Europe used the swastika to symbolize good. Way before Adolph Hitler adopted it, the Company printed the swastika on business papers, advertisements, and signs; each coal car was emblazoned with a swastika.

For our Brilliant tour, a yellow school bus pulled in front of the first-grade building. We marched out with Miss Blackerby in the lead.

"Now boys and girls," Miss Blackerby laid down the law, lining us up to board the bus, "you may speak with each other—quietly."

After we were all seated, Mr. T. J. Floyd, the owner and bus driver, turned and glared through his sunglasses: "No horsing around! I'll take a strap to you!"

Mr. Floyd was an imposing, rotund man with dark hair and big hands. He wore a wide leather belt and cowboy boots. His son Stan was in our class, sitting behind Geno and me. He whispered:

"Don't turn around. Don't worry. His bark is bigger than his bite." Geno and I felt better, but decided to talk only when necessary.

Brilliant was a lot like Chicorico. As Mr. Floyd drove the bus through Brilliant, he pointed out the Company store, clubhouse, and Brilliant School, a two-story building. Unlike our school, the Brilliant school had playground equipment. I'd never seen, much less played on, a teeter-totter, merry-go-round, giant strides, and jungle bars, but the swings weren't new. In our front yard, we had a tire and rope swinging from the cottonwood. Because there were no kids playing when we arrived, we were allowed to play on the equipment. We settled down to good, honest play, taking turns on it.

After a while, some Brilliant kids arrived. It was their recess time. One kid shoved Geno off the teeter-totter. Geno shoved back, and they wrestled to the ground. The kid held Geno, socking him hard. I wedged between to break them up.

Sock! Someone socked my back. I turned.

Sock! Right on the lip.

"Ouuu-eeee!" I tumbled on my back. Stan jumped to my defense; another kid from Brilliant sprang at him. Not to be left out, Louie joined the brawl—kicking feet, flying fists, whimpering grunts.

"STOP!" Mrs. Marjory Leason, the Brilliant principal, shouted above the hubbub. "IN THE OFFICE!"

Mrs. Leason grabbed Geno and the other kid by their ears. I was flat on my back, lip bleeding. I rolled over, standing. Mrs. Leason marched us into the office. She glared:

"What gives with you boys?"

Geno and the other kid argued:

"You went and shoved me!"

"Did not! You did!"

Other kids chimed in from both sides:

"Did too!"

"Did not!"

"We're getting nowhere! Fighting's no way to settle differences. I want you boys to shake hands and apologize."

"But!" Geno protested.

"No BUTS! We don't settle differences by fighting in my school."

Geno sulked, then swaggered, apologizing to the kid who shoved him, shaking his hand. The kid grinned sheepishly and apologized to Geno. That broke the tension and we all took turns apologizing.

Mrs. Leason ordered Miss Blackerby: "You mete out punishment to your boys when you're back in Chicorico. I'll talk to the teachers of our boys. Go enjoy the rest of the visit."

We shuffled out of the office. Mrs. Leason grasped my chin, "Drop by the nurse, for your lip."

I wasn't keen on seeing the nurse. My lip wasn't bleeding anymore, but I obeyed. The nurse wiped my split lip with alcohol, and I rushed out to catch up with the class. They were in the foyer, inspecting the five-foot Statue of Liberty, standing tall. Miss Blackerby explained:

"This is a likeness of the real Statue of Liberty that stands near Ellis Island in New York Harbor. Only the real statue is thirty times taller than this one, standing 151 feet high. You've seen its picture in our classroom. It was made in France and given to us as a gift for our friendship. It was placed in New York Harbor to welcome newcomers to America, the land of the free and the home of the brave. See how Lady Liberty is stepping from broken chains; her uplifted right hand is holding the torch of freedom, and her left hand is holding the Declaration of Independence."

"My Mom and Dad," Sava explained, "saw the Statue of Liberty when they came from Yugoslavia."

"Really?" Miss Blackerby asked, "What about others?" A lot of the kids raised their hands. I didn't.

"Matt, what about you?"

"My Dad said we weren't immigrants to America. We lived here, and America came to us."

"Oh." Both Miss Blackerby and the other kids just looked at me with a blank stare.

I was uncomfortable—always the oddball. I should just keep my mouth shut. To relieve my discomfort, I asked,

"Miss Blackerby, please read *that* on the statue."

"Certainly, it's a poem by Emma Lazarus. She was a poetess in New York City."

She read loud and clear for us to hear:

"Give me your tired, your poor
Your huddled masses yearning to breathe free. . . ."

12

YO SOY LA LLORONA

Clouds rolled over the Raton mesas and snowed on Chicorico. The piñón and spruce trees sagged under the snow's heavy weight, and branches of the cottonwoods splintered from their trunks. For a few days, a calm fell over Chicorico. Yards, meadows, hillsides, and the school playground were carpeted white. Only Chicorico Creek, the railroad tracks, and main road stood in stark contrast. The snow did not last. Within a week, the snow melted and Chicorico returned to dry normalcy.

"Soon we'll go for piñón," Dad announced.

During the summer, José had scoured the hillsides, looking for the piñón trees. On a mid-October Sunday afternoon, Dad and Mr. Heard took us piñón picking.

"Matías!" Dad decreed as we hiked up the hillside. "Watch out for Ramona."

"Ah, Dad!"

"That's okay," José encouraged me, "I used to watch you. It's your turn now."

That made me feel better—big brother in charge of little sister. I took Ramona's hand. She put her soft little hand in mine. Marian took her other hand.

"Weee!" Ramona liked being tugged when we boosted her over parts of the rocky trail.

"Keep a lookout for rattlers!"

"Huh?" Marian was frightened.

"Nah! Don't worry." José overheard my comment. "They're under rocks, where nobody'll bother 'em. But watch out for yellow-bellied horny toads."

"What about yellow-bellied horny toads?"

José warned again: "When you see one, shut your mouth. You'll die if it counts your teeth!"

"Ü-ü-ü!" Ramona cried, "I don't want to die!"

"José!" Dad chided. "Comfort Ramona."

"Don't worry," I hugged Ramona. "I'll take care of you."

"Yeah!" Marian patted Ramona's back, "José's just trying to scare us."

Ramona wiped the tears from her eyes and took our hands, and we continued. Ramona, a sweet, gentle girl with a broad smile and twinkles in her eyes, was a lot like Mom. Whenever Dad did things with us boys, she always wanted to join us.

Picking piñón was harder than picking chokecherries. Chokecherries grow in clumps. When they were ripe, we could pluck the clumps from their branches. Piñón nuts have to be coaxed from the tree. José took us to a tree ready for harvest. He and Juan laid a white sheet beneath the tree. Dad and Mr. Heard got on opposite sides of the tree, grabbed a branch, and swayed the tree back and forth. Gobs of piñón nuts tumbled onto the sheet. We knelt around the sheet, picked the piñóns, and dropped them into our bags. We repeated the procedure with each tree till our bags were full.

We headed home with more work to do. At home, Juan and José placed the piñóns in a cajete and poured hot water over the nuts to sterilize them just in case a bird had pooped on any of them. The piñóns sank to the bottom. Some dead bugs and twigs rose to the top of the water. The guys picked out any bugs, rocks, or twigs, throwing them away; there weren't very many. They drained the water and then spilled the nuts onto large cookie sheets. Mom slid the brimming sheets of piñóns into the oven. In about five minutes, Mom removed the cookie sheet and stirred the piñón seeds. She put them back in the oven.

After about ten minutes or so, she removed the nuts from the oven. The guys filled another cookie sheet, repeating the process. Again, like baking bread, Mom timed the roasting instinctively, lightly feeling and then smelling the piñóns as they roasted. Over-roasted piñóns taste like charcoal. Perfectly roasted, they taste exquisitely yeasty. By the time Mom had baked all the nuts, a pervasive, yeasty odor of piñón whiffed through the kitchen.

Mom and Dad didn't ration the piñóns. We could eat all we wanted. Nevertheless, the rules were strict. We couldn't eat them shells and all. Some kids would throw a gob of the nuts in their mouths, crunching the shells, blending the crushed shells with the pine nuts, swallowing them shells and all. We were told the broken shells could lodge in our appendix, causing it to burst. So we had to shell them, one at a time, by cracking each one between our teeth. Another rule: when done shelling and eating, we were to discard the shells in the wastebasket. If we left the shells lying around, we lost the privilege of eating piñóns.

Juan and José liked to sit on the back porch with a gob of piñóns in their mouths. They'd crack one at a time, jamming the shells to one side of the mouth, the nuts on the other side. Then they'd spit out the shells, scattering the husks onto the ground. Juan and José seemed to have forked tongues, going by the way they spit out the shells and held onto the piñón nuts. I couldn't do both—hold the nuts in my mouth and spit out the shells.

I loved to crack one nut at a time, feeling the shell cracking between my front teeth. I'd remove the cracked shell from my mouth, wedge the nut open with my fingernails, drop the seed into a cup, and discard the shell. I'd repeat the procedure till I had ten or eleven shelled nuts. Then, I'd raise the cup to my lips and slowly drip the nuts into my mouth, sucking on them to taste the yeasty, oily secretions of the piñón. With my tongue, I'd press the piñóns onto my palate, and then slosh the nuts over and around my tongue to embellish the full-bodied texture and taste of the piñón gob. Finally, I'd swallow—another divine taste of heaven on earth, like chokecherry jelly on Mom's homemade bread.

Like Mom would say, "No hay mal pan con bien hambre," or food tastes a lot better when you don't have very much. To us, Mom's home-baked bread and tortillas, her chokecherry jelly, and her roasted piñóns were delectable, delicious treats in a time of scarcity. Like many other foods in October of 1944, candies and nuts were rarely found on store shelves. A bag of ordinary, salted peanuts was hard to find, and when one was available, it cost a whole nickel; money was just as scarce. Besides, the piñóns were free for the picking—Mother Nature's gift to anyone who took the time to pick them. Besides, gathering piñóns took me back to the hills again, where I belonged along with the creepy, crawly critters, even if, at times, I was a little leery of them.

Each day school became more enjoyable, especially when we were given maps showing current events in the world. Miss Blackerby had us take the maps home so our families could locate their countries of origin. We could also show where in the world our brothers or sisters in the armed services were at the time. In class, we shared this geographic information. Sava's family was from Yugoslavia. It was under the control of the Germans. Mr. and Mrs. Vuicich were worried about their brothers and sisters. Many of them still lived in Yugoslavia. Ever since Germany took over the country, letters from their relatives had quit coming to Chicorico. Mr. Vuicich feared for their lives.

Geno's parents were from Sicily, which is an island at the toe of Italy. We discovered Italy was shaped like a big cowboy boot. Mr. Chicarelli told Geno to tell the class that people from the island of Sicily "got the boot" from Italy. Geno explained his Dad was joking about how Sicily got kicked by the boot of Italy. I thought that was a pretty funny joke! Most of the other kids didn't get it, but then, I knew Mr. Chicarelli's wry sense of humor. We were disappointed to find out that Italy's leader, Mussolini, sided with the Germans, so the United States army was invading Italy. Mr. Chicarelli was glad. He didn't like Mussolini.

I was disappointed to find out our country of origin, Spain, was ruled by a general who sided with Germany. I showed everyone where Arturo was in the Pacific—the island of Guam. But his letters were censored. Many of the words were cut out with scissors so we barely got any news of his whereabouts, except he was feeling okay. Mostly he flew supplies to different bases on various islands so I assumed he didn't go on bombing missions.

Marian showed us the coast of Africa and told how her people were brought to the New World as slaves:

"Negro people were brought to America as slaves. Most were kidnapped from the western coast of Africa. After the Civil War, our relatives went to West Virginia where many of them still live. My brother, Eddie, is in France right now. He's an army truck driver delivering supplies to the fighting soldiers. He drives in a long caravan of trucks called the Red Ball Express. He has a partner. They take turns driving the truck night and day, stopping only for gas. They eat and sleep in the truck. When he gets to the front, he leaves off the supplies, and then drives back for more. There's hundreds of trucks driving night and day to keep the supplies moving to where they're needed."

"My, you certainly know a lot about your brother." Miss Blackerby was surprised.

"Mama said the army wants people to know our soldiers are doing good, so they let the letters go through."

The next day as we were picking up the messes we'd made from finger painting, Miss Blackerby gave us a slip of paper to take home to show our parents.

"Boys and girls, when you've cleaned your desk, come get this paper. This slip of paper is very important. You must bring it back tomorrow, after your parents sign it."

"Oh, no!" I thought. "Here we go again. This time it's a note to our parents. They have to sign it. We're in trouble for something!" Somewhere I'd heard about this. The teacher keeps it a secret, sending notes we can't read to our parents. They have to sign the note to prove we gave it to them. I decided to take a chance and ask Miss Blackerby, but instead of asking her in class where her answer might embarrass us,

I waited till she dismissed us from school. After all the kids left the room, I approached her:

"Miss Blackerby, I hope we're not all flunking first grade." I decided to be indirect as a way to find out what the note's big secret was all about.

"My land! Matt, where did you get that idea?"

"Well, are we?"

"You're all doing fine. You kids are full of curiosity and eager to learn!"

"Hmm," I thought, "maybe she's afraid she might hurt my feelings." I persisted:

"No, really, I won't mind. You can tell me!"

"Matt, I just don't understand!"

She appeared to be sincerely perplexed. To me, it was obvious. She was sending an important note home to our parents. Something was amiss. I could tell my indirect approach wasn't working. I decided to take a chance with my direct style for asking questions—a style I had been criticized for using:

"What's so important about this piece of paper?" I wagged the paper in her face.

"He-he-he-he-he!" Miss Blackerby giggled, "That's what put the idea in your head. Well, the note's about getting shots."

"Shots? Dynamite? Whiskey?"

"No, no, Matt." Miss Blackerby giggled again. "Tomorrow, Dr. Monty and his wife will be here to give all of you vaccinations."

"Whatever that is? It can't be so serious to tell our parents!"

"Oh, yes it is! Shots and vaccinations protect you from childhood diseases, like measles and smallpox. They'll hurt a little bit, but that's better than dying! Now, I've said enough. Take the note to your parents . . . have them sign so Dr. Monty can give you shots tomorrow."

I was silent. The way Miss Blackerby ordered me to get my parents to sign the slip of paper, it sounded like a done deal. Of course, I was unaware of the seriousness of childhood diseases and how they used to kill many children in the coal camps.

"Okay, ma'am. Bueno-bye!" I folded the note, put it in my pocket, and left the classroom.

"Goodbye to you, too. Don't lose that note!"

As soon as I got home, I showed Mom the note. She read it, found a pencil, and immediately signed it without hesitation. She had lost three children in infancy. She didn't want to lose another in early childhood. She explained:

"The shots will hurt a little. But this is a good thing. Tomorrow, you give it to Miss Blackerby." She placed the paper on her bedroom dresser.

I went outside to check on the chickens. Every day after school I'd been putting chicken feed in their trough. As I poured the chicken feed into the trough, the hens pounced upon it, pecking every which way as though they'd never eaten. Going by the way they pecked so furiously, they would have eaten the trough—if it weren't made of tin! The rooster, on the other hand, ate alone. He expected the feed piled in his corner of the henhouse.

As the hens frenetically feasted on the feed, I put chicken feed for the chicks in a smaller trough I'd constructed out of some old boards. They just couldn't compete with the hens, and would never eat if they had to eat out of the same trough as the hens. By now, though, the chicks were pretty big. It wouldn't be too long before they could hold their own against the older hens. I was pleased to see how they'd grown since I brought them home in June.

Next day after breakfast, Mom neatly folded the medical-release note and tucked it in my pocket.

"Don't take the note from your pocket till you give it to Miss Blackerby." Mom winked and ruffled my hair.

When I got to school, Miss Blackerby asked me for the note. Proud as can be, I whipped the note out of my pocket and handed it to her. Without even checking to see if it had been signed, she plopped it in a pile of notes and turned to the whole class:

"Boys and girls, stay standing after we sing. We're marching to Mrs. Hilliard's house for our shots."

"Ou-ee!"

"Ü-ü-ü!"

"Yi-e-e!"

A rumbling of grumbles tumbled through the room. The kids weren't exactly ecstatic about getting their shots. I was pretty saucy, thinking "what a bunch of sissies!" They'd never been shot with an arrow! Of course, they didn't know that I really yelped when José shot me or how much the Novocain had stung. Today "America" and "O, Fair New Mexico" were pretty puny renditions. Miss Blackerby marched us out of the schoolhouse.

"It's just shots," I told Geno as we walked over to Mrs. Hilliard's house where Dr. Monty and his wife were waiting. "What can it hurt?"

"Oh be quiet, you dodo!" Geno was in a sullen mood and didn't want to talk very much.

Geno and I were about in the middle of the line of first graders. We lined up single file. As Geno and I got close to the front door, we could hear some of our classmates weeping as they pulled up their sleeves. When I stepped into the front room, I was overcome by the spirited aroma of alcohol and the muffled whimpers of my classmates. When my turn came, Mrs. Monty told me to pull my sleeve over my shoulder. As I tugged the sleeve, she used a cotton pad to dab alcohol on my upper arm.

"Hi there, pistol!" Dr. Monty addressed me. "How you doing?"

"Ouch!" Just as I went to answer, he pricked my arm with a needle, and I whined, "That hurt." Any hope of being a hero was fading fast.

"Now," Dr. Monty directed me, "turn around so I can vaccinate your other arm."

"What? Did you miss the first time?"

"Haw!" Dr. Monty laughed loudly. "No. The first one was for measles. This one's only a scratch—to give you smallpox."

"Huh?" I recoiled—a doctor giving smallpox didn't sound right.

"Matías, a little bit of smallpox is good for you. It makes you immune from a big dose of smallpox."

I wasn't sure what Dr. Monty meant, but given how readily Mom had signed the note I took home last night, and the confidence Dr. Monty placed in the shots, I didn't question any further. Besides, discussing the shots made me queasier.

"You might have a little scar on your arm, unless you don't react to the shot. Never mind, the little pick is worth it," Mrs. Monty assured me.

I joined the other kids outside the back door. When everyone had their shots, Miss Blackerby marched us back to the schoolhouse. Once inside, she had us put our heads on the desk. I rested my queasy head on my hands. A faint odor of alcohol perfumed the room. I dozed, dreaming of Eagle Nest and the time I spotted a grackle harassing a raven over Chicorico Canyon.

The raven had just caught a rodent and was speedily flying across the canyon. The grackle tormented the raven by swooping down and around it several times, swooping dangerously near. When the raven ignored the grackle, the grackle swiftly dived toward the raven—a kamikaze plane heading for the kill! The grackle struck the raven in the back—feathers flew off the raven's back! It floundered, plummeting, plunging toward the ground. The grackle swooped below, slightly in front of the raven, then rose swiftly and pounded the raven in the belly just below the breast, knocking the raven to the side. The raven dropped the rodent and hurriedly flew away, hiding in a ponderosa.

"Ding-a-ling! Ding-a-ling!"

Miss Blackerby's bell jolted me out of slumber. I think a lot of us fell asleep because other kids were stretching and yawning. She directed us:

"Go out and play a while. Get plenty of exercise! To wake up!"

By the middle of October, thoughts about Halloween caused us to forget about the smells of alcohol, the stings of needles, and the scars of vaccines. Our thoughts turned to ghosts, goblins, and great times trick-or-treating. Halloween could get rough in Chicorico. Some Halloweens the older guys really made a mess. While the younger kids were making the rounds trick-or-treating, some of the older guys snuck around smearing soap on windows and screen doors and splattering crude, blue hieroglyphics on outhouses. Once, Mrs. Heard made the mistake of leaving her wash on the clothesline. Mostly it was Mr. Heard's long johns, the cotton underwear miners wore when it was cold in the mine. The guys tied up the long johns so the legs were attached, like connected paper dolls. When they dried up, they were very hard to untie.

The roughest and stinkiest thing they did last Halloween was tip over outhouses. While the younger kids were running around trick-or-treating in sheets, hobo clothes, cowboy outfits, and pirate eye patches, the guys were sneaking around doing their mischief. Usually, the outhouses in the backyards sat pretty far from the houses. The rectangular, frame sheds were made of Number Three pine, a scrub wood full of knotholes. A few fancy outhouses had pitched roofs that sloped back and down so the rain and snow could wash off. Often, a stovepipe was stuck in a round hole in the roof for ventilation. The door was usually in front.

Inside was the potty, a two-foot-high bench with a hole in the middle of it; the bench extended the full width of the outhouse. Fancy benches had two holes, a bigger hole for adults and a smaller hole for kids. Most had only one. We smaller kids had to pull off our pants and shorts, pushing them down around our ankles, and climb up on the bench, our feet dangling over the edge. In the winters, the outhouses were cold and drafty. Snow would drift through the cracks, powdering the floor. In the summer, they were hot, smelly, and full of flies.

Outhouse sittings were short, except for certain idyllic times of the season. Then I could scrutinize the old Montgomery Ward catalogs Juan placed there. José teased that I used the pages of the catalog for toilet paper. I don't remember doing that! I do remember seeing all kinds of curious things, such as a lawn mower with little blades that cut as they circled. I remember thinking about how lawn mowers were impractical because it would take a long time for a farmer to mow a hay field with such small mowers! And I liked looking at the pictures of the classy bikes. There were all kinds, even ones with a gasoline motor. These were motor bikes—not motorcycles.

Anyway, last Halloween, Mr. Malcolm's outhouse was tipped over with Mrs. Malcolm in it! The guys tipped the outhouse from the back, knocking it over with the door to the ground. Poor Mrs. Malcolm couldn't get out.

"Hello! He-looo! He-looo!" She yelled and yelled till Mr. Malcolm finally heard her. He came next door to our house and got Dad to help tip the outhouse upright.

"Just sit tight, Mary!" Mr. Malcolm advised her.

"What do you mean? I can't sit or stand or anything! Get me out of here," she pleaded as her voice quivered.

The two men struggled to hoist the outhouse upright. It was extraordinarily heavy, and while the two men were accustomed to lifting heavy objects, they didn't want to lift the outhouse too abruptly. Boy, was Mrs. Malcolm frightened! And Mr. Malcolm was really angry. When Mr. Malcolm and Dad realized that Mrs. Malcolm could've been hurt, they concluded they needed to do something about the vandalism.

To prevent vandalism this Halloween, Dad called a meeting of some of the neighbors in our kitchen. They couldn't see me hiding behind the Mom's cooking fogón while they tried to figure out a way to put a stop to the Halloween vandalism.

"Some of the boys go too far!" Mr. Heard complained. "We should just keep our kids home. Don't let them go out for Halloween." That was easy for him to say. He didn't have any big kids at home.

At first, this sounded good, till Mr. Malcolm—who had two bigger boys at home—reckoned, "Boys will be boys. We used to do much the same mischief when we was boys. Better yet, we have to figure a way to scare the bejeezus out of them!"

"Oh, yeah."

"Sure."

"But how?" They muttered among each other, some saying they never did such things.

Mom had an idea:

"Dress up like La Llorona and scare the boys at night when they go out to the toilet."

La Llorona is a legendary Mexican character who drowned her kids in the river to please her lover. When she died, God wouldn't let her into Heaven until she found the souls of the kids. So she searches for stray kids and kidnaps them, taking them to God, claiming these are the souls of her kids. All of us kids, even the ones who weren't Mexican, feared La Llorona. She would kidnap you without compunction!

The minute Mom suggested the idea, she knew she had to be La

Llorona. For a costume, Mom borrowed a pattern from Sister Mary Caramel at St. Patrick's Academy. Mom made a nun's habit. It was entirely black. Mom's face was shrouded by the hood so you barely could see her face. She stood long and tall and looked very eerie in her La Llorona shroud. Dad suggested a chant in Spanish, coaching her to elongate the vowels for an eerie, sorrowful effect:

Waa-ee-ee-ee-ee-ee-ee-ee
Yo soy la Llorona
Y vengo por ti-iiiiiiiiiiiiiiiiiiiiii

Mom—also known as La Llorona—started to show up at night about a month before Halloween. She'd wait until one of the older guys went to the outhouse. Our dads made us go to the toilet before we went to bed so we wouldn't get up late at night to use the pot in the house. By morning, it stunk and was used only for emergencies.

La Llorona would sneak up to the side of the outhouse, rap lightly on the wood panels, and then say softly while elongating the vowels:

Waa-ee-e-e-e-e-e-e
Yo soy la Llorona
Y vengo por ti-iiiiiiiiiiiiiiiiiiiiii

Then she'd walk in front of the outhouse and slip away into the dark of the night. There were no street lamps in Chicorico. The guys making toilet would peek out of the door and see a long, tall phantom, draped in a flowing black gown, drifting away into the dark, apparently floating rather than moving across the ground.

¡Yo soy La Llorona! The closer to Halloween, the more the La Llorona sightings, and the word spread fast and furious among the older guys in Chicorico. Like experienced fire bosses, they presumed to be cool and calm, but when alone they spoke of the impending doom. This was a gas-filled mine waiting to explode! They would laugh feebly and warn all us littler kids to watch out. La Llorona would get us!

Juan was not convinced. Now that he was in the ninth grade, beliefs in La Llorona were for little kids, so he scoffed:

"Sssssss! There's no such thing as ghosts!" Juan acted cocky. "They're just in your imagination!" But the other guys weren't so sure. Mom knew that Juan must be convinced. He was a ringleader. Though they were afraid, many of the guys would follow his lead. Mom talked the situation over with Dad. They hatched a plan to scare Juan.

October 28th, 1944—the Saturday night just before Halloween—La Llorona made her strike! On Saturday nights, my Dad allowed Juan and José to stay up late to listen to the radio. About 11:00 P.M., Dad made them go to the outhouse. Juan and José went out together, but our outhouse had only one hole in the bench so they had to take turns. Juan said:

"I'm going first. José, you stay outside! Watch out for La Llorona! Haah!"

José didn't laugh—no joking about La Llorona. José stood outside the door while Juan pulled his pants and shorts down to his ankles to sit on the potty.

A soft rapping . . . tapping on the outhouse's east side.

RAP——RAP—

"Quit that, José!" Juan shouted at José. "You're just trying to scare me!"

RAP——RAP—

José was speechless, frightened out of his wits, and afraid to look behind the outhouse. Juan could hear José sucking in his breath. Above the sucking sound of José's breath, they heard:

Waa-ee-eeeeeeeeeeeeeeeeee
Yo soy la Llorona
Y vengo por ti-iiiiiiiiiiiiiiiiiiiii

"José! For crying out loud, quit horsing around!"

No answer—nada. When José heard La Llorona the second time, he didn't waste any time high-tailing it back to the house.

"José, I know it's you! Just trying to scare me! But I'm not afraid—"

Cre-e-e-e-e-k! The outhouse door creaked as La Llorona pulled it open, poking her hooded head into the doorway.

Cr-e-e-e-e-e-k—the door opened wider, hinges screeching. La Llorona loomed over Juan. Caught with his pants off!

José's plaintive, barely audible warning came from the kitchen door:

"Juan. I'm in the kitchen! I can see! It's La Llorona, really! Run for it!"

José's distant warning made Juan realize he was alone on this chilly October night! Surprisingly, he was sweating because he was in the worst possible place. There they were—La Llorona, a dark, gloomy, faceless shroud, cloaked in black, hovering over Juan and blocking the door—and Juan sitting in the outhouse with his pants and shorts down around his ankles.

In a desperate attempt to escape, Juan abruptly lunged toward La Llorona as though he was trying to tackle her. She stepped aside. He grabbed a handful of thin air and empty cloth!

"Egad! Yikes!" he thought. "It's true! La Llorona doesn't have any feet. She floats like a ghost!" Juan kept on lunging, catapulting away from the outhouse by pushing back with his toes. Stumbling, he landed on his chest, got up, and tried to beeline toward the house. He tripped and fell, hobbled at the ankles by his pants and shorts. He tripped and fell! Tripped and fell, hopping toward the house, his pants and shorts down around his ankles! La Llorona kept floating toward him. He stood up, and like a jack rabbit with one good leg, he hopped up and down with his shorts and pants still twisted around his ankles. He hopped and jumped till he got onto the porch.

José opened the kitchen door a crack wider, stuck out his arm, and pulled Juan through the door into the house just as La Llorona disappeared on the dark side of the house. Juan's pants and shorts were still tightly tangled around his ankles. Juan struggled to gain his composure, claiming:

"I'm not scared! But, don't tell nobody!" He huffed and puffed, out of breath. He made José pledge not to tell, as he untangled the shorts and pants and pulled them up around his waist:

"Don't tell nobody! And, I'm not scared! Don't tell nobody!"

For a guy who wasn't scared, he sure sounded frightened!

"I won't tell nobody," José pledged; he'd been frightened, too. "Cross my heart and hope to die."

Although there was little talk of it at home, somehow the word got around. Juan almost bought the ranch. La Llorona almost got him. Of course, Juan didn't know I saw the whole thing and didn't make a pledge of silence. At school, all the kids wanted to hear my version of Juan's near miss with La Llorona. Geno heard me telling the episode to so many kids, he started bragging how he saw the whole thing. The kids wanted to know his version. He stayed close to my version, but he added a twist:

"When La Llorona opened the door," Geno added, "a big gust of wind almost blew her away. She held onto the door with one hand. Juan saw she didn't have any legs or feet. She was all air—like a ghost! She talked spooky-like:

Wa-a-a-a-a-e-e-e-e-e-o-o-o-o-o-o-o-o-o-o-o-o-o-o-o-o-o-o

"That's when Juan tore out of the outhouse, tripping over his pants and shorts all the way to the house, when José pulled him in!"

Halloween came the next Tuesday night—only three nights after Juan's escapade with La Llorona. Most of the other older guys volunteered to trick-or-treat with us smaller kids, "just in case La Llorona comes around." That night we got plenty of apples, piñón nuts, and dried fruit. Not a single outhouse was tipped.

13

DE LA MUERTE Y DE LA SUERTE NO HAY QUIEN SE ESCAPE

November brought good news from the war fronts. In the Pacific, American forces had retaken the Philippines. Arturo's letter from Guam reflected the optimism of our forces on the move. Lucky for us, he was still flying supplies behind the front lines. In Europe, Germany was pinched in a vise between Allied forces from the west and Soviet forces from the east. German armies were in hasty retreat from both directions. Eddie Heard's letters, like Arturo's, reflected the optimism of eventual victory.

Eddie sent a photograph of himself in uniform with two French women by the Arc de Triomphe in Paris. The women were waving small American flags, sitting on the truck's front fenders. Eddie sat on the hood. He marked the photo "Paris, August 25, 1944," the day the Allies marched into Paris.

For me in November, life looked pretty good. Dad was training on a Continuous Miner rather than being displaced by it. For him, there would be no more drudgery of undercutting, boring, and blasting coal.

The machine would do most of the work. Professional shooters would assume the high-risk task of setting charges and dynamiting coal.

On Thanksgiving morning, Mom gave us a man's job—kill, pluck, and gut a chicken to bake for Thanksgiving dinner. Juan was in charge.

"Sharpen the *hacha*," Dad directed, "so you'll make one clean chop to her neck. Don't torture the hen with a blunt hacha that requires many more chops."

José located the hatchet and metal file. Juan held the hatchet on the step of the back porch while José sharpened the blade. After filing for a while, José raised the hatchet: "Looka here!" He pretended to pluck a hair from his scalp, dropping the imaginary hair over the blade. "See! The hair split in half."

"¡Wat-chá-le!" Juan yelped. "It's sharp."

When they finished sharpening the hatchet, Juan joked: "Let's chop off the heads of the chicks. They're easier to catch. They're suckers for Matías—the way they come running to him. He can catch them!"

"Hey! No fair! They're just babies!"

"At ease, disease!" José quipped.

"There's malaria in the area!" Then Juan got serious. "When we get to the henhouse, I'll distract the rooster. José, remember the brown hen?"

"Yeah, Mrs. Brown!"

"You grab her while I'm distracting the rooster. Matías, you hold the gate closed. Open when José comes out with her, and after I'm out, you lock the gate."

Juan distracted the rooster by trailing chicken feed in a line away from the henhouse. The rooster started pecking, following the chicken feed trail to one corner. In the meantime, José sneaked into the henhouse and grabbed Mrs. Brown.

"Pawk! Pawk!" She squawked erratically! The rooster darted toward José. Juan tripped the rooster and ran through the gate behind José. I slammed the gate, the rooster angrily protesting *"Pok-ta-pok! Pok-ta-pok!"*

Mrs. Brown calmed down. She knew us and was no longer startled. José had gathered her eggs when Juan had not. I had fed her most of the summer. She didn't suspect her caretakers were about to execute her. José held her by the legs, head hanging. She peered up at José, craning her neck, calmly cackling "*Paw-aw-aw-aw-aw-awk.*"

She trusted us unquestionably. She didn't know to be afraid. She didn't struggle, protest, or attempt to escape. José cradled her in his arms and stroked her small crown, speaking in a fake falsetto:

"Mrs. Brown, I wish I had a pretty feather coat like you!" He patted Mrs. Brown's feathers, sliding his palm lightly down her wings. "Such a pretty coat. My favorite color!" José could've thawed an iceberg with his soothing falsetto.

Mrs. Brown was very calm and relaxed although a bit baffled by the sudden attention. Innocent of her impending fate, she didn't realize her head would soon be chopped off. Naïvely, Mrs. Brown appeared to be asking José to explain what was happening to her.

I was starting to feel sick.

"We're gonna chop your head off!" Juan accommodated her curiosity. "Don't worry, you won't know what happens!" Juan gently placed Mrs. Brown's head on the stump, sliding his fingers down her neck. He positioned her neck. Mrs. Brown complied, readily laying her head on the stump. José deftly slid his fingers out of the way, down to her feet again.

"Stop!"

I couldn't take it. This hen was once a chick, like the ones I'd raised during the summer. We ate her eggs. For Easter, we boiled and colored her eggs! She was always generous. Now, we were going to kill her.

"You can't kill Mrs. Brown!"

"Are you a man or a mouse?" Juan bluntly challenged my manhood.

"Matías, Mrs. Brown hardly lays any eggs." José tried to be conciliatory. "Mom told us to kill the one that lays the least eggs."

"I don't like it. This is murder."

"Mrs. Brown's not a *real* person!"

"It's *still* murder."

"So is war!" Juan injected. "Let's finish the job."

"Yeah," José agreed, "take her out of her misery."

Juan again positioned Mrs. Brown's head and neck on the stump. Her wings flopped, drooping to the sides. She was totally calm. Whatever our game was, she relaxed. With naïve, trusting eyes, she gazed at her executioners, including me who had just fed her that morning. My stomach tightened. Juan raised the hatchet—Whack! A swift, definitive stroke, the severed neck and head tottered on the stump, tongue dangling to one side of the beak, eyes wide open, peering. . . .

Alarmed at the sight of her open eyes, Juan flinched, releasing Mrs. Brown. She fell to the ground, landing on her feet. Erratically she sprinted around the backyard without her head, blood spurting out of her neck. She bumped into the outhouse, bounced off it, and ran the opposite direction, bumping into the coal shed. José and Juan laughed raucously as she skittered about without her head.

"Boys! Stop that chicken!" Dad hollered sternly from the back porch. "You're torturing her!"

José and Juan stopped laughing. They chased down Mrs. Brown. She finally collapsed in Dad's garden patch. I was mortified. My brothers had killed Mrs. Brown and callously laughed as she randomly ran and bumped her way around the yard. Blood was spurting everywhere, gushing out of her neck! I felt wretched and dirty inside. I was a part of a conspiracy that tortured a living creature, a hen that had given freely of her eggs, asking nothing more than a nest to lay and feed to eat. Now, with one sharp chop of the hatchet, she had given her life so we could eat—and my brothers laughed, mocking her generosity as she ran frantically toward her death.

"Bring her here—pronto!" Dad was livid. "Pluck it—after you dunk her in the water!" Dad slammed a bucket of boiling water on the back porch, glaring at the guys.

Lifting the hen by the legs, Juan dunked her in the steaming water. The steam emitting from her body smelled putrid. She was dead, though a few nerves still twitched. José held the hen while Juan plucked, tossing feathers on the ground. The feathers were wet, but felt silky. They had little beads of water on them and no longer smelled putrid.

"Get Dad's knife," Juan ordered me, afraid to ask Dad himself. After Dad had spied the guys raucously laughing at Mrs. Brown running around the yard, he stayed on the back porch to keep an eye on them. Dad was none too happy with the way they had treated Mrs. Brown. I walked over to Dad with my head hanging low, asking him for the knife. Dad could tell I was distressed. We had just killed a living creature. We scorned her. Now, we planned to eat her.

"Hito, everything we eat was once alive." Dad offered condolences. "Even the onions we planted this spring."

To me, there was a vast difference between onions and Mrs. Brown. I knew her as a chick. I had watched her fend for herself for the feed I put out. I had come to admire her spunk. She didn't let the other chickens push her around.

Dad could tell I was in pain. He put his hand on my shoulder, trying to console me. "Still, it's no fun killing a chicken." Dad patted my back sympathetically, handing me his pocketknife.

I gave the knife to Juan. He opened it and cut into Mrs. Brown's soft underside, much like gutting catfish. He pulled out her steaming entrails, cutting them loose and tossing them in the bucket of water.

"Here! Give these to Mom." He handed me the liver, heart, and gizzard.

I reeled back! Jerking my hands away, I poked my fists into my pockets.

"Hey! Are you a man or a mouse?" Juan had a way of making me angry by challenging my manhood. I extended one hand.

"You need two hands!" He jerked my pocketed hand, pulling it out, plopping the heart, liver, and gizzard into my hands. The organs were warm and wet. "Now, hurry! Go!"

Dad opened the screen door, letting me into the kitchen. Mom motioned to a bowl of cold water on the kitchen table. I placed them into the bowl. Outside, Dad took the plucked and gutted Mrs. Brown to the stump. He grasped her by the neck and chopped off her feet. As he carried her into the house, he ordered:

"Bury the hen's remains on the side of the hill beyond the llano."

"Even the head?" Juan asked, laughing.

"O, sí!" Dad exclaimed. "But don't enjoy it so much. Show respect! You have killed a living creature so we may eat."

Juan found Mrs. Brown's head and feet, putting them in the bucket. I pitched the excess feathers into the bucket also. Juan and José carried the bucket. I carried the spade, crossed the llano, and followed the guys as they searched for a good burial spot. A chill ran down my back. I shuddered, thinking, "Someday my little chicks will be our supper!"

Dad made us wash and dress up for Thanksgiving dinner. We washed our hands and face, and combed our hair. When we went into the bedroom to dress up, I was still bothered by the execution of Mrs. Brown and couldn't believe Juan and José were going to actually eat pieces of her.

"Are you guys really going to eat Mrs. Brown?"

"Yeah."

"Sure, why not?"

"That makes you no better than a cani—, uh cani—, uh can-o-bull!"

"Haah!" Juan laughed. "You mean a 'cannibal.'"

"Yeah, a can-o-bull!"

"Su-u-un!" Juan exclaimed, "If eating Mrs. Brown makes us a cannibal, what do you think about eating her babies every morning?"

"Eating her babies? I'd never do that!"

Juan and José chuckled.

"What do you think eggs are?"

"Huh? They're not babies."

"Sure they are. Where do you think your precious little chicks come from?"

"Oh."

Mom called us to dinner. She had prepared a wonderful fare of freshly baked bread, corn, peas, and sweet potatoes for dessert—and yes, baked chicken. We could have milk or water. I chose water. Dad led the blessing, giving thanks for the health of our families and safety of Arturo and Eddie Heard:

"*Gracias a Dios para esta comida; gracias a Dios para la buena salud de mi familia; gracias a Dios para la salud de Jesús, Baltazar, Feliz, y los jóvenes; gracias a Dios para la seguridad de Arturo y Eddie Heard. Amén.*"

Dad led us in prayer to the Virgin Mary: "*Dios te salve, Maria, Madre de Dios. . . .*" After a decade of Hail Marys to end the blessing, we feasted.

The former laying hen now lay dead on our kitchen table. I hadn't forgotten my anguish over Mrs. Brown and was determined not to eat her. Dad carved the hen and served everyone. He started with Mom, then Angela, and so on. When my turn came, I told him I didn't want any.

"Here, try these crispy chicken wings." Dad placed the wings on my plate.

The aroma was enticing. I peeled the skin from the wings and bit into the crispy skin. I succumbed and savored every bit. So much for my high ethical ground.

Right after Thanksgiving, things were buzzing at school. Everyone was involved in preparation for the Christmas pageant. It was a community-wide affair, organized in the school, and was highly attended by Chicorico folks. Mrs. Hilliard had organized the Parents' Christmas Pageant Steering Committee, consisting of three mothers and the teachers involved in producing the pageant. Mom was on the committee.

When the committee met in September, they decided mothers would make the costumes. Everyone was pleased with the decision, especially Mrs. Hilliard. Also, she had a lot of help from Mrs. La Mont and Miss French, music teachers for all the camps. Mrs. Hazel Durham, the drama teacher at Raton High School, assisted with the Nativity play. Mrs. Hilliard made one cardinal rule: any child who wanted—or whose parents wanted—could be in the pageant.

The Parents' Steering Committee selected all the actors. I wanted to be one of the Wise Men, but I was too small to be a Magi and too big to be the Baby Jesus. Donald Vuicich, Sava's brother, got to be Baby Jesus. He was four months old. He did okay. Last year the Baby Jesus cried all during the pageant. Donald only cried once, during the Adoration when his brother Sava tickled his stomach too hard.

Geno and I got to be shepherds. There were a lot of shepherds in the pageant—almost all the kids in my grade except some who played "being kids." Seventh graders Lucy Barselli and Mike Pappas got to be Mary and Joseph. José got to be in a legion of angels. The lead angels were Vido Appoloni and Annie Aguilar.

Friday, December 22nd, the pageant was held in the clubhouse theatre, El Carbon, where movies were shown. During the pageant, Mrs. La Mont and Miss French took turns playing the piano. The Nativity play was a colorful spectacle based on a grand story. Yet I remember little about it, except the kids all sparkled splendidly in their homemade costumes, considering money and materials were scarce. The colors, fabrics, and styles were dazzling, especially when everyone blended together. I liked my shepherd's costume; it would have won a blue ribbon if prizes had been given for the most resourceful and inexpensive costume. It consisted of a chicken feed gunnysack, turned inside out so the Purina Chow label didn't show. Mom cut holes for my neck and arms. Around my waist, she tied one of Dad's red and white neckties, and for a headband, she used one of Dad's red bandanas.

No one missed their lines, even though a few new lines were improvised. Everyone sang with vigor and joy, without stumbling too much on the high notes. After the Nativity play, Peter Peralta sang "*Tres Años Hace*" and "*Adelila*" in Spanish; Selimo Flores followed with an accordion solo. The evening ended when all the actors came on the stage to lead the audience in singing "Silent Night." The audience stood to sing. As the last notes of "Silent Night" faded, Mrs. Hilliard stepped to the front of the stage and signaled for everyone to join her in singing Christmas carols. Mrs. La Mont joined Mrs. Hilliard, and Miss French stayed at the piano.

The audience stayed standing and all of us kids stayed in our places on the stage. Mrs. Hilliard and Mrs. La Mont made quite a duet, waving their arms and leading everyone through the lyrics and refrains with gusto. Miss French accompanied on the piano:

"Jingle bells! jingle bells! . . ."

"Jingle Bells" was followed with "Joy to the World," "O Come, All Ye Faithful," "O Holy Night," "Deck the Halls," "The First Noel," and "O Little Town of Bethlehem."

After the last song, Mrs. Hilliard lifted both of her arms:

"Merry Christmas everyone! God bless you!"

"Ha-a-a-ppy New Ye-e-e-ar to y-o-u!" the jubilant audience shouted back to Mrs. Hilliard and applauded vigorously.

People started milling around, visiting with each other as they prepared to leave. Some mothers came on stage to retrieve their little ones and left carrying parts of costumes or props. I saw Mom cutting through the crowd toward the stage. Standing there in the jovial scuffle, with kids removing their costumes, parents jostling through the happy crowd of students, parents, and friends, I was swept by a feeling of warmth and security. We were blessed, surrounded by adults who loved and cared for us.

On the 23rd Dad decreed, "I got a good job for you boys. Go to the *montaña*. Find a good Christmas tree. Juan's in charge. Be careful. Take your jackets."

"Wow!" José exclaimed. "This will be fun!"

He had already put on his jacket and hat. Juan helped find mine as he looked for his. We went outside to the coal shed to get the axe and started our trek across the llano and into the hills. At first the walking was easy. Juan carried the axe, leading the way across the llano and up into the hills that loomed over the coal camp. The snow wasn't deep. Before long, the snow got deeper, and we had to slow down considerably. Without snowshoes, walking in deep snow requires slow, deliberate steps. The trees changed as we climbed higher; below were junipers, scraggly piñóns, and scrub oaks; above were tall ponderosas, spruces, and some cedars.

We were perilously close to Eagle Nest. As much as I yearned to visit it, I held back. About one hundred yards away, Juan spotted a huge Colorado blue spruce, and beside it was a smaller one, about five feet tall. José and I hurriedly joined him while he chopped off the branches around the bottom of the smaller tree. Juan and José took turns chopping.

"E-e-a-sy!" Juan cautioned José, who whacked at the trunk with rapid, short swings. The tree started to tip. Juan held the tree as it leaned to one side. José moved to the backside of the tree and finished chopping through the trunk. It was a well-shaped tree. Juan and José took turns carrying the axe or the tree. Sometimes I helped with the tree. Whenever they could, they slid the tree down the steep slopes. Other times, they carried it when it was impossible to slide it along the top of the snow. After we got home, Dad made a makeshift tree stand with two boards. He nailed the boards to the bottom of the tree trunk. Mom already had the decorations out. They were old, from Mexico, given to us by Abuelo Ribera, who got them from his father, Pablo Ribera. Angela and Ramona were in charge of decorating the tree.

When Angela and Ramona finished, we complimented them. It was a swell tree, simply decorated with lights, painted-paper angels, and saints, as well as imploded glass sunburst balls. Angela had clipped some tin candleholders onto the tree, but she didn't put any candles in them. Years ago, Mom and Dad would put candles in the holders, and on Christmas Eve, light the candles right there on the tree! They'd watch the candles burn for a short while, and then put them out. As our family grew, Mom and Dad thought it best not to take chances with a live flame. Besides, the tree was decorated with electric lights. So they discontinued the custom. To save money this Christmas, Dad planned to plug the lights in for only a short time tonight. Tomorrow night would be different.

As a reward for a job well done, Mom treated us to some warm tortillas and chokecherry jelly. After eating the tortillas, I lay under the tree, the living room filled with the pine needle smell of the hills.

On Sunday afternoon, Christmas Eve day, some of the families returned to the clubhouse to prepare the union gift bags. Ever since we had the union, families took turns stuffing small paper bags with nuts, peanuts, apples, and candies purchased by the union. Every kid in the camp got a bag full of the sweet treats. Mostly, the candies were of the hard variety in all kinds of shapes and colors. It was our turn to stuff bags this Christmas. And, no eating!

"I could be playing," I complained, "if I didn't have to fill the bags!"

"Hito, in the union, we all have to do our share. This year it's our turn. Christmas is about giving gifts—we're lucky to be the ones to give."

After we finished stuffing the bags, we delivered them around Chicorico to every home. I knocked on each front door. When open, we greeted, "*Feliz Navidad!* These are from the union."

By the time we finished delivering the bags, I felt exhausted and happy. Dad was right, giving gifts was fun.

Christmas Eve, Dad and Mom took us to midnight mass at St. Joseph's Church in Raton. Located on Martinez Street across from a Lebanese mom-and-pop grocery store—Sawaya's Food Market—St. Joseph's felt like down-home to Mom and Dad because it was an old adobe church in the heart of the Hispano barrio. On its walls, a Hispano artist had painted all the Stations of the Cross. Close to the altar, he had painted angels. They were splashed on the walls in soothing hues of blue and white, accented with gold. With their elongated golden trumpets, they seemed to be heralding the birth of Christ. These angels were a year-round reminder to the parishioners of that wondrous event.

Now, at Christmas, on both sides of the altar was a *bosque* of Christmas trees. A Nativity scene, with the Baby Jesus, Mary, and Joseph surrounded by farm animals, was next to one of the bosques. During mass, the choir sang songs in Latin and Spanish. A few adults got carried away, singing along with the choir in Spanish, adding to the Christmas festivities. After mass, we all lined up to kiss the Baby Jesus before we left the church.

On the way home after mass, the night was dark and deep into the winter solstice. The sky blazoned with a million bright, beaming stars sparkling from rim to rim of Chicorico Canyon. Dad commented, "Santa will make good time with such a clear night."

Christmas morning, Santa had arrived, leaving gifts under the tree. Most were articles of clothing. Each of us boys got a plaid flannel shirt. Angela and Ramona received new sweaters, socks, and mittens, too. Juan and José each got a book. Juan got *The Call of the Wild* by Jack London, and José got *The Adventures of Tom Sawyer* by Mark Twain. Angela got a Spanish prayer missal, *Misal Diario San José.*

Most of the toys we received were homemade. Arturo sent Juan, José, and me a whoosh-whoosh whirligig. The toy consisted of a large button. A piece of 12- to 14-inch string was strung through two of the button-holes. To operate the whirligig, the string was looped over both thumbs. Then, with a clock-like motion, the string was wound tightly, thus pulling both thumbs away from the center where the button was suspended in the air. The wound string whirled the button rapidly—the strings vibrated, making a whirring *whoosh-whoosh* sound as the button spun and the strings untwined. Juan and José got a walkie-talkie—two tin cans connected with a long, waxed string. They rigged it up to talk from their bedroom window to the outhouse in the backyard.

I got a homemade wind-up tractor. Dad made it with an empty spool of thread, a burned-out match, a rubber band, a piece of soap, and a wood splinter. The rubber band was stretched through the spool's hole. At one end, the match was slightly larger than the spool's circumference. The piece of soap was at the other end, serving as a washer. The splinter held the rubber band against the soap. I wound up the rubber band and watched the tractor go. On the floor, it skittered like a jittery stinkbug running from a bird.

Ramona's toy came from the store. It was an expensive doll with a porcelain head and eyes that moved. Ramona was delighted; she called the doll "Mimi." When laid down, Mimi's eyes closed. Her cotton-stuffed body was made of high quality cotton cloth. A neatly folded wardrobe of clothing accompanied the doll in a little cardboard box. Immediately, Ramona started dressing and undressing Mimi.

The day after Christmas, a soft, powdery snow started falling, covering everything. It fell softly and steadily, not giving a soft white care where it fell. Dad sent Juan and José outside to shovel paths to the coal shed, water pump, and outhouse. Otherwise, the backyard and the llano were entirely blanketed with snow. The light, powdery snow was only a calm prelude to the maelstrom that followed.

On the second day after Christmas, squalls of snow came blustering over the north rim of Chicorico Canyon. We were in for a "norther," an arctic cold front that howled from the North Pole, blowing frigid air and packing the snow into hard dunes. Everybody hunkered in their homes . . . work ceased at the mine . . . all morning . . . all afternoon . . . into the evening, the wind howled and the snow blustered and swirled before it died, falling heavy on the ever-deepening pack of snow.

Sometime late that evening, the snow lost its bluster, but continued to fall sporadically. A freezing cold air slumped over Chicorico, socking us in. The canyon bushes and boulders were entirely covered with white. Even the mighty yucca plants with their long, sharp spires did not pierce through the deep, white blanket of snow. Only the barren cottonwoods remained visible. The piñón, ponderosa, and spruce trees were heavily laden with piles of snow and blended with the landscape. A white Christmas was common in the southern Rockies, including the hills of Chicorico.

On the afternoon of the third day, the snow gradually stopped falling, the gray sky opened, and the clouds disappeared. The sun shined brilliantly, although it was frigid outside from the frosty arctic air. Dad sent Juan and José out to shovel the paths they'd made to the coal shed, water pump, and outhouse. They slipped on their heavy cotton underwear and tied bandanas over their mouths and faces to brave the cold while digging out from under the snow.

The mine wasn't working. The snow pretty well closed everything. Dad had a bad case of cabin fever but resigned himself to an afternoon of reading and smoking his pipe. He hadn't left the house for three days. He sat in his chair in the living room and located a white tobacco can with a red label, Middleton's Cherry Blend. Dad stuffed his pipe after clearing out the stem with a pipe cleaner. He lit it; the smell of cherry tobacco whiffed through the living room.

"Dad! Dad!" José yelled from outside the kitchen window, "Look who's coming!"

The jingle-jingle bells of a sleigh announced the arrival of Mr. Sandoval and his wife with a team of horses pulling a sleigh loaded with logs. Used by *properos* in the wintertime to deliver props to the mine, the properos' sleighs were converted buckboard freighters—the large, high wagons once used to haul coal. The buckboard's wheels were rigidly rigged, enabling it to ski across the snow when pulled by a team of horses. The props were cut from the timber in the area hills to support the tunnels of the mine.

Dad happened to know one of these properos, a Mr. Carlos Sandoval, who was from down-home in El Pueblo near Ribera where Mom grew up. He was a wiry, thin man with a ruddy complexion, a large, scraggly mustache and beard. He was dressed like a lumberjack—high laced boots, wooly red cap, a plaid flannel shirt, dark wool pants, and a thick black leather belt. Like most of the miners and section-gang workers in the winters, he wore a brown sheepskin jacket.

"Whoa!"

Dad and I heard Mr. Sandoval stop the team as we hastily located our coats, caps, and gloves. Dad snuffed out his pipe. I don't remember who was more excited—Dad or me. But Dad beat me outside! I held the door open for Mrs. Sandoval. I stayed outside with Dad and Mr. Sandoval, watching them unload and stack the neatly chopped and split piñón logs.

After stacking the logs, Mr. Sandoval offered Dad some chewing tobacco. Without speaking, both of them bit off a cud and sloshed it in their mouths for a while, spitting the tar spittle on the freshly fallen snow. I thought someday I'd be just like them. When they weren't looking, I puffed out my checks and made chewing motions. Then I turned sideways and spat in the snow.

After they spit out all of the tobacco, we went into the house, where Mom and Mrs. Sandoval had prepared a large meal of leftovers from Christmas. I hadn't noticed that Mrs. Sandoval had brought a huge pot of chili.

Angela had the table all arranged. The adults sat together on one half of the table, squeezing the rest of us together at the other half. Angela placed the washbasin cabinet at our end of the table, providing two more settings. Mr. and Mrs. Sandoval sat in our chairs. José and I sat on powder boxes.

Dad led grace; he thanked the Lord for giving us friends like the Sandovals. After a decade of Hail Marys, we got directly down to the business of eating. The leftovers were okay, but Mrs. Sandoval's chili was a sensational hit. Mr. Sandoval showed us how to eat chili with our hands, a down-home tradition.

"*¡Mira! De primero*—you pour the chili in the bowl." Mr. Sandoval carefully dipped the ladle into the chili pot, holding the bowl close to the pot's rim. "Chili is gold in the winter. So don't spill," he grinned, ladling the chili into his bowl. "Now, take a tortilla, *como esta!*" He lifted a warm tortilla from beneath the towel of the tortilla plate. "Be sure to put the *toalla* back, so the other tortillas will stay warm."

We were all eyes. We loved chili—and to think we could eat it with our hands!

"Tear the tortilla in half." He ripped the tortilla apart, holding half in each hand. "Hold both pieces with your thumb and fingers, over the bowl. With your right hand, scoop up some chili; put it in the other piece." He scooped up some chili and deftly brushed it into the other piece. "Now, you've made a *taquito,*" he explained, lifting the folded tortilla and chili to his mouth. "Now you try."

At first, I was pretty clumsy at getting the chili up to my mouth. The chili kept running out of the tortilla before I could get it to my mouth. Luckily, it spilled back into my bowl rather than on the table. Out of desperation, I lowered my face close to the chili bowl where I could more easily scoop up the chili into my mouth. I thought Mom or Angela would object till I looked around, noticing everyone else doing the same thing—even Mom and Dad.

After supper, Angela, Ramona, and the adults gathered in the living room. We boys stayed in the kitchen to wash, dry, and put away the dishes. Juan was put in charge. He made a good boss. Surprisingly, José and I obeyed and our after-supper chores were finished in no time flat. We joined the adults in the living room. Mr. and Mrs. Sandoval shared news about la plebe down-home. Mom told the sad news about Abuelo's passing, sparking stories Abuelo used to tell.

Mr. Sandoval remembered Abuelo's story about a boy who disobeyed his parents by going to a dance during Lent with a beautiful girl who worked for the Devil. His story scared me to death! Stories about the Devil doing his dirty work always gave me the creeps. The Devil was very good at tempting kids to do bad things.

Dad remembered a chiste Abuelo told about La Muerte:

"*Es que,* many years ago two *novios* from Las Vegas had a grand wedding. For their honeymoon, they went to the Montezuma Hotél in Gallinas Cañon right north of Las Vegas and stayed in the most expensive honeymoon suite in the hotél. They were *todo enamorados.* I mean they were deeply in love—so they claimed. Pues, they spent the first night of their honeymoon bragging about their love.

"The groom said, 'Honey, my love for you is deeper than the ocean.'

"'O-o-o-o-o!' his bride answered, 'my love for you is even more. I have more love for you than there are stars in the heavens!'

"'Bueno, pero, let's agree to return here when we are old.'

"'Ah—then we shall see whose love is the greatest.'

"Many years pass. The novios raise a family. Their children marry and move away. Fifty years later, the novios—now they're viejitos—return to the same honeymoon suite in the Montezuma Hotél. Pero, they're very old, and they've forgotten their pledges of love. Instead, they bragged the whole night of their aches and pains:

"'A, yí–yí,' the viejita complained, 'my *estómago* is killing me. I will surely die before you do.'

"'*Y, mis rhuemos,*' the viejito complained, '*duelo mucho.*'

"'Pero,' the viejita bragged, 'my pains are greater than yours.'

"'*Mucho más,*' the viejito bragged, '*mis dolores* are greater. I will be the first to go.'

"So the viejitos bragged about how each of them had the greatest pains and would die first. Now, as they were bragging, La Muerte happened to be flying by the hotél. She stopped to rest, landing her carreta on the ledge of the viejitos' room. Right inside the window, La Muerte could see and hear the viejitos. They could not see her.

"Hmmm! When La Muerte had overhead the two bragging about their aches and pains and how each would be the first to die, she decided to test them. She entered the hotél, knocking at the door of the two viejitos, announcing in a rhyme she made up:

"'*Yo soy un Angel de Dios*
Y vengo por uno de los dos.'

"*Silencio!* All of a sudden, the two viejitos were very quiet. La Muerte was at their door, saying she had come for either one of them. They said nothing, hoping La Muerte would go away.

"*KNOCK! KNOCK!* La Muerte banged on the door, announcing again,

"'*Yo soy un Angel de Dios*
Y vengo por uno de los dos.'

"Still yet, the two viejitos were very quiet. They knew one of them must die, for no one can escape La Muerte. She was asking for either one of them. Both had said they would be the first to die, because they had the greatest aches and pains. Finally, after a long while, both of the viejitos said the same thing to each other—at the same time. They both said:

"'Go see who's at the door!'"

"Haah!" Mrs. Sandoval laughed heartily. "Ah, true love! The viejitos loved each other so much, but when their time came, whoa! What's the rush?"

"¡Qué va!" Mom chuckled. "The righteous have nothing to fear of La Muerte, but even the righteous aren't in a rush to take a ride on her carreta!"

Laughing energetically, the adults really enjoyed Dad's chiste—mostly because they understood it. I didn't laugh, and I didn't understand it. La Muerte was no laughing matter. When Dad noticed how quiet we kids were, he advised:

"Don't worry so much about La Muerte. Just be happy to be alive. Anyway, 'de la muerte y de la suerte no hay quien se escape,'" Dad moralized with a down-home dicho: "No one can escape from death or fate."

Friday evening, December 31, 1944, everyone from Chicorico gathered at the baseball field with their Christmas trees. The evening was a perfect Chicorico December night. Not a cloud in the sky, the stars beamed brightly in the dry, dark sky. The air was completely still, and it was cold, but not too cold. This was a perfect night for the biggest bonfire of the year. People piled their trees into a very tall heap in the middle of the baseball field. The field was still covered with at least two feet of snow so there was little worry the bonfire might spread to the rest of the coal camp. Everyone gathered around the tall heap of Christmas trees.

The Super stepped forward with a flaming torch: "Happy New Year!"

He threw the torch onto the huge pile. Slowly, the flame spread—hissing, popping, roaring. High above, surges of sparks and smoke billowed and twirled, dimming the stars above.

Singing welled from the crowd:

"Should auld acquaintance be forgot. . . ."

After two renditions of "Auld Lang Syne," other songs welled up in Italian, Slavic, and Spanish. I didn't understand the Italian or Slavic songs, but the Spanish song was "Las Mañanitas," a traditional Hispano song sung at birthdays and Christmas.

After all the singing, people milled around wishing each other a "Happy New Year," visiting as the bonfire dimmed. When most of the trees had burnt, the men kicked snow onto the fire's borders, leaving a large mound of charred logs and dying embers smoldering on the baseball field. Sometime in the spring, baseball players would rake and haul them away.

Gradually, everyone scattered, walking home humming, singing. Once home, we went right to bed. After I said my prayers, I lay awake from all the excitement. The rest of the house was quiet. Angela, Juan, and José were asleep. Outside, the snow seemed to muffle sounds, and unlike the summer, there was no concert of crickets chirping a chaotic symphony. The glow and glare of the huge bonfire lingered in my eyes. I wondered how such a fire could get so bright . . . hot . . . slowly fizzling back into darkness. And the powerful smell of dry pine and spruce lingered in my mouth and throat. The glow and the roar of the fire were still alive in my mind's eye and the hardy voices of the people resonated, singing in all the different languages—their voices echoing in my head, even though I didn't understand the Slavic and Italian songs.

Eventually, my eyelids drooped, nodding to sleep, the smells and sounds of the New Year's Eve bonfire slowly receding. I'm not sure if I dreamed or actually heard Mom and Dad slipping out of bed. They walked gingerly, the wooden floor squeaking as they tiptoed into the kitchen. They spoke softly:

"Let's have some of Onorio's wine."

A twinkle of time zipped by, and—*CLINK!*

"Happy New Year, honey!"

"You, too."

14

FROM DUST THOU ART, AND UNTO DUST SHALT THOU RETURN

Crunk! Crun-ka—crun-ka! 5:00 A.M. Dad stoked the living room stove, removing the dead ashes, dumping them in the black coal bucket.

Crunk! Crun-ka–crun-ka–crun-ka! 5:05 A.M. Dad stoked the kitchen fogón, removing the dead ashes, dumping them in the coal bucket. He opened the kitchen door, slamming it shut, leaving with the bucket full of ashes:

Cre-e-ch!—Blam!

Bucket full of coal, Dad opened the door:

Cre-e-ch. Cold, frosty air surged into the house. Dad dumped the coal into powder boxes beside the fogón and living room stove. Outside, it was pitch dark—darkest time of night just before the sun rises.

"Daa-aad? What ti-i-ime is it-t-t?" I sputtered, more asleep than awake.

"Time to get up," Dad proclaimed matter-of-factly. Every morning Dad arose early to make the fire, even in the mornings when he wasn't working, like this cold January morning. He was none too quiet about the task, believing we should all enjoy the nippy, frosty sting of the cold

January morning. When Dad awoke, it was time for everyone to get up, even us kids who didn't have to go to school. Colfax County schools were supposed to open that Tuesday, January 2, 1945, but the snow that had started yesterday was still blustering, drifting on many of the county roads. The Superintendent called a "Snow Day." Mr. Floyd spread the word in Chicorico.

Brrrrr! Barefooted, I tiptoed briskly across the cold, bare, wooden living room floor—pants, shirt, socks, and shoes in hand, slipping behind the living room stove. Behind the fogón the floor was still warm from the evening before, the evening embers slowly kindling the new morning coal—the perfect place to dress.

Dressing behind the living room stove, I was shielded from the frosty sting of the cold winter night that still tarried in most parts of the house. The living room stove was just starting to heat up the surrounding area. Outside, the sky was just beginning to lighten up. Whiffs of brewing coffee floated through the kitchen air. Dad sat at the kitchen table, waiting for the coffee to finish brewing, pouring coffee. Mom joined Dad at the table. I sat behind the living room stove, crouched against the wall, drowsing.

Usually, Dad was a calm man, but when cold winter days kept him confined in the house, he grew restless. He was overly anxious, not knowing what to do with himself. He was used to working. Not one to sleep in, he didn't mind women's work, like washing floors or cleaning house. In fact, Mom was happy to have him home because he busied himself around the house. This particular morning, Dad took it upon himself to fix José and me, even though we weren't broken.

"Make sure the boys get a good washing!" Dad declared. "There's an outbreak of lice."

"Head lice? *¿En enero?* ¡Por Dios!" Mom was surprised. The lice usually flourished in the summers and falls, when we played hard, sweated a lot, and didn't wash our hair.

"Do you still use kerosene to remove the lice?" Dad alluded to the old remedy for removing head lice—cutting the infected hair entirely off and scrubbing the head with liberal portions of kerosene. If it didn't slay the lice, it drowned them!

"Some people still use it," Mom noted. She was concerned. "But the boys have clean hair—no lice. I bathed them only Saturday."

Sometimes we contacted lice by wearing somebody's hat; sometimes, the lice leapt from one person's hair to another. But the lice couldn't fly around in the cold, frigid January air. No matter! Today, Dad was afflicted with a bad case of cabin fever, and head lice were the bogus enemy.

"Better to be safe than sorry." Dad's coal mining wisdom was at play.

"Well—if you must—give them a good washing." Mom took some soap out of the wash basin. "This Ivory soap will do it for now, if you scrub hard enough!"

"I'll give Matías a bath!" Dad suggested.

"Before breakfast?"

"¡O, sí! ¿Cómo no?" Dad turned a powder box over, so the bottom could serve as a platform for the cajete. He poured water from the hot tank on the fogón, calling for me.

"Matías, *ven pa'cá.*"

I pretended to be sleeping, faking deep breathing.

"Ma-tí-as, *tiempo para tu baño.*" He spoke softly.

I gave no answer and didn't move, still pretending to sleep. As far as I was concerned, it wasn't even time to get up. Even the rooster still slept.

"Ma-tí-as!" Dad gently tugged my sleeve.

No answer.

"Matías!" He meant business.

"¿Sí, papa?"

"Come! The water's getting cold."

The kitchen was warm. I undressed. Mom replaced my dirty underclothes with a clean undershirt and shorts.

"Now, sit still!" Dad curtly ordered as he lathered the soap, wetting my hair.

"Ouch!"

Dad threw himself into the task, rubbing my scalp as though my hair were infested with lice. Head lice were pesky, difficult to remove once they've moved into a head of hair.

"Don't rub so hard! I don't have lice!"

Dad rinsed me quickly, lifted me out of the tub, placed a towel around me, rubbing my back. He called for José:

"José!"

No answer.

"José!"

Still no answer.

Dad firmly ordered: "¡José! ¡Ven 'acá!"

Still no answer. It was cold in the bedroom and José was warmly snuggled under the blankets. Dad left me to finish drying and dressing. He opened the bedroom door and poked his head into the room, forcefully whispering:

"¡José! ¡Ándale! ¡Ven 'acá!" Dad's icy whisper penetrated the blanket José had pulled over his head, piercing José's stupor in slumberland. Dad retreated to the kitchen, confident José would soon be in the kitchen. José crawled from bed and tottered to the kitchen, his fists rubbing the sleep out of his eyes.

"Wha-a-a-t's wrong?" he sputtered, glancing around in a daze.

"Water's getting cold!"

"Water?"

"Yes! For your bath!"

"Jeeps! A bath? Now?"

"¡Ándale, José! Take your clothes off!"

"B-u-u-t! Mom gave me a bath Saturday!"

José's eyes darted toward Mom's. She turned away from José, sipping coffee. José undressed by the fogón, skittering into the kitchen. Dad lifted him into the tub, starting the Chicorico—

rub-a-dub dub
give-the-lice
a good scrub
hair treatment!

If there were lice in José's hair, they probably were crushed to death by Dad's strong fingers.

"Mom gave me a bath! Just Saturday!"

"You already said that!"

"I don't have no lice!"

Dad tired of José's protests. Dad stopped scrubbing, crossed his arms in firm resolve, and tapped his foot.

"I swear I don't have lice—"

"Don't swear, hito," Mom advised. "More you complain, longer your bath takes."

"Here!" Dad handed José the Ivory soap. "Wash yourself! While I prepare the kerosene."

"Kerosene! D-a-d! I-don't-have lice, honest! Just look!" José parted his hair in different places.

Dad ignored José's desperate pleas. He found the kerosene. Placing it on the kitchen table, he searched for Mom's olive oil and vinegar to mix: one part kerosene, one part vinegar, one part olive oil, and two eggs. Before the concoction was applied, usually the hair was cut entirely off a boy. After the haircut, the concoction was rubbed into the remaining stubs of hair and then thoroughly rinsed. You learned to keep your eyes tightly shut.

"We have no eggs!" Mom mentioned to Dad.

"I'll go see if the chickens have laid any." Dad found his coat and cap. He quickly opened and closed the kitchen door, keeping the cold from spilling into the warm kitchen.

Frantically, José glanced at Mom. She signaled him to start washing. Maybe he'd be finished before Dad returned. Quickly, José started to wash, spreading soap evenly over his body. Dad's behavior was a break from family tradition. Mom gave baths. She always bathed us on Saturday mornings until we were old enough to bathe ourselves. Juan and Angela now bathed themselves. I never thought I'd hanker for a Saturday morning bath till that cold January morning when Dad took it upon himself to bathe José and me. If he applied the lice concoction on José, he would surely apply it on me; we shared the same bed and blankets. He would do it after cutting our heads bare!

Just getting a bath from Dad was bad enough. He was rough, got soap in my eyes, and wouldn't let me linger in the water. It was all work and no play. Mom was just the opposite. On Saturday mornings, only a few years ago, Juan and José would haul enough water from the pump into the kitchen to fill a cajete. Sometimes, in the winters, they would take hot water out of the fogón's boiling pan to pour over the pump's faucet to thaw the ice out of it. They'd fill their buckets with water and haul them back and forth into the house, pouring the water into the cajete. When the tub was about half full, they'd bring in two more full buckets and place them on top of the stove so they'd warm as Mom was bathing us.

Mom would add hot water from the fogón's tank to the tub's cold water. Because I was the youngest of the boys, I went first. Ramona was the youngest of the family, but she was given a bath about midday when the kitchen was cozy and warm. We weren't allowed to watch. We joked we weren't allowed to watch because she didn't have to take a bath! Of the boys, I went first, which was perfectly okay with me. The water was the warmest and the cleanest. However, more hot water was added with each additional boy.

Mom would wet my hair and gently scrub it. She handed me the soap bar and I washed everywhere I could reach. Mom rubbed soap on my back and rinsed my hair, back, and chest with the tub water. She handed me the bar of soap, or a wooden clothespin, to float in the tub. I liked to sink the soap and let it slip back up through my fingers. With the clothespin, I liked to sink it and watch it pop back up, always in a different place. Play was okay when Mom gave us a bath. When the rinsing was done, I was allowed to fidget with the soap or clothespin for a short while. The short time was never long enough. I had to be considerate of my brothers, who would follow me in water that was getting colder by degrees.

After fidgeting and floating the soap and clothespin for a while, Mom signaled me to stand up. I would, and she would wrap a Gold Medal flour towel around me, lifting me out of the tub and placing me in front of the living room stove where she'd rub me dry. As she dried and helped me dress, José would undress and stand ready to be lifted into the tub for his bath. After José, Juan would be bathed, in that order from youngest to oldest. The three of us always got to linger a while in the water after Mom

When Mom gave us a bath.

had bathed us, allowing us to float the soap or a wooden clothespin like little boats. Because Juan was last, he got to linger the longest. That was the only advantage of bathing last.

Dad stomped back into the house, kicking the snow off his boots as he entered the house. "Doggone it!" Besides "bad egg," the word "doggone" was the worst swear word I ever heard Dad use.

"*¡Manuelo!*" Mom accosted Dad, "Watch your language."

"I'm sorry, honey. But, no eggs! Those lazy chickens—"

"I took all they had yesterday!"

"O-h-h," Dad conceded, "must be too early."

Whew! José sighed in relief. "Look, Dad, I'm all washed up. Even my hair!"

"Good boy, José. Let's get you out and dry." Dad lifted José from the tub, wrapped a Gold Medal flour towel around him, and stood him in front of the living room stove. I had already dressed so I watched as Dad rubbed José dry. Again, Dad could be pretty rough. Twenty-some years working as a miner made him strong, and he didn't always know his own strength. Oddly, José didn't complain. Guess things could be worse—kerosene, vinegar, olive oil, and eggs worse.

Time flies when you're having fun . . . or avoiding your father's cabin fever! The January 2nd Snow Day reprieve passed quickly. I admit it: School was least on my mind, although I often wished I could read better. I wanted to read Juan and José's new books.

"Hey, Juan?" José described an episode from his new book. "This Tom Sawyer, he knows how to have fun. One time he had to paint the fence. All the guys came around, teasing him—that he had to work. He pretended it was an honor to paint the fence. He tells the guys only big-shots get to paint the fence! Before you know it, all the other guys are busy painting the fence! They even pay him to do it! And he's just standing there, acting like he did them a favor!"

"Ho-boy! They were stu-u-u-u-pi-d!"

"Yeah. Tom's fooling the other guys. Right now, I'm at a place where Tom is gonna explore a cave. . . . How goes it with your book?"

"It's okay." He didn't sound enthusiastic.

"Have you started your book?"

"Oh, heck ya! It's just different than your book! It's about a dog, Buck, that gets kidnapped and taken to Alaska. He's learning to be a sled dog. Boy, do they treat those dogs rough!"

That sounded good to José:

"Does he fight with the other dogs? Is he any good at pulling a sled? How come somebody kidnapped him?"

Listening to the guys discuss their books made me even more eager to learn to read. All I could read were books written for first graders. Reading, I reckoned, would be a way for me to have a lot of adventures all over the world—and be safe and sound right here in Chicorico.

We returned to the workaday world on January 3rd. We were in school, Dad was in the mine, and Mom was always at work. With the house, Mom was a stickler for cleanliness. Heating and cooking with coal was a dirty, dusty business. Every day she followed a housecleaning routine. She started by dusting over picture frames, the books in our little library, and the furniture in each room. In the kitchen, she washed the floor each day after she thoroughly washed the table and breakfast dishes. Once a week, she washed the outhouse with lye, a thankless task that kept the outhouse spotless and sterile.

Ramona was the only one who didn't have to return to work after the holidays. She was now four years old, getting saucier by the day. She knew how to use her feminine wiles, especially with Mom and Dad. She was a New Year's Eve baby. Mom made a pretty big deal of it, even baked a cake and put four candles on it. None of the rest of us ever got a birthday cake for our birthdays. Mom and Dad never made too much of birthdays, except Ramona's.

"Honey," Mom explained to Ramona, lighting the four candles, "make a wish just before you blow out the candles."

Ramona puffed up her cheeks, puckering her lips, blowing hard:

F-o-o-o-o! She blew out the candles, resting her elbows on the table, hands in her chin. She proudly watched the smoke weave toward the ceiling.

"Ramona, what'd you wish?" I was curious.

"Well, I wished—"

"*¡No digas nada!*" Mom advised Ramona, "or your wish won't come true."

Ramona put her small hands up to her mouth, clamming up, refusing to say anything. She glared at me as though I'd asked her to do something bad. So, I got angry and was about to say something mean to Ramona, but Mom gave me a stern look. If looks could kill, I'd been dead! And I was easily placated . . . a piece of cake . . . a glass of milk. Politely and contritely, I asked for a piece of the birthday cake. No use to make enemies over a wish when a piece of cake is at stake.

"Plee-ease? May I have a piece of cake—and some milk?"

What I didn't realize was that Ramona had wished to have toys like the guys' walkie-talkie and my little tractor. As soon as I was back in school, Ramona had the whole house to herself while Mom busied herself cleaning, dusting, and doing all those housecleaning chores we never appreciated. Ramona was infected with a powerful childhood virus called "envy." The other side of the fence started looking greener to her. She soon tired of her new porcelain doll. I don't blame her. All it did was open and close its eyes.

Ramona rigged up a walkie-talkie system. Mom lent her two empty soup cans. She put one in the kitchen, the other in the bedroom. She'd pretend to speak to someone by talking into the kitchen can. Then she'd put it down, go to the bedroom, pick up the other soup can, listen to herself, and reply to herself—talking into the can.

As a six-year-old, I also suffered from the childhood virus of envy. I envied Ramona. To me, she was a mama's girl. She didn't have to go to school. Mom made a big fuss over her, fixing her a birthday cake every December 31. The rest of us never got a cake for our birthday—not even Dad. Too young to understand Mom's feelings, I didn't realize how much Mom treasured Ramona as God-sent after having lost two other little girls. Her oldest girl, Angela, was practically grown and would soon leave home to go to college. In Ramona, Mom had a kindred spirit in a family dominated by males.

Anyway, Ramona got tired of talking and listening to herself on the makeshift walkie-talkie cans. She extended her play world to her second wish—to have a tractor like mine. Since I wasn't home, she played with my tractor. She liked to play on the soft, stuffed living room chairs. She'd wind the rubber band, place the tractor on the cushion, and watch the tractor trudge over the dips and swells of the chair's seat. Sometimes the tractor wedged in a crease in the cushion, spinning. Ramona nudged the spool forward with her little fingers; the spool wobbled out of the crease, gyrating onto its path.

The tractor did run kind of slow. Ramona wanted it to move faster. She twisted the rubber band extra tight. Sure enough, the tractor spun off much faster. Whee! She really liked to see it go fast on the living room floor. As soon as it stopped, she'd rewind it tightly and watch it go. After a while, the rubber band snapped from being over-wound. Wups! She broke it. Instantly, she hid it beneath the chair's cushion. She must have assumed no one would know she put it there. After a few of us sat in the chair, it follows, the tractor would get broken. Of course, Ramona wouldn't have to explain how sitting on the tractor would cause the rubber band—which was inside the spool—to snap. But her telltale heart did her in.

One cold January evening I searched and searched for my tractor. It wasn't where I'd left it on the stand beside our bed. I searched in our small chest of drawers. I found Juan's bag of marbles tucked in an old woolen sock. In the matching sock, I found one of Dad's discarded Prince Albert tobacco cans. Something rattled inside the can. I opened it, hoping to find Prince Albert's rattling skeleton. Instead, I found twenty-five political campaign buttons: Wendell Willkie for President.

¡Hijo, mano! This was *real* contraband. Willkie ran against Roosevelt in 1940 as the Republican presidential candidate. Juan would be in big trouble with Mom and Dad if they found out he had hoarded the political campaign buttons of a Republican! I tucked the can back into the woolen sock.

I rummaged through the bottom drawer where Mom stored our summer clothing. I spotted a bulge in one of José's pants pockets. Inside the pocket was another of Dad's discarded cream-colored tin tobacco cans, brand name written in red: Revelation, the Perfect Pipe Tobacco. I opened its red lid. Lighting wasn't good. I couldn't see into the can. Whatever was in the can, it felt dry and rough and wouldn't shake out.

I shoved the can back into the pocket, slamming the drawer shut! I glanced around. I was alone. Opened the drawer again. What was in that tin can? I couldn't stand the mystery.

This time I reached into the pocket, stealthily lifting the can. I opened it slowly, focused on the contents, and pulled out the carcass of a dead yellow-bellied horny toad. Holy cow! Just be to be safe, I quickly closed my mouth so it couldn't count my teeth. I put the carcass back in the can, shut the lid, and shoved the can into the pocket. Shutting the drawer, I wondered, "Was the toad alive when José put it in the can?"

Still, I couldn't find my tractor! Desperately, I asked Angela, Juan, and José if they'd seen it? No. None of them knew where it was.

"Maybe it drove itself away," Juan joked, "when you were in school."

Ramona overheard Juan say "when you were in school." Her telltale heart told on her. She went over to Dad, tugging at his pant leg as he sat in the soft, stuffed easy chair, reading the *Raton Range*, pipe drooping from his lips. Dad put down the paper, stooping over to hear Ramona whisper,

"Somebody put the tractor down there. You're sitting on it."

"¡Matías, *aquí está tu máquina!*" Dad reached under the cushion, and eureka, the tractor. Dad smiled, handing it to me.

Eagerly, I attempted to wind the tractor. No matter how much I turned, the rubber band had no tension. I tugged at it. The rubber band fell out of the spool, broken.

"Ramona, you broke my tractor!"

"N-o-o, I di-dn't!" Denying her guilt, she grabbed Dad's pant leg.

"It's a sin to lie!"

"W-a-a-a-a!"

Ramona started bawling, rubbing her fake tears out of her eyes, sweetly and sadly looking at Dad.

"Daddy! Daddy! Matías said I sinned! Waaaaaaa!" She bawled some more, again faking. She was more afraid than she was hurt, but Dad was a sucker for her crocodile tears. He again put down his paper and pipe, picked up Ramona, and put her on his lap, comforting her.

"There, there, Ramona. Matías is mad because his tractor's broken."

Darn tootin' I was mad. And she broke it. Now I was between a sow and her cub. If I came down hard on Ramona, Dad would come down hard on me. His little girl could do no wrong. Yet I had to say something. I couldn't just accept the fact she broke the rubber band and lied about it. But Dad protected her. I decided to let the liar come to proof. "Sooner or later," I thought, "she'll get caught in her own lie."

"You can play with my doll," Ramona whimpered to me, offering a solution.

"Your doll! That's no good! It don't do nothing!"

"It *doesn't* do *anything,*" Angela corrected me; I ignored her. I didn't have time to split hairs on grammar. My precious tractor was broken!

"Pl-ea-se, Dad! Can you fix it?"

"O, sí, *no te apenas.* I'll make two of them, so both of you can play!"

Ramona crawled off Dad's lap, wiping her eyes. Dad found Mom in the kitchen. She showed him where she kept her sewing basket. Mom saved empty spools for just such needs. Angela had brought some rubber bands from the store. They were the most difficult item to find for the tractor; rubber was strictly rationed during the war. Using his pocket knife, Dad notched the spool wheels into treads; he found some soap to use for washers, using burnt-out matches for levers. Before long, both of us had brand new tractors to race.

"They're off!" Dad called the race; our spools sped across the living room floor. "At the break, it's Ramona by a nose—coming up the stretch—Matías is sliding against Ramona. Now, Ramona's moving to the side—Matías is passing, going to the finish! Matías wins as Ramona goes to the side!"

"W-a-a-a-a!" Ramona wailed again, complaining, "Matías won because his tractor pushed mine away!"

"Don't cry, honey!" Dad tried to console Ramona. "Maybe next time yours will push his aside."

José, who was watching the race, went into our bedroom, returning with one of his arrows. I reckoned he moved them from the coal shed. No one else seemed to notice the arrow.

"Here, put the arrow in the middle. That way, when the tractors go, they'll bump the arrow instead of each other."

"Hey, yeah!"

This was a good idea—a guardrail to keep the tractors apart. Ramona and I were back at it. José dug up my old tractor, got a rubber band from Angela, and fixed it. He joined us, bringing another arrow. He laid down a second arrow. Again, no one questioned the arrows. I kept quiet. I should have told on him months ago if I had wanted him to get in trouble.

"Gentlemen, start your engines!" Again, Dad called the race. We wound our tractors.

Pop! Ramona's rubber band broke. She handed the tractor to Dad.

Dad called, "Angela, bring another rubber band!" Angela came from the kitchen, where she was trying to do homework.

"This is the last one. Don't wind so hard!"

Ramona didn't know her own strength. She knew the tighter she wound the rubber band, the faster the tractor would go. Dad reassembled her tractor and wound, handing it to Ramona. We positioned our tractors on the line caused by a strip in the flooring. We raced across the grain of the wooden floor.

"Gentlemen, start your engines!" Dad started the race just like the Indianapolis 500, which we heard on the radio.

We held our tractors between our fingers at the starting line. Mom, Angela, and Juan gathered around, forming a circle around the tractors, concentrating on the race.

"Get ready. . . . Get set. . . . Go!"

We released the tractors.

"They're off! At the break, they're neck and neck! Ramona's pulling forward! Matías is spinning to the side—Oops! He's spinning on the guard rail—José is catching up to Ramona! In the home stretch, Ramona's still going strong! José is gaining. Oops—José stopped! Ramona stopped! No one crossed the finish line!"

"I came in first!" Ramona claimed, clapping her hands.

"Nu-uh!" José protested. "You didn't cross the finish line!" He pointed to Ramona's tractor, stopped an inch before the finish line.

"Neither did you," Ramona claimed, "but I was ahead!"

I didn't have much to say. I'd crashed into the arrow, spinning my wheels till the tension in the rubber band ceased and my tractor stopped.

"Nobody won! Nobody lost!" Dad declared. "Let's go again."

While racing our tractors that cold January evening, we weren't aware of the howling wind or the driving snow, which Mom kept at bay by rolling towels along the window sills and door jams so snow couldn't blow into the house. Nor did we think that somewhere in Europe and the Pacific, men were shooting at each other in deadly warfare. Even La Muerte's presence wasn't felt. We were totally engrossed in the race with toys made of household throwaways and scraps. For a brief moment in our small, warm Chicorico living room, nothing was more important than the race—to put up a good show . . . the agony of accidents . . . the ecstasy of victory. Except for Arturo, our family was together in serene communion, engulfed in the moment and oblivious to the cold world outside. . . .

Ash Wednesday started with a feast and ended with a famine. We started the first day of Lent with a full belly and ended the day by agreeing to sacrifice chokecherry jelly. Father Stanley came from Raton late Tuesday evening before Ash Wednesday, sleeping on our sofa. At 5:00 A.M. Ash Wednesday morning, he and Dad awoke the rest of us. Dad dressed for work. The rest of us dressed for school. Angela and Juan ate breakfast before catching the bus to St. Patrick's. Father Stanley dressed in his vestments, wearing a large black topcoat over the priestly regalia. We walked up the tracks to the boarding house, where monthly Father offered Sunday mass. He also came every Ash Wednesday to administer Holy Ashes. This was the first time for me to receive Holy Ashes.

We had to be at the boarding house by 6:00 A.M. José and I took the lead walking up the tracks, stepping lively to reach the boarding house quickly. The wind blustered, piercing through my coat and cap and bringing tears to my eyes. I was cold, quaking with hands in pockets and face to the railroad bed, carefully stepping on the ties to prevent tripping. Father Stanley nudged my shoulder, signaling me to let him pass. I stopped. He moved in front of me, serving as a windbreak. José and I weren't so cold now. Mom, carrying Ramona, walked in back of Dad.

At the boarding house, Father Stanley offered a very short mass to a very large crowd of Chicorico folks. When done with mass, Father administered the ashes, requesting that the miners step forward first.

"From dust thou art . . . ," he recited the doleful Biblical reminder of our mortality, smudging Holy Ashes on the miners' foreheads in the shape of a cross.

The luscious smell of sizzling bacon, the aromatic odor of perking coffee, and the fragrant aroma of freshly baked tortillas wafted from the kitchen into the large sitting room where we were receiving Holy Ashes. All the food in the kitchen was prepared in large quantities in huge pots, pans, and coffeepots. Even the fogón was twice as large as Mom's. Though the Lenten season had officially started, the miners and their families were allowed to eat one last meal with meat in it.

I tried to concentrate on the occasion's solemnity. The reminder that I would return to dust evoked Abuelo Ribera's last words, *bien o mal, todo acaba.* But I couldn't concentrate. Right now I was thinking about staying alive by eating. Yes, my spirit was strong, but my flesh was weak. The call of my appetite was compelling. My watering mouth and growling stomach swayed my spirit. I hadn't eaten anything since suppertime. Outside, the weather was forbidding. Inside, we were toasty warm, causing the food to smell all the better. As the miners received their ashes, they walked into the dining room and sat for breakfast. Some of us boys jostled toward Father to receive our ashes so we could follow the miners into breakfast.

"Perhaps the children should go next?" Father chortled.

Our mothers laughed! They knew a stampede when they saw one.

"Only, boys, don't crowd out the girls!"

We lined up for our ashes. When my turn came, Father Stanley winked, rubbing the ashes on my forehead.

"*¡Dios te bendiga!*" He blessed me instead of reciting the perfunctory ashes to ashes.

I scurried away, crossing myself while rushing into the dining room. Dad caught my eye, waving for me to join him. I elbowed between the crowded tables. The miners were all enjoying themselves, conversing in hardy guffaws as they wolfed down the bacon, eggs, and tortillas, washing it all down with huge gulps of coffee.

Dad grabbed a nearby chair, pulling it next to him. The miner next to him made room for a place setting. Dad waved at Mr. Apple, who was serving everyone. Mr. Apple was an elderly disabled miner. He'd been injured in a cave-in years ago when there was no workmen's compensation. For employment, the Company hired him to manage the boarding house.

"Chief cook and bottle washer," Mr. Apple described himself.

"What does that make me?" Mrs. Apple assisted him.

Mr. Apple hunched his shoulders, setting a plate, fork, and spoon in front of me, pouring coffee in a cup. Mrs. Apple came by with a large tray of bacon and eggs; she slapped two eggs and a batch of bacon on the plate. Dad handed me a plate covered with a towel. I lifted the towel and took two warm tortillas. I started to eat, taking a sip of coffee.

"Ouch!" I shoved the coffee cup back. The coffee was too hot.

"Milk for the boy!" Dad waved. Mr. Apple brought a glass of milk. "Like some honey for the tortillas?"

"Su-ur-re!" I was in hog heaven.

Mr. Apple dipped a spoon into the honey jar and sloshed a gob of honey on each tortilla. I spread the honey evenly across the tortillas and continued to gobble breakfast.

"*¡Despacio!*" Dad advised. "Savor the food."

Mom, José, and Ramona joined us. Dad gave Mom his seat; he stood up with the other miners, preparing to walk to work. He motioned to Mr. Apple to serve the rest of the family. Mr. Apple approached, his wife behind. He hesitated when he saw me eating.

"Feed my roly-poly some more." Dad tapped Mr. Apple's shoulder, "His legs are hollow!"

"Growing boy, huh?" Mr. Apple smiled as Mrs. Apple plopped two more eggs on my plate. I reached for more tortillas. They were still warm.

After such a scrumptious, savory breakfast, going to school was anticlimactic. When I arrived, many of my first grade colleagues were already there, whispering to each other like birds twittering in the early spring. I asked Geno, "What gives?"

"Shh!" He whispered cautiously, "Not so loud. Look around the room. What's different?"

I glanced around the room, but didn't notice anything unusual. Louie was checking his homework. He was a very conscientious student, especially good in arithmetic. Stan was humming a tune, using two pencils for drumsticks, rapping his desk with the pencils. Marian was cleaning out her desk, putting everything in order from the day before. Becky was pounding the chalkboard erasers, removing the chalk dust from them. In other words, I didn't see anything different or unusual, except that everyone else was twittering extra loud. I whispered to Geno, expressing my confusion:

"There's nuthin' different. What gives?"

"Looka Becky! And Miss Blackerby! Don't stare! Pretend you're checking everythin' out."

Again I took a sweeping gaze of the entire class, surveying the serene pre-class hubbub of early morning activities. As my eyes swept across the room, they briefly stopped on Becky and Miss Blackerby. I noticed nothing unusual.

"What's the deal?" I whispered to Geno, nudging him, "I don't see nothing."

"Look at their foreheads."

Again, I discreetly swept my gaze around the room. Unnoticed in the bustling chaos of the early morning, I looked at the faces of Becky and Miss Blackerby. "Holy cow!" I thought, "no ashes on their foreheads." I looked at Geno, alarmed. "They don't have no ashes!"

"Shh! They're not Catholics!"

"Huh?" Turning to Geno, I capped my lips, whispering so only he could hear:

"They don't believe in God?"

"Course they do, dodo! They're Protestants!"

"What's a Protestant?"

"I dunno."

"Boys and girls, before we go start class, I'd like to explain something. By now, you've noticed Becky and I have no ashes on our foreheads."

She always knew what we were thinking.

"Becky, would you mind telling the class about your religion?"

We didn't know that Miss Blackerby had asked Becky ahead of time if it were okay to draw attention to her lack of ashes. Becky crossed her hands at her desk as though praying, saying, "In my church, we don't believe in using ashes, Miss Blackerby, but we do have Lent."

"Thank you, Becky."

Wang! Ten different hands shot into the classroom sky, fingers waving, including mine. Miss Blackerby called on Stan:

"Yes, Stan?"

"What's your religion, Becky?"

"I'm a Lutheran."

Miss Blackerby called on Sava:

"Yes, Sava?"

"Miss Blackerby, are you a Lutheran?"

"No, Sava. I'm a Methodist." Miss Blackerby introduced us to religious diversity. "Both of our churches are Protestant. There are many Protestant religions in America, boys and girls. Not everyone is Catholic."

More hands went up. Miss Blackerby called on Marian, who asked politely, "Miss Blackerby, what's a Protestant?"

"Wh-y, Protestants are Christians."

Finally, Miss Blackerby called on me. My arm was getting tired.

"Yes, Matt?"

"Are Catholics Christians?"

"Well, yes. Why do you ask?"

"Well, that means everyone's Christian, then?"

"Well, not altogether." Miss Blackerby found herself in the quagmire of religious pluralism, but she wasn't one to avoid the truth. "There are many religions in the world. Christianity is one of them. Later, in the third grade, you'll learn about the many different religions. Just remember, in

America everyone has freedom of religion—to believe and worship as they wish. Methodists and Lutherans don't smudge their foreheads for Ash Wednesday. Catholics do."

The Lenten season started with a feast Ash Wednesday morning and a lesson on religious diversity during the day. That evening the feast ended, the famine started, and my religious education continued.

"We must all give something up for Lent," Mom decreed at suppertime.

"I'll go to mass every Friday and Sunday," Angela announced. "And, no movies for me."

"Me, too," Juan injected, "I'll sacrifice like Angela." Of course, the nuns took Angela and Juan to mass every Friday. And our family went every Sunday. We hardly attended movies—no big sacrifice for Angela and Juan.

"José?" Mom waited for his answer.

"I don't know what to sacrifice. I can't ever get candy. And I don't go to the movies."

"Me, too!" I went along with José. "I don't get nothing, so I can't sacrifice nothing."

"You don't get *anything*, Matías," Angela corrected my double negative.

"Yeah, what Angela said!" I thought she was agreeing with me—that I didn't get anything. So how could I sacrifice anything?

"Don't be a smarty-pants, Matías!" Angela quipped. "There must be something you and José can sacrifice."

"Um-m-m . . . n-o-o-o?" José cautiously mumbled, sensing he and I were walking on eggs. He kicked my shin under the table, signaling me to go easy.

"How about chokecherry jelly?" Angela went for the jugular vein. She knew how much we loved chokecherry jelly.

"Son of a gun, chili con pan!" José whined.

Gasp! I was speechless, contemplating the unthinkable sacrifice—chokecherry jelly.

"¡Bueno!" Mom declared, "No chokecherry jelly for José and Matías till Easter."

"B-u-ut Mom." José hunkered with his tone of voice, making a last-ditch effort.

"Easter's not so far away," Dad attempted to console us, but he went along with Mom.

I was dejected. My favorite snack was a warm tortilla with chokecherry jelly, same with José and Ramona. I thought I'd bring down Ramona with us. I asked,

"What about Ramona?"

"*¿Mi muñeca pequeñita?* She's too young."

"No fair!"

Now I was treading on eggs, challenging Mom's sense of fairness.

"What's fair?" Angela asked.

"To be treated the same," I answered. "Ramona should be treated the same."

"Our Lord doesn't believe so," Mom added.

"Huh?" Mom was implying that our Lord discriminated against people.

"Mi hito," Mom explained, "if one man is rich and the other is poor, our Lord would give to the poor but take from the rich."

"That's different!"

"No, hito, we're all different. If we treated you the same as Ramona, then we would be unfair to her."

"So not making her sacrifice is fair to me?"

"No, hito. It's fair to her."

I admit I was too young to understand Mom's sense of equity. Somehow, none of the family really was sacrificing for Lent, except José and me. Yet, part of respect is built on trust. I didn't like what Mom told me, but I trusted her judgment. I sulked a little bit, but not much.

In bed, I told Juan about the religious lesson at school.

"Good! Good!" Juan was delighted to hear about my religious curiosities. "Religion's very interesting, and it keeps people out of trouble."

"Huh?" I didn't quite understand the last comment.

"Well, religion teaches the differences between right and wrong so you can do the right thing and keep out of trouble."

"Oh! Is it true that we all have freedom of religion?"

"Yes! Yes! It's in the Constitution, the first Amendment."

"Gosh! You're smart."

"Naw! You'll learn about it in government, in the eighth grade."

"I think I'd like to be a Methodist! Or a Lutheran like Becky Ruker!"

"Wha-a-a-at?" Juan's inflection implied that I had spoken something blasphemous. He was concerned that I was falling from Catholicism. "Where'd you get *that* bad idea?"

"Well, Miss Blackerby said they don't believe in ashes, and they don't have to give up chokecherry jelly and tortillas, like we do."

"She said that?" Juan was skeptical.

"Well, not exactly, but—"

"Matías! Matías!" Juan was dismayed, "Next thing you'll say is—you wanna be a Republican!"

"What? No! No! I'd never be a *Republican!*" I pronounced the word "Republican" with as much venom in my voice as possible, wiping my lips with my hand—the down-home custom when one utters blasphemy. I wanted to demonstrate I was a die-hard Democrat like Dad and Mom.

"Besides," I defended myself, "you're the one with Wendell Willkie buttons!"

"Well, that's different. I'm just a collector; someday they'll be valuable." Juan discounted my challenge to his political loyalty. He frowned, sighing:

"I don't know about you, Matías. Before you know it, you'll be a Republican and a Protestant! Maybe you should go to St. Pat's—right away!"

José, who'd been listening, piped up, "Yeah, Matías, you better pray—right away."

From the kitchen Mom called, "Quiet, boys."

15

WE LIVED IN FEAR, LA MUERTE LURKED NEAR

Terr! Terr! Terr! The mine whistle blew and blew, blasting out in short, sharp shrills. There was trouble at the mine. All work and play stopped till everyone knew the trouble. Only school continued as usual. We stayed at our lessons with no talking, laughing, or horsing around. We just did our lessons. Mrs. Hilliard took off her rubber hose spanking belt to go to the mine to find out what was wrong. There would be no trouble in school when there was trouble in the mine. We were afraid. One of our fathers might be killed. This was such a day.

Mrs. Hilliard rushed to the mine. Miss Blackerby kept us at our lessons. It was hard to memorize figures from a card or the spelling of new words on a list. We were afraid . . . wasted lessons . . . what about Dad? . . . Mrs. Hilliard returned from the mine and came to our class. Sometimes when she came, she looked cross, especially when we were horsing around. Today, she looked sad, whispering to Miss Blackerby:

"Dismiss school. Accident at the mine."

Miss Blackerby didn't have to tell us. We knew by the sad look creeping over her face. Right away we put our pencils down, straightened up the papers in our desks, took our workbooks to finish our lessons at home, and quietly lined up to leave the room. As I walked up the aisle, I glanced at pictures of George Washington and Abraham Lincoln. I almost cried, thinking, "Abraham Lincoln was like Dad—a common man. He was killed and left a son. Maybe. . . ."

Marian and Geno waited for me at the schoolyard gate. Without talking, we crossed the road to walk the tracks. We trudged home, solemn and sober, worrying about our fathers. They were on day shift . . . in the mine . . . when the accident happened. We were afraid to speak. La Muerte's chill had frozen our tongues.

Geno finally broke her icy silence. "Wonder what happened?"

"Dunno," Marian muttered, "some kind of accident."

We continued walking, groping for words to mollify our fears. Again Geno broke the icy silence. "Wish we could go see."

"To the mine?" Marian exclaimed, "Are you crazy?"

"Naw," Geno defended himself, "I know! Company's closed the gate. Won't let kids through."

"I know a way," I uttered without thinking, endangering my secret Eagle Nest hideaway.

"Huh? What?"

I was as surprised as Geno and Marian. I didn't ever want to divulge Eagle Nest. I stalled, "Tell you what! Ask your moms if you can play with me. Then, meet me in the llano."

"What for?"

"Yeah, what for?"

"Never mind. Just do it."

We split up, each going home. I assumed they wouldn't show and Eagle Nest would remain a secret. When I entered the front door, Mom was in her bedroom, kneeling before the Sacred Heart of Jesus statue and praying the rosary. Ramona knelt beside her. José was shredding Holy Palms and tossing them in the fogón.

"What happened?" I whispered to José, trying not to bother Mom.

"I don't know. Somethin' at the mine."

Our eyes met momentarily. We were anxious about Dad—he might be dead, crushed by boulders and props. My thoughts flashed to the summer Sunday when he took us to the mine—the bleak darkness . . . dampness. I shuddered; a spasm bolted down my back, buckling my knee. The nightmare last summer . . . after the meteorite shower flared . . . Dad running out of the mine, clothing on fire . . . La Muerte in hot pursuit. Terror obliterated my qualms.

"Let's go to the mine. Find out for ourselves 'bout Dad."

"Can't! There's a blockade. Won't let kids through."

"I have a way!" I snatched my coat and put it on, throwing José's coat to him. "Come on!"

"Huh?" He glared at me, putting on his coat.

I remembered Mom and Ramona were still praying. I hollered from the kitchen, "Mom, me and José—we're going to play."

"Okay, hito. Stay close by the house."

"Okay, Mom!" I scurried out; José followed. I ran across the llano. To my surprise, Geno and Marian were there.

"Follow me!" I darted through the bushes that concealed the trailhead to Eagle Nest.

"Hey! Wait for us," I heard the others puffing behind me.

I didn't answer—no time for small talk. Time was wasting. I clambered up the trail as fast as I could. Soon I stopped, winded.

"Hu-uh! Hu-uh!" José, Marian, and Geno caught up with me. They were really puffing.

"What gives?"

"Be quiet. Don't ask."

I was puffing too. I scrambled ahead (this time walking as fast as I could), slipping on the wet grass and sometimes plopping into drifts of snow. The others followed. The snow wasn't deep, but it was melting, slushy and slippery. I'd never been this high in the hills this time of year. The snow was usually too deep. But this winter we'd had some earlier warm days, causing the snow to thaw.

At Eagle Nest, I signaled how to climb up the wall. As we scurried up the dike, I noticed its surface—cold and clammy to the touch. Upon reaching the dike's peak, I pointed to the canyon floor. Nothing had changed. Eagle Nest was just as I had left it, except now frozen snow etched the dike's cracks. Nearby, a spring was frozen where it had trickled from the boulders, freezing as it cascaded through the crevice—blue, red, and pink from the minerals in the boulders.

A clear, crisp March afternoon, the sun blazed in the sky, and the snowcapped Sangre de Cristos dominated the northwestern horizon, shimmering in their majesty. It was wonderful to be back at Eagle Nest—just as I remembered, with a clear view of the entire canyon, especially the area by the main mine entry and tipple.

"Gosh!" José was awestruck. I smiled at him. He smiled back, "You have a swell spot here, little brother!"

I felt great! José liked my hideout! We kept gazing across the canyon, trying to absorb all of the beauty stretching out before us. For a moment, we'd forgotten about the trouble at the mine. I told about my love affair with Eagle Nest—how we had met by accident as I followed the tracks of a deer higher and higher into the hills through the ponderosas and then here . . . on this ridge.

"¡Hijo, mano!" José exclaimed, "looka that big slack pile."

"Classy, huh?" I was fascinated by its growth, enthralled about the production of coal, even the slack piles.

"Classy, nuthin'! Don't you know? Someday slack piles will cover the whole canyon. Even our houses."

"Hey! Don't be such a spoilsport!"

"It's true, Matías. It can only get so high, then the Company'll start another pile."

"No foolin'?" Marian was surprised. "Sure is big."

"Can't go nowhere with the slack, except down the canyon."

"Shh!" Geno shushed, pointing toward the scrub oaks growing at the dike's base. A sparrow flitted in her perennial search for seeds and berries.

"We're too high here," José spoke in a hushed tone, like in church. "Can't see much down below."

Down below, we could see people milling around in front of the entry. They looked puny. A gnawing dread crept into my head . . . my mind

At my Eagle Nest hideout, I had a clear view of the entire mining operation. Courtesy of the Raton Museum.

drifted, morbid thoughts: "People down below . . . so small, like ants . . . could be crushed in an instant by a cave-in, or explosion in the mine! That's what Dad said, the day he took us in the mine. He was like a little ant. He could be crushed. La Muerte lurked near, grinning insidiously, aiming her deadly bow. With one powerful thrust of an arrow, Dad could be killed—"

"Hey, we need to be closer!" José admonished, breaking La Muerte's grip on my thoughts. "Let's sneak down. Nobody'll see us."

José crawled down the dike. We followed, descending cautiously and quietly, tearing and dirtying our clothes. We wove through the spruces, ponderosas, and scrub oaks, sometimes slipping on the icy grass. Approaching near the mine entry, we sat down. One hundred yards below we could see the concrete abutment framing the mine entry. It rose above the ground about four feet. We could hide behind it and watch what was happening down below.

We crawled on our bellies, using our elbows and knees to propel us, crawling like bullsnakes in a big rush! The grass was wet, covered with snow in places. The elbows of our jackets and knees of our pants were soaked. That didn't slow us down. We reached the abutment and stood behind it, peeping over.

We saw a lot of people we didn't know. They were rescue crews from the other camps, other miners from Gardiner and Brilliant—trained by the union in first aid and evacuation. But they were just standing around, talking to each other, waiting for something to happen. Why weren't they doing anything? The Super was holding his chin, tapping his foot. I spotted Dr. Monty with Mrs. Monty by his side. He'd brought his car, a 1940 Buick, a stretcher resting against its side. Oxygen tanks and gas masks rested in its open trunk. Mrs. Hilliard and some other women were setting up a food table to feed the rescue workers, though the workers weren't doing much to work up an appetite.

The table was set up to give the women something to do—something to alleviate the helpless fear in their hearts. At this point, Mrs. Hilliard and the women were the only ones doing anything. Everyone else was standing around, waiting for something to happen. Just then, everyone turned, looking down the canyon road.

"Er-r-r-r-r-" A flatbed truck was gearing down, creeping toward the tipple, heading for the mine entry. The truck belonged to Raton Public Service, the electric company in Raton.

"What's the truck for?"

José didn't answer, preoccupied, watching the flatbed truck trekking toward the entry. It edged close to the entry. Two men jumped out of its cabin and ran back to the bed, loosening cables from a large gasoline generator.

"Isn't that a generator?"

"You bet!" José responded. "Hold your ears, they're gonna crank it up."

Bu-r-u-ummm - - - - The generator's loud motor resounded, echoing up and down the canyon. We held our hands to our ears.

"What are they doing?" Barely hearing myself, I shouted, my voice muffled by the generator's roar.

José cupped his hands around his mouth, shouting, "They're trying to get electricity back in the mine!"

Momentarily, the generator's pounding roar muffled the familiar sound of the electrically powered Jeffrey trolley motorcar creeping out of the dark shaft into the entry and outside the mine. Mr. Malcolm was driving the motorcar. Behind the motorcar, men were sitting in coal cars, their faces dusty black except their eyes and teeth, which glistened as they smiled weakly.

Mr. Malcolm stopped the motorcar and looked back. Miners trudged out of the mine . . . faces to the ground . . . caps shoved back. They walked slowly, like in a funeral procession, hardly talking—lost in their own thoughts of the dark tomb they were leaving. More miners paraded by in solemn strides . . . forcing smiles of recognition, the sun washing over their faces.

The procession ended. Most miners had left the mine. Yet no Dad, nor Mr. Chicarelli. We spotted Mr. Heard. Marian held her hand to her mouth in astonishment, blocking a shout for joy. We looked down again. More miners trekked by. Where was Dad? Mr. Chicarelli?

¡Todo acaba! ¡Todo acaba! Abuelo's last words: All things pass. . . .

We didn't notice Marian slip away, but there she was next to Mr. Heard. She wrapped her arms around his legs. Mr. Heard leaned over, asking her something. She answered. Mr. Heard looked in our direction. We ducked and crouched behind the abutment for a long time. We gradually popped our heads up, looking for Dad and Mr. Chicarelli. Yet no sign of them.

"Pete, Tony, Dominic, Sal, Alex! You too, Jack!" Dr. Monty decided. "We're going in for 'em. Rest of you men," Dr. Monty addressed the entire crew, "stand by. We'll send for you, if needs be." Dr. Monty handed gas masks to his six-man task force. "Probably won't need 'em, but just in case, wear 'em around your neck."

Already the task force had donned their hard leather caps with attached battery-powered lamps. Readily they followed Dr. Monty into the mine. Everyone else cloistered around Mrs. Hilliard's table, munching on sandwiches, engrossed in anxious conversation about the accident, the missing men. . . .

"Come on," José whispered, "nobody'll see us. Too busy talking about the accident."

Without delay we sneaked down the side of the abutment. We stood at the mouth of the entry. José was right. No one noticed us. We slipped into the entry, walking on the ties of the narrow tracks. The tunnel lights were back on, but still the coal dust blurred our vision, coating my tongue with the taste of sulfur. I closed my mouth. The tunnel turned darker as we plunged through the dust, slipping on the ties. I shuddered. La Muerte was . . . in the shadows . . . in the crevices . . . watching . . . waiting.

¡Todo acaba! ¡Todo acaba! Abuelo's words again.

Up ahead, we heard Dr. Monty barking orders while the task force scrambled around, moving fallen props and rocks. We were near Dad's office—near the room Dad showed us in July. Rocks and props blocked the entrance to the room. Dr. Monty speculated, "Why! A cave-in right here! Probably caused the electrical short, too." He barked out more orders. "Move them props and rocks, slow-like! Be careful! Manuel and Onorio may be under 'em." And then in a quiet, sad voice he added, "Be careful, blast it."

The men proceeded cautiously . . . carefully. Haste could make more dead, and if Dad and Mr. Chicarelli were already dead, then there was no need to rush. My stomach wrenched. I held back the urge to cry, hoping against despair they were trapped in the workroom—alive and shaken, but alive. The task force removed the fallen props and rolled the smaller boulders to the side, digging into the rock pile with their hands, removing the rubble one rock at a time.

José, Geno, and I slinked in the shadows of the walls, creeping close to the rock pile.

From beneath the rubble, a muted, mournful moan:

"Oh-oh-oh."

I prayed, "Oh, God, let Dad be alive."

¡Todo acaba! ¡Todo acaba!

"Somebody's here!" Dr. Monty crackled.

The task force dug faster!

"O-O-O-O-O."

"Why, it's Onorio!" Dr. Monty exclaimed. "Go slow. He's pinned under that big boulder."

"AAAAAA," I gasped a selfish sigh, praying, "O God, Mr. Chicarelli's alive! Please make Dad so!"

¡Todo acaba! ¡Todo acaba!

"Wa-a-a-ah!" Geno wailed, startling us. He darted underneath Dr. Monty's legs and tried to see his father.

"What you doing here, boy!" Dr. Monty gruffly jostled Geno. "Step aside. We got work to do! And quit cryin'!"

Geno fell to his knees, crouching beside the rock pile. José and I slinked along the wall to join Geno. After Dr. Monty's admonition, Geno was afraid to cry. Sobs, deeply felt silent sobs, surged throughout his body. But where was Dad? He probably wasn't in the workroom—meaning he was under the rocks, like Mr. Chicarelli. I shuddered. An icy waft of air . . . La Muerte . . . slinking by . . . to get Dad. Geno and José felt the cool air. They frowned, sensing La Muerte as she crept—

¡Todo acaba! ¡Todo acaba!

"Tony! Gimme that plank!" Dr. Monty barked, reaching for a 2 x 18 x 6-foot board. He wedged it under the large boulder. Alex slid a rock under the plank for a fulcrum. Dr. Monty, Pete, and Sal slowly pulled down on the plank as Jack and Dominic painstakingly lifted the large boulder, rolling it away from Mr. Chicarelli.

"Don't touch him, fellows!" Dr. Monty laid down the plank and knelt beside Mr. Chicarelli, positioning his lamp light on Mr. Chicarelli's mouth, speaking normally:

"Onorio, can you hear me? See me?"

A muffled murmur.

"Yes!" Dr. Monty popped his head up, "He said yes! He's alive!" Dr. Monty jerked his head down, his right ear near Mr. Chicarelli's mouth.

"What? Can barely hear you." Dr. Monty struggled to hear Mr. Chicarelli.

"Oh! Can't move, you say! Fellows, Onorio can't move. But he's conscious. Look for Manuel while I tend to Onorio."

"O Lord, say it isn't so! Is Dad dead?"

¡Todo acaba! ¡Todo acaba!

All this time, José and I looked on dumbfounded. We couldn't stifle our sobs anymore; we cried urgently, snorting repeatedly.

"Oh, GOD! Oh, G-O-D!"

We weren't crying for Mr. Chicarelli. He was alive. We cried for Dad—and ourselves. If Mr. Chicarelli couldn't move, then maybe Dad was dead!

We wailed. Geno, no longer muffling his sobs, wailed with us:

"No-o-o-o! This can't be!" Gurgling . . . sobbing, waves of sobs surged, "Daddy, oh Daddy, don't die . . . don't die."

"Hush up, boys! How in the world did ya get in here?" Dr. Monty glared at us. "Never mind! Just hush! You're making it worse!"

"But he's our dad!" I blurted, wailing.

"And Manuel's my friend!" Dr. Monty yelled, stung by my comment. "I love him just as much as you do!"

Wap! José punched me, a stinging jab to the ribs!

"Be quiet! We gotta act like men!"

I was in pain. José scolded me. Dr. Monty scolded me. I was just a big baby in the eyes of my heroes—just a roly-poly baby. What was I thinking? Dad was somewhere beneath the rock pile. He might be dead! And here I was, feeling sorry for myself.

Coal mining's not the movies, Dad said. It's a way for men to work to live, but sometimes mining kills men while they work. La Muerte doesn't kill miners—the mine does. Oh, how I wished this would all go away. I wished I would wake up from a bad dream, and everyone would be okay. But Abuelo's words wouldn't go away—

¡Todo acaba! ¡Todo acaba!

I bit the inside of my cheek, tasting the blood oozing from the cut. The sharp pain kept me from crying.

"Over here!" Tony yelled, "He's over here, by the props."

The task force hustled to the left side of the rock pile where props and railroad ties had been neatly stacked and stored for future uses.

Tony shouted excitedly, "He's beside the stack! Come here! Help me move these props!"

"He's down here."

"Here he is!"

"He musta rolled over!"

Fearfully, José and I edged close to where the men clustered. Geno stayed by Mr. Chicarelli. The men hovered over Dad, who lay on his belly, cringing up against the bottom layer of props and ties.

"Dr. Monty, better get over here."

Everyone made room for Dr. Monty to slip through. He lay down on the rocks and spoke to Dad:

"Manuel, can you hear me?"

A low, soft mumble—

"Manuel?" Dr. Monty raised his voice. "Can you hear me?"

"Uh, huh." Yes. Dad's voice was very low.

Dr. Monty slid down the rocks and put his face next to Dad's.

"Move your fingers if you can hear me."

Dr. Monty popped up his head:

"He can hear me! He moved his fingers real well."

AAAAAAAAAA! Another sigh of selfish relief. Dad was alive. José put his arm around my shoulder. I put my arm around his waist. We were still very frightened, but Dad was alive. His time hadn't come. José and I watched as the men carefully shoved aside the smaller boulders. Dad was pinned under the bedrock. Luckily, the stacked props and ties provided some protection from the massive bedrock.

¡Todo acaba! ¡Todo acaba!

Jack pulled Dr. Monty out of the wedge created when the massive bedrock had fallen on top of the stacked props and ties.

"Manuel had some protection with the ties, thank God. But I think both have broken backs." Dr. Monty sighed, his voice trailing off, "Blasted mine."

Everybody was silent. A broken back meant Dad and Mr. Chicarelli could never again work in the mine. They might not ever work . . . or walk . . . again. Anger surged into my heart. My head felt like it was going to explode. Rage. . . . I hated the mine—not La Muerte, but the mine. . . . It repulsed me.

"O-o-o-o-" Geno, José, and I moaned, tears flooding out of our eyes.

"Don't die, Daddy!"

"Don't die."

"Here, here," Dr. Monty softened his tone. Up to this time, Dr. Monty had been very gruff with us, showing his dissatisfaction at us for coming into the mine. Now, he hugged us. "Your fathers are tougher than buffaloes. They're not gonna die."

Geno wiped his eyes on a sleeve. "How do you know, Dr. Monty?"

"Because I have faith in God. He doesn't want them yet. Now, it's up to us to get them out of here."

Again, the icy air whiffed by. . . . La Muerte mounted her carreta, leaving the scene empty-handed . . . her bow unstrung . . . arrows in her scabbard. I knew she'd never scare me again.

"José, you're the oldest." Dr. Monty peered over his wire-rimmed glasses. "Take the boys out. Tell the rest of the rescue crew we need their help—to get in here, pronto! Tell them to bring a pair of thick, wide planks for stretchers. Make sure they know it's for stretchers."

"But, I—"

"Out! José, it's time for you boys to grow up! You're needed now to do what you're told. That's an order."

We didn't want to leave Dad or Mr. Chicarelli. Yet José respected Dr. Monty and complied:

"Okay. Matías, come on. You, too, Geno. Here, take my hand."

Geno and I tried to stand our ground. Neither of us wanted to leave. José gruffly yanked my hand, pulling me with him. José grabbed Geno's hand and nudged him gently, pulling him away from Mr. Chicarelli. Geno took one last, long look at his father, and then plodded alongside José and me. José broke into a brisk pace, forcing us to keep up with him. Soon we were running hand in hand. When we reached the mouth of the mine, people were surprised to see three little boys. Geno spotted Mrs. Chicarelli and ran to her. Mom broke through the crowd that had gathered at the entry. Someone had gone for both of them when the other miners had realized Mr. Chicarelli and Dad were still in the mine.

Mom didn't mince words:

"Where's your father?"

"He's alive," José spoke softly but clearly. "But his back may be broken."

"He's alive. ¡Gracias a Dios!"

"Yes, I saw him," I tried to sound grown up and comforting. "And Mr. Chicarelli, too."

I started to tell them where the rescuers had found Dad, but José curtly interrupted:

"Shut up, Matías. Dr. Monty wants all the rescuers to go in right away. They should take thick, wide planks with them—a couple of them for stretchers."

The rescue squad rushed into the mine. A couple of them carried the makeshift stretchers. Neither Mom nor Mrs. Chicarelli asked us any questions. Both had faces shrouded by shadows of worry. No one spoke. Everybody just crowded around the entry and waited with anxious anticipation. . . .

After what seemed like an eternity, we could hear Dr. Monty encouraging the task force as they carried Mr. Chicarelli and Dad out of the mine:

"Easy! Easy! Don't jolt 'em!"

The rescue squad trudged from the mine slowly and cautiously, warily pacing themselves. The squad was evenly divided—half of them carried Mr. Chicarelli on a plank, and half carried Dad on another. The planks were rigid and made excellent but narrow stretchers. Dad and Mr. Chicarelli were bound in place by rolls of bandages, but still the men of the rescue squad gritted their teeth and the jugular veins on their necks protruded as they strained to carry them without jolting.

The men holding the planks at the center strained the most, their tight neck muscles bulging. They carried the brunt of the weight and had to keep the planks from bowing in either direction. Walking on the rocky, irregular floor of the mine's tunnel was normally difficult, but now the rescuers were carrying two very heavy miners as well. Both injured miners were not tall men, but they were stocky and muscular, and on the planks they were solid, deadweight. An abrupt jolt could cause even more severe damage to their broken backs.

Dr. Monty walked behind the rescue squad, still commanding as he paced the rescuers out of the mine:

"Easy, fellows! You're almost out. Easy!"

The men came out carrying Dad, followed by the men carrying Mr. Chicarelli.

"Manuel! Manuel!" Mom leaned over Dad.

"Onorio! Onorio!" Mrs. Chicarelli went next to Mr. Chicarelli.

"Can't hear you. They're sleeping. I shot them up with morphine. Better that way."

"Oh, thanks be to God!" Mrs. Chicarelli tried to stifle her sobs, but she couldn't hold them back.

"¡Gracias a Dios! ¡Gracias a Dios!" Mom crossed herself, tears welled in her eyes as she broke out in sobs.

Softly, Dr. Monty issued his last command to the rescuers:

"Set them down gently."

Slowly and cautiously, the men lowered Mr. Chicarelli and Dad to the ground; the men fell away from the planks, sprawling onto the ground. Mom and Mrs. Chicarelli dropped down on their knees beside the stretchers. Dr. Monty knelt between the two of them. He placed his arms on their shoulders, hugging and assuring them:

"They're going to be okay. Won't be long, they'll be back on their feet."

Mrs. Chicarelli brushed a kiss on her husband's forehead. Mom gently touched Dad's head. It was a timid touch. She was afraid she might cause further damage. She lowered her head to his hand and kissed it.

Dr. Monty turned his attention to the rescue squad:

"Boys, your job is done. Sorry I've been so gruff," Dr. Monty apologized to the rescue squad, who were arching their backs and twisting their torsos. "But you did good by Manuel and Onorio; you're all heroes far's I'm concerned. Thanks a bunch for helping. Someone called Miner's Hospital, right?"

"The ambulance is on its way," Mrs. Hilliard assured him.

"Yes, Matthew," Mrs. Monty added her assurance. "It's on the way."

He shook hands with each of the men as they discarded their gas masks in his car. Mrs. Malcolm, carrying Ramona, made her way through the crowd.

"Come on Geno, Matías, you're going with me." Mrs. Malcolm nudged both of us. "You, too, José." She turned to Mom and Mrs. Chicarelli. "I'll watch the boys. You go with your men to the hospital."

"Geno, go by the house. Take your schoolwork."

"Ah, Ma, schoolwork!" Geno blurted out. "Who can think of schoolwork—"

"You can!" Mrs. Chicarelli bluntly interrupted. "You gotta get a good education, Geno! Starting right now! Or you'll end up like your father! You, too, Matías! You're both whipper-snappers, you know!"

"¡Sí, Matías, José! Do your school work!"

I couldn't believe Mrs. Chicarelli's sharp tongue. Usually she was soft spoken, nurturing—always a smile. And Mom too. Both mothers had a tough side to them. Neither Mom nor Mrs. Chicarelli had a mean bone in their bodies, but they believed school was the way to keep us out of the mine.

We walked home the same way Dad and Mr. Chicarelli had come to the mine that morning—on the tracks. We got home about four o'clock. Angela and Juan were now home from school. Angela gave José and me a stern look. She knew we'd gone to the mine. No one truly knew how badly our fathers had been injured. Mrs. Malcolm didn't want us to worry so she had us sit at the table and start our homework. She put Angela in charge of us, including Geno, while she went to her house to prepare supper. When supper was ready, Freddie came over to our house to get us. We all washed our hands at our house, including Geno, and quietly walked next door to the Malcolm's for supper. After supper, Juan and José helped Freddie and Petee wash and dry the dishes. There was little of the usual banter.

When dishes were done, Mrs. Malcolm sent Angela, Geno, and me back to our house to finish our homework. Ramona, Juan, and José stayed at the Malcolms'. With such a short school day, Geno and I had finished our few workbook pages before supper, so Angela took it upon herself to read to us. She sat us down in the living room, where she read from *The Adventures of Tom Sawyer.* After reading a paragraph or two, she spewed out questions like a machine gun, scolding us if we answered wrong. We were afraid to enjoy the story because Angela was so cross. After the second series of questions, tears welled up in Geno's and my eyes.

"Pay attention, boys!" Angela wailed. Then she burst into muffled sobs and hugged us both. "Don't you know, you have to get a good education. You have to get a good, safe job."

We all hugged each other, overwhelmed with sobs. It really felt good to cry. Then we started to laugh; that felt good too. When we finally stopped, Angela wiped all our tears and washed our faces. She got out milk and oatmeal cookies, and we sat in the kitchen and ate while she read some more to us.

About eight o'clock, Mrs. Malcolm brought Ramona, José, and Juan back to our house.

"Do you think you can manage?" she asked Angela while she buttoned up Geno's coat.

"Of course, Juan will help me."

"I'm gonna take Geno to his house; get 'im ready for bed. We'll wait for his mother there."

I tried to watch them as they trudged to Geno's, but it was pretty dark. In a short while I heard the happy bark of Twal and knew they were at the Chicarelli's.

Juan got out the Chinese Checkers and we all played as we waited for Mom. Angela and Ramona were a team and used only one set of marbles between them. It wasn't much fun; no one was competing; we all just went through the motions.

About ten, Juan thought he heard a car. I ran to the window and peeked out. I heard Twal again and figured Mrs. Chicarelli was home.

"Mom's coming! Mom's coming!"

José ran to the door and threw it open. Dr. Monty's headlights flashed into the house for just a second before he turned them off. José was out the door and pulling Mom and Dr. Monty back in with him.

Mom invited Dr. Monty into the kitchen and started to heat coffee for both of them.

Dr. Monty dropped wearily into a chair at the table. "José, Matías—you shouldn't go into the mine ever again. Do you understand?" Dr. Monty wasn't scolding; he was pleading.

We both nodded solemnly—yes.

Mom brought him coffee; he blew on it. We anxiously waited for him to go on. An eternity passed as he took a sip.

"Your dad's back is broken."

Angela was on the verge of tears. I'd never seen her cry, and now—twice in one day.

"It could be worse; he's not paralyzed, and his back will heal. He won't be able to work in the mine again. Mr. Chicarelli is pretty much in the same shape." Dr. Monty took another sip of coffee while avoiding our eyes.

Mom smiled. "He's alive."

Suddenly all of us felt better.

"Six years ago, I sat in this kitchen with Manuel. We witnessed a miracle. I had all but given up on Matías—and on my ability as a doctor. Your father told me never to lose faith . . . that God provides life for all of us, but we got to care for the living. Today, another miracle—not a single man killed."

No one spoke. We were worried, concerned . . . relieved. Dad was alive.

¡Todo acaba! ¡Todo acaba!

Abruptly, Dr. Monty's mood shifted. With an ornery glint in his eye, he jostled José in the arm and quipped:

"So you still want to be a miner?"

Nada . . . no answer . . . José was momentarily surprised at Dr. Monty's sudden playful mood. The rest of us were just as surprised.

"I-I don't think so."

"Me neither!" Ramona chirped.

Ha! Ha! Ha! Ha! Rowdy, raucous laughter—we rocked and reeled in mirth. Ramona's sparrow-like chirp sprung our overwound springs.

Ha! Ha! Ha! Even Mom and Angela writhed in the laughter.

Ramona didn't understand. First she smiled. Then she was unsure; she hooked the little finger of her left hand in the corner of her mouth, contorting her mouth like that of an unhappy clown. She glanced around. Tears trickled. These weren't the copious crocodile tears she shed for Dad to get her way. She was hurting. She batted her eyelids at me. How could I resist her plea for sympathy? I hugged her, and in my best sparrow voice, chirped:

"Don't cry, Ramona. I don't want to be a miner, either."

GLOSSARY

Words are listed in order of appearance.
NOTE: Words are listed and italicized only the first time used in the book, unless they occur again as part of a Spanish sentence. In most cases, words are included in the glossary for consistency's sake even if they are translated within the text.

CHAPTER I

panza ▪ stomach
fogón ▪ stove
Sí! Entre ▪ Yes! Come in
mi hito, qué ▪ My son, what
ojos lindos—claros y morenos ▪ pretty eyes—clear and brown
cabrito ▪ kid
Abuelo ▪ grandfather
platos ▪ plates
La vecina ▪ the neighbor
También ▪ Also
No sé ▪ I don't know
A, qué lindo—tu nombre ▪ Ah, how nice—your name
Espérate ▪ Wait
En español se dice ▪ In Spanish, it's said
Escríbale ▪ Write it
y con ▪ and with
qué bueno ▪ how fine
Válgame Dios ▪ Oh, my goodness
padrinos ▪ godparents/sponsors
bautismo ▪ baptism
Pero ▪ but
qué mal ▪ how bad
Su tristeza es del ▪ Your despair is of the
corazón y alma ▪ heart and soul
pero los viejos del país ▪ but, the old timers at home

Dios da, pero no acarrea ▪ God provides, but he does not carry anyone
dicho ▪ saying
remedio ▪ remedy
como los viejos en el país ▪ like the old timers at home
Dios te salve, María, Madre de Dios, el Señor es contigo ▪ Hail Mary, full of grace, the Lord is with Thee
Sabes qué ▪ You know what
ruega por nosotros ▪ pray for us
Biblia ▪ Bible
La Muerte ▪ Angel of Death
la carreta de los muertos ▪ the cart of the dead
cuentos ▪ stories
Comadre Sebastiana ▪ Godmother Sebastiana
llena eres de gracia ▪ full of grace
el Señor es contigo ▪ the Lord is with you
bendita tú eres entre todas las mujeres ▪ blessed are thou amongst women
y bendito es el fruto en tu vientre ▪ and blessed is the fruit of your womb
Matías vive! Ven acá! ▪ Matías lives! Come here!
huevos rancheros con jamón ▪ bacon and eggs with chili
niño ▪ son
por favor ▪ as a favor to me
Cansada, no más ▪ She's tired, that's all
después de mal panza ▪ after an upset stomach
Nada ▪ Nothing

CHAPTER 2

Respeto de los derechos de tu vecinos/Es la salvación de todos ▪ Respect for the rights of your neighbors is everyone's salvation
Angelitos de Dios ▪ Baby angels of God
Ándale ▪ Hurry up
muy sabroso ▪ very tasty
quelites ▪ wild spinach/pigweed
llano ▪ plain/meadow
pues ▪ Well, hmmm
Como no? ▪ Why not?
Con cuidado ▪ With care
yo creo ▪ I believe
vaquero ▪ cowboy
Cállate la boca ▪ Shut up!
Con respeto ▪ With respect
Un hombre muy bueno ▪ A very good man
Bendito sea Dios, bendito sea Jesucristo, bendito sea la nombre de María, Virgen y Madre, bendito sea sus Angeles y sus Santos ▪ Blessed be God, blessed be Jesus, Blessed be the name of Mary, virgin and mother, and blessed be your angels and saints

CHAPTER 3

qué lindas ▪ how fine
genízaro ▪ Mexican Indians
chili con pan ▪ chili with bread
Qué pasó con mi hito ▪ What happened to my son
Vamos rezar a Dios y la Virgen María ▪ Let's pray to God and the Virgin Mary

CHAPTER 4

¿Quién sabe? ▪ Who knows?
¡Hijo mano! ▪ Oh, man!
chiste ▪ joke
Mira, aquí ▪ Look here
No importa ▪ never mind

CHAPTER 5

Camino Real ▪ royal road
hormiga ▪ ant
no le vale la pena ▪ It's not worth the pain
No te penes ▪ Don't worry about it
abrazo ▪ hug
Qué lástima ▪ What a pity
Tiene una toz muy mala ▪ He has a bad cough
Ojalá ▪ I hope to God
mentirosos ▪ liars
Hola, Tío. ¿Cómo le va? ▪ Hello, uncle, how goes it?
Aquí, no más, trabajando ▪ Oh, I've been here, working mostly
¡Qué va! ▪ Goodness gracious
Dale gas ▪ Give it gas
Hola, ¿Qúe tál? ▪ Hello, how's everything?
Aquí, no más jugando ▪ Oh, I've been here, playing mostly
¿Y, sus hermanos? ▪ And, your brothers?
familia ▪ family
Hermana mía, mira la telegrama ▪ My sister, look at the telegram
está muy enfermo. Venga a la casa adelante ▪ he's very ill. Come home right away
mañana ▪ tomorrow

CHAPTER 6

de este tiempo ▪ of this time

CHAPTER 7

viga ▪ beam
horno ▪ adobe oven
Como esta ▪ Like this
Es muy enfermo ▪ He's very ill
Allá ▪ Over there
leña ▪ wood
Breques ▪ brakes
por qué ▪ what for?
La Iglesia ▪ The Church
borreguero ▪ sheepherder
Cuantas borregas, tienes ▪ How many sheep do you have?
ranchito ▪ small ranch
lemíta ▪ squawbush
gracias ▪ thanks
Aprovecharse ▪ Come here
Una día, se va a ser un hombre ▪ One day, you'll be a man
Y luego es su tiempo pa' ayudar a mi Clarita ▪ And it'll be your turn to help my daughter Clarita
Ella trata a usted muy bien, ¿que no ▪ She treats you well, yes? no?

Mamá me trata muy bien ▪ Mama treats me very well
Respeto pa' sus parientes es muy importante ▪ Respect for your parents is very important
Ayudar a ellos en los años ancianos ▪ Help them (your parents) when they're old
como su Tío Baltazar me ayuda a ahora ▪ Like how your Uncle Baltazar helps me
Bien o mal, todo acaba ▪ Good or bad, all things end
Buenas noches ▪ Good night
Pobrecito ▪ Poor man
De la muerte y de la suerte no hay quien se escape ▪ No one escapes from death or fate
Vamanos ▪ Let's go
ratoncitos ▪ little rats/mice
Como el jardín ▪ Like in the garden
Verdad ▪ True
Acequia Madre ▪ Main irrigation ditch
camposanto ▪ cemetery
velorio ▪ wake
compadres ▪ godparents
todo la familia ▪ all of the family
Madre mía de los Dolores Tú has de ser intercesora pa Pablo Ribera ▪ Mother of God, please intercede for Pablo Ribera
En la hora de la muerte Tu sí defiendas, Señora. ▪ Please defend him in this hour of death
ofrecimiento ▪ offering
Los Ángeles en el cielo Alaban con alegría Y los hombres en la tierra Responden:—¡Ave María! ▪ Angels of heaven praise the Lord and men on earth respond, Hail Mary!
ruega por nosotros pecadores, ahora y en la hora de nuestra muerte ▪ pray for us sinners, now and at the hour of our death
santero ▪ sculptor of wooden statues of saints
retablos ▪ painted wooden panels or tablets
Polvo y polvo ▪ Dust to dust
Dale, Señor, el descanso eterno y la luz perpetua ▪ Give him, Lord, eternal rest and your perpetual light

CHAPTER 8

No hay mal pan con bien hambre ▪ There's no stale bread when you're hungry
cajete ▪ tin washtub
bizcochitos ▪ small cookies, often with anise or cinnamon
Un cuantos minutos ▪ In a few minutes
Un algo más ▪ A little longer
hefe ▪ boss
Dios tí bendigo, hermano cariño ▪ God bless you, dear brother
Vamos, tomar un snacké ▪ Let's eat a snack
Pero, se come quélites ▪ But we eat wild spinach
Y tambien la té de yerba buena del llano ▪ And we drink peppermint tea
¡Qué va! ▪ Goodness!
Como ▪ How
En el nombre del Padre, del Hijo, y del Espiritu Santo ▪ In the name of the Father, the Son, and the Holy Ghost
Padre nuestro, que estás en los cielos; santificado sea el tu nombre ▪ Our father, who art in heaven, hallowed be thy name
Escucha ▪ Listen
Que suave al tacto—como lana ▪ How nice to the touch—like soft wool
No tenes miedo ▪ Don't be afraid
muy sabroso ▪ very tasty
Un poco, no más ▪ Just a little, that's all

CHAPTER 9

como se llama ▪ what's it called/how are you called
Buenos días, perezoso ▪ Good morning, sleepyhead
polla ▪ little chick

CHAPTER 10

Mida ▪ Look
No se ▪ I don't know
Mi plebe ▪ My people/My friends
Silencio ▪ Silence
Mucho gracias ▪ Thank you very much
sala ▪ social hall
Pues, quién sabe ▪ Well, who knows?

CHAPTER 11

Juan, y tu? ¿Como se fue? ▪ And you, Juan? How did it go?
No tí penas ▪ Don't worry about it
posiblé, era una hija adoptiva ▪ maybe she was adopted

CHAPTER 12

Yo soy La Llorona ▪ I am the Wailing Woman
Y vengo por ti ▪ And I come for you

CHAPTER 13

hacha ▪ hatchet/axe
Wat-chá-le ▪ Watch it
Gracias a Dios para esta comida ▪ Thank you God for this food
gracias a Dios para la buena salud de mi familia ▪ Thank you God for the good health of my family
gracias a Dios para la salud de Jesús, Baltazar, Feliz, y los jóvenes ▪ Thank you for the health of Jesus, Baltazar, Feliz, and their young ones
gracias a Dios para la seguridad de Arturo y Eddie Heard ▪ Thanks for the safety of Arturo and Eddie Heard
Tres Años Hace ▪ It's been three years
Adelila ▪ Adeline
montaña ▪ mountain
Feliz Navidad ▪ Merry Christmas
bosque ▪ woods/grove of trees
properos ▪ lumberjacks for mine props
Mira! De primero ▪ Look! At first
toalla ▪ towel
taquito ▪ small taco
la plebe ▪ the people/the family
Es que ▪ They say that
novios ▪ newlyweds
todo enamorados ▪ all in love
viejitos ▪ old folks
estómago ▪ stomach
mis rhuemos ▪ my rheumatism

duelo mucho ▪ It hurts a lot
Mucho más ▪ Much more
mis dolores ▪ my pains
Yo soy un Angel de Dios Y vengo por uno de los dos ▪ I am an Angel of God and I've come for one of you

CHAPTER 14

En enero ▪ In January
Por Dios ▪ Good God
ven pa'cá ▪ Come here
tiempo para tu baño ▪ Time for your bath
No digas nada ▪ Don't say anything
Hijo, mano ▪ Oh, man
aquí está tu máquina ▪ here's your tractor
no te apenas ▪ Don't worry about it
Dios te bendiga ▪ God bless you
Despacio ▪ Slow
Mi muñeca pequeñita ▪ My little doll